PRAISE FOR
FROM THE MOON
I WATCHED HER

"*From the Moon I Watched Her* is an achingly beautiful, brutal, coming-of-age struggle about a young girl's yearning for truth, love, and loyalty as her family and faith rip apart.

Against the honky-tonk landscape of 1970s small-town Texas, Medley artfully and brazenly exposes the evils of religion, the tragedy of mental illness, and the cruelty we humans do while exploring a troubled mother-daughter relationship amid a family in crisis. But the ferocity of the human heart, Medley reminds us, can survive a multitude of sins if we immerse ourselves in the cleansing waters of truth and reality instead of lies and myth. Packed with sin, secrets, and sex, this book rubs your senses raw a dozen different ways and then offers hope and healing. Just like real life."

—NATASHA STOYNOFF, co-author of
*The King of Con: How a Smooth-Talking Jersey Boy Made
and Lost Billions, Baffled the FBI, Eluded the Mob,
and Lived to Tell the Crooked Tale*

"In our current climate of hyper-partisanship, this book gives insight on how someone's perspective can become so hardened it seems impossible to change.

Medley has created a page-turning adventure where the reader is never sure who are the heroes and who are the villains. The characters inhabit a world of oil rigs, Texas heat, and the repressive nature of their church—yet they fit together like puzzle pieces, each affecting the others, sometimes by happenstance and sometimes by choice.

This book is a powerful work of fiction that makes you wonder how much of it might be based in reality. Once I started it, I flew through it and couldn't put it down."

—ETHAN MINSKER, New York writer, filmmaker,
artist, fanzine publisher, and founder of
the New York Antagonist Movement

"*From The Moon I Watched Her* is the riveting coming-of age-story of a girl from the deep South raised within the Church of Christ. The book dives into the implicit and explicit messages, and pervasive roots of religious control, oppression, and abuse towards women in the South. From the first page, the author instantaneously transports you to the mind, perspective, and vivid inner world of young Stephanie Walters. As she navigates her youth and teen years, Stephanie overcomes sexual trauma and loss. Her story educates and informs on the profound impact of mental illness on family dynamics and the development of identity over time."

—JAIME COHEN, PhD, LLC, Adjunct Professor,
Clinical Mental Health Counseling, University of St. Thomas

"The voice of this book is astonishing, engaging, and real. Medley captures the heartbreaking innocence and sturdy hope of a growing child as she desperately tries to believe in her parents and in the 'parents' of her church—who try to blind themselves with a similar willful hope. As they cling to the hope that would prevent them from questioning the structure of their lives, they depend on that hope to cover their illness and their secrets, but as ever, it is always the children who pay."

—LEAH LAX, author of *Uncovered: How I Left Hasidic Life and Finally Came Home*

"*From The Moon I Watched Her* is a powerful, compelling, horrifying, disturbing, cruel, and beautiful book. Medley forced me to look inside and see through the fresh, wounded, and tender young eyes of Stephanie Walters as she tries to build a life on solid ground but is continuously destabilized by her shaky world.

In describing Stephanie's trauma of being isolated from healthy, adult human connection in her broken culture, Medley's work reveals the way the vulnerable are forsaken for the reputation, pleasure, and comfort of those in power. The author's juxtaposition of incredibly beautiful spiritual experiences with horrific portrayals of religious and sexual abuse were especially haunting.

Medley describes a horizon . . . a place where one can't really distinguish boundaries at the hazy meeting of reality and unreality."

—SUSAN MILES, women's recovery and addiction minister and pastor of First United Methodist Church, Jonesboro, Arkansas

FROM THE MOON I WATCHED HER

A NOVEL

EMILY ENGLISH MEDLEY

GREENLEAF
BOOK GROUP PRESS

Published by Greenleaf Book Group Press
Austin, Texas
www.gbgpress.com

Distributed by Greenleaf Book Group

For ordering information or special discounts for bulk purchases, please contact Greenleaf Book Group at PO Box 91869, Austin, TX 78709, 512.891.6100.

Design and composition by Greenleaf Book Group
Cover design by Greenleaf Book Group
Cover images: paper burned old grunge abstract background texture; Full Moon; Night starry sky, dark blue space background with stars; Portrait of little poor girl posing in profile, used under license from Shutterstock.com

Publisher's Cataloging-in-Publication data is available.

Print ISBN: 978-1-62634-744-1

eBook ISBN: 978-1-62634-745-8

Part of the Tree Neutral® program, which offsets the number of trees consumed in the production and printing of this book by taking proactive steps, such as planting trees in direct proportion to the number of trees used: www.treeneutral.com

Printed in the United States of America on acid-free paper

20 21 22 23 24 25   10 9 8 7 6 5 4 3 2 1

First Edition

This book is for my precious husband, Jason, and the voiceless.

Burn for a Burn

CHAPTER

1

Pasadena, Texas, 1977

THE CHRISTIANS WERE COMING IN and sitting to the right of the stage and The Devils were sneaking in from the left.

"The auditorium is noisily brimming with enthusiasm tonight folks, as we wait to hear two outspoken opponents debate the question that is arguably permeating our decade . . . Is abortion murder?" The pretty lady with black hair and a red-and-white scarf around her neck tapped her microphone. "Testing, testing, one, two, three. Am I on? I don't think this is on."

I looked up at her and tugged on the bottom of her striped skirt, "Miss? Miss? Can I talk in that?" She patted the sides of her hair, but it didn't move at all. I tugged her skirt again, this time harder, and thought about poking her but didn't. "Ma'am? Please?" She didn't answer me. "MA'AM! Can I *please* hear my voice in that thing?"

She leaned down and smiled at me and her lips shone like ham in the sun and her teeth were big like a horse. She pushed her wide glasses up on her nose and waved to the man with tight brown curls who held a big black camera. She bent down and patted me on the head. "Run along, kiddo, okay? I'm tryin' to work here. You're cute, though." She stood back up, whispered to the cameraman, and pointed over to the stage showing him where to stand. "No, not there. Here," she said.

Everyone at church said I was a "little Paul" because I looked so much like Daddy. They called him "Deacon Paul" at church on Sundays when he passed the collection plate. My daddy was an extra good Christian, but he was a banker at First Community Bank every other day. We both had red hair with freckles and white skin, but I didn't cry if someone said "carrot top" besides it's not bad to be one, no not at all. In fact, "God made me something special. I'm the only one of my kind. God gave me a body and a bright, healthy mind," my Sunday school teacher sang while we got out our carpet squares.

And guess who the teacher was? Mother, that's who! I was not tall like Daddy because I was five, but my sister, Katherine, was tall because she was seven.

Mother's father, Daddy Black, was a big, strong, loud preacher at Bayside Church of Christ in Pasadena, Texas, where we lived, and that's who everyone was here to see. Daddy Black was bald and had a pointy nose and everyone in Texas knew that the Church of Christ was the best. And everyone in the world knew that Texas was the best. We were the biggest state in this world and Daddy said there was wildness in Texas you just couldn't find anywhere else.

"Darling, there you are. Stephanie, stay close to me. This is not a playground." Mother knelt down and put her face *riiiiggghhht* up next to mine and licked her finger and cleaned my cheeks. "Don't dawdle off again," she said.

I held Mother's hand very tight while we walked up to the front by the stage. There were very many people there and I did not want to get lost in that big place, so we went *right* by that pretty lady with the microphone and the man with the camera like we didn't even *see* them. *That will teach her to tell me run along, kiddo.* Mother's fingers were boney like the chicken Hansel and Gretel gave to the witch to trick her and her nails were long and red and her rings were big. She held my hand just a little too hard, but I didn't tell her because that would make her so sad. You have to think about other people's feelings.

Daddy swooped me up and heads were everywhere under us and I could see this whole place like I was a bird up in the sky and the people were squirrels. "I've got her, Lily," he said.

"Let's change angles," the lady with the microphone said. "Let's try to face the stage. There's too much light. I want a good shot of both debaters." And the man with the camera minded her.

I didn't know what abortion was. I did know murder meant killing God's creatures on purpose. And I was proud tonight because Daddy Black was going to be on TV; he was a Christian soldier and fighting The Devil, Madalyn Murray O'Hair, a big, old, fat, ugly atheist. An atheist does not even believe in God which makes them black inside their hearts. That's what Christian soldiers do. We fight Devils, but we fight them sweetly.

Daddy told Katherine and me before the debate that Daddy Black was fighting for little babies who got lost inside their mommies and floated away forever and some mean, murdering people didn't even ever try to find them. "That's a-bor-tion," Daddy said. "And it's against God."

"But why wouldn't people try to find them? And where do they float away to?" I asked. I thought of tiny babies floating around in the stars with the big moon beside them.

"Does it happen by accident?" Katherine asked.

"Sometimes," Daddy answered. "But sometimes, no. Sometimes it's on purpose. They let the babies float away. Now, Stephanie, come here and let me tie your dress in a decent bow."

I rubbed my eyes and started to cry, "But Daddy I don't want a decent bow. I just want a regular bow." Daddy laughed and put his sweet hand on my cheek and then tied my dress in a decent bow anyways.

"Paul, don't lie to them and tell them it happens by accident," Mother said. "Katherine, sit up straight and hold your stomach in." And Katherine sat up straighter and sucked in so I sucked in, too.

Last night, I saw *sooooo* many tears fall down Daddy Black's face when he thought of the tiny souls that he said were never launched into eternity. Daddy Black says eternity means forever and ever and ever amen. He tapped on his typewriter and said don't bother him and don't jump around because he was writing to our new president Jimmy Carter. Then he pulled out his paper and threw it on the floor and opened up his Bible and cried some more because of lost babies.

He grabbed Mother and hugged her tight and cried for the lost souls and Mother wrestled him a little and turned her face but he kissed her over and over. "Oh, Lillian, my sweet little angel, precious, perfect sweetheart, beautiful jewel of a daughter. Thank you for having such sweet little believing girls and a wonderful servant of a husband and for remaining pure and holy and perfect."

"Dad, I am not perfect," Mother would say. "Please don't call me that. It's way too much pressure. And don't kiss me on the mouth." And she wiped the kiss off that Daddy Black had given her and he let her go.

"Oh, but you are, Lily. Everything about you is good and precious and pure and perfect," Daddy Black would say.

Because of Daddy Black, my family got to be in charge. We were like line leaders at school, and we got to sit on the very front. He knew everything there was to know about God and the Bible and nobody could top him ever in a million years so don't even try because he knew *everything*. Daddy Black's voice was sometimes too loud when he preached and it did not always feel like he loved our church when he slammed his fists on the pulpit and it scared me and woke me up during church even if I was dreaming. "Dogs without a bark!" he screamed and screamed at us last Sunday because there were not many of us there. "That's what this congregation is if we forsake the assembling of saints!"

"What is forsaking saints?" I sat up on my knees and whispered into Mother's ear.

"He's not talking to us, sweetheart," she said, and she sat me back down on my bottom. "He's talking about people who don't come to church regularly. Like, people who only come on Sunday mornings, but then don't come on Sunday nights, Wednesday nights, or Tuesday home group," she whispered back. "Not us, baby," and she put her arm around me and pulled me tight to her.

My first best friend, Simone, only comes on Sunday morning. Simone's family was dogs without barks. Poor Simone. Simone will burn in hell.

Daddy Black smells like green mouthwash and he wears a suit every day even when he sleeps, even when he mows the grass, and he makes Mother very, very nervous and that makes me nervous, too, and Mama Black calls him "House O'Fire," because he goes and goes and goes and preaches and preaches and preaches and Daddy Black never gets tired of preaching God's Word. Never. *Ever.*

I wore a poufy slip under my dress and lace knee socks with cotton balls that hung down on the sides. I twirled around before sitting and fanned my dress out like a princess.

"Y'all look so dadgum cute," the lady at the dress store said to Katherine and me when Mother bought our matching dresses for Daddy Black's debate. Mother said, "Well, these dresses are for a very important night, aren't they, girls?" We don't say, "dadgum" because that sounds an awful lot like "darn," which is very close to saying you-know-what.

Mother had just cut my hair even shorter last night. She said it made it easier on her nerves to fix it and that made me feel very sad because my hair did not hurt her nerves, it could not even talk and now it made me look like a boy. My bangs were short and stiff across my forehead and looked like my baby doll's hair, the one whose eyes open and shut when I picked her up or lay her down. I ran my fingers through it and across the back of my neck, and pretended it was long and flowing like Wonder Woman or the lady with the microphone. This place smelled like the perfume at our church and I sneezed and wiped my nose on my sleeve. But if I could have had some perfume, I would have gotten *Charlie* because that's what Mother wore.

Katherine was sad.

Her hair got cut, too, but even shorter and more slanted on the bottom than mine because she would *not* sit still when Mother tried to curl and tease it last night. A teeny-tiny red curling iron burn was behind her ear.

"Katherine, does your ear hurt?" I whispered.

She put her finger over her mouth. "Hush, Stephanie!" she hissed like a snake.

I did not want Katherine to be burned or have slanted, short hair. But Mother said Katherine needed to sit still when she was getting her hair put in a bun. Otherwise, it could make the curling iron drop, and boy, she was really right. Daddy was mad and said, "Lily, how dare you be so careless?" but I patted Mother because I knew she did not mean to burn Katherine.

"I don't have to hush yet, Katherine. Daddy Black and that mean lady aren't even on stage yet!" I yelled as loudly as I could above all the voices around us because yelling loud made me stronger than Katherine telling me to be hush. Mother's eyes got big and flickered scary green and she looked like Maleficent from *Sleeping Beauty*. She folded her arms slowly like Maleficent, too, and stared at me until I looked away.

Daddy handed Katherine and me each a Sprite. We held them close to us. "Maybe this will buy us a few minutes. We can bribe the little knuckleheads," he laughed and winked at my mother and found his seat. Mother laughed and smiled back at him. I smiled because he called me knucklehead.

"Excuse us, Judy." Daddy passed Mama Black. He gathered Katherine and me up and sat Katherine nearest to him. His freckled hand rested on Katherine's shoulder, and I scooted in closer to brush up against it and tried to force my head underneath his hand for him to rub and pretended I was a puppy and stuck out my tongue and pretended I had paws and panted. "Stephanie, relax," he said gently. I looked around the auditorium. There were no other kids here tonight.

We were the only church in the world who knew the truth. We were daughters of The King, and that made us real life princesses. We were members of the Church of Christ, and we didn't have pianos or organs when we sang and we baptized with water to wash our sins away and took communion every Sunday not just when we felt like it. Plus, we had the right name, "Church of Christ," when other people like Baptists worshipped John the Baptist but he was not Jesus, he was only Jesus's cousin so that was a big sin to be a Baptist.

I felt very sorry for my friends in kindergarten who were not in the Church of Christ, because even if I loved them, they were going to burn in the flames of hell forever. This Devil who didn't believe in God would believe by the time Daddy Black got done talking to her. The crowd was not as good as us because they hadn't even found their seats and at least we had found ours.

I looked over at Mother. Her blonde hair was swept back in a tight bun. Her face was perfect and thin like a triangle; her black eyeliner made her eyes look sleepy and pretty. At night without her makeup she looked weaker and a little bit sad, but with her makeup on tonight, she looked stronger than she did at home. "Mother, you look pretty," I said and tapped her on the shoulder. She smiled at me and I felt rich.

I knew best the Mother whose eyes were good with no painted lids or lashes, the eyes only I got to see because I'm the only one she shared them with, not Daddy and not Katherine. Only I knew the Mother whose eyes were kind because she loved me more than anything in the world. Even though Mother was thirty-three years old, her eyes were the eyes of a little girl like me. They were nice and sometimes afraid and very sad so I helped her when she cried. "Shhh . . . Mother don't cry," I patted her head when we were in secret.

"Thank you, sweet Stephanie; you make me feel so much better. You are such a precious baby," she said.

But she was my baby, too, and I was hers and she was mine and we belonged to each other and without me, my mother would die or be very cold and lonely because Mother said that we were two bodies but one heart. *Two bodies but one heart.* And without her, I would die and be cold and lonely, too. I looked at her shoes. They had tiny mirrors on them and were very high heels that sparkled up onto the ceiling like diamonds. Each time she moved the sparkles on the ceiling moved and danced with her.

We were all seated now, even The Devils, and the loud talking became a low buzz and then everyone was quiet. I straightened up and folded my hands.

"Good evening, Ladies and Gentlemen." A gray-haired man in glasses cleared his throat and spoke into the microphone on stage.

"Daddy, who is that old man?" I got down out of my seat and asked loudly, tugging at the sleeve of Daddy's brown suit. He had his bellbottoms on tonight and looked so handsome and his thick red hair was combed over to the side and he had used lots of hairspray from a can. I reached up and patted his hair and it felt like sticks.

"Shhh, Stephanie. Be quiet." He put a finger sweetly up over my lips. He leaned over and whispered, "He's the moderator. He tells people when their time talking is up. Now, go sit down."

Moderator. He looked like he might also be a Devil, because he looked like he didn't care one way or another and that is just as bad as not loving God at all, because Daddy Black says God spits people out like that, people who don't care one way or another. Better to hate God than to not care about God. I couldn't tell whose side the moderator was on, so I got up on my knees to try to figure it out. Too many gray heads in front of me to see anything.

The moderator said, "Tonight we are proud to present two distinguished guests, Ms. Madalyn Murray O'Hair, outspoken atheist, who proudly wears the title given to her by *Life* magazine as the 'most hated woman in America.' Ms. O'Hair is the founder and president of American Atheist and is best known for her advocacy of complete separation of church and state.

"Also joining us tonight is Mr. Victor Black, minister of Bayside Church of Christ in Pasadena, Texas, and prolific writer on the topic of abortion. He is joined tonight by his wife, Judy, his children, and grandchildren. He's best known for his controversial book, *Abortion in America: The Silent Holocaust of Our Nation's Policies*. He argues regularly on the public debate circuit, and has spoken in front of senators, congressmen, and medical boards as has Ms. O'Hair. This debate should prove interesting and relevant to many of us here tonight who stand on opposite sides of a heated topic. Our speakers have a lot of ground to cover, so we'll get started. Folks, please be respectful, hold your comments and questions until the end when our speakers are finished, and I'm sure they'll be happy to stick around and answer questions."

Mother's shoes sparkled on the ceiling.

Daddy Black started by being nice and calm because you can't win over a Devil by yelling. He spoke in his deep, happy tone and that is the same way he talks to Catholics when he teaches them the Bible and Catholics are really going to burn in hell because they don't even worship Jesus's cousin. They worship Mary, which is even worse but I don't know why. Maybe because she's a girl. One night when I was very little, much littler than now, I woke up from night-time and went into the living room and Mother and Daddy were still up and watching the news and there was a man in a white nightgown and he was waving to a big crowd and I rubbed my sleepy eyes and said, "Daddy who is that?"

and Daddy said, "That's the Pope. He's one of your enemies," and that scared me very much because I didn't even know I had enemies.

"Stephanie, sit up straight," Mother whispered. "Stop slouching. And sit on your bottom."

"I'd like to begin my stance with describing and defending the position of the early church on abortion by bringing in non-canonical writings of the first few centuries," Daddy Black said. I hoped Mother was happy over there and not too nervous. She tapped her bright red nails on her cheek and I smiled big at her so she would be happy. She smiled back but her smile didn't look nice and she motioned her eyes and nodded her head up to the stage, reminding me silently to focus on the debate but I really could not think about the debate anymore and it had only just started. I looked up at the stage at Daddy Black and wished him good luck and stuck my tongue out a little bit at The Devil but I could feel Daddy's eyes looking at me so I pulled it back in.

"The Church, from the very beginning, according to The Epistle of Barnabas, branded abortion as a form of murder (Barnabas 14:11). We find that in very direct teaching, Ms. O'Hair, 'Thou shalt not destroy thy conceptions before they are brought forth; nor kill them after they are born,'" Daddy Black said. The light was shining on his bald head.

Ms. O'Hair laughed at Daddy Black and pushed her wiry gray hair over tighter to the side. She adjusted her glasses and shook her head. The Devil's tights had a red hue and I was pretty sure I saw horns and I looked closer and those were not red tights. That was her skin! Both of their words sounded very much the same, like the teacher on Charlie Brown, but I was rooting for Daddy Black.

"Says whom? A bunch of prehistoric, nonsensical, barbaric baboons that had no intellectual or scientific basis for their belief system? Oh please." She reached for her water glass with her large, wrinkled hand and took a sip without looking up as she spoke back to Daddy Black. She was writing something while she spoke.

Daddy Black did not say anything mean back when she called our Bible a baboon bible. I felt sorry for Ms. O'Hair because she had gone up against Daddy Black. He was trying to get the Devil loose from her. What a victory for Jesus! Devil knocks you down, Jesus lifts you up!

Daddy Black wrote now while he talked. "From the time of the very beginning of the work of the Church of Christ on this earth, it has spoken out strongly against abortion as being the equivalent of murder in the sight of God. The early Christians knew not to grieve The Lord."

I wiggled in my seat. My Sprite was gone. I pried off the metal flip-top from the top of the can and played like it was a wedding ring, holding my hand out in front of me and waving it around. I fluttered my hand from side to side to show myself and everyone else my new ring. Daddy looked at me and shook his head.

I slowly reached over and tried to take Katherine's Sprite out of her hand but she yanked it back, spilling a little on her own leg. She turned away from me so she couldn't see me scowling at her for not sharing. Daddy looked at me and warned me with his eyes. Mother scowled back at Katherine for not sharing and then Mother warned Daddy with *her* eyes because he had warned me and not Katherine and Katherine was the one who was not sharing. Selfish Katherine.

Daddy Black stood up now and took his place at the podium. Daddy Black was God and he would beat this Devil. I looked around the auditorium and the crowd was listening carefully. "They knew the languages in which they were written, Greek and Hebrew, better than we. Their testimony that abortion is equivalent to murder, a testimony which is unanimous and without dissent, should go a long way towards settling the question for those who seek the truth."

The Devil's eyes flashed with red light and her fangs grew longer down to her chin. *Oh, Jesus help poor Ms. O'Hair. Jesus save her!* She snorted like a pig. "Truth? You think you hold the truth? There is no god, no 'truth.' The truth lies within each human and is up to autonomous interpretation. You have no truth. No god has ever been revealed nor answered any prayer and no god ever will. The relationships that people have that are sexual, psychological, emotional—these relationships are not open to supervision by parents, schools, churches, or government. Nobody has any right to intervene at all in any kind of relationship like that. Are you saying that abortion should be a *crime?* Punishable by *death?*"

Daddy Black opened his Bible. His voice got louder and I pictured him sprouting holy angel wings.

"The Unborn are just as precious in His sight as those who have come forth from the womb. Exodus 21:22-25 is powerful teaching from God, and if we had no other Scripture pertaining to the valuation that God places upon life in the womb and the punishment He will visit upon those who destroy it, this passage settles the matter once and for all. 'If men who are fighting hit a pregnant woman and she gives birth prematurely but there is no serious injury, the offender must be fined whatever the woman's husband demands and the courts allow. But if there is . . . ,'" he raised his fists up in the air and shook them at the ceiling, "'SERIOUS injury, you are to take A LIFE FOR A LIFE, EYE FOR AN EYE, TOOTH FOR A TOOTH, HAND FOR A HAND, FOOT FOR A FOOT, BURN FOR A BURN AND WOUND FOR A WOUND. What gives you the right to snuff out a life?'"

"What gives me the right? The Supreme Court gives me the right. That's who," she said.

I turned around in my seat to look at a woman who was sitting behind me breastfeeding and smoking and I couldn't believe she could do this because she was *very* good at doing two things at once. I really liked her because she must be very smart because her cowgirl hat was white with a peacock feather on the side. Her long brown hair was silky.

I walked down the aisle and whispered in Mother's ear, "Mother, she's smoking."

"Stephanie, she can smoke in here. It's a free country. Now go sit down and don't get up again."

I got back up in my seat and stared at the woman in the cowgirl hat. I pretended to smoke. She did the *you need to turn around, sweetheart* motion with her hand and I really was about to, but then I started licking the back of the chair pretending I was a giraffe and my tongue was reaching a leaf. Then suddenly I felt the warm air of the auditorium underneath me as I was whisked towards the back of the building, flying through the aisles being careful not to get in anyone's way or step on feet. The floor was the only thing I could see as I faced down, a hand on my back and underneath my stomach. I was being marched out the door by Daddy.

We pushed open the back door using his hand and my body. "Mathew, Mark, Luke, John." My bottom lip started to shake and my feet touched down on the parking lot gravel.

"Stephanie, stop reciting the books of the New Testament," Daddy said.

"Daddy, don't spank me! I'm sorry." I started jumping up and down and crying. "Acts, Romans, First, Second Corinthians, Galatians, Ephesians." I wanted God to know I knew His Word so that if the spanking killed me I would close my eyes and wind right up in heaven.

"I am going to spank you. Do you know why?"

I did know why.

Whack, whack, whack. I knew what I'd done wrong. And I knew to sit still better than that and to leave my sister alone. I knew to be silent like we are in church; it just wasn't something I was very good at.

He picked me up and I buried my face in his shoulder, hugging him and hiding my face from the crowd. It was none of their business that I got spanked and I will spank them if they look at me. We made our way back to our seats. This time the auditorium felt hot, not warm. My mother and aunts and grandmother shifted their legs making a way for us to get by. I sat in my father's lap because even though I was on her team, Mother was too fragile to have people sit on her; it hurts her bones. I put my hands over my ears but could still hear Daddy Black. "What sayeth God's Word?" He shouted and pounded his fists.

The Devil said slyly, "You can't create law with Scripture, Mr. Black. We don't base the laws of our nation on your Bible or anyone else's."

"Behold, children are a heritage from the Lord! The fruit of the womb is a reward. Like arrows in the hand of a warrior, so are the children of one's youth. Happy is the man who has a quiver full of them. Psalm 127:3-5." Beads of sweat were now dripping from Daddy Black's head as he shouted about lost babies floating in outer space. "Children are gifts from God."

Katherine turned and looked at me and smiled and was ready to play. I turned my head away from her. I reached out for my mother; my sadness had turned to anger and shame about my spanking and her love made me feel better. She waved me off. She agreed with my spanking so I sat back down in my empty seat and let Daddy Black's deep voice rock me to sleep as the debate went on and on and on like the sound of Katherine's record player when I held the needle down, "Chhhhiiiiillllldddddrrreeennn aaarree gggiiiffftttsss fffrrrooommm GGGOOOODDDD." Daddy Black fought The Devil. He fought her as best he could that night with the sword of truth and the shield of faith and the breastplate of righteousness, but the newspapers and reporters said he lost. He lost because The Devil was just plain stronger and trickier than him. That old red Devil was just plain trickier.

LEARNING TO READ IN FIRST grade was the greatest thing that had ever happened to me. We were having a big party and only Mother, Daddy, Katherine, and I were invited. Daddy had gotten his braces off and tonight we were celebrating. He was raised on a farm and could never get braces when he was a kid because his parents didn't have enough money so he got them when he was a man. His smile had been a jumbled, metal clump since I was a baby and tonight, we were going to get to see his real teeth!

Mother was very busy fluttering through the house like a butterfly filling bowls and plates with food for our party. She was wearing her black sparkly heels that glittered under her black satin bathrobe with a real mink fur collar. It was tied loosely at the waist over her special dress that no one would see until the party because she was beautiful and she saved things like that to surprise us. She cheerfully told Katherine where to place the food and showed her how to blow up balloons, and we tried to help her as much as we could. I was happy but nervous because it was very important to Mother that everything be perfect for Daddy's Braces Party. Mother was happy so I was happy too.

Because it was such a special night, Daddy had given Mother money to buy something very special: a La-Z-Boy recliner! Katherine and I were so excited we were about to burst like bubbles! The only thing we needed after a La-Z-Boy was a ceiling fan. Or an Atari. But that was just dreaming, I knew. It's not like we were rich or anything.

Our party menu had all the things Daddy couldn't eat with braces . . . pink bubble gum, caramel popcorn, and salt water taffy. Katherine helped set the table and filled the sparkling sterling silver bowls—gifts from Mama Black—with small and large pieces of gum. Mother told Katherine the gum needed to be unwrapped and colorful and standing up straight like they were saluting soldiers, not lying like death in a plastic coffin. She showed Katherine how to salute and we giggled because Mother was no soldier. "Presentation is very important," she said.

Katherine was already dressed for the party. She wore a smocked yellow dress with a pink-and-green watermelon embroidered on the side and tiny black buttons sewn into the lace collar like they were little lost seeds. A few shiny buttons were also placed down and around her dress as if they had fallen from the watermelon. I was allergic to watermelon. I was also allergic to many other foods like milk, eggs, wheat, and lots of fruits and vegetables, chocolates, and any and all fabrics that Mother didn't touch first to make sure they were gentle enough. I could only eat pears and cashews and goat's milk and a few other things if Mother smelled them first and said they were safe for me to eat. Everything else gave me asthma and made my legs itch because I had eczema that bled and bled if I ate something that was not safe. I was also allergic to cats, dogs, smoke, dust, grass, all weeds, and any sheets that were not satin, but I could wear clothes as long as they were washed in laundry detergent with no scent. It was very important that I had Mother nearby at all times because she was the only one who could help me if I got asthma or rolled around in grass or sweat. Katherine could eat every food and Mother didn't have to test it first and that's why Katherine was a little bit fatter than me and I was a skinny girl and she was a fat girl.

"Katherine, make sure he can see the taffy. And don't eat any of it. It's for Daddy and you need to start thinking about your figure, anyways." I sucked my stomach in and decided I would start thinking about my figure, too, even though I was not eating the taffy because I was allergic to it.

"And I don't want the bubble gum getting all the attention so make sure both bowls are filled to the rim," my mother sang from the kitchen. "Yes, Ma'am," Katherine answered back, because Katherine and I both wanted to please Mother and we were working as hard as our hands could work to make the Braces Party good.

"I want to help," I said. Mother passed by me and her perfume got into my nose and made me sneeze.

"No, Stephanie. You're allergic to dust and we're stirring up dust. See? You're already having a bad reaction and having a hard time breathing." I hadn't noticed I was having asthma but now that she mentioned it my chest was beginning to feel heavy and my face was starting to itch. "Go rest. You look pale and weak. Katherine and I will do everything."

Katherine rolled her eyes at me. I lay down on the couch while they worked around me and I smiled at the way the room was transforming into a wonderland. Mother strung lights across the wood-paneled living room walls and covered our plants with aluminum foil. She made them sparkle and twinkle like a fairy tale forest. She was amazing.

I wandered up behind Katherine who was blowing up balloons and I took one out of her pile. I put it up to my lips but she took it from my hands. "Stephanie, go lie down. Mother said no. Now scram."

"Stephanie, *lie down!*" Mother yelled from the kitchen, this time very forcefully. "You'll get asthma and break out if you are around latex." My throat itched and I scratched it with the back of my tongue. Mother opened the oven and the heat singed her long false eyelashes together until they looked like spider legs. "Well phooey!" she yelled with her eyes squinted shut, suddenly feeling around frantically and holding on to the walls like she had just gone blind. I hopped off the couch and Katherine and I ran into the kitchen to see if we could help. Katherine handed her a paper towel and Mother peeled off the burned eyelashes.

"You looked prettier without those, Mother," I said, but she didn't listen to me because she was trying to see. I worried that Mother was running out of time and that the party wouldn't be ready for Daddy. I was cross that she wouldn't let me help because I could've been a good help to her.

The corn on the cob sizzled in butter and the spareribs bubbled in the oven in oozy-gooey barbeque sauce and the house smelled like the rodeo from my place on the couch. Daddy would be so happy to have these foods again! It felt like a home. Katherine fluffed up the couch cushions and when she came by me, I popped my head up and said, "Katherine, I can help. I don't need to lie down."

She sighed and looked around the room for a job for me. "Okay, Stephanie, I'll tell you what. Hold this." She handed me some glitter, patted me on the head, and walked away. I tried to tell her I didn't want to just hold glitter but she passed by.

Daddy was out today running errands while we got ready for his Braces Party. Daddy took care of our home and made it beautiful, so he always ran errands on Saturdays. He fixed things when they were broken and even built a tree house for us in the back yard. He did the grocery shopping, the laundry, and all the cleaning. He mowed the yard and planted every flower in it. He was careful, my daddy. His voice was sweet and kind when he was kind. He blew my eczema with a cold hair dryer and told me to picture myself well and calm and he rolled a cold Coke can on my legs when they were bleeding if I scratched them hard because I had eaten something I was allergic to that Mother didn't test or if I broke out because Mother and I got nervous. He played with us at the park, read books to us at night, and he coached our little league teams. He preached once a month at a stinky old folks' home and his Lion's Club got money every year to give eyeglasses to kids my age who couldn't afford them. I loved Daddy and wanted more of his hugs. But Katherine was his real daughter, not me. I was more Mother's.

I threw the glitter on the floor when she walked away. Stupid Katherine. "I don't want to hold glitter," I told her, but she was already gone.

I rolled off the couch and wandered down the hallway into the back of our one-story, ranch-style home. Our street was called Orchard Lane, and it was in the middle of a neighborhood not far from Pasadena, the home of smog-burping oil refineries and Gilley's honky-tonk.

I ran my finger down the wall of the hallway down to my parents' bedroom. I quietly went in and shut the door behind me like I had done so many times before. Daddy had a bathroom that belonged just to him, so my mother and Katherine and I shared the pink one down the hall. His had black wallpaper with shimmering orange roses and big, round lights around the mirror like a movie star's dressing room. Mother said his bathroom was "elegant for a man," but I thought *Daddy* was elegant for a man. He loved his telescope and folding his clothes neatly and shining his shoes and one of his biggest dreams was that one day he would have all matching walnut hangers in his closet and I hoped I would be the one to buy them for him. He had glossy nails and he ran them through his thick red hair. His hair was the kind of hair I ran my fingers through too, and I prayed the whole time while I did it, *Dear God, oh please don't let anything ever happen to change Daddy's hair or make it different than it is right now. Jesus name, Amen.*

Everyone at church said my hair was a gift from him and I believed that was true, but just because I looked like Daddy did not make me a pretty little girl. I had a pug nose and small gray eyes that were a little too close together, and one was slightly larger than the other. When my hair was short I was not pretty at all, but Mother said I was the sweetest and prettiest little girl in the whole world and she said that if she could've lined up all the little girls in the world and chose one she would have chosen me.

I made my way to the back of Daddy's toilet and picked up his little black gun off the large stack of *Playboy* magazines that were neatly placed on the back of the bowl like I had done so many times before. Daddy's *Playboys* called to me when no one was watching because they were sexy and they made me feel sexy, too. It made me happy to know they were there and I could see naked ladies any time I wanted to and that made me feel close to Daddy because my daddy liked naked ladies so I wanted to be a naked lady, too.

"Stephanie, don't tell your Daddy I'm telling you this because he would be so embarrassed, but I saw Daddy kissing Katherine and touching her you-know-where and they played hobby horse naked." Mother puts her finger up to her mouth. "Shhhh," she says. "That is our secret." I kept her secret because I was a good girl and Mother knew she could trust me.

I held the gun carefully by the wooden handle between my pointer finger and my thumb. I made sure I made it face the floor. I put it down very, very carefully on the bathroom countertop because guns could shoot you. I turned back to pick a magazine and came across one with a girl on the front of it and she was dressed up like a kitty so I took it. I also took three more magazines, too. I picked the gun back up carefully. I knew I had done the wrong thing by even touching it and Daddy had warned us not to touch this gun time and time again but I couldn't help it. I was lonely.

I snuck back through my parents' bedroom and down the hall to my own room. I could hear Katherine and Mother in the living room hurrying to finish up the final touches for our Braces Party.

Mother said, "Katherine, the cotton candy should look fluffy, not depressed like it just came out of a sad movie. And serve that crunchy peanut butter in the crystal wine glasses, not the everyday bowls."

"Yes, Ma'am," Katherine answered back.

I peeked out of my bedroom and down the dark hallway; my heart was racing with excitement. Mother caught my eye from the kitchen, and I could see that her hand was wrapped up in a dripping white towel and she hurried over to the sink. "Dammit, Katherine. I reached into the hot oven without that potholder on again. Can you get me some ice?" Katherine stopped what she was doing and rushed to help her as best she could. "Goddammit, nobody ever helps me," she said, as Katherine reached in the freezer for ice.

I closed the door to my cornflower blue room with a white-laced canopy bed and got into my closet and closed the door there, too. I pushed past my frilly dresses and warm winter coats to make my squirrel nest in the corner of the closet, lit with one flickering light bulb, threatening to go out. I crouched down in the corner and just couldn't wait to open them. My body was warm and my heart was beating into my chest. I opened up the magazines and flipped one open to the first page. Nothing but words, words, words. I went straight to the big page in the middle and opened it up, letting the three pages flap open, my heart pounding like the hooves of the fastest horse winning a race. I was breathing very fast and hard and my face was hot.

I studied her body, devoured her with my eyes, her breasts and bottom and the look in her eyes that said, *I love you, Stephanie.* I started rubbing myself all over my body and in between my legs. Her lips were shiny red with clear lip gloss like every pretty girl and she was lying across the rumpled purple satin sheets and was turned halfway around with one smooth leg over the other. I pretended like I was older. I pretended like I was a teenager. I purred like a cat and like I bet the woman in the picture must be purring and I wanted to be just like her.

I reached up and touched my own short hair, and I promised when I was a grown lady one day I would have long hair like this lady and I lay down on my side like her but my knees were scuffed from playing too hard, so I put my hand over my scabbed knee so I couldn't see it and I pretended to moan sexy and move my body like the woman in the magazine. I pulled my white cotton panties down and rubbed myself. I felt good and hot and sexy in my body. I saw the shadow of myself on the wall and tilted my head back so that my hair in the shadow looked longer like a sexy lady. I knew all of this was icky and wrong because I was little and Jesus was watching but I always loved so much looking at Daddy's *Playboys* and if he knew they were missing, he didn't seem to mind.

My closet door swung open and there stood Mother. She had changed out of her bathrobe and was wearing a bright green dress with sequins and a white feather boa. Her neck and shoulders were covered in glitter. Her eye shadow was white and sparkly and was up to her eyebrows that were now drawn on with brown eyeliner; and underneath the brown pencil was a bald, angry red spot where her natural eyebrows had been only moments before. She looked like the surprised Queen of Hearts in my *Alice in Wonderland* book.

I tried to slam the magazine shut and hide it as I scurried to sit up but she had already seen. "Mommy I'm so sorry," I started to say.

"Stephanie, what do you have here?" She clenched her teeth because she was about to spank me harder than she'd ever spanked me before in my life. She jerked the magazine up and looked at it. I was a dirty, filthy little girl. Her eyes darted around my closet at the pile of *Playboys* I had hidden behind my clothes from all the other times I had looked through them before. She saw them. *She's going to hurt me or flush me down the toilet.* I closed my eyes and tried to pretend I wasn't in the closet; I pretended to be in the clouds where the sun shone through

but it didn't work. I opened my eyes and I was still there in the closet
with Mother and the *Playboys*.

"Nothing Mother," I said very sorry-like because I couldn't pretend
not to be there. I looked down at the ground and was embarrassed
about how short my hair really was. This would have been so much
easier if I could've had some hair on my head that I could've swished
around or run my hand through or hid my eyes behind. I looked and
felt like a boy and knew I would never be pretty enough to be in
those magazines. She took a deep breath and smiled. She had *a lot*
of makeup on tonight and I wanted to reach up and feel her eyebrow
because it did not look real, but she took me by the hand and pulled
me up to my feet. My bottom was about to get spanked very hard and
I squinted my eyes, "Mathew, Mark, Luke, John, Acts, Romans." My
panties were down around my ankles so that meant a bare bottom
spanking. I wanted to be a baby again. "Mommy I'm so sorry." I tried
to climb up into her arms but she waved me down, so I just stood
there. "It's time to pick out a pretty party dress for your dad's Braces
Party!" Mother said. Oh, I was so happy she pretended like nothing
was happening. *She's happy not sad but I'm sad and sorry.* "Which one
do you want to wear, sweetheart? The blue-and-white polka dot or the
crushed red velvet dress you wore on your birthday?" She was acting
happy so I acted happy, too.

"The polka dots please," I answered, looking down at my panties
without her seeing. I was burning to pull them up but if I moved, she
would remember that they were down because she found me in here
with Daddy's magazines and she would whip my bare bottom. She
quickly pulled my Underoos off over my head, flicking my nose on
their way up, and just as fast pulled the pretty dress down over my head.
I acted excited and happy about my dress because it was covering my
bottom and I talked fast about the pretty bows on it and while I was
talking, I quickly pulled my panties up so then I was dressed. She licked
her fingers and rubbed the grape jelly smudges off my cheeks and left

behind her fingerprints. She took my chin in her hands and moved my head from left to right. "You look so precious," she said, "just like always, you little cutie." Mother and I, we now shared another secret.

We left the magazines in my closet and marched into the living room and it was lit up and beautiful and it was a twinkling Braces Party. "Mother, everything is so pretty!" I said. We waited behind the couch and when he walked in, Mother whispered, "One, two, three!" We jumped out and shouted, "SURPRISE!" even though he knew we'd been home getting ready for his party. My eyes filled with happy tears and we were all smiling because this was the most wonderful party ever and Katherine and I held hands and jumped up and down because we were delighted to see our parents laughing and happy together. My mother handed me a plate of pears and we had the best Braces Party in the world. We were a team. We were a very good family.

After the party, Mother held her hands out for the money to go buy the La-Z-Boy. Daddy was silly and he slowly counted out the bills and Katherine and I yelled with him getting louder and louder with each word, "One hundred, two hundred, three hundred, four hundred, five hundred . . ." Oh, our excitement was big now!

Daddy whistled and had a dish towel thrown over his shoulder while he washed the dishes and cleaned up after our party. He listened to Willie Nelson while we waited for Mother to come home with our new chair.

Katherine and I waited in the garage with the door open so we could be the first to see the La-Z-Boy. I sat on my Big Wheel and Katherine sat on her bike and we looked out onto the driveway at the night rain. The Texas air was hot and steamy. The back of my neck started to sweat and the mosquitos were really biting. We waited and waited, and it was starting to feel like an awfully long time had passed.

Katherine said, "It's ten o'clock at night. She's not coming." Katherine had a watch and could tell time. "I knew she wouldn't come."

"She's coming," I said. But secretly, I started to worry that maybe

Mother had gotten into a car wreck. Maybe her car slipped off the road in the rain. Maybe she had gotten lost. I should've gone with her. The backs of my legs started to itch, and I scratched them until they hurt instead. I pushed my fingernails into the whelps and made crosses so Jesus would take away the itching.

We sat with our faces in our hands until finally Daddy walked into the garage. He was in his blue pajamas now and wearing his glasses instead of his contacts. He looked worried. He smelled like shampoo and he wasn't wearing his watch. He patted Katherine on the shoulder and said, "Hey, Ace, thanks for the party tonight. Let's turn in," and they walked arm in arm inside. I got up and followed them.

"Deeddy, you're weeeelcome!" Katherine cooed like a country girl or a baby or something. She reached up to kiss him on the cheek and he smiled and pointed right to the center of his cheek for her to kiss it again like a target.

"Well I tried to help get ready for your party but they told me no. They said I would get asthma," I said. "They said 'go lie down, Stephanie.'"

But nobody heard me. I hated myself for not having done more to make his party special. *Dumb Stephanie! Dumber Katherine!* There was something wrong between my daddy and me but I could not decide what it was. I could not get his attention. *Is Daddy mad at me because Mother is late?* I didn't make her be late.

And then the front door of the house flew open and my mother blammedy-blammed in, and she was still in her ball gown and high heels with a plastic bag over her head and she was now soaking from the rain. Her hair was stuck flat to her forehead even though she had that plastic bag on. Her mascara was dripping down her face, but her smile was big from ear to ear. My favorite person in the world was home.

"Oh, *Stephanie*, come here, sweetheart! I got it! I got it!" she yelled. My heart was jumping with joy and I darted past Daddy and Katherine, shoving them as I ran to the front of the house. *I told you she was coming, Katherine!* I wanted to jump up in her arms and hug her like people on *The Price Is Right* but she was so small under her wet clothes I thought I might break her so I didn't. I just stopped and patted her arm. "Where?!" I asked. My eyes were wide and wild, and I smiled so hard.

"Here!" she said, and she moved her body to the side of the doorway, and Katherine and Daddy and I all stood in amazement at what sat out on our porch protected from the rain that fell hard right in front of it.

Daddy's mouth actually fell wide open. He could not even talk.

"Mother, what *is* that?" Katherine asked. "Daddy, tell me what this is, please, right now." She looked up at him and tugged on his sleeve. She sounded scared. Daddy closed his eyes and tilted his head back and took a big breath.

"What we have here sitting before us is a shiny, spit-polished, real, one-of-a-kind, totally unique, irreplaceable, antique hospital wheelchair," Mother answered.

We stood there staring at her and none of us could think of what to say. I was trying very hard to think of something but I couldn't because I kept looking at Katherine who now looked angry. *Katherine, be nice to her! Don't you dare say something ugly.*

Mother talked fast. "The wooden legs are absolutely without blemish. The marbled wood is swirling with natural detail, and it has brass decorations on the hinges that have been painted black, giving it a feeling of being . . . well . . . art," she said.

We kept staring at her. Daddy tilted his head to the side and raised one eyebrow higher than the other and folded his arms.

The rain poured behind her and dripped off the corner of the roof and fell into the flower beds. The porch light shone yellow and some bugs zapped into it. She wiped her hair out of her eyes and giggled like a little girl and I was getting nervous because everyone knew Mother had made a mistake.

"Mother, I love it!" I rubbed the wooden arms. But I did not love it at all. "It's really pretty."

She smiled and slowly breathed out and said, "Well thank you, Stephanie. The back was made of wicker and was spray-painted a mahogany brown."

"Oh, I can see that. It seems really special," I said.

"It is." She struggled with it through the doorway and set it up in the sparkling forest of our living room. I looked at Katherine who was fuming! I glared at Katherine until she turned and looked away. *Katherine, don't you dare look at her that way! She did her best! She tried!*

Katherine said, "Mother, this is not a La-Z-Boy. And I don't think it's art *or* special. It's embarrassing and stupid." She looked up at Daddy and he just nodded, giving his unspoken permission for her to go to bed. Katherine walked out of the room without saying anything else and I knew that Katherine felt let down and I didn't want her to feel let down and now I felt like I had let Katherine down because Mother and I were both embarrassed now that we had bought the wrong chair.

Mother waved her hands like she didn't care so I didn't care what Katherine thought either. "Look at this! Isn't this great?" she squealed. "Stephanie, darling, come get in it."

But I was afraid of the wheelchair. It looked like a chair a ghost would sit in. "Will it pinch her?" Daddy asked. "It looks like it'll pinch her, Lillian. There's nails attaching the hinges."

"Oh, Paul, don't be a stick in the mud. It's not going to pinch her. Come here, baby," she patted the seat.

"It's going to give her splinters," Daddy said.

I went over to it and sat down on the hard wood seat, and the center of it was wicker too, and it felt like my bottom might be too heavy for it because when I sat down, I sank down low. I couldn't do anything but sit up very, very straight because the back of the chair was very straight.

"It does everything a regular recliner does but *better*, Paul," Mother said. "And it isn't ordinary like everyone else's chairs. It *reclines*." She pulled a lever on the side and I went flying straight back and was looking right up at the ceiling of our living room and holding on tight to the wooden arm rails so I didn't accidentally turn all the way upside down.

"Lily, the chair we agreed upon in the store also reclined," Daddy said.

"Right. I know. But, it also sits up *straight*," she said. And with that, she huffed and puffed behind me using her shoulder to push me straight back up fast and her ball gown almost got pulled down but she hoisted it up over her chest. "Paul, it wheels *everywhere* and *anywhere*, which a modern recliner *will not do*." She pushed me through the living room, whipping the chair around, showing that it could swerve side to side, but the big wheels kept catching on our shag carpet.

My lip started to quiver and I was getting scared now. "Mother, I want to get down," I said.

"Even the legs come up, Paul, if you want to relax and watch a game or just rest." But the legs had to be raised one at a time and that took a lot of strength, and even I could tell they were there for the care of a real broken leg, not for a Daddy watching the Oilers.

Daddy's face looked like an old man. He looked like he might cry but he tried to be kind because he loved Mother and didn't want to hurt her, but his eyes looked a little mad, too. I couldn't tell what Daddy was thinking.

"Thank you, Lillian," he said. "This was real sweet. Real, real sweet." And then I knew he must be sad because he doesn't always call her Lillian. He kissed her on her wet forehead and walked inside and started taking the foil and lights off the plants that Mother had so carefully hung so our living room would look like a pretty forest. He turned off the record player that had stopped playing a while ago and had been skipping but none of us had noticed, and he turned off all the lights in the living room except one lamp. The party was really over now. The wheelchair stayed right there with me still in it. Mother said, "They don't appreciate unusual things with potential."

"Nope," I said. "They don't." The back of the chair fell all the way back again and once again, I looked at the ceiling. I held my head up but then let it lie down again. She straightened it up and smiled at me.

"I feel better tonight than I've felt in *years*," she said. "More vibrant. More in control. Able to take on the world." She knelt down to my level and looked into my eyes and got quieter. "Stephanie, what do you think?" She smiled and squeezed my cheeks. "Did Mommy throw a great party or what? Does Mommy have a good eye for art? Can Mommy take on the world?"

3

We are one in the Spirit
We are one in the Lord.
We are one in the Spirit
We are one in the Lord.
And we pray that our unity
  will one day be restored.
And they'll know we are
  Christians by our love,
By our love
Yes, they'll know we are
  Christians by our love.

"LILLIAN. PLEASE. LILY. PUT THE gun down." Daddy's voice trembled like a little boy talking to a bear. He stood still by the stove in his "Super Dad" apron. Our pork chops were burning on the stove making the whole room smoky and hot. The dark smoke under the pan was full of fire Devils and they snickered their way up into the overhead oven vent and then sunk into the flowered wallpaper of our yellow kitchen.

I crouched down in the corner of the kitchen with my back turned against them and hid my face in my hands. "Jesus loves me. Jesus loves me. Jesus loves me this I know. Jesus loves me. Genesis, Exodus, Leviticus, Numbers, Deuteronomy, Joshua, Judges, Ruth. Help us live!"

I tried to breathe but I shook hard because Mother was *really* mad at Katherine and when I breathed, I felt a sharp pain in my chest. I closed my eyes tightly and tried to hide myself because if I couldn't see them, they couldn't see me. I pushed my body into the corner as best I could, pushed my shoulders into the wall, and tried to find a hole like a squirrel does in a tree when it rains. I imagined a black tornado behind me tearing through our house picking everything up, everything up . . . things like mothers and daddies and sisters who love one another. It swirled everything and everyone I loved through the air. I closed my eyes tighter and pictured everything in our house being destroyed by the winds and the pouring rain and I felt as though logs and bricks, wood, and roof shingles were hitting me in the back and I could not get far enough away, I couldn't run, and the wall would not let me in. Plants, furniture, dishes, and books and toys were swirling in the air too and slammed into my back and knocked the breath out of me. But no that's not what was really happening. It was just Mother and Daddy fighting again.

Mother was sitting at the table in a chair that faced Daddy in our kitchen. She held Katherine in her lap and pushed the gun up near her face with the round part sticking hard into Katherine's bright red cheeks. They looked hot and tears spilled over her lips and the creases of her neck. The tears got in her mouth and she could not talk, she could only keep crying and spitting. I was so sad for Katherine but very scared for me too because Mother hated that gun but she was holding it like she *loved* it. Katherine's blonde hair had grown a little and she had just gotten a perm yesterday, and the tight curls were wet against her forehead and her nice blue eyes were giant. "I want Daddy. I want my *daaddddyyy!*" She screamed the word *daaddddyyy* so hard that she sounded like she was dying.

I turned and looked because I thought Katherine had actually died but she was still alive and Daddy's hands were still shaking and Mother was shaking with the gun. The more Katherine wiggled, the tighter Mother gripped her hard around the tummy. She dug her nails into Katherine who tried to get Mother's hands off, but she couldn't because Mother's hands were just plain stronger.

Daddy's voice got slow and careful behind me. "Katherine, baby, please be still, little one. Breathe slowly and be very still. Lily, please let her go. Nobody meant to violate you." His bottom lip quivered like mine and I thought he might cry like Katherine, but he didn't because he was very strong and daddies don't cry.

Violate. I did not know what that word meant but I thought I must have done it to Mother. It was me and not Katherine who was bad but I couldn't tell anyone because I might have died with Katherine so I tried harder to get into the wall. I was not brave enough to stay and die with Katherine.

Daddy turned off the stove. I heard it click and turned to look. He took a step back and let his arms fall to his side and he was careful. Very careful. Katherine was still crying but less now and she was trying to wiggle loose.

"Why did you let them open my mail?" Mother was crying too like Katherine. Beside her on the table was a Christmas package that had been unwrapped; its shimmering gold paper that should have been pretty had been torn apart by me. Inside the box was a new pair of beautiful red satin gloves with pearl buttons that lined the wrist. There was a glittered card also opened by me. It sat beside her on the table and she was now *violated.*

My mother had smiled at first when she picked up the card. "Merry Christmas to my perfect, irreplaceable, totally unique, one of a kind and precious niece, Lillian. All the Best. Love, Uncle R.L."

But when she read the card out loud, I watched her smile melt away and her face change into someone else's face, and not only could I *see* her change, I could *feel* it because I felt what she felt because I was her and she was me because I was her favorite, favorite, favorite six-year-old in all the world.

Dr. R.L. Black was Mother's uncle, brother of Daddy Black. They called him "Ronly Lonly," and they said he was brave to serve in a big war and the whole wide world was fighting for a second time but America was so strong and the officer that took his papers asked, "What does R.L. stand for?" You can't just go by letters for your name. It has to be short for something.

"It stands for nothing. It's 'R' only and 'L' only." So that's what the men who fought that war with him said his name was and so did Mother and Daddy. Mother and Daddy laughed and laughed at the name Ronly Lonly. Daddy said isn't it strange that Ronly Lonly had a name that stood for nothing and how sad would that be to be a Methodist who stood for nothing. But at least he was a doctor. That was something.

Uncle R.L.'s pictures looked like Daddy Black. They both had sharp cheeks and chins that pointed out ahead of their faces. I was afraid of Daddy Black but not of Uncle R.L., because he was a nice doctor who lived far away and sent Christmas gifts to us each year.

"Why did you open my mail?" Mother gritted her teeth and growled like a wolf. "You had no right! It was addressed to me. 'Lillian Walters.'" Her eyes burned red and her tears got far down into me and I could feel her pain so I started to cry too, because I didn't plan on any of this happening and I didn't mean to *violate* her and Katherine was taking my blame that's why.

"Lily, the girls thought there may be a Christmas gift in there for them. They didn't do it on purpose. They thought it was toys. Please, please put the gun down. Give Katherine to me."

It wasn't "they." It was me who opened her gift. The kitchen filled up with the last of the smoke now from the skillet. Our food was burned and it smelled yucky. Mother pulled Katherine closer. I wanted to raise my hand and say, "Take me! Mother, take me! Not her! I opened your present!" But I was just too afraid. I was not brave enough to help Katherine.

Stupid, stupid, bad Stephanie! I tapped my head on the wall. When Katherine and I had seen the new Christmas gift lying under our lit-up Christmas tree we were both so excited.

"Katherine, what is it?" I asked. "Maybe it's my doll!"

"No, silly goose. It's too flat to be a doll," said Katherine. She shook it gently and we listened for what was inside. "Stephanie, it's not a doll. I think it's crayons," she said. I thought maybe Katherine knew because she was big and very smart and in third grade.

"Santa came early!" I said. I grabbed it from her and shook it hard because that's what it needed if we wanted to listen for crayons and really know what it was. "It's a bell for a bike!"

Katherine took the box out of my hands. Her eyes were happy too because we were kiddos and Christmas and Santa were coming and that made us happy. "No, Stephanie. It's not a bell for a bike. Put it back before Mother sees or she will be mad." She gently placed the pretty box back under the tree because Katherine was a good girl and could wait on things much better than I could. "Let's go play," she said. So we did . . . we went to play.

But when Katherine played by herself outside, I snuck back and opened the present by myself because I just couldn't help it. The wrapping paper was lined in smooth green velvet and looked very expensive. I opened it because it might've been candy. Santa was coming soon! But it wasn't candy. It was gloves for Mother and I was sorry because now I had opened her present.

Daddy put his hands up in the air like Mother was the police. He said, "Lillian, everything is going to be okay. I promise. Nobody here wanted to hurt you. We are all on your side." Mother looked like she trusted him. She let go of Katherine with one arm. Daddy took off his apron very slowly and moved in closer and Mother handed him the gun. He put it in the cabinet above the stove and fell down at her feet and started to cry too because he couldn't help it but neither could I. Mother trembled as she held Katherine and then hugged her and loved her again. She wasn't mad anymore. "I'm so sorry, baby. I'm so sorry. I love you so much, sweet, sweet, little baby Katherine." She kissed my sister who arched her back to try to get away. I was hurting now because Mother was sorry and Katherine wouldn't take her hug or forgive her and she was trying to say she was sorry. Daddy took Katherine out of Mother's arms and into his room and I heard him lock the door. Mother put her head down on the table and cried and cried. She was sorry and it hurts very badly in our hearts to be that sorry when we are people and other people won't forgive you. I hugged myself and I cried in the corner, too, because I was sorry too.

I felt Mother's arms around me from behind, lifting me up and carrying me to the chair. I put my arms around her neck very tight like I was holding a teddy bear. I patted her on the back of her head and kissed her cheeks. There were salty tears all over them and I told her she was very pretty and good but she was just too sad. She didn't believe me but I told her again. I listened to her cry but I did not cry because she was sadder than me and I wanted to make her feel better and not cry. "Don't be sad, Mother. It's okay now, Mother. It's okay. Please don't cry, Mother." I patted her until she slowed down her breathing and didn't cry as hard. The fighting was over and Mother felt better and so did I.

The next morning was Christmas Eve, and we woke up early to the smell of cinnamon rolls and the sound of Christmas songs on our record player. It is not a sin to play music in our house, only in church. Daddy was waiting for us in the living room; his eyes were red.

"Girls, your mother is in the hospital because yesterday her head really hurt. She is a little bit sick right now, but I don't want you to be afraid. She is very safe and warm and is not hurting anymore and some nice doctors are giving her some very good medicine." He smiled and nodded and I understood and I also thought that maybe she felt sick.

"I'm glad she's gone," Katherine said. Her voice was too calm, and she looked down at the ground and wouldn't look at me when I tried to make her. "She's not sick. She's mean."

"Katherine, no, she's sick," Daddy said. "She's beautiful and kind. There is a side to her that is very beautiful and kind."

I wanted Katherine to forgive Mother quick so we could be happy and together and have Christmas. Yesterday was a long time ago and I forgave her when she said sorry. "She's not mean! You're mean! And Santa is watching! So is Jesus!" I yelled at Katherine to make her forgive my mother who was very sorry.

"Girls, stop. No one is mean. Your mother is *sick*. If she had two broken legs and could not run with you, you wouldn't be angry with her, would you? If she had no arms and could not reach out, you wouldn't be angry with her. We would hand her what she needed because we love her. This is the same thing, girls. She is crippled like a person in a wheelchair. She's handicapped. Her head hurts sometimes, but she wants to love us the right way and she needs help doing that. Please don't hate your mother, Katherine. She loves you and she cannot help it." Daddy was telling the truth. I forgave her right now and I wanted Katherine to forgive her right now, too.

"Daddy can I go play?" I asked.

"Not yet, Stephanie. Be still."

He told us he had just spoken with her nurse and that our mother had scrambled eggs and toast with jelly for breakfast. He told us we are not telling anyone at church that Mother is sick. He said they will want to pray for us and bring us food but that some things are just private. He said if anyone from church asked, we would tell them Mother was visiting a friend.

The house was quiet for the rest of the day. Katherine and Daddy did not seem to be sad. When they thought I was playing, I heard Katherine ask, "Why can't we just leave her and get away?"

But Daddy said God hated divorce and that it would be a sin. He said he made a promise before God to stay married to Mother until death do us part in sickness and in health. He said Mother was his cross to bear and that everybody had one. *Don't you dare leave her. I will throw rocks on you if you do!*

That night, Katherine and I slept together in Katherine's room and waited on Santa together.

"Katherine, is Santa real?" I asked.

"Yes, Stephanie, now go to sleep." Katherine yawned and pulled her covers up over her head.

"Do you think he'll bring my two-wheeler?"

"I don't know, Stephanie. But if he doesn't, you better be happy for whatever you get. Don't be selfish. That's a sin," she said.

I thought about it, and because she was my big sister and she told me to, I decided I would be happy even if I woke up and there was no two-wheeler. I would be happy if there was no bike but I hoped there would be a bike because I could be selfish Stephanie.

"But do you think he will?" I poked her because she seemed like she was falling asleep and I wanted to talk. "Katherine, do you think Rudolph will come, too? What if Rudolph can't come because he gets sick like Mother? If Rudolph can't lead the sleigh, then none of them could even come."

Suddenly, Katherine jumped out of bed and ran over to the window. Her eyes were wide and she was very serious but she also smiled so I smiled too.

"Stephanie! I heard him! I heard Santa! I heard Rudolph on the roof! Go to sleep, Stephanie, or Santa won't come in!" I closed my eyes tightly and laughed to myself when she got back in bed. I wrapped my arms around her body. I held Katherine with all my might but she did not hold me back because we both knew she was brave and I was not and that I opened Mother's present and didn't speak up. Even so, she was warm and she felt so good, and I prayed that this feeling of being close to her would last forever and ever, not just for tonight. But I knew it would not last. It was only for Christmas.

We were quiet for a while.

"Katherine, are you really glad Mother is gone?" I asked because I didn't want her to be glad.

"Yes," she answered.

"She's a good mother and she loves us."

"No she doesn't. She only loves you." She was falling asleep.

"I'm sorry," I said, because I knew in my heart that she was right. Mother had a headache and she only loved me but I didn't want her to only love me because it was scary love and I had to be very strong to bear it and I was not strong.

"But *I* love you," I said. And I did love Katherine.

She was asleep. I was awake and kept holding her. I listened for Santa and prayed to God. *Dear God, please help Santa come. And please when I wake up make Mother's head not hurt that way.* I snuggled in close and held on tight to Katherine because she was my only sister.

• • •

God answered my prayers because if you even have the faith of a mustard seed, He will do anything you want. It took a looonnngg time, but He healed Mother's head because when she came home from the hospital, she felt better and was smiling and her eyes were smiling, too. She came home with a box of Valentine's candy for Katherine and me and I ran to jump in her arms but Daddy said don't jump on her. So I just whispered, "Surprise!" and smiled big because I knew she felt better because the makeup on her face was not too much and not too little and her lips were pretty with pink gloss, not red. Katherine loved her again and forgave her because deep down Katherine was not really glad when Mother was gone. Katherine forgave me too because the days have been coming and going and Katherine forgot that I was not brave enough to die with her and she and Daddy and I had lots of fun days at the park that helped Katherine forgive.

Daddy went to work at the bank and Mother taught school for a lot of days in a row and we were very happy. They put their coffee cups down softly and Mother didn't lose her keys or lock herself out of her car once for lots and lots of days so I stopped watching where she puts her keys down because I don't have to do that right now. She went to school at night to get a master's degree while we stayed home with Daddy because Mother said a master's degree is the only thing nobody can ever take away from her. She said they can take everything else, your home, your husband, your babies, your car, but they can't take a master's degree.

Daddy made us chicken pot pies when she was at school and I ate them and didn't get asthma or allergies at all. He fed me other foods, too, like grapes and enchiladas and I didn't get allergic once. Daddy said, "Stephanie, don't tell your mom I gave you this," and he gave me a popsicle. I told him I couldn't eat that but he said for me to give it a whirl so I did and I was fine.

We watched *The Hulk* because Mother's school nights weren't on a church night so we could relax. Katherine and Daddy laughed and laughed together and set their TV trays riiiggght up close to the screen because they couldn't *wait* for *The Hulk* to come on, but I was very scared of the nice man who has the mean man inside him. I hid behind the couch and watched through squinty eyes when he started to get angry. "Oh Stephanie, come out from behind the couch and sit with us. It's not real, it's just TV," Daddy said. But I just couldn't because it looked very real. David Banner was going to get angry and *The Hulk* was going to come and I just couldn't look at that.

Mother and Daddy both came home from work and poured glasses of wine in the kitchen together. She leaned on the counter in her pretty Gloria Vanderbilt blue jeans with the skinny gold belt. She ran her long clear fingernails through her hair and laughed when Daddy told a joke. Because she laughed, he laughed, and he leaned in and kissed Mother on the cheek. Her head is *so much* better and she is pretty with a smooth face. She touched Daddy's shoulder and his eyes looked so kind and they had some tears in them that looked happy and he moved a piece of her thin brown hair off her forehead. The sun came in the kitchen and made Daddy's face look gold and he was happy because Mother felt better. When they finished their wine, they giggled and told us girls to huddle up, huddle up. The four of us, we ran through the house to see who could do it the fastest. We grabbed the blankets off our beds and pulled the folded blankets out of the closets and threw them in the middle of the living room floor. Mother was laughing because Daddy tickled her. "Tickle me too, Daddy!" I shouted, and he did. The blankets were a mountain of fluff and we piled them up very high, as high as we could get them.

"Stephanie, come get in with me!" Katherine held the blanket open because it was a secret door so I could climb in. I climbed in under the mountain and she climbed in, too. We couldn't breathe but we didn't even care. "Hide! They're coming!" she giggled, and she forgave me and Mother and we didn't think about *violate* or guns or being sick anymore.

Mother and Daddy went to all our rooms and turned all our lights off in the whole house so that it was dark. They went to close the curtains and the blinds so our windows wouldn't let in any light at all because the sun was going down outside and tried to shine in on us. Mother looked out the window. "That rent house is empty again. I guess the last people just up and left it. It's such an eyesore," Mother said as she pointed down the street.

Our neighborhood had lots of families just like us, and we all lived in our houses for a long time, but the rent house down the street only had people live there for a little while, and then they would be gone again. The real owners lived somewhere else and only renters lived there who didn't care about it, so it was ugly and when Mother and Daddy talked about "the rent house" we all knew which house they meant.

"Someone needs to just march over there and mow the yards and plant some flowers," Mother said. "You'd think they'd hire someone to at least maintain the yard since mostly the thing sits empty."

"Maybe the landlords will get some new tenants soon," Daddy said. "Let's don't worry about it." He closed the curtains.

"Well, Paul, *somebody* needs to worry about it. If it's abandoned it's going to bring down the value of the whole neighborhood."

He smiled and took her chin in his hands. "Well, let's not worry about it tonight, Lily, okay?"

The house was as dark as when I closed my eyes. Totally black, totally silent, and I couldn't see my hands or Katherine's face. I could only hear the quiet and Daddy and Mother laughing and getting ready to get in with us. No strangers could get in to be near us and nobody needed to pray for us or think Mother was visiting a friend when really she was sick, because it was just our family. Nobody knew where we were and nobody was with us but the four of us. Katherine and I waited under the blankets for them and they came.

Katherine let me get close to her because we were happy and have the same blood on Friday nights because we were sisters. I didn't belong to Mother and Katherine didn't belong to Daddy but she belonged to me and I belonged to her and they belonged to us and we belonged to them and we belonged to each other because we were a family on Friday nights.

Daddy turned on the TV and they were both under the blankets with Katherine and with me. *Dukes of Hazzard* started, and they held us tight and said they loved us girls and that we were both great kids no matter what, no matter what. It was the greatest love in the whole wide world, and it was inside me and God was *with* us under those blankets and my parents, and Katherine's and my love and Jesus's love was very, very, very real.

THE A CAPPELLA SINGING BEGAN harmoniously from inside the double doors of the worship hall led by a few elders who were already in their pews. The rest of the congregation filed in while simultaneously singing, too, winding down their happy conversations in the foyer between Sunday school and Big Church. Lots of kids grabbed one last donut from the table in the entryway that was supposed to be reserved for visitors. They ran crazily through the legs of the adults, laughing and tagging one another, but ever since I'd turned eight and started third grade, I didn't act like that anymore. I was even allowed to carry a small purse to church like Katherine. The mothers held armfuls of birdseed-covered pinecones and papier-mâché with strings and other Sunday school crafts while they talked with each other and found their usual seats.

I walked out of the bathroom drying my hands on my dress and looking around for my family when Brother Hazel caught me by the shoulder coming around the corner. "Hello there, Stephanie!" He crouched down as best he could to my eye level and put his face riiiiggghhht up next to mine. I heard his knee crack and I reached out and touched his shoulder to help him get steady.

"Young Lady, why don't you reach into my pocket and see what you find." Brother Hazel was very special to me and when I was with him, I understood I was loved. I didn't feel any age when I was with him, not eight or five or one hundred. I wasn't younger *or* older than anyone and neither was he.

Brother Hazel was our church song leader, but he also read scripture sometimes in the pulpit. Every Sunday he wore the same forest green suit with a crisp white handkerchief in the front pocket.

I loved him because his eyes danced when he laughed and that made him seem young but they were also sad at the corners because I think there were things he'd cried about that made him wise. But he didn't show any sadness on Sundays because this was the day that the Lord hath made!

But I knew his wife was dead. And I knew his son had died in the Vietnam War because I'd heard Mother and Dad talk about that, how it had "leveled" Brother Hazel. He had deep lines in his face so I hugged him every chance I got. He understood me and I understood him, too. He smelled like Old Spice and spearmint and a little bit of cigarette smoke, and his gray hair crinkled against my cheek when he hugged me.

"Brother Hazel, gimme some gum." I ripped back his suit coat and plunged my hand down into his satin-lined pocket and pulled out a piece of pink bubble gum that was meant just for me. He laughed and took off his cowboy hat and walked with me into the worship hall where my parents and sister had found their seats. He shook Dad's hand. "Good mornin'. Bless y'all," he said. He nodded his head at Mother, "Sister Lily."

She smiled.

"Why, thank you, sir. And God bless you." Dad shook his hand vigorously. Brother Hazel leaned down to hug me but instead pulled a quarter out from behind my ear before he went to sit down. I laughed and put the quarter underneath my sweaty thigh to see if it would make a mark in the shape of a circle by the end of the service.

The men sang the melody and the women sang harmony and our voices bounced off the bare walls and wood-paneled ceiling, beginning to reverberate, calling our flock to worship. *There is a God, He is alive, in Him we live, and we survive* . . . My heart started settling down because the sound of our congregation singing was the most calming sound in the whole world to me.

More families, men and boys in suits, women and girls in their starched, finest dresses, were sitting down now and kids got out crayons and candy. The moms wagged their fingers saying, "Not so fast," and handed them a hymnal instead. The morning sunlight streamed through one window and across the pews in our very plain building. Over the years, the light had warmed a spot on the flat, once-red carpet that was now faded to a dull maroon. The Church of Christ took pride in our plain buildings. Things like stained glass, candles, crosses, and figures of Jesus were considered idols, graven images according to the Ten Commandments. Our church met in a small wooden building and we had no fabric on the pews, no kitchen, no images of Jesus on the walls. Many Churches of Christ did not have windows at all, but ours had a few.

Daddy Black began the sermon. "Good morning, Bride of Christ! Are we, the Church of Christ, the only ones going to heaven? Of course we are. Jesus said He was the way, the life, and the truth, so a person can't be saved outside of the Church of Christ, because we are His one true church. Indeed, we are His bride." I took out a piece of paper and wrote what I learned in Sunday school.

God's plan of salvation for Stephanie Olive Walters in third grade:

1. I have to hear the gospel. I have to know without Jesus I am lost no matter what. I know this is true.

2. I have to believe in God and have faith because without faith I cannot please God. I need to be more faithful. Starting RIGHT NOW.

3. I have to repent of my sins but repenting is not enough because I have to obey, too, and I don't obey because I won't stop looking at Dad's magazines and touching myself you-know-where.

4. I have to confess that Jesus Christ is the Son of God, but this is not enough to save me.

5. When I am baptized and not one minute before, my sins will be forgiven. I will be baptized soon, when I can stop sinning.

6. Once I am baptized, God writes my name in His book of Life but I have to be faithful until the time of my death or my name will be blotted out of His book and I already have a very hard time being faithful.

"And why are we the True Bride? Because of baptism by immersion, our participation in communion, and our lack of 'strange fire.' We are the only church who only makes music with our voices, not with a piano or organ. The Bible doesn't tell us one way or another about instruments, but it does say, 'Make a joyful noise unto the Lord and come before Him with *singing*.' Make a joyful noise unto the Lord with your heart, and nowhere in the Bible does it talk about pianos or organs. See, these things are strange fire like what Aaron's son in the Bible used. The verse in Leviticus said, 'Aaron's son Nadab and Abihu took their censers, put fire in them and added incense; and they offered unauthorized fire before the Lord, contrary to His command. So fire came out from the presence of the Lord and consumed them, and they died before the Lord.' And that's what pianos and organs and drums are to the ears of God . . . noise . . . strange fire."

I looked up and noticed a young blonde woman sitting on the front row next to Mama Black with her head bowed down towards the floor and her shoulders slumped. I waited to get my drawing pencils out because I was trying to get a better look at her.

She was unsmiling and thoughtful but she didn't look like she was crying. Mama Black was whispering in her ear and she was nodding her head up and down. In the Church of Christ, women were not allowed to speak unless they had their heads covered or their husband's permission, but I'd never seen anyone cover their heads. Come to think of it, I had never seen a woman even try to speak in a service. Women also weren't allowed to teach Sunday school to boys over the age of twelve and they were not ever allowed to teach men. Brother Hazel walked over to her and touched her shoulder like a father, and with shaking hands, she handed him a crumpled piece of paper. Mama Black patted her on the back and then coldly folded her arms and nodded to Brother Hazel. After the sermon, he walked up to the pulpit and handed the letter to Daddy Black to read it out loud to all of us.

• • •

"Dear Brothers and Sisters,

As you know, a year and a half ago, my three-year-old daughter drowned in a pool. The pain of this eventually led to the breakdown of my marriage. My husband and I were not able to overcome the deep divide of grief between us after her death. We were so sad and blamed one another, even though that wasn't right, and as you know, we recently divorced. Since then, I have not been faithful in my attendance, and have tried to console myself with any earthly comfort available to me . . . drugs, alcohol, and sometimes sex with men who are not my husband. However, these earthly comforts have not comforted me at all. In fact, some days the pain of her death causes me to pray that the love of God will keep my legs holding me up so that when my feet hit the floor in the morning, I will have the strength to stand. But some days, even the love of God can't do this for me, and I fall down right there beside my bed. But I want to come back to my church. I need the love of my brothers and sisters in Christ. I ask your forgiveness for seeking the comforts of the world, and I am humbly standing before you willing to absorb any consequences you as a church may have for me."

· · ·

"Mother, what is she talking about?" I whispered. "Mother, what consequences?"

"She's talking about being shunned or disfellowshipped," she answered.

I knew what disfellowshipped meant. It was when someone was unfaithful and the church loved them *so much* that they had no choice but to shun them until they got their life back right or got rid of their sin.

I sat still like a stone and watched carefully. Being disfellowshipped sounded so scary.

Daddy Black folded the letter back the way it was, put it in his pocket, and said, "Because of your repentance, we will honor your request." Just, "we will honor your request." No happiness. No sadness. No nothing in his voice. No care. No one said a word. I looked up and down the pews and moms were opening up mints and some other people were reading their bulletins. It was almost as if people weren't even listening.

I wanted to run down the aisle and hug and pat her and give her my pencils. I squinted my eyes as tightly as I could and folded my hands until my knuckles turned white, because when you are worshipping God the more it hurt the more it counted.

I shot light and love into her back. *Dear God, please bless Sister Tammy. Jesus, calm her down, and let her feel your love. Heal her heart and keep her baby close to your face forever. Pleeeaaassse don't let her little girl be afraid without her mother. Oh, I sure would be so afraid if I were her, Lord.* I pictured her little girl somewhere far away, floating in the nighttime starry orbit, with her chubby arms outstretched for her mother, but then, just as quickly as the image came, the little girl's face became my face, and then I was also floating in space. Then the image left.

It was replaced by a vision of the little girl happy and playing in a dazzling, splendid world with colors that we didn't even have here on earth. Instead of being green, the plants were iridescent shades of purples and oranges, like opals, and they swayed each time a soul passed by. The plants got their energy from these passing souls instead of the sun. The little girl was holding fluffy baby lambs and bunnies and she was lying down with kind lions and gentle cobras who didn't want to hurt her at all. The snakes slithered up out of their holes, poked their heads up, and grinned at her in a game of peek-a-boo. Every animal and human soul was in harmony and the little girl wasn't crying or drowning anymore. There was no water filling up her lungs. She was not gasping for breath or struggling; she was breathing easily with a deeper, loving understanding that I wanted, too.

I wanted to go tell Sister Tammy not to cry, that she was forgiven, because I loved her so much her sin didn't count. I wanted to tell her not to worry or be afraid or blame herself anymore. I wanted to tell her none of that mattered now.

But that's not the way we did things.

Brother Hazel walked up to the pulpit and blew into his pitch pipe. He coughed a bit after deciding on a note, and said, "Brothers and Sisters, let's stand and sing page 225, 'How Great Thou Art.' We'll sing all four stanzas."

Shoot. We always have to sing all four stanzas. That's too long.

I looked down at the floor at Mother's high heels. They were fire-engine red with hot pink tips on the toes. It was coming. I waited and cringed. My forehead started to feel like it was swelling and heating up. Oh, goodness, here it came. I looked over at Katherine and she had her head cocked back, her eyes closed. She was facing up at the ceiling and rocking back and forth on her ankles. Mother stood erect in her lavender suit, cinched at the waist with a thick canvas belt and bright plastic buckle in the shape of a rose. Her hair was cropped and dyed red and her makeup looked . . . almost right but the black eyeliner swirled up too high towards her brow and her lids were covered with bright white eyeshadow and she looked like Endora from *Bewitched*.

"Oh, Lord my God. When I in awesome wonder."

At first, we all started singing together and at roughly the same volume.

"Consider all the world Thy Hand hath made. I see the stars; I hear the rolling thunder. The power throughout the universe displayed."

Mother's voice started to rise loud like an opera singer because she loved "How Great Thou Art." Her voice got louder and louder and pretty soon the other voices began to trail off. Then it was just our family and a few old people who couldn't hear who were still singing. Stanza four was coming and that was the worst part of the song because it was the most powerful and she usually got so worked up on this part that I wanted to climb under the pew and die but I kept singing in support of my mother.

"Then I shall bow, in humble adoration, and there proclaim, MY GOD! HOW GREAT THOU ART! Then sings my SOOOUUUL,

my savior, God, to THEEEEEE. How Great thou ARRRRRRT. How Great thou Art!"

And it was done. There was nothing anyone could say or do. We closed our hymnals and replaced them in their pockets on the backs of the pews. The congregation sat down. Everyone was silent. And nobody dared laugh, because who were we to judge the sounds being lifted to God? But the youth group and some toddlers did laugh and I looked down the pew at Katherine fuming and she scowled at me. *It's not my fault, Katherine. I know she sounds awful.* I snuggled up to my mother and buried my hot face in her suit. She put her arms around me and looked down at me. I looked up in her eyes and she winked at me. She looked . . . clueless. Helpless.

Daddy Black walked up to the pulpit and began. "Brothers and Sisters, this is the day that the Lord hath made, Amen. Good morning and isn't God good? Rejoice ye heavens, and ye that dwell in them. Woe be to the inhibiters of the earth and of the sea for the devil has come down unto you, having great wrath, because he knoweth that he hath but a short time! Turn in your Bibles to Revelations 12:12."

CHAPTER

5

IN THE CAR ON THE way home we rode in silence with our Bibles stacked in the back seat between Katherine and me. Dad loosened his tie and gripped the steering wheel. Mother popped her crossed leg up and down and tapped her nails against her cheek. I stared out the window and thought about the consequences but then gathered up the nerve because it needed to be said.

"Mother, you sing too loud at church," I said softly. "Your voice is really pretty and all; it's just a little bitty, teeny, weeny bit too loud." I made the "tiny" symbol with two of my fingers when I said, "teeny," and I put her head between my fingers and my line of vision. Immediately after the words left my mouth, I was sorry.

"Well, Stephanie, darling, I'm so *sorry* if you are embarrassed by my signing." Her voice sounded like a song, but not the happy kind. She didn't really sound sorry.

"I am not singing to you, however. I am singing to God. He is the only one who needs to be pleased with my singing. And one of these days, I will be dead. That's right. I will be dead and gone and shut up in a coffin and you will just wish in that little *selfish* heart of yours that I was here to sing you just one more song. You will wish you could hear me sing again, even if it's loud. But I'll be dead. Dead."

Okay, Stephanie, you big stupid jerk. I'm sorry!

Then a stream of slow, steady tears fell out of her eyes and she stared out the car window. Noooo! My skin started to itch and my stomach got queasy and I lightly tapped my head up against the car window. I made a promise even though it was a sin to promise because the Bible said let your yes be yes and your no be no that from now on I was going to like her singing, no, I was going to *lllooovvve* her singing and never say anything bad about it again. I didn't want to kill my mother or be sorry that I would never hear her singing anymore if she died, so starting next Sunday I was going to scowl very meanly at anyone in the congregation who laughed at her because she was singing to *God*, not man. The next time somebody laughed at her for singing loud I would scream bloody murder at them.

"I'm sorry, Mother. I didn't mean that," I said.

"No! The damage is done, Stephanie. I'll never sing again. Okay?" she answered.

I glanced over at Katherine who shook her head and mouthed the word "stupid."

Like you care about her, Katherine. At least I care about her. Brat.

"Lily, is that necessary?" my father asked. "Are you listening to yourself?"

Mother turned her head and slit her eyes at him. "Shut up, Paul," she snarled. "You wouldn't know anything about it. *I'm* the one who fell off a horse when I was young and pregnant and my baby died. Okay? He *died*. And I would be the one to ask how that felt, okay? I sing loudly because it makes me feel better. I'm singing to *God*, not you or anyone else. Stop trying to humiliate me!" She gritted her teeth and tapped her red nails harder this time on the dashboard.

"Oh great. Here we go again. Lily, don't do this, please," Dad sighed. His gray eyes relaxed and so did his voice. He put his hand on hers but she quickly pulled it away. "Last week you said you ran through a red light when you were young and pregnant and your baby and boyfriend both died. Remember? Just stop it. Please?" he pleaded. "Nobody is dead. Everyone is safe. Maybe you should call your psychiatrist, Dr. Leatherman, again and talk to him about this *baby*? We could go together. It's not healthy if you are having these thoughts, Lily."

Mother's head is hurting again and her heart is hurting too. And it is my fault because I said she sang too loud.

"You'd like that, wouldn't you, Paul? Well no thanks. I'm not crazy," she said.

"I'm not saying you're crazy. I'm saying there's no dead baby." She stared out the window and her eyes looked far away. We all rode in silence.

"Mother, I love you," I said.

Nobody said anything.

"Mother, I really do love you. And I know God really loves your singing." More silence.

"Mother, Katherine called me stupid," I said.

Mother whirled around and faced us in the back seat. "Katherine, shut up, you fat little brat. Don't you dare call your sister names! You treat her worse than a bum on the street!" She grit her teeth through every word.

"Hey!" Dad stopped the car and yelled. "Stephanie, you are the one instigating all this! Why don't you stop tattling on Katherine, and Lillian, why don't you just stop, too! You're hurting both of them, not just Katherine. Stephanie, when we get home, go to your room! Katherine, you and I are going to take a walk." I wanted to go walk with them, too, so when Katherine looked at me I mouthed the words, "Can I come?" But she scowled at me, turned, and faced the window.

When we got home, I went into my room and shut the door. "I

don't know why you don't divorce her," I heard Katherine say to Dad from down the hallway.

"Katherine, you know that is a sin in the eyes of the church," he answered back.

Don't you dare divorce us.

I took off my binding dress and stripped down to my cool satin slip with the little pink rose at the neckline. Goodness, I loved it when church was over. I was finally able to breathe now that we had a few hours before it was time to go back for evening services.

I tied a blue scarf around my head so that the material hung down my back like long hair and I put a rubber band around the top so that I looked like Mary Magdalene, best friend of Jesus. I surveyed my look in my dresser mirror and whooshed my long, flowing "hair" from side to side.

I didn't look half bad. Next time Mother said my hair made her nervous and that she needed to cut it off I would run away.

I picked up my stuffed animals off the bed and lined them up on the floor so I could talk to them for a little while. "Come here, babies. You are all very precious and perfect, but I'm angry with you even though I love you all because you are all little brats, too."

I explained to them that as their mom I loved them very much, but that there had been some behavior among them lately that I didn't approve of. Some had been smarting off; some had just been down-right lazy.

"*We're not lazy.*"

"Yes you are," I replied. "In fact, you aren't memorizing your scriptures at all and some of you have even tried to sneak out and run away." I looked straight at Elle, my elephant that sang the tune of "You Are My Sunshine," when I said that. She tried to avert her eyes, but she knew who she was.

My poodle puppy looked up at me with his deep black eyes and cocked his little white head to the side. "Don't try to change my mind,

Singing Puppy." His little blue velvet necktie was crumpled from me loving and hugging him at night when I was afraid. *"But I've always been there for you,"* said Singing Puppy.

"That doesn't matter. I'm your mother and I say what goes, and you're a little brat."

Tiger, who was always shy, buried his little head in his paw. And my Cabbage Patch Kid, Renee, smiled. Like that was gonna help. I put my very favorite teddy bear at the front of the line and turned all their backs towards me.

I gritted my teeth at him. "Don't you DARE ignore me," I said. I took one of my dad's belts out from my closet and spanked each and every one of them over and over again, leaving my favorite teddy bear for last. When it was his turn, I turned him to face me and explained to him that I'd saved him for last because I loved him the most, and that he made me have to beat him this way. "I love you and you are my special little baby. You and I really need to stick together, and I really feel like you are trying to pull away from me. This is going to hurt me so much more than it's going to hurt you, believe me. It's just, I really, really, really need for you to behave and not hurt Mommy so much."

"Mathew, Mark, Luke, John," he said. He almost changed my mind.

I hugged him tightly and kissed his face desperately, "I love you I love you I love you I love you sweet, precious baby," and then because he was my favorite, I whipped him hardest of all.

• • •

That night after church I waited in my bed for Dad to come lie down with me, but he never came. I lay in the dark and stared at the ceiling listening to him and Katherine laughing in the next room. He was tickling her and talking to her and telling her favorite stories from when she was little. I could hear him making the "ahhhooooggggaaa" sounds of the fog horns as he told her the story of Captain Horn Blower. This was one of my favorite stories. I loved it when the Captain saw the light of the lighthouse far away in the distance.

"Daaaddd! Come tickle me!" I shouted.

"Just a minute, sweetheart," he called back from down the hall.

"No! Dad, come now! Dad! It's my turn!" I shouted again.

"Stephanie, stop it. I'll be there in a minute." Their voices muffled.

I pulled my teddy bear towards me being careful not to touch his hurt bottom and whimpered and whined to myself turning over towards the wall, towards the door, towards the wall.

As I waited and faced the wall, I felt the pointed, tender scratching of long nails on my bare back.

Mother was with me now.

"Shhh. Sweetheart, you go on to sleep." She slipped in under the covers with me; her satin robe cooled everything inside me down.

"You know this is their special time together. It's not for you, Stephanie. He loves her in a very special way, and I love you in my own special way. You should be glad he doesn't come lie down with you and tickle you and play kissy face with you. It's just not right what they do when they're together and I wouldn't want that for you. Be glad he doesn't come. It's not appropriate."

She came closer now and whispered in my ear. Her breath smelled like wine. "Stephanie, I want you to be careful of your dad, okay? He really is a wonderful daddy in many ways, but I want you to be careful of him, and I don't want you to ask him to tickle you anymore because I don't want him doing to you what he does to Katherine, even if she does seem to just jolly well love it," she snorted. "If he comes in to tickle you, I want you to pretend like you are asleep, okay?" There was a panic in her voice. She was saying something very important. She was saving me.

I felt cold all of a sudden and I slowly closed my eyes and my breathing got heavier as I faced the darkness of my bedroom wall. Eventually, she quit scratching and I could tell she was thinking of something else because she was rubbing but just here and there, then finally she thought I was asleep so she tapped my back and left.

A few minutes later I saw Dad's strong shadow on the wall being lit up by the warm hallway light. He stood in the doorway and watched me for a second but I was thinking about what Mother had said. *Stay away from him. Be glad he doesn't come play kissy face with you.* "Stephanie?" he whispered. "Stephanie, are you asleep? Hey, Sport, you sleeping? I can tickle you now."

But I lay still and didn't say anything. I pretended to sleep like she said to do and prayed for him to go away and he finally did. And there was pain and anger inside me because I was very confused about what my dad and Katherine were doing when they tickle and what kissy face meant for a father and a daughter. I was afraid my mother may be getting sick again and I could feel my anger starting to grow thorny. It wasn't something that I wanted to happen. It just did. It just did.

"**WANNA GO DING-DONG DITCHING? C'MON,** Steph. It's no fun to go alone." Simone was at my window crouched down in our bushes with her dirty knobby knees in the dirt. She had painted "I hate cheerleaders" on her brand new, high-top Reeboks and I made a mental note to ask her about that later. That, and her jelly bracelets. I needed to know how she'd connected them together like that. She just knew things. She was wise. She had, like, tons of knowledge because she was in sixth grade and I was only in fifth. I opened up my window for her; she was tapping on it with a rock. "You're gonna break it! Sheesh!" I tapped on the window back at her harder than I meant to as I opened it. "I'm supposed to be resting before Sunday night church. Everyone's sleeping!"

Simone's blonde hair blew in the breeze and with the sun lighting up the ends of her curls, her silhouette looked like an angel with a halo. Her long, tight curls sprung across her forehead, and she gently shook them out of her eyes. "You're ten years old. Why do your parents still make you take a nap on Sundays? Don't you think that's a little dumb?" she asked.

My eyes got used to the shadows and sunlight and I could make out her face and could tell she had a cold sore in the corner of her mouth, probably from too much time in the Galveston sun again wearing nothing but baby oil and iodine. And even though she was only twelve, her skin looked like rough brown leather, cowhide. God, I was so jealous of her.

"Why didn't you just come to the front door, silly goose?" I opened up the window the rest of the way so she could climb in and she tracked black mulch all over the carpet.

"I don't know. So do you wanna come or not? I'm so bored. That guy across the street was standing in front of his pantry *naked* again. I looked through his window and he caught me peeking at him but he couldn't get covered up fast enough to chase me. What a fat ass hog. You'd think he'd at least take the Popsicle out of his mouth before trying to grab a towel. I swear to God, Steph, if I ever get like that, just take me out in the woods and leave me to live on my fat reserves alone, okay?" She sat down at my dresser and puffed up the sides of her hair, spraying the last of my Aqua Net on the sides so they would fan out.

"Shhhh! You'll wake up my mom and dad!" I took the Aqua Net from her and placed it back on the dresser, shaking the last remaining drops and hoping she would catch my drift not to waste any more of it because it was almost empty.

"Oh, whatever, Stephanie. Then get dressed and come outside with me. Church isn't for like another two hours."

I took off my slip and put on my shorts and T-shirt and grabbed my backpack full of Cheese Nips and Dr Pepper and other private foods that I had stashed in the back of my closet. I had been eating almost every food and none of it made me sick, but Mother didn't know. I poked my head out of my bedroom door and peeked both ways down the hallway. All the lights were out and the house was napping peacefully. I heard Dad snoring from down the hall and Mother quietly washing dishes in the kitchen. She was talking on the phone to Mama Black about a fellowship meal for the next week. "Well Mother, if you're bringing the whole brisket, then I think I can swing bringing the sides, good grief." She finished drying the last dish, flipped off the kitchen lights, and plopped down on the couch with the telephone cord stretching from the kitchen to the living room. "No, it won't work for me to bring potato salad. Sister Davis is already bringing chips and macaroni. That's too much junk. Plus, the last time I brought potato salad to a church picnic, nobody ate it. Don't you think people would prefer something green? I'm trying to keep Katherine's weight down." Katherine's door was closed but I could hear Air Supply crooning that they were all out of love.

"It's safe," I whispered. We climbed out the first-floor window, shut it behind us, and made our way down the street like we had no one to answer to in the whole wide world.

"Wanna go do that Elvira lady with the black Corvette's house? Or the Embrorskys?" The Embrorskys were a Pentecostal family with five daughters and they lived in the corner house down the street. The father, who I had never seen in anything but a three-piece suit, like Daddy Black, made all his daughters and his wife constantly wear pink. Not just to church, but every day and everywhere they went; to school, to the store, everywhere. They had pink dresses, long pink skirts, and pink pedal pushers. They had pink hair bows, pink rabbit fur coats, and pink patent leather shoes. Also, the carpet inside of their house was pink, and so were all the flowers in their garden. They had pink wind chimes that swayed when the wind blew and a huge Texas flag that hung outside their pink door. I seriously could not tell the daughters from one another no matter how hard I tried. They all looked exactly alike. In the springtime, their blonde hair got lighter and in the winter it got darker. But their tight braids were the same throughout the seasons, and the youngest, Julie, was my age.

"Let's do the Embrorskys, because I think that Elvira lady who lives in that ugly rent house is actually a witch. Have you seen her *makeup*?" I asked, hiding my backpack underneath a car that was parked on the street. I looked down the street at the rent house. The witch had painted the shutters black but the paint was chipped and one was crooked and hanging off the hinges.

"Well, at least she mows the damn yard and keeps the porch light on," Simone said. "Plus, she's got a Stingray. I'd give anything to have a Stingray."

"Oh, I know. Me too. I would give anything, too. I love stingrays. Everything about stingrays is so awesome," I said.

"You like 'em, huh?" she asked.

"Oh, gosh yes. I love everything about stingrays," I answered.

"Really? Everything? So, you believe in them, huh? Think people with Stingrays are on the right track?" She stared at me. Her cold sore had a yellow scab forming in the corner of her mouth. She took out a small jar of Carmex and rubbed it on her lips with her finger.

"Yes. Of course I do. I agree with having stingrays," I said.

"Stephanie, do you know what a Stingray is?" She tried not to laugh but couldn't help it.

"No." I looked down at the ground. She patted me on the head and smiled.

We crept up to the Embrorskys' front porch and rang the doorbell several times then took off running across the street and hid behind the back of the parked car. Mr. Embrorsky opened the door in his boxer shorts and tight white T-shirt, his black nylon socks pulled up to his knees.

"For once, no suit!" I whispered.

"No shit. He must be gettin' lucky, a little afternoon delight," Simone said.

He peeked out the door but couldn't see us. He stepped out onto his porch and stood there for a minute with his hand up like a sun visor, peering around from the left to right.

"Did you see that? He scratched his big, disgusting balls." Simone laughed.

"Yes, I saw. Now hush!"

He picked up his newspaper that was behind the potted plant and shut the door and went back inside. We watched and waited.

"Let's go back," Simone panted. Her face was serious. The competitive side of her had kicked in.

"Okay. But let's wait a little longer just in case he's coming back out." We waited a few seconds more and then went back up to the door and both of us banged on it about ten times with our fists as hard as we possibly could. We took off running and giggling and crouched down behind the car again to watch. Nobody came to the door.

"Maybe they didn't hear us," I gasped, squinting through the sunlight, not taking my eyes off the strawberry-frosting-colored door. "Maybe we should've rung the bell instead of banged?"

"No. He heard. He hears everything. He's probably busy locking his wife and daughters in a dark closet and making them pray. Let's go back," Simone said.

We got up and boldly walked across their yard, past their pink rose bushes, and up to the door. Simone pointed her magic, ding-dong ditching finger like Elliot in *E.T.* towards the doorbell, and right as she was about to push it Mr. Embrorsky threw open the door. His face was scarlet and his nose was bulging like a hilarious cartoon character, and had I taken the time to look closer, I might've seen steam coming out of his ears like one too.

We didn't even speak; we just both took off running like we were on fire down the street. He was after us but we were younger and faster than him even though I was barefoot. We didn't have to say it, we just divided and conquered. Simone ran through Elvira the Witch's rent house yard, jumped her crooked fence, and she was home free. Mission accomplished. No hard feelings.

I stayed the street course and he hunted me down like an animal as I zigzagged through manicured yards and down the wide concrete sidewalks. I turned over my shoulder to look at him, and his greased black comb-over was actually blowing so hard from his speed it was sticking straight up in the air like a wall. I took off to the left, running with superhuman speed, my arms at the side of me like blades cutting through the air, and I jumped the fence of the old people with the koi pond in their backyard.

"You girls better stay away! I'll tell your parents, you little punks! Stephanie Walters! I know your grandpa!" Mr. Embrorsky was chasing far behind in my dust now, screaming and shaking his fists. He couldn't keep up. I kept running and jumping fences until I was back on Orchard Lane, two streets over. The humid air sunk into my lungs and coated them with balmy Gulf Coast moisture with each breath I took. I slowed down to a comfortable stride.

When I turned back onto our street, Simone was sitting behind the parked car casually leaned up against the bumper with my open backpack beside her. She had gotten the box of Cheese Nips opened and helped herself to a warm Dr Pepper. She wasn't even sweating. I sat down beside her and reached into the box and took a handful. We rested in comfortable silence with our faces towards the sun, relaxing and knowing we could totally live in the wild if we needed to as long as we were together.

"Dare me to go ding-dong ditch Mr. Greg? Did you see him in his yard practicing those karate moves Saturday morning in that *kimono*? I mean, who *does* that?" She shoved a handful of the atomic gold crackers in her mouth and swigged a huge sip of soda at the same time and swished everything around in her mouth.

"No, I didn't see him. And no, we can't. We need to get home to get ready for church," I answered.

"Dare me to go knock on his door and act like I'm out of breath and ask to borrow a condom?" Her eyes lit up like she'd just won a zillion dollars and she started panting.

"Nah. We don't have time. Our parents are going to know we're gone if we stay out any more." I stood up to my feet and gathered up my Cheese Nips and decided there wasn't enough in the box to save.

Simone motioned for the box, and when I handed it to her, she tilted her head back and ate the last of the crumbs. "Okay. You're right. See you at church." And we parted and went back to our houses just a few feet apart. I climbed back though my window and the house was still sleeping. No one was the wiser.

We gathered up our Bibles, me looking for mine up until the last minute and Katherine helping me to find it again. My parents laughed and talked lightly on our way to church about what it would be like to go to Gilley's and ride the bull, and about whether or not the Astros were having a good season. Dad thought Jose Cruz should retire, but Mother said he still had a few good years in him yet.

I thought of a verse I had learned in church about Mary when she looked at her little baby boy, Jesus. It said, "And Mary treasured up all these things in her heart and thought about them often." I closed my eyes right then and there and took a snapshot in my mind of my parents being friends and decided to treasure up the memory of their hands touching and put it in my heart for later if I needed a memory to wrap myself up in, in case these good times didn't last. I decided that if it was good enough for Mary, it was good enough for me. I smiled at Katherine and she smiled back at me. "I love you, Katherine," I said.

"I love you, too," she answered.

We snuck in a little late through the back of church and found a seat on one of the middle pews. Katherine made her way up to the front of the church where the youth group sat together because she was twelve and she inched in past Simone, who was sitting next to the new girl, Valerie.

Valerie's parents didn't come to church. Her father was sixty-five years old even though she was only eleven, and her mother was thirty but she had a full head of gray hair and looked as old as he did. They dropped Valerie off for services, but they never came in. Valerie didn't care; she really wanted to be here. She searched the Bible constantly for Scriptures, way more than I ever did. She tried to memorize them and look for answers to her biggest questions and most of the time she listened even more than I did to Daddy Black's sermons.

Valerie's house was dark and depressing. On the rare times when we went there to play, the lights were usually off throughout the entire home and it felt empty and depressing . . . we felt alone there. The only light came from the flickering blue hue of the TV that shined under the crack of her parents' closed bedroom door. We could hear the occasional rising and falling of the laugh track of the TV audience and the low murmurs of her parents' voices, but we rarely saw them.

Valerie's parents were both heavy smokers and even though she was just a kid, Valerie was allowed to smoke in her house, too. She carried a cigarette between her fingers like it was the most natural thing in the world. She also carried loneliness behind her brown doe eyes, but it wasn't enough to spoil her beauty. She had a very sweet smile and she loved everybody the same, black or white, fat or thin, rich or poor. She didn't judge anybody and she wasn't prejudiced like so many other people in Pasadena were. When Simone and Valerie saw Katherine, they looked right past her with their eyes lit up because they knew I couldn't be far behind. They both turned around and waved at me and smiled.

Katherine shrugged her shoulders and scooted past them and sat down by the guys. She positioned herself between her two best friends, Devin and Trent. I didn't like those boys one little bit. They were older and rough and I knew that they hung out down by the ditch and smoked and started fires after school. Once, when I was outside playing, I saw Trent throw a frog up in the air and Devin skid on it with his bike. "Why do you hang out with those guys?" I asked her once. "They're jerks, Katherine. And their parents don't even know it."

"Butt out, Stephanie. You don't even know them," she said. So I did. I butted out.

. . .

"How important is your soul?" Daddy Black was already deep into his sermon. "Your soul is the real you, who dwells in your body, and when it departs from your body, your body is dead. Your soul is that part of you which will live forever, somewhere. Where? There is an endless expanse of time stretching out before us, after we leave this world. Where will you spend eternity? The Bible informs us that we are either going to an infinitely better world than this one when we leave here, or to an infinitely worse one—depending upon whether we hear and obey God's word while we are in this life, or not."

I thought of running up and down the street today with Simone and laughed to myself about Mr. Embrorsky's comb-over that looked like it had been greased with motor oil. I chuckled when I thought about Simone running so fast and him chasing us. I looked up at Simone and Valerie; they were passing notes and snickering. I couldn't wait until next year when I could sit with the youth group. Valerie looked like a full-blooded, full-bodied goddess, and her raven black hair hung down her back and touched the pew. She always dressed up for church, even at night services, because she didn't really know how things worked around here yet, that we only wore dresses on Sunday mornings. Nobody wore dresses at night except the really old women, but the lacy sleeves of her dress hugged her smooth brown arms, and when she ran her fingers through her hair, I could see even from where I was sitting that she had painted her nails bubblegum pink. When she turned to laugh at whatever Simone said, I could see the tiny chicken pox scar on her cheek right under her eye. It looked like an unusual beauty mark without the color. There was nothing about Valerie that wasn't pretty inside or out.

"To ask, 'By what are we saved?' is like asking, 'By what is physical life brought into being and sustained?'" Daddy Black paused and stared out at the congregation for an uncomfortable effect.

"Of course, the answer to both of the above questions is, 'by *many* things.' To say that we are saved by God's grace and mercy is preeminently true! To say we are saved by the blood of Christ is true! To say we are saved by our faith is true! To say we are saved by baptism or by living a Christian life is also true! But to say we are saved by any of these things alone is false." He wiped his forehead with a white handkerchief.

"These, and many, many other things, are absolutely necessary components of our salvation. We receive salvation by obeying the word of God and by being members of The True Church. God gives his holy spirit to all those who obey him." He pounded his fist on the podium waking up the sleepers. "All who do not obey the gospel will be severed from the Lord and from the glory of His power forever." He toned down his voice. "God's Word will be the basis of the final judgment of our souls. John 12 tells us that 'he who rejects me, or in other words, rejects The Church of Christ, and does not receive my words, has one who judges him, the word that I have spoken will judge him in the last day. For I have not spoken on my own authority; but the Father who sent me gave me a commandment and is everlasting life. Therefore, whatever I speak, just as the Father has told me, so I speak.' You have a choice tonight, brethren, whether to live eternally or die. Who'll come forward with a decision to live and be baptized? Now let's all stand and sing." Brother Hazel came up to the podium and led us in all three stanzas of "Seek Ye First."

Severed from the Lord forever. Forever. Was there even such a thing? That's really serious. I wondered if that was what God wanted from us . . . to be afraid of losing Him, or if Daddy Black could have been wrong. Maybe Daddy Black thought he was giving us life-saving information. Or maybe Daddy Black and maybe God, too, were just plain mean. I thought about what that really meant . . . to be without Him, without God, in coldness, freezing or burning from lapping flames in a lake of fire, doomed to complete separation from the one who made me. Amputated from the only one who really knew me. Floating in total silence, in darkness, in a world where I could scream but no voice could be heard, only silence, only struggling effort but void of noise. I shuddered with a fear somewhere so deep inside of me, so private to my soul that I couldn't even get the words out to the song. I wondered what would happen if I ever got outside of the Church of Christ. *I will never have fellowship with God outside of this system.*

Simone and Valerie stood behind me with the other kids from youth group in the foyer as everyone mingled around and talked after the service. Out of the corner of my eye, I saw Katherine laugh with Trent and Devin.

Mother looked wonderful and well in her starched white shirt and jeans. Her thin gold belt was wrapped twice around her tiny waist and she held her Bible loosely at her side as she talked and laughed. She had a platinum blonde pixie cut that shaped her face in a way that showed off her diamond earrings, a gift from Uncle R.L. Her blue eyeliner swirled up at the corner of her eyes giving her eyes a cat-like appearance.

Dad and Brother Hazel chatted it up about different types of pipe tobacco while Simone, Valerie, and I waited. "So what's with the shoes? Why do we hate cheerleaders?" I poked Simone's Reebok.

"Oh, I just did that because Lynne said I couldn't wear white T-shirts anymore or she'd take my phone out of my room." Simone referred to her parents by their first names, Ron and Lynne. Lynne couldn't stand it for Simone to do anything that wasn't ladylike, such as cursing or listening to rock music like Mötley Crüe, and Simone knew that Lynne's Achilles' heel was for other people to think that they couldn't afford nice clothes for Simone. So Simone threatened her constantly and usually got what she wanted by saying she would only wear white T-shirts if Lynne wouldn't let her do this or that.

"So you ruined your new Reeboks just for that? I wish I had Reeboks!" I exclaimed.

"Oh, who cares? And yes, of course I ruined them 'just for that.' She can't *control* me. Lynne didn't pay for them anyways. She's just a housewife. A stupid *housewife*. My dad paid for these and he's too busy golfing to care," she snorted.

Still, I felt bad for Lynne because I saw her every day outside working really hard in the yard, watering flowers and trimming the hedges, washing the car and the windows. Lynne didn't look stupid to me; she looked loving, and Simone's house was beautiful. It looked like a perfect little blue birdhouse, with white trim around the door and overflowing flower boxes that hung under the windows as a perpetual message to the rest of the world that all was well in that house. Secretly, I was jealous of the fact that someone waited for Simone to come home from school every day with a warm snack like French bread and marinara sauce or chocolate chip cookies and that their house looked like a birdhouse. It was so . . . *normal*.

"Still, Simone, you need to take care of what God gives you. Lots of people would give anything to have what you have, especially because your mom and dad are so nice," Valerie gently reminded her. I walked over and put my face right up between Brother Hazel and my dad. I smiled so big I felt like I was stretching my face out being with the two of them. I put my head against Brother Hazel and inhaled his familiar scents. He seemed tired tonight. His eyes looked milky and as he held his cowboy hat down by his side, I noticed that his hands were pale. On the way out to the parking lot, he didn't pretend to wring my neck or play with my hair or get quarters out from behind my ear. My dad helped him into his car.

Simone had the whole youth group's attention. "Oh my god! Did you hear the one about all the Catholics who were at the well with Jesus and that prostitute? Jesus said, 'Let any one of you who has never sinned cast the first stone. One by one all the people hung their heads and turned in shame and left. Finally, a woman came up and pegged the woman at the well in the back of the head with a pebble. Jesus said, 'Oh, hey, Mom.'" We all laughed but felt so sorry for the Catholics at the same time. We knew they were going to burn in hell, but we couldn't really teach them about Jesus because they were so wrapped up in the Pope and busy worshipping Mary and being an evil political machine. Also because that would mean we would have had to actually talk to them and that could've truly contaminated us. They were the ultimate anti-Christians for their Pope worshipping. Also they had priests and that was like totally against God because the Bible said, "Call no man Father."

Mama Black overheard the joke and took Simone aside. "Young lady, let's watch our language, yes?" she asked.

"What'd I say?" Simone asked.

"G-O-D is taking our Lord's name in vain," Mama Black reprimanded.

"Oh, I'm sorry, Ms. Judy. I shouldn't have said that at a church group," Simone said.

"You shouldn't say it in *any* group," Mama Black cautioned. "Do I need to speak to your mother about the example you're setting?"

"No." Simone folded her arms and was blushing, ticked off.

"No, what?" Mama Black asked.

"No ma'am," Simone answered.

Mama Black threw her black silk scarf over her shoulder and patted her freshly dyed, winter-wheat hair. She smiled and passed us by. "That's what I thought," she said, over her shoulder. "And Stephanie, don't let me hear you joining in that. And stand up straight."

"Your grandmother needs to get the stick out of her ass," Simone said.

We laughed and talked until the parents worried we wouldn't be able to get up for school the next morning. On the way home, I rolled down my car window and watched the evening sun slip back behind the gulping refineries in the distance. I thought about Daddy Black's sermon tonight. *Dear God, are you going to amputate me from your love?* I put my head out the window and faced the sky and the gentle wind revealed to me that Daddy Black was wrong, that I not only needed God, but that God needed me, too.

. . .

The next morning, Mother knocked on the bathroom door while I was in the tub. I covered my body with my washcloth as she made herself comfortable on the commode. I turned off the water because she looked serious. "Stephanie . . ." she stammered.

"Do you know how it is when you drive down a street and you look in the windows of houses that have no owner? You can tell that the spirit of the house is gone, can't you?"

"Yeah. I know what you mean." I thought about it. I pictured the rent house down the street that was empty now that Elvira had moved out, and how the windows were dark even in the daytime and how the yard had turned into a patch of overgrown weeds. It had an old, rusty bicycle leaned up against the side that had been there a long time now.

"Do you think the owners were bad? Or, what I mean is . . . is it . . . is it *sad*? Because they left and went to a newer, better house?" she asked.

"No, of course not. It's never sad or bad to buy a prettier house. Why?"

"Well, Stephanie, sweetheart. Our body is just our house for our soul. And, oh, I'm so sorry, baby; I don't know how to tell you this. But last night Brother Hazel died in his sleep. His body was too old. He moved to another body, a better body. He's in heaven now, and he is young and healthy again. He is probably handsome and twenty again, Stephanie! He's with Jesus and his wife and son. Oh, sweetheart. He knew you loved him." She looked like she wanted to hug me but I was naked so she sat on her hands, not knowing what else to do with them.

I stared at her blankly and it occurred to me that now my water was getting cold. I understood his body was just a house for his soul. I sat up and turned the water back on as hot as I could get it.

"He knew that you loved him, Stephanie," she repeated.

"I know that, Mother. I don't need to be told that. Can you get out?" I turned the water up higher and waited for her to leave before I started to cry.

That afternoon when school was out I rode my bike alone up to the Pasadena funeral home. The blazing Texas sun beat down and the air stunk like rotten eggs from the refineries. The kickstand on my bike was stuck, so I tossed it down on its side in front of the big white steps, not bothering to lock it up. The air-conditioning felt as cold as Alaska when I entered, and I was immediately taken in by the opulence of the thick red carpet and soothing music that played overhead. It kind of made me wish I lived there, it was so peaceful. There was a bowl of plastic fruit on the table in the lobby, and white flowers placed at every doorway. The plump old woman at the front desk nodded her head at me like she knew exactly who I was, and it didn't matter to her that I was young. It was like I had every right to be there. Her big gray hair didn't move at all.

I licked my hand and straightened my windblown hair. "I love this song," I said and motioned to the music overhead playing "Jesus Is Tenderly Calling." She smiled and nodded like she did too, and I made my way down the dim hallway until I found the room with a sign in front that said, "In Loving Memory of Brother Robert Hazel 1901–1983." The first line was blank so I was the first to sign it, "Stephanie Olive Walters." I made little hearts above the "i's" in my name.

The door was already open, and I could see the outlines of his face lying in the white satin-lined coffin. I took a deep breath and strode reverently up to the shiny black box, the house that now held my friend's old house. I wasn't sure why, but I saluted the coffin and curtseyed, feeling stupid after I did it. I stood over him. He didn't look like himself. His smile that used to be so big and warm was now a thin, pursed line. He wore his favorite suit, the one I was used to seeing him in, the one I was used to touching, the one I knew well, but I could tell there was nothing in his pocket for me now. I leaned down to kiss his face but quickly jerked back when my lips touched his cheek. *Oh my goodness, he's frozen.* The light in him was gone. His soul was not there. I bowed my head and folded my hands on top of his coffin.

Dear Lord, I love you, God. Lord, I know you don't do this kind of thing normally. I know that. But your word says you can do anything. Your word says that if I ask, and have the tiny faith of a mustard seed that anything will be done, that you will even move a mountain if I ask it in Jesus's name, because all things work together for good for those who love you. Well, I really, really, really, love you, God. Lord, will you please raise Brother Hazel from the dead today? Please? You could if you wanted to. You could. You can. Your word says you are the same yesterday, today, and tomorrow. You raised Lazarus from the dead because he was special to Jesus. Well, Brother Hazel was very special to me, God. Please raise him up and let us have him for a little while longer, Lord. You are mighty. I ask this in Jesus's name. Amen.

I blew out my breath hard, not realizing I had been holding it. I patted the coffin like everything was taken care of now and turned around and walked out the door with total confidence.

On the way out through the lobby, I caught the old woman pulling an unexpected pencil from her hair. "Sweetie Pie, was that your grandpa, you sweet young thang?" she asked. She pulled up her dingy bra strap that had been hanging down her arm.

I pictured Daddy Black pounding on the pulpit and wiping sweat off his forehead saying words like "gnashing teeth" and "lake of burning fire."

"Yes, Ma'am, he was," I lied.

"Bless your heart," she said, turning back to her typewriter. I pushed the door open with total faith and joy and forced my eyes to adjust to the sunlight because I knew an amazing miracle was about to happen. God was good.

7

GOD DIDN'T ANSWER MY PRAYER to raise Brother Hazel from the dead. All the Scripture I ever knew came flooding back . . . the sound of Daddy Black's voice like a tape recorder in my head . . . all the messages from Sunday school . . . and they felt like lies . . . pray without ceasing . . . knock and the door shall be opened . . . seek and ye shall find . . . anything you ask in the name of Jesus will be done . . . the faith of a mustard seed moves mountains . . . say to that mountain, "Go throw yourself into the sea," and it will . . . the prayers of a righteous man availeth much . . . none of it mattered now. And if one part of it was a lie, maybe all of it was. And if all of it was, then maybe all of us were one of two things, either liars or fools who believed in lies.

We buried Brother Hazel on Wednesday. I didn't go to the funeral. My parents felt like I was too young to see a dead body, and I saw no need to tell them I had already been to the funeral home, so I stayed home. I said goodbye to him privately and sincerely from my heart in the privacy of my own bedroom. I let him go.

Wednesday night church went on as usual with a message about Jesus in the upper room. There wasn't a single mention of Brother Hazel or his funeral that morning. We were very aware of the verse in Luke 24 that read, "Why do you seek the living with the dead?" We knew that to mention him in any commemorative way other than at his funeral would be wrong. It would be like worshipping him and not accepting God's timing for his death.

The congregation led itself in singing tonight, spontaneous melody erupting from whoever felt prompted. Daddy Black preached about how our blood relatives weren't necessarily our family, that only church was family.

"Jesus says to his disciples, 'Who are my mother and brothers? My mother and brothers are the ones who obey my will.' Brothers and Sisters, the Word of God is powerful, like a double-edged sword. It divides joint and marrow. It divides families. Who is your family? Your family is those who listen to and obey the word of God. If your earthly mother and father are not in accordance with the will of God, that is, baptism for remission of sins and into the body of Christ, the Church of Christ, pray for them. Pray for them, but know they are not your family. If your brother says to you, 'I am a Christian, but I refuse to be baptized,' he is counterfeit. If your mother says to you, 'I am a Christian, but I have been sprinkled as a baby,' they are lukewarm and will be spat out from the mouth of the Lord. You will know your family by their obedience to God. There is one way, one truth, one life, and that is through baptism in Christ Jesus. Without that, we are lost and undone, left to burn in the flames of hell forever."

Simone turned around and motioned to me from her seat with her eyes towards the back of the sanctuary. She stood up and walked out the side door coughing. A few seconds later I tapped my mother, "Can I go to the bathroom?" She furrowed her eyebrows and put her finger over her mouth to "shhh" me and nodded her head. I stepped over everyone's legs and made my way towards the back and out the door. Simone was waiting for me in the foyer.

"Suckers!" we laughed and did a quick "apples on a stick-makes-me-sick makes my tummy go two forty-six" game with our hands. Valerie just walked out like a grown person into the foyer because she could. She didn't have anyone at church who really even knew she was there except the two of us.

"Let's play hide and go seek in the dark classrooms!" Simone said.

"Okay. You count," I said, and Valerie and I started to run off.

"Bullshit!" she yelled after me. "Stephanie, you're it."

I sighed. "Okay. Fine. But you better hurry because I'm only counting to ten. One, two, three . . ." I could hear them giggling and their voices got smaller.

"Eight, nine, ten. Ready or not, you will be caught!" My heart was pounding and I smiled and bit my lip running through the hallway. I turned down the first hallway lined with second grade artwork and photographs of new members. There weren't many new members. I passed by the "Look who's expecting" board and remarked to myself how many women were pregnant. Geez. Now there were some new members, right there. I went into the first classroom and flipped on the light. It was so empty I could hear the buzzing of the fluorescent bulbs overhead kicking on. I stood in the doorway for a moment and looked around. The classroom had a banner up with the name of the class, "The Do Gooders." I surveyed the room, but no one was there so I turned the light back off and left. I was getting spooked.

Daddy Black was still preaching. We had lots of time. One by one, I went into every classroom and flipped on every light, but each classroom was empty. I looked under the tables and behind the doors and in the supply cabinets. Even though I knew my way around these classrooms and hallways like the back of my hand because I had grown up in them, because I was alone, it was creepy.

I went into the bathroom and kicked open all the stalls. "A-HA!" I shouted and did my best karate-chopping stance when I kicked open the handicapped one. Nothing. By now I was too tired to run so I walked on to the other side of the church. I did the same thing in the other dark classrooms. "Simone! Get out here! This is stupid now! Valerie! Where are y'all?" I heard the faint voices of the congregation from inside the sanctuary rise to sing, and I knew the service was almost over; they were in the invitation. I went back through the lobby and out the front door. The night air was cold and the stars glistened in the sky even though the parking lot lights shone brighter. I was excited because I knew exactly where they were. My heart started pounding because I knew when I found them, they were going to tear off running back to base, and Simone could run unusually fast. Valerie would laugh so hard she would give up and let me tag her, but Simone, she would take off and not even look back. She was merciless at hide and go seek. But so was I.

I turned my walk into a skip, laughing again at the thought of capturing them. There was only one way out from behind the back of the church, and that was also the way in; so all I had to do was block it. I got so excited and full of adrenaline that my skip turned into a run and I ran around to the very back of the brick building. I turned the corner yelling, "Sillies! I CAUGHT YOU!" But I stopped dead in my tracks and my eyes met with Katherine's.

She was completely naked, her smocked sundress rumpled up on the gravel concrete with her panties twisted around the arm straps. Devin was in front of her rubbing up against her and moaning like an animal with his pants down at his ankles. Trent was behind her at the same time with his pants pulled down to his ankles thrusting himself into her. Devin squeezed the fat part of her bottom, being careful not to touch Trent, and Trent had his hands on her almost-flat breasts, squeezing them as if he hated her. They were scalding red, but his white handprints lingered. But Katherine didn't look sad. She looked like she was used to it. The parking lot lights flickered and I saw that her skin had blue marks under the handprints, and it looked as though she would be bruised tomorrow. Both Trent and Devin looked at me and smiled and waved. Katherine's face was flat. Her eyes were dark, like an empty house. "Get out of here, Stephanie," she said, almost whispering. I stood there for a moment staring into her eyes, not knowing what to say, and not being able to move, either. "Get out of here!" she screamed.

I took off running, running for my life. Running for Katherine's life, too. *And if you do not obey the will of God, you will be severed from His love forever.* My grandfather's voice boomed in my head. I slammed my hands over my ears. *Stop it!*

I wanted to run so fast that I disappeared like a puff of smoke in a cartoon. Running for my father and the distance between us. This church building was everything that was safe and good and true and clean in my life. I turned the corner and ran my hand down the hardness of the outside wall and for the first time ever it just felt like bricks and mortar.

My cheeks shook each time my sneakers hit the pavement. The cold night air felt like I could break it into pieces like tiny shards of glass. I flung open the door to the church and everyone was happily mingling around in the bright, warm lobby trying to decide who all was going to Frish's. Simone and Valerie stood in the corner drinking Cokes, both of them waving at me. They were laughing with their eyebrows raised.

"Ready or not you *will* be caught? We were in the first room you looked in, Genius. What are you, blind? We were behind the curtains. You didn't see Valerie's big hair sticking out?" Simone and Valerie laughed, sticking out their tongues and putting rabbit ears up. "Nanny, nanny, boo boo!" They circled around me and hugged me so I would know they loved me.

I forced a smile but my face burned. "Ha ha. No, no. I, I, I, I just didn't, I didn't, see anyone in there. I went in there, but I didn't, I mean, I, I couldn't, I couldn't see you." I wasn't really in control of my words. They were tumbling out through spit because my lips felt as if they were big fat pieces of ham and my head was spinning. Coming in from the darkness of the night and into the lights and warmth of the church made me feel like I was falling.

Fainting.

Dying.

The lobby came into sharp focus through tunnel vision and the laughter from the congregants that I had known and loved all my life now sounded like witches in an evil, scary fairy tale.

"Good grief. What is *wrong*, Stephanie?" Valerie narrowed her eyes. She put her cold Coke can on my forehead. "You look gray. Come sit down." Simone didn't notice and she took off with her parents, saying something to Lynne about how, no, she *would not* spill her Coke in the car and to stop treating her like a baby.

But Valerie and I went into the sanctuary together, now emptied of people. She sat down beside me and put her arm around me. "What's wrong?" She rolled her cold can all over and up and down my arms and it cooled me down. Then she put her sweater around my shoulders and it warmed me back up.

"I think I just got some asthma or allergies or something when I was running," I said.

"Well, you shouldn't have gone outside, goofy. You know that cold air isn't good for you if you have asthma." She patted me sweetly. "Slow your breathing down. Steph, slow down. I'm sorry we hid from you for so long."

We sat in silence for what seemed like a long time. Valerie was a true friend. I wished she were my mother.

"Young ladies, we need to turn out these sanctuary lights," a frosty voice called from behind us. Mama Black stood in the sanctuary doorway.

I turned and put my finger up, "Yes ma'am. Just one minute, Mama Black. We're coming," I said.

She began to replace the hymnals that had been left haphazardly in the pews back to their proper slots muttering something about why people couldn't just take responsibility for their things and clean up after themselves.

I cleared my throat and held my head up. "I know. I'm sorry, too, Valerie," I said, although I wasn't sure why I was apologizing. "I'm better now. Thank you. I really am. Do you need a ride home?" I stood up and tried to forget what I had just seen. My sister was not Katherine anymore. I didn't know who she was now. "My parents will give you one."

"No. That's okay. I'll walk. It's a nice night. You gonna be okay?" She stood up, too, smiled and took her sweater back.

"Yes. I'm fine. Thank you, Valerie. Love you."

"I love you, too." And she blew me a kiss and left.

Katherine and I both stared out opposite windows of the car on the tense ride home and my mother stared out hers and tapped her nails on her Bible. The tapping made me nervous. I wanted to ask her to please stop but I wasn't stupid. I didn't want to do anything to set her off. My father drove dutifully, safely, every turn taken slow, every rule of the road followed with care.

When we got home, I was combing my hair and I found a cigarette in the bathroom drawer. I called Katherine into the bathroom and shut the door behind us. "What is this?" I snarled. I was so confused and angry about what I had seen Katherine doing behind church and I wanted to kill those boys because it looked like they were forcing her but I couldn't tell for sure. I was too embarrassed to even speak it out loud. Why hadn't Katherine fought back? Where had she learned all this? *Katherine, why is what those boys do to you okay with you? Why is kissing with Dad okay with you? Katherine, stay with me!*

I pictured my sister as a little girl again and the image of her harmless smiling face and innocent big blue eyes became dimmer as I looked at her now . . . I didn't know her anymore. I held up the cigarette like it was the most important evidence in a capital murder trial. And I was the detective who had it.

Katherine's eyes were huge when she saw what I had in my hand. "Stephanie, listen to me. About Devin and Trent . . ."

"Don't talk to me about that!" I growled. "I don't want to talk about those boys! I didn't see anything!" If I said it enough, maybe it would be true.

She put her hands up like I had held a gun to her. "Okay . . . it's okay, Stephanie . . . we don't have to talk about what you saw behind church."

But I was shaking. "Don't you dare. I don't want to hear about it! I do not want to talk about that!" My lips started quivering and my cheeks burned. Tears welled up and boiled over in spite of myself.

"I won't. Please, Stephanie . . . please don't tell Mother. I'll flush the cigarette and I'll never smoke again. I promise."

I handed it to her and folded my arms. "You better not! You'll get cancer! Your lungs will turn black with soot! Don't you know that?" I started crying because I really wanted to scream at her, to make her explain to me what I had just seen. I wanted to scream to my parents for help, but I didn't know how to find the right words because I didn't understand it myself. We needed help! She took the cigarette out of my hand and quickly flushed it down the toilet.

"Yes. I am so stupid. I'm so sorry, Steph. I'm *really* sorry. Please don't tell Mother."

I sighed and wiped the tears off my chin, so angry at Katherine but for what I didn't know. "I won't. But that better be the last of it. Who have you been smoking with? And when? And where?" I knew. Those jerk boys.

"It doesn't matter. I swear it is the last of it. It was just that one time. Please promise me you won't tell."

"DON'T SWEAR! And I shouldn't have to promise." I folded my

arms and turned my head to the side. "The Bible says, 'let your yay be yay and your nay be nay.' But since you flushed it and repented, I won't."

"Oh, thank you, Stephanie. Thank you so much. I owe you one big." She hugged me but I kept my arms folded.

When I left the bathroom, I went into my mother's bedroom. She was lying in her bed in her black satin gown. She had taken her makeup off, revealing deep ravines in her forehead and beside her eyes, so many for a woman of only thirty-eight. "Mother, can I talk to you?"

"Not now, Stephanie. I have a headache," she answered. She flipped through her magazine without looking up.

"Mother, it's important."

"Honestly, Stephanie. Can I ever have just a moment to myself? Do you constantly need my attention?" She looked up.

I paused. "I need your help. It's about Katherine. Katherine and I really need your help."

"Well, spit it out," she said. "What?"

I didn't know how to reach my mother in a normal way but I needed her so much. And the further away from Katherine she got, the closer I felt to her, and I just couldn't help it because I needed her that much. It seemed the only way to draw her close was to divide her from Katherine, because those were the times where she loved me the most.

"Katherine has been smoking. I found her cigarettes in the bathroom myself."

Mother slammed down her magazine. "*Excuse* me? That little brat." She went into the closet, grabbed a belt, and blew past me. *Sic her,* I thought.

I could hear her whipping my sister and my sister begging her to stop. "Mother, please! I'm sorry!" Katherine sobbed.

"Shut up! I ought to take this belt and smack it across your face! You little liar! We do not lie! We do not hide things from our mothers! And we *certainly* do not smoke!" The belt smacked down hard on

Katherine's skin. Twenty-seven lashes. I sat on the bed and counted them, and I cried quietly to myself. I was so confused.

"I hate you, Mother!" Katherine cried.

Dad stepped out of his black wallpapered bathroom with a toothbrush in his mouth like he hadn't heard anything. He was probably looking at the stack of *Playboys*, thinking about those pretty naked girls, I thought. I pictured him in my mind, a deacon in our church, holding out the collection plate to old ladies, waiting for their coins. He heard what was happening, and as if he were bored, he said, "Stephanie, what's the matter with you?" He turned his back and stepped back into his bathroom as if he couldn't hear my sister crying, as if there was nothing he could do. He ignored it.

Katherine would never forgive him for ignoring this. Maybe then he and I could be closer. She would hate me. But I needed him. I belonged nowhere. I couldn't stop myself.

I went into my room and threw myself on my bed and sobbed from deep within me. I heaved until I couldn't anymore, then wiped the tears and saliva from the side of my mouth as rage and confusion burned and smoldered within me. I picked up my favorite teddy bear and slammed him onto the floor over and over and over again, screaming, "My father does not LOVE me!" Dad heard me screaming and burst into my room. He was now wearing his pajamas. His face looked angry. I had gotten to him. My eyes flashed at him when he opened the door.

"What the hell is wrong with you, Stephanie? You are ten years old and screaming through the house like a baby that I don't love you? Why? You think I don't love you? Why? WHY? That makes me want to go out into the front yard and fucking throw up! I do love you!" I was shocked at his language, but I didn't show it. He pounded his fists on my wall.

I spit in his direction and screamed back at him. "No! You don't love me! Get *out*! Get out of my room! I hate you so much!" And I did hate him, too.

"Stephanie, what the . . ." he wiped the spit off his glasses and his eyes. I had scared him. Good. I hated him for playing hobby horse with Katherine and teaching her to do the things I had seen her do behind the church. I ran at him like a bull and shoved him out the door. I heard him crying in the hallway. "What the hell is wrong with her?" he asked my mother as she passed him by.

I could hear her voice muffled through the door and down the hall. "I don't know, Paul. She's just at that age. Just leave her alone." I heard him sobbing but I didn't care. I was glad he was crying and hoped he felt as helpless as I did.

I turned off the light and the darkness soothed me. It halted the rage, blacked out the images in my mind of Katherine and those boys together behind the church, of Katherine and my father having a special love that was meant for only them, not me, her wrapped around him and him wrapped around her, rocking back and forth playing hobby horse. Just as I caught my breath and could control my breathing, my mother opened the door slowly. "Sweetie, are you okay?" she whispered.

I stood in the dark in front of the door. "Yes. I'm fine." I stilled my shaking because the truth was, I was still crying and very much not okay.

"You stay away from them," she whispered. "Do you understand me? He will do nothing but hurt you. Do you know that he is already turning your sister against me? He's done that since she was a baby. And he's turning her against you. He's been doing that to both of us for years. He'll call it 'love,' but you don't want that kind of love."

"Yes. Thank you. I know."

I fell off a horse and my baby died. Your father and sister have a special kind of love, but it's not appropriate.

I didn't want to stay away from them, and I did not know what the truth was. I wished I could be close to them all. I wanted us all to be close but it seemed like that could never be. I didn't know how to make us all close at the same time or what to believe. Why would a mother lie?

"Good night, sweetheart. Don't forget to say your prayers." She closed the door, turning the knob silently, leaving me standing alone in the darkness. I didn't forget to pray . . . and I hated myself because I knew what I had done.

8

THE AUTUMN PASSED AND TURNED to winter and one afternoon when spring rolled around, I rode my bike through our nicely manicured neighborhood. Each house on our street stood up straight and tall with pride. Shutters hung on each of them, freshly painted and white beside the windows. And even though they looked similar, each house was unique and charming in its own way. Some were pink, like the Embrorskys, and some were sunshine yellow, and some, like Simone's, were robin's egg blue. Ours was a pale mint green with black shutters, and it stood firmly on cinder blocks like everyone else's, the first line of defense against Pasadena's hurricanes and flooding. We had a beautiful fig tree in the corner of our yard that bloomed with fruit almost yearround. Ours was a neat and clean street with lawnmower tracks in the small green yards and mid-priced station wagons parked in some of the driveways, pickup trucks in others.

As I passed by Trent's house, I noticed a faded "Find a Tot" sticker on his bedroom window. I laughed to myself, because Trent was fourteen, hardly a tot anymore. I guessed it was to let firefighters know it was the room of a cherished child; that they should look in that room first if the house was ablaze because that's where the most important and helpless person in that house slept. Everyone knew that Trent's parents adored him. He came from a good home, with good parents, a pretty mom and a handsome dad who were kind to each other and to our church. Mother and Dad said they were good members of the church because they were "givers." Trent Dawes had Cherokee Indian in him, obvious by his tan skin and chiseled bone structure and deep-set brown eyes. His dad was a blue-collar factory worker who commuted to the refineries of Pasadena every day, and his mother was a housewife who crocheted doilies and led her daughter's Girl Scout troop.

Devin came to church with Trent, and in my ten years of life, I had never seen Devin's family. Not even once. But I had seen the bike trailer attached to their car parked in their driveway with big bubble letters that said "Racin' Devil Devin" airbrushed on the side. Devin was a semi-professional bike racer with a white-blonde rat tail. He was so skinny; it's like his body was the prototype for what the manufacturers had in mind when they created parachute pants, which was all he ever wore. All of us kids knew that his dad was pretty strict with him, and pushed him to be good at his sport, and he was good at it. He was very good at it. Sometimes he would go long stretches of time without coming out to play and Katherine said it's because she thought his dad beat him, but she couldn't be sure.

The weather was nice and breezy today and the sweet polluted smell of the Pasadena oil refineries filled me with a natural calm. Silver smokestacks blustered orange fire in the distance, making everything around them hazy. The tops of our neighborhood houses divided the line between the sky and the smokestacks. My handlebars shone in the sun as I rode down my street.

As I passed by the rent house a few houses down from mine, I noticed it was dark and vacant. I felt the energy of the house reach out to me. *Stephanie, come back here . . .*

I turned around and went back and stopped beside the curb in front of the house, cocked my head, and took it in. At first glance, it seemed like it had a right to be there on our pretty street; it was as though it could whisper, "*I belong here, just like you do.*" After all, it was built at the same times as ours, so it must've been part of the plan. I wasn't sure of the house's history, only that it was always for rent, never for sale, which was unusual in our neighborhood where most people had lived for years and years and years. The door appeared to be a mouth, and it murmured, "*But I am not usual . . . I am empty.*" At first glance, it looked like one of ours, but I knew better. It beckoned me, "*Stephanie, come inside . . .*"

I wondered why the owners never lived in it, why they just rented it out. Maybe it was just built to be a rent house and was never meant for a family to stay. Or maybe the landlord lived somewhere far away and didn't care if it sold, and just paid to take care of it from afar.

As I stood and stared at it longer, I realized something more: This house *knew* it was a rent house. I could tell it knew. The windows, with their shutters askew, looked like two sorrowful eyes that pleaded, "*Please invest in me permanently, not just for a little while. I really need an owner. Someone who cherishes just me. Please come get me, make me yours. Make a claim.*" The roof shingles hung crooked. The posture of the house was mournful, and the yard was messy and overgrown. I bet somebody could get this house for cheap.

I sent a message to the house through my mind and it understood. I told it not to worry, and started to pedal off again. I sailed down my street and turned around the corner, but I stopped because Devin and Trent were standing beside the stop sign and in my path.

"Hey, girly! Whoa! Slow down! Where's the fire?" Devin laughed and stepped aside as if I had almost hit them. Trent backed up and acted like he was falling against the pole, exaggerating his movements, flailing his arms as if he were moving in slow motion.

"Shut up. I wasn't going that fast. I didn't almost hit you. Not even close, you jerks," I said. I started to ride around them, but Devin put his hands on my handlebars and stopped me. I put my feet on the ground and met their glances head on. This was the first time Devin and Trent had spoken to me since I was a little kid. I pictured them behind the church with Katherine.

"Stephanie Knievel, eh? Hey, have you been inside that empty house a few doors down from yours? We were just about to sneak in it and check it out. The back door is open, and I heard vandals have been in it and stolen all the A.C. units," Trent said.

"No, but I don't care. I don't think we're supposed to go in there, anyways. Y'all don't know, there could be rats in it or something," I said.

"Well, we double-dog dare you to come in there with us and check it out." Devin was the leader.

"I'm not afraid of that house. And I'm not afraid of you silly boys." I stuck my tongue out at them both. As I looked at them more closely, I could see that they were actually pretty cute. I smiled at them and then acted shy. "Sure, why not?"

We jumped the fence and wandered into the backyard, which had a swimming pool that had turned pitch black from lack of care and use. Enormous flies buzzed wildly around it, and hundreds of frogs croaked from underneath the stagnant, murky water. Devin came up behind me and grabbed me like he was going to push me in, but I screamed and he laughed and pulled me back. I nervously laughed along with him and his hand touching me sent tingles down my spine.

We didn't have to force the back door open; the old thing opened with ease, and we entered in through the kitchen. The house was entirely empty of furniture and the front windows were boarded up. A strong smell of Pine-Sol sliced through the must and cat urine hitting us all hard in the faces. The electricity had been shut off for a long time I guessed, because a hush occupied the whole place. There was a single glass ashtray on the kitchen counter with the stale butt of a cigarette smashed out in it. Trent walked up to it and took a lighter out of his pocket and lit it. They both dragged on it until it was gone, filling the room with smoke. I was excited and thrilled and afraid at the same time. I felt like I was one of the crowd, one of the cool kids, like Katherine.

We walked into the living room and talked there for a while, sitting on the flat, diarrhea-colored carpet. The vacuum cleaner marks disappeared the moment we sat down. I was enjoying their attention so much that my heart started racing and I felt giddy and warm. Devin reached out his hand, and without saying a word, we went upstairs to one of the empty bedrooms. Trent waited downstairs.

He closed the door behind us and started kissing me on my lips and neck. My body went berserk with this first kiss from a boy. I knew the feeling well; the feeling of feeling sexy and stimulated. I felt like a gorgeous girl from my father's magazines. I escaped to the inside of a *Playboy* in my mind, to their dazzling beach locations with waterfalls and tropical flowers . . . my hair was long and flowing and my face was foxy. My breasts were full and suckable, with large brown nipples; not tiny pink buds inside a white training bra.

He led me down to the floor and took off my clothes one piece at a time, tossing my jeans into the corner. He kissed me on my neck while he unzipped his jeans. His eyes bugged wide and he laughed out loud when he took off my panties. "Oh my god, Stephanie, you don't have any crotch hair! Shit! What the hell is this? A little cherry? Oh this is gonna be so good."

"Well, I'm only ten," I answered. "But I'm gonna get hair really soon. And I'm on a diet, too," I lied.

I thought about the look on my sister's face at church that night, the aloneness and darkness in her eyes, but pushed the image out of my mind, burying it down deep in the pit of hell.

He rubbed up against me, and I didn't stop him. I wanted him to touch me. The attentive warmth of his hands drove me wild. His jeans up against my leg were rubbing me raw. I wanted him to stop hurting my leg, but not to stop touching my body. I didn't ask him to stop; I let him do whatever he wanted to me. I wanted his focus. I pictured myself in the land of Oz, when Dorothy stepped out of her spinning house, where everything had gone from black and white to Technicolor. I pictured a place where everything was wonderful and whole, and my senses were heightened as I floated away. He was with me, and we shared the quiet moment together. I could see in his eyes that he loved me. Didn't he? I couldn't believe I never noticed him in this way before. I wanted his attention, wanted to be touched. I arched my back like a *Playboy* model and moaned. My father said he read those magazines for the articles, but they had taught me everything I needed to know. This is what women do. This is what we love and are made for. Look at him; I am in complete control of him. I finally closed my eyes and snuck out of my body and allowed my spirit to hover above and watch us from the other side of the room.

I noticed that this carpet was a different color than the one downstairs. This carpet was dingy gray, and I was getting rug burn on my back. He climbed on top of me, more assertively now and pushed his way inside of me; he really had to work at it. It felt like sandpaper shoving up inside, but I grabbed on to the back of him and pulled him in closer until he was inside of me. He thrust his tongue deep into my mouth and I almost gagged as he moved up and down, but I didn't mind. I fixed my eyes on the ceiling, and I took it. I just took it. He was like a bucking bronco trying to throw a rider off, oblivious of the consequences. Even though my bones felt like they were exploding at the pelvis I reminded myself to act sexy and make noises, so I said, "mmmm" and "aaahhh," because that's what sexy ladies do, and I tried to fan my short hair out onto the floor to make it appear longer but it didn't work. When it was over, he pulled up his jeans and walked out of the room.

I stayed right where I was, lying naked in the middle of the empty room. I stared up at the wobbly brown ceiling fan with thick hunks of dust hanging from the blades and down at myself from where my spirit hovered on the other side of the room.

Something was dripping between my legs and I dried myself off on the dirty carpet. I pretended to be in a beautiful pink satin nightgown as I put my white cotton panties back on, the ones with a single rose in front, a gift from Mama Black for Christmas.

Not even five minutes later, Trent walked in the room. I made a shy face at him like I was a baby kitten and purred a little, draping my leg seductively. He forcefully spread my legs open and climbed on top of me avoiding eye contact. He was fast and mechanical, going up and down and up and down as fast as he could. My bottom and back hurt because he was heavy, and tears trickled down my cheeks. Again, I tried to leave my body, tried to picture somewhere safer to go, some-where prettier than Oz, some shelter where my spirit could go and leave the rest of me here, but I couldn't think of anywhere to go. So I booked a rocket and shot off to the moon where it was silent, dark, and cold, safe and far away from everyone. It was quiet . . . noiseless there . . . and I floated in outer space in blissful weightlessness. The planets and twinkling stars were so close I could've reached out and touched them. I didn't need to breathe . . . God was doing it for me, and there was no time . . . no yesterday, no Wednesday night church, no today or tomorrow or five minutes from now or a hundred years ago. From the moon I watched her, the little girl naked on the carpet; far down below me on the swirling blue and green earth, a tiny speck from the galaxy above, the little ten-year-old down on the floor with Trent in The Rent House, pushing her innocence away, and I watched her push and push and push without using any force at all.

Until the innocence left her.

From the moon I watched her and it was what she wanted; her innocence floated away, up into the room, and then it seeped into the walls and cracks of the ceiling of The Rent House.

And then it was over.

I came down from the moon and entered back into Stephanie again, and when I stepped out of the house, I left her purity and innocence behind to live there together and become part of The Rent House for all I cared, and I walked away from that part of her forever and decided when I left that place I would never, never, never tell anyone what had happened that day.

Afterward, I got on my bike and rode as fast as I could through my neighborhood, doing hard wheelies up onto the curbs, making the flowered basket in front shake as it tapped up against the handlebars. I rode as fast as I could, past Simone's house, past mailboxes, and past happy folks washing their cars and dogs with sudsy buckets of bubbles. I darted around cul-de-sacs and back up again, and around the woods by a marshy creek. I didn't take time to put down the kickstand, but instead I laid my bike on its side and wandered down to an overlook to sit awhile and breathe. Between my legs and down my thighs I was throbbing, throbbing, throbbing. What did all this mean about me? Was I bad? I hoped I wouldn't get pregnant. I was pretty sure you couldn't get pregnant unless you were at least thirteen. I decided to try to forget it, told myself it meant nothing; that it didn't really happen. I took off my pinky ring and twirled it around in my hand, but it accidentally fell through the overgrown thorn bushes and into the creek. I carefully tried to go down after it, but I lost my footing and careened through the thorny bushes, grasping in vain at each one trying to save myself. My face sped by the wet moss, filling my mouth with dirt, as I plunged into the water, knocking the wind out of my stomach on a rock.

I landed with a splashy thud, the mossy scum separating beneath me. My legs were bloodied from cuts and I struggled to gasp for air.

Slowly, my breath came back to me, and I tried to wipe the leaves and the sticks out of my hair.

I picked myself up and brushed off, got back on my bike, and started home. This time, I glided slowly, carefully, feeling the breeze on my face and desperately needing it. By now it was evening and some stars were out in the cool blue sky. I could smell charcoal from the neighbor's grill and hear laughter and the sounds of families coming from backyards. A few houses showed warm, flickering lights through their windows and I could feel the neighborhood settling down. I could even smell dinner cooking from inside as I passed by some, and I saw a dog playing tug-of-war with a man who had not yet changed out of his work suit. My street gave a collective sigh of relaxation as another peaceful week was winding down. I rode past The Rent House and tried not to look at it, but it called to me, "*Stephanie* . . ." I didn't feel anymore as though I didn't know its history. In fact, I felt like I knew *everything* about it now. And as I rode past, I felt the haunting window eyes as they eerily followed me home just a few houses away. They weren't sad or even hopeful or vulnerable anymore. They were sinister and mean.

PART 2

And Jesus said,
"Anyone who drinks
of this water will never
be thirsty again."

Two Years Later

> *Just as I am, and waiting not*
> *To rid my soul of one dark blot,*
> *To thee whose blood can cleanse each spot,*
> *O Lamb of God, I come. I come.*

IT WAS 6:30 AM AS Simone and Valerie made their way towards me with their pillows and sleeping bags and shoved them under the seat of our bus. We were on our way to Camp Blessed Rock, a Church of Christ camp in the piney woods of Arkansas. Our youth group went every summer, and Daddy Black had served as a board member there for twenty years.

"This sucks so bad." Simone blew a big pink bubble and dug feverishly into her bag for her Walkman. "I could punch Ron and Lynne in their throats for making me come here. Here we get to go again, an eight-hour trip on Onward Christian Soldier Bus line up to Butt-Crack-fucking, Arkansas."

"Simone, don't have a cow. We get to go to Six Flags this year. And the eighth graders get to tour a real-life college." Valerie applied more powder to her face and examined her face in her compact.

Simone crinkled her face. "Yeah, *Harding*. And they tour us now so they can brainwash us before the 'evil influences' of high school. I don't even want to go to fucking *Harding*. For what? So I can get hog tied to some big caveman of a husband and a bunch of his screaming-ass kids only to spend the rest of my days breastfeeding and cleaning skid marks out of his giant underwear with an old toothbrush? No thanks." She found her Walkman, placed the spongy black headphones over her ears, and closed her eyes.

"Okay everyone needs to find their places!" Dad was relaxed and dressed in his short blue shorts with his knee socks pulled all the way up. He wore an old yellow baseball cap from Katherine's Little League Softball days with the word *Pixies* emblazoned across the front. His tight First Community Bank of Houston T-shirt hugged his belly and said in large black letters, "Integrity. Service. Community." There was a picture of the Houston skyline behind it.

Daddy Black stepped onto the bus wearing his three-piece suit as usual. We all hushed to hear what he had to say. My dad removed his ball cap and stood up straighter. My mother started tapping her nails on the seat in front of her. I felt nervous the minute I saw him. His booming voice struck fear into me and I felt an immediate urge to get away from him.

"Young ladies and gentlemen," Daddy Black began, "I want to ask you a question. Does Jesus tell the truth or is He a liar?"

We all sat mutely because we weren't sure if he really wanted us to answer or not. "Katherine, Darling Angel. Does Jesus tell the truth?" Katherine sat up straight and answered, "Yes, Daddy Black. Jesus tells the truth."

His eyes twinkled and he smiled at her because she had answered correctly. "Thank you, Darling. Of course He does. The goal over the next two weeks is to impart to each camper a knowledge of what God's Word says about salvation and to make you aware of your own personal need for salvation and what Scriptures say you must do to be saved and to stay saved. Stephanie, what do you need to do to be saved?"

I looked at my mother who nodded at me, so I answered, "We need to be baptized."

"That's right. Because of sin you are all unclean and ruined. Without baptism our dreams will turn from ashes to dust; we will be full of hopeless gloom, our lives a big revolving graveyard. Stephanie, what is the solution?"

My heart beat faster and faster into my chest and I wondered if he could see the big graveyard of my soul and all the lies I had hidden and marked with tombstones titled "innocence" and "purity." "Baptism by immersion?" I answered robotically. I turned and looked at Katherine for support and she nodded.

"Yes. Baptism for remission of sins. Campers, think on these things these next two weeks. Accept Jesus as your Lord and Savior and be baptized into His church and be faithful to Him until death. Obey Him as long as you live." He hugged my dad and whispered into his ear and got off the bus taking my trembling worry about the flames of hell with him. When the doors closed, my dad put his cap back on and turned to us and smiled. He looked so much younger than Daddy Black with his thick red hair wavy under his ball cap.

"I will be your bus driver today." And the whole bus gave a big cheer because my dad was known to be a fun-loving guy.

"Thank you, thankyouveramush." My dad took a bow. "I will be your bus driver and Sister Lily will be the bus mom." Everyone turned around to locate my mother, who sat in the middle row and waved and gave a pursed smile. "If you need anything, come to one of us. In the meantime, I want you to keep it to a dull roar. No fighting, no biting, no itching, no kicking. We'll stop once on the way to Dallas for lunch before we get to Six Flags." We all cheered again. Simone ripped off her headphones like she was the only one there and whipped her head around scowling like everyone needed to shut up because it was too early for cheering. Valerie elbowed her in the ribs.

"We'll be at Six Flags about noon and we'll stay until seven o'clock. From there, we'll drive on up to the lovely state of Arkansas where we'll enjoy a nice time at Camp Blessed Rock. So get seated and we'll be leaving here shortly." He turned and settled himself into the driver's seat and pulled out a humongous map and started drawing on it with his pencil.

Katherine, Devin, and Trent had been the first ones on the bus and had designated the last seats as their official domain. They set up a barrier of boom boxes and pillows to prove it should anyone try to infringe. Neither of the boys had spoken to me since the day in The Rent House and I hadn't tried to speak to them, either. I was twelve now, and I tried not to think about it much. The image of myself with them in The Rent House stayed locked away inside of me and it was part of my pelvis and the rest of my bones that had stretched and opened up that day; it was part of my back that rubbed on the carpet; it was part of my bottom that was burned from the friction of having them on top of me; it was part of my skin that was cold from my nakedness and hot from being grabbed; it was part of my cells that mixed with Devin and Trent's DNA; it was part of my heart, that when they entered my body, they also entered my soul, but it wasn't part of my working memory most days. I packed it down deep, hiding it in the base of my core so it was in me and it was true that I carried it, but I told myself I was hiding it well by dressing like a little girl of twelve and talking like a little girl of twelve and the more days that went by, the more I was able to lie and pretend to myself that it never happened. But when I told myself that it didn't happen and almost believed it, too, a dark, menacing voice inside me reminded me, *yes it did*.

We took off out of the pebbly parking lot and began on our way. My dad started the first round of a song about Jonah. The singing filled the bus with excitement and early morning cheerfulness as we drove up the Texas highway in the early morning light. As we passed through Houston and drove out onto a long stretch of road, I looked out the window at the wide-open spaces. We passed by a ranch with a group of Black Angus cattle eating the dewy, sunlit grass. How did the whole herd know to face in the exact same direction? Was it something they were born knowing how to do, or did they learn by watching the others? I glanced around the bus and noticed we were all looking out the windows in the same direction.

At that very moment, we all broke out in spontaneous song, and we all participated whether we wanted to or not. It was just good Southern Christian manners. Music was so much a part of us in the Church of Christ; it permeated our lives. Since we didn't use instrumental music we learned to rely on the most artistic things we had: our voices.

At our first stop, we got to choose between Burger King and McDonald's. I ordered a Happy Meal and Valerie and Simone ordered salads. They walked over and sat down at the table where I was sitting with my cheeks full like a squirrel. "Why did you order a salad?" I asked, suddenly cognizant of the fact that I was shoving fries down my gullet faster than I could chew them.

"Oh, I'm just trying to be skinny," Valerie said.

"Yeah, me too. I don't want to be a beached whale this summer. I already feel like that rolling hog on *Sixteen Candles* who wore the neck brace." Simone had new braces on her teeth and she was self-conscious about them. She took exactly three big bites of her salad and it was completely gone.

"You eat too fast," I said. Simone shrugged and picked at her teeth, examined a tiny seed she found there, and then swallowed it.

"But is eating salad enough to make you skinny?" I asked.

"Of course it is," they both sang in unison. All of a sudden, I was keenly aware that my belly was hanging over the edge of my white shorts, which were pulled up high around my waist with a striped shirt tucked into them. My shoulders felt broad and my thighs were touching each other on the warm brown and yellow bench. *Note to self: Start ordering salads. I'm not allergic to food, and now that I eat everything and don't get sick, I'm getting fat like Katherine.*

When we pulled up to Six Flags, we all tried to charge off the bus at once up to the ticket box. My father and mother walked behind us calling us back. "Hey, hey, hey!" they shouted through cupped hands. We reluctantly stopped running and waited for them. "Listen up, gang," Dad declared. He had sunglass lenses attached to his glasses, and they were popped up like visors so he could make eye contact with us. My mother wore big round green frames that made her look like a grasshopper with frosted hair. She had a large "L" monogrammed in rhinestones into the corner of one of the lenses.

"We need to meet back here at six thirty because we are pulling out at seven o'clock sharp. Do *not* come to the bus hungry. Your parents should have given y'all money to buy your admission tickets and eat like kings today here at the amusement park. We will stop twice on the way to camp from here, but only to go to the bathroom, not to eat. Stay together. Be careful, and have fun!"

"I think Katherine should have some girls with her," my mother said. "It's inappropriate for her to be with just boys."

"Lily, let the kids have fun," my dad answered.

"I want them to have fun, Paul, but I think Katherine should be chaperoned if she's going to be alone with boys all day, don't you?" my mother asked. "For the sake of propriety?"

"Lily, once again, you're overreacting and making something out of nothing," he answered. My mother looked at Trent and Devin suspiciously.

"Katherine stays with me," my mother said.

"Katherine, sweetheart, don't pay attention to her. Go have fun. Lily, don't be crazy."

"She stays with me, Paul! No going alone with the boys!" my mother shouted. People stopped and turned to look.

Dad patted Katherine on the head and rolled his eyes at my mother. They both just laughed at her.

"Thanks, Daddy." Katherine kissed him on the cheek and the rest of us broke up into our groups and took off, nodding casually at the instructions.

Six Flags was fiery hot. The Dallas sun scorched the cement park, causing a thin mirage of water everywhere we looked, but we didn't care. We were in heaven; free like birds. Simone, Valerie, and I trotted all over the park, waiting happily in the long lines and the heat without complaint. Simone wanted to ride The Screamin' Demon, the biggest roller-coaster in the park with a drop four hundred and fifty-six feet down. I looked at it hesitantly.

"Simone, I don't know. That looks pretty high." I squinted in the sun as I looked up at it.

"Oh, c'mon," Simone said. "It'll be fine. It's three minutes of your life. You can do it." So I blindly followed her up to the line.

"I'm going to wait right out there," Valerie said, as she pointed to the bench down by the exit.

"No, come with us, V," I answered. "We're supposed to stay together and not leave you. We'll feel bad."

"Well, you are my group, and my group is choosing to go on a ride that I am afraid of. And since I'm not riding, technically, I'm leaving *you*. So y'all go on and have fun. I'll be waiting right here. Here, give me your money. I'll hold it so it doesn't fall. Now don't forget to wave to me from up high."

"Valerie, you sound forty when you talk, 'essentially, I'm leaving you, don't forget to wave, blah, blah, blah.'" Simone mocked. "You don't have to be so careful and polite all the time."

But to me it made total sense the way Valerie put it. She was right. There was really no reason for us not to have fun just because she was chicken. Valerie was careful. She was mature. So we left her there alone on the bench like an old grandma who was responsible for holding all our stuff. We took off running and rode the roller-coaster, not once, not twice, but three times. Valerie sat and waited patiently and waved each time she saw us get back in line.

We came down the ramp laughing and sweating, our heads spinning elatedly. Valerie's face was lit up as she waited for our report.

"It was awesome!" we both yelled. We spent the rest of the day in the park laughing and talking and eating. We turned the corner into a tree-lined walk and saw the Six Flags outdoor theatre. There was a sign in front of it that said, "Duran Duran Strange Behavior Tour Tonight at 7:00." Simone got a wicked twinkle in her eyes and jumped out in front of us both, stopping us in our stride.

"Oh, no," I said.

"Attention: We Are Going," she pronounced. She jumped up and down, threw her head back, and laughed.

"Simone, stop it. There's no way," I said. "We have to be back at the bus at six thirty. It's six fifteen now."

"Oh, hell yes, we are, Stephanie. There is no law against this. We are *going*."

"There is a law against it! It's called stealing! Or lying or something. I don't know, but no, we can't! Do you know how much trouble we will get in with Daddy Black? Now shut up and let's go ride one more ride before we go." I secretly wished we could go, but there was no way.

"Simone, I have a tape with 'Rio' on it on the bus. I'll let you listen to it," Valerie soothed. But Simone wasn't listening.

She brazenly walked ahead of us and started to climb the fence over into the seated section. People were already forming a line. I pulled her back down by her jeans; there was concert security milling around everywhere. "Are you out of your damn mind? Get down and stop acting like a fool!" I shouted at her this time and then lowered my voice when I realized I was shouting.

She got down and took a breath as if she was trying to collect her thoughts and show restraint. She sighed and spoke very slowly like at any moment she could bite our heads off if she let herself. "Valerie. Stephanie. My esteemed colleagues." She stood facing us now, clasping her hands calmly in front of her face, and used a tone on us like we were first graders drooling into our milk cartons. "I have always wanted to go to a Duran Duran concert, but there's no chance in hell of Lynne ever letting me. We will never, and I mean *never*, have this chance again. I am going. What are they going to do? I'm fourteen years old; they can't beat me anymore! They can't be mad at me, because I don't give a shit. And your parents will be so embarrassed that they lost me that they'll never call mine. The bus won't friggin' leave without me, and the worst thing that will happen is that they'll send me home and not let me go to Camp Dogma In Your Face All Day Long, a place, incidentally, that I would rather stick a spoon up my ass than attend. I'm going to the concert." She turned around and tried to scale the wall again but couldn't get up high enough.

We just stood there and watched.

"I'm going, too," Valerie said. My mouth almost dropped to the ground. "Hold my purse!" She shoved her big bag into my arms, took her shiny black hair down out of its ponytail and shook the curls out excitedly, and then scaled up and over the wall in five seconds flat. She looked so strong, so sure of herself. I pictured her going over the wall and sprouting wings and flying high up into the air like a bird.

Simone stared up after her, and then she climbed up and over the wall. Third time was a charm. They were gone.

I stood there like a buffoon holding Valerie's bag and looked around. There were people everywhere across the grass, but nobody was watching. I called after them in a strong whisper. "Guys!" I breathed. "Simone, get back here! We're going to get in big trouble, you know!"

But they didn't hear me, and they didn't come back. I waited and waited for them, looking up at the top of the wall hoping they would come back down, but they never did, and it was getting dark and was time to get back to the bus. So I walked obediently back by myself having a conversation in my head about how much trouble they were going to be in and how I wished I had gone to the concert, too. Why couldn't I be braver?

I stepped up onto the bus, now dim inside from the evening glow, and slid into my seat. The smell of dirty socks and hot dog mustard was foul. Everyone was shuffling about, making room for their bags of unfinished cotton candy and all things that glowed. As it seemed we were all on board, my father and mother stood up at the front of the bus with the map, making a plan for the four-hour trip that lay out before us. They collaborated about where our next stop would be, and finally, they seemed satisfied with a strategy.

"Okay, Faith Finders! Listen up!" My mother was at the helm now wearing my dad's baseball cap. "Everyone get to your seats so I can do a head count." She took her index finger and started to tap the air one by one above our heads. "Two, three, four, five . . ." She went through us one at a time, walking up and down the aisle. She frowned, and under her breath said, "Hang on. Here we go again. Two, three, four, five, six, seven, eight, nine, ten. Eight, nine, ten. Paul, we're missing two." My father looked up from behind the big steering wheel like a mole poking his head up out of the mud. His eyes were magnified three times by his thick glasses.

"What do you mean? Everybody, get in your groups so we can count you." But we *were* in our groups. He went through again and counted.

"Simone and that quiet girl aren't here!" shouted Big Boned Becky, the known tattle tale in the group. I turned around and slit my eyes at her. She stuck her tongue out at me and I flipped her off.

"Stephanie, where are your friends?" my mother asked.

"Um, I think they went to the bathroom on the way out. They'll be here," I said, trying to buy them some time. We all waited. Ten minutes went by. Then twenty.

"This is ridiculous. Where could they be?" my mother said.

I was trying so hard to come up with something, anything that would suffice. But what? There was nothing I could do to cover for them. *Think, Stephanie! Think!* A kidnapping? No, too atrocious. A watch malfunction? No, not believable. They witnessed a crime and had to give a statement to the police? Too elaborate. I had nothing.

"They may have gotten trapped in a ride line. Some of 'em, once you get in, you can't really get out," Katherine piped up from under her mountain of quilts in the back of the bus with Devin and Trent. I turned and looked at her pleadingly, and her eyes said, "Hey, I'm trying." *Thank you, Katherine.*

"Yes, that could be," my father said. "Those lines are certainly frustrating. I wish there were a way to get in touch with them. I'm sure they're fine, Lily. We'll give them five more minutes. We're still good on time."

When four and a half minutes were up, my mother stomped back into the park to look for them, her heels lifting up a cloud of parking lot dust behind her. She came back an hour later, fuming.

She and my father whispered to each other as to what to do, and I could tell Simone had been right. They had no intention of going back into the park and calling the church or her parents. That would make them look incompetent. They couldn't leave her, which would be criminal. And they couldn't punish her because she wasn't theirs. We sat on the bus waiting as the sun sank into the Texas sky.

As night fell, the parking lot became emptier, as one by one, park visitors who were parents went home with sleeping children draped over their shoulders looking dog-tired and like all their money had been spent. And still our bus waited like a lone island in the vast parking lot, with a few other cars that were parked on the very last rows, obviously having come late to the park specifically for the concert. The oomph of our group fell flat as the moments passed slowly.

And we waited some more.

For another two hours we waited like dim-witted fools who all secretly wished we were at the concert, but of course it was too late to get off the bus now. We were trapped like Duran Duran–loving rats. We were hushed now, and some of us had even fallen asleep. I sat in my seat staring out the window at the lit-up entrance, when without warning, Simone and Valerie strolled out through the gates. They were arm in arm, laughing and hooting. They both had black concert T-shirts on over their other clothes. I straightened up in my seat waiting for the punishing whirlwind that was about to happen.

They were dead meat.

They stepped up on the bus and stopped on the second step trying to contain their glee. Their smiles faded away. I stopped breathing and fixed my eyes on them because my mother met them at the doors. They were seriously dead meat.

"Sit down!" she growled. She took them both by the shoulders and forced them into the very front seat beside her. "Where have you girls been?" She yelled the question more than asked. "This whole bus has been waiting for the two of you little brats for hours! Shut up! Answer me!"

Valerie looked like she might start to cry.

Simone innocently looked directly into my mother's eyes, shrugged, and calmly answered. "We came to the bus at 5:30 like we were told and there was nobody here, so we went around looking for you."

"You were told to be back at the bus at 6:30," my mother said.

Simone stood up and positioned herself eye-to-eye with my mother. Her face became that of a little innocent, naïve child. "Mrs. Walters, we came to the bus early even before we had to be here. We got here at 5:15 so we could help you and Mr. Walters if you needed. When no one came by 5:30, we got worried. So we went to the lost child claim center. We've been waiting for you at the Six Flags lost child claim center since 5:30 because we didn't know what else to do. Nobody found you to tell you we were without supervision and frightened? The nice security guard was looking everywhere for you! We were lost and we asked for help and we waited and waited because we knew splitting up might get us even more lost, so we stayed put, but you never came to get us. We have been so terrified that we would never get home or to camp. Finally, we just took a chance again and came looking and found the bus running in the parking lot, luckily before you left without us. Thank goodness we weren't kidnapped."

My mother slit her eyes at Simone and Valerie and snorted sarcastically. "Sit down and shut up, do you hear me?" my mother said.

"Yes Ma'am. We're sorry to have gotten confused and lost. But luckily everyone is safe now, right? And the important part is that Val and I didn't get hurt." Simone patted my mother on the shoulder and my mother looked like she actually might murder her. And that was their one and only punishment: They had to ride up in the front of the bus for the rest of the way to camp. Simone had been right . . . they would not do anything because it would mean admitting they had lost control. What's done was done.

My father started up the bus and we drove out of the litter-filled parking lot in silence. None of us said a word for the rest of the trip, and nobody ever said anything else about the concert. Simone had taken a risk. She took a beautiful, marvelous, calculated risk, and it paid off like gangbusters. And Valerie went right along with her because she knew enough about herself to know when the risk was worth it to her. I shook my head, laughed at them, and turned and looked out the window. I was so crazy nuts about them both.

● ● ●

Nine hours of driving through the night, four bathroom stops, and two wrong turns made by my mother later, we maneuvered through the winding, cliff-flanked roads of the rocky state of Arkansas. It was quiet outside on the misty, meandering road as our bus drove the last morning stretch of our journey. We passed by trailers and small wooden houses tucked deep off the road behind tall pine trees. Some had old cars jacked up without tires and a few had trash in the yard. Some had Confederate flags flying on poles in their fronts, and scraggly dogs searched their food bowls for breakfast. I was the only one on the bus who was awake besides my parents, and I took in the feeling of togetherness and tradition as we drove towards Camp Blessed Rock. I looked at them as the sun came through the front window and I watched my mother pour my father a cup of steaming coffee from their thermos.

"So are you worried about staying in the cabins with the middle school boys?" Mother whispered so as not to wake anyone up. "You've never been around boys. Think you'll know what to do with them?" She laughed.

"Ha. We'll be fine," Dad answered. "I think you're going to have just as much of a handful staying in the girls' cabin," he said. "What if they all fight? That age can be terrible."

"Oh, I'm sure," she said.

Why couldn't they always be this way? There was still love between them. It was real. I could see it.

I adjusted the blanket that was propping my head up and thought about how much I loved this time of year at camp. I cherished the feeling of consistency, serenity, and tradition, and I enjoyed getting away from the Sunday morning, Sunday night, Wednesday night tempo that governed our lives. In this quiet moment, I felt clean.

The mountains and woods were so picturesque and different than the hot, concrete town that I was used to where every store was part of a strip center. The gentle morning sun streamed across the bus, but no one stirred. Simone and Valerie were still up in the front next to my mother, their heads resting on each other like pillows, a mess of blonde and black hair streaming across their faces.

It seemed as though every time I closed my eyes and opened

them again, I saw another Church of Christ. Each building was the same as the last: plain, unadorned, and palpable with autonomy from one another. Some had a few windows, but mostly they didn't. I wondered if these congregations ever got together to eat or visit with one another or to break out some fried chicken at a potluck. I bet they didn't. They were so close to one another in proximity, I didn't understand why there were so many of them, why they couldn't just join together. As we snaked deeper and deeper into the woods, I got a profound sense that this area was *Church of Christ*, not only in denomination, but the pulse of this place, the blood flow; it was the religion here. I didn't see any other kinds of churches at all, no Baptist or Methodist anywhere. I saw no police stations, fire stations, or hospitals. The area seemed lawless and remote. I shifted uncomfortably in my seat, wondering if that meant anything about *us* that we would come here. I had never noticed the isolation and seclusion of Camp Blessed Rock before this morning.

That first night, our camp groups met at A Rock, B Rock, and C Rock . . . three mountains with a wide valley in between. Three of the groups sat on opposite ends of the valley while the rest of us hiked to the tops of the mountains and hid in crevices and caves. As night fell upon us, we silently waited in a spirit of worship. Nobody spoke, we just waited together for the sun to disappear and the moon to take over.

When the sky turned black and the stars revealed themselves, the oldest group of girls, who were inside a cave on A Rock, began to sing. Their voices floated out into the valley in a soprano harmony.

Jesus is Lord, my Redeemer
How He loves me. How I love Him.

And from across the way, voices began to fill the air from B Rock, the guys this time. Their voices soared into the sky with bass, baritone, and tenor melodies.

He is risen. He is coming.
Lord come quickly, Hallelujah

And the voices from C Rock joined until they were all singing together, but no one could be seen. Only the power of song was present in the air, the voices harmonizing as one, and we were deep in worship. We who were in the valley began to round, adding to the music with only the sounds of our soprano girls. The altos respectfully sat quietly. This was the kind of singing and music that the Church of Christ was known for and that we took so seriously.

Jesus came to die on Calvary
To redeem all lost humanity
After death He rose triumphantly
And now He reigns for all eternity

The boys took on the melody of the groups in the mountains as if they had been doing complicated rounding since the day they were born. Many of them had been. Pretty soon, we were all singing into the night with worshipful song that was so powerful, I could feel the love of God permeating through my bones and down into my spirit. When our words floated up into the cool mountain air, I knew that God heard them, and I deeply loved my Lord and this part of our lives and the movement of the Holy Spirit among us in the still night air. I could feel God . . . He was back . . . He was here. Master. Savior. Redeemer.

As the song came to an end, we focused our eyes on what we had all been waiting for in the center of the mountains, the Burning of the Cross. A lone, anonymous voice began to sing.

Oh, how He loves you and me
Oh, how He loves you and me
He gave his life. What more could He give?
Oh, how He loves you. Oh how He loves me.
Oh, how He loves you and me.

Two gasoline-drenched ropes hung from the rocky mountain and strung across and met in the middle. The saturated ropes suspended a wooden cross high into the air and situated it inside a cleft of a rock that was cut out on the front of the mountain. Simultaneously, the ropes were lit and the fire traveled across them in the darkness and set the cross—which appeared in the night to be hovering—ablaze with golden fire that lit up the night sky like a million suns. The wooden cross burned and smoldered, the crackling embers floating out and then to the ground, dying before they reached us like shooting stars. Our faces were drenched with cleansing tears as the spirit of love overtook us. As the cross burned above me, I felt so close to God, so full of joy and tenderness, that somewhere deep inside of me, something started to hurt. And as our singing grew more powerful and intense, I knew that the time had come. For the first time ever since that day when I was ten years old, the memories of The Rent House and the understanding that my purity was gone for good and the awareness of the size of the blame that Jesus took for me on the cross felt like it was swallowing me whole. I was blemished, tainted, and dirty and I had been since I was a little girl. I closed my eyes and listened to the cross crackle and I pictured the mark of sin on me, an ugly spirit mark across the face of my soul if my soul had a face that others could see if they looked closely enough and searched, the mark that was unique to us children who had no innocence. Across my soul face were slashes and gashes that left my soul skin tattered and dangling like a ghoulish Halloween mask; too ugly to be real. The indignity of it all was giant and it covered me . . . and I looked up at the heavens and cried with shame for who I already was at twelve years old; a sinner from the moment of my birth. So in worshipful adoration of God I begged Him to forgive me for being born bad. I didn't hate Devin and Trent. I hated myself for needing them and for wanting what Katherine had. I begged God to make me clean.

So I decided it was time to be baptized.

10

I WALKED WITH MOTHER THROUGH the campground that night to the one and only cabin with a payphone. The darkness of the campgrounds was broken up only by the occasional firefly and the glow of our flashlights that pointed out sticks and rocks on our way to the old cabin that held our only portal of communication to the outside world.

She waited outside but with her ear close to the door, and I put my quarter in and dialed the number. The crickets chirped lyrically outside the quiet, screened-in room and the coolness of night was soothing after the long walk back from the Burning of the Cross. The phone rang several times and finally he answered.

His voice wasn't sleepy. I knew him well enough to know he was wide awake and separated from the rest of the house, holed up in his office writing sermons. I could picture right where he was sitting at his dimly lit desk among stacks of papers and books, writing away inside his own mind the words that he knew would never need correcting.

"Hi, Daddy Black. This is Stephanie," I said. I shooed my mother away who was listening outside. "Mother, give me some space!" I hissed.

"Well, hello, darling angel precious sweetheart. How is camp?" he asked.

"It's fine, it's fine. The showers are freezing," I said.

He laughed. "Well, it builds character, darling. Makes you appreciate what you have, doesn't it dear? Just a moment, Stephanie. I spilled my coffee. Goodness." He rustled papers in the background. The cabins didn't have actual walls, just screens, so that it truly felt like sleeping outside. I ran my fingers against the mesh and made the rip that was already in it bigger by accident. "Crap," I whispered, but he didn't hear me.

"Yes. It sure does. Um, Daddy Black. The reason I'm calling is . . . well . . . I wanted to tell you . . . I mean, ask . . . well . . . I made a decision for my life tonight after devotional. I want to be baptized."

Silence.

"Daddy Black? I want to be baptized?" I shifted my weight from one foot to the other. My eyes caught my mother's outside and I waved my hand and scowled and shooed her away again. She looked down at the ground like she was seriously focusing on something down there.

Silence.

"Hello? Daddy Black?"

"Yes. I heard you, Stephanie. The answer is no." One of his other telephones rang in the background. He picked it up and had an entire, several-minute conversation about giving someone a ride to church tomorrow in the background while I waited. He told whoever it was that he had to pick up four people on the way, so it would be a tight squeeze, but that he would be there. I sat on the line waiting and fuming and pictured him on his big black telephones with curly wires, one in each ear, sitting at his messy desk covered in notes he had written or Scripture references. He came back on and sounded surprised that I was still here. "Hello?" he said, as if I hadn't said a word yet and neither had he.

"Daddy Black. It's still me, Stephanie. I was trying to tell you I wanted to be baptized. Why do you say the answer is no?"

"Well," he cleared his throat. He didn't need his Bible because he had it *memorized*. "For starters, in Acts 2:38 Peter states, 'Repent and let every one of you be baptized in the name of Jesus Christ for the remission of sins,' and again in Acts 22:16, 'Arise and be baptized, and wash away your sins.'"

We sat in uncomfortable silence before I said, "Well . . . I know. That's what I want to do, Daddy Black. I want to have Jesus be the Lord of my life. I want to walk with Him in newness of life and take communion and be in the body of Christ. I want to let the world know that I'm not ashamed of Him. I want my sins washed away. Is that okay?"

"Well . . . no, it's not okay. You don't have any sins, Stephanie. You are twelve years old. You are a young child, still not at an age of accountability. You don't have any sins for which to be forgiven, so you aren't in need of baptism tonight. You're really not old enough to make that decision. Now, good night, dear."

And with that, he hung up the phone. I stood there on the line waiting for him to say something more, but no, he was gone. The dial tone turned to a busy signal and I slowly placed the receiver back on its base, feeling embarrassed. I looked out at my mother who had been looking in but then quickly acted like she was trying to get mud off her stark white sneakers, which looked out of place on her. I walked out the screen door and down the wooden steps out to the side of the cabin to meet her. "He said, 'no,'" I told her. I walked past her and back to my cabin, leaving her there in the dark.

By the time I got to my cabin all the other girls were asleep. I didn't want a cold shower. I fumbled around in the dark taking off my sweaty camp clothes and changing into my nightgown with the pink hearts on the sleeves. I climbed up the ladder to my top bunk with my flashlight in my mouth and slid into my sleeping bag. I turned on my flashlight under the covers so that I wouldn't wake the others and shone the light onto my toes and up my bare legs, examining myself for ticks. *How dare he tell me no.* I shone it in between my toes and onto the soles of my dirty feet. I dug the dirt out of my toenails and flung it over the bunk. *It's none of his business. Yes, it is. No, it's not. Yes, it is. He knows better than anyone the Scripture.* I shone it up to my knees and turned my legs from side to side. I saw what looked like a tick but it was just a piece of bark, easily wiped away. *He can't tell me no. How would he know if I have sin that needs to be washed away? Why does he consider himself to be more powerful than the spirit of God? What makes him so all-fucking-powerful?*

I opened up my thighs. I wasn't stupid; I knew they could be anywhere, even in my private parts, so I pulled down my panties just enough to see what I needed to see. I searched myself thoroughly, making sure to hold my covers up with one hand. My sleeping bag was heavy enough to hide the light; everyone else snored peacefully. Ticks totally freaked me out. I was damned if I was going to have one blow up on me without my noticing. *I have sinned. I have. I have sinned more in my short life than most people have in a lifetime. If I don't get baptized now, I could die tomorrow and burn in hell for all the sins I've committed.* I stretched out my arms and did a quick once over. But ticks weren't stupid, either. They weren't going to get me on such a prominent place like my arms. *Daddy Black will be furious if I go against him. So will Mother. I don't want anyone to be mad at me. I wish Brother Hazel was still alive.* I pictured him in his polyester suit and cowboy hat, his eyes twinkling and his smile warm with acceptance. I wished he could've baptized me. I looked at my hands and felt all through my scalp, running my fingers up the base of my neck and onto the top of my head. I was satisfied. I had managed to survive another day at Blessed Rock without all my blood being sucked out of my body. I lay still and tried my best to fall asleep. I closed my eyes and pictured Katherine being whipped the night I turned her in for smoking; pictured myself on the floor underneath Trent, moaning and arching my back, pretending to be a sex kitten at the age of ten; pictured the hazy memory from a long time ago, Katherine taking the blame for me because I had unwrapped the Christmas gift; pictured myself touching myself in my closet with my father's *Playboys* at five years old; imagined having sex with my father; being held like my sister; being loved by him like she was because my mother told me so. *God, I'm sick. My sins are like ticks. They hide in the most private places in me. Forget Daddy Black. Forget age of accountability. I'm doing it.*

I flipped off my flashlight and carefully climbed down the ladder so as not to wake the other girls. I put a sweatshirt on over my gown. I didn't bother to put on shoes, and I softly crept out the screen door and walked out into the night. I walked across the camp to the other side, to the boys' side. I counted the cabins until I found the right one, the next to the last one in the row. I walked around the outside of the cabin peeking inside, listening for sounds of familiar breathing. I couldn't see anything; it was so dark I could barely see my hand in front of my face. I was getting cold without shoes. No one sounded familiar so I went around to the other side. I stood outside the screen and put my face right next to the sleeping heads on the other side, pressing my nose to their hair, smelling, staring, and listening. I moved down the cabin one bed at a time and put my face near each sleeping camper, listening to the sounds of their breathing. Finally, I put my ear up to one that sounded like what I was looking for. I put my mouth right up to the screen and whispered straight into his ear, "Dad."

His breathing continued, slowly, peacefully, in rhythm with the croaking of the frogs far off in the distance. I cupped my hands around my mouth and pressed in more. "Dad!" I whispered again. Now, my eyes were adjusted to the camper's head. I was next to my father. "Dad! Wake up!" My dad shot up and ripped his covers off his legs and tore outside.

He came barreling around to the side of the cabin in his pajamas, arms folded. The cold night air smoked with the heat of his breath. "Stephanie, what on earth are you doing out here?" he whispered, hopping from one cold foot to the next and peering over his shoulder to make sure we hadn't woken anyone up. "Your mother will kill you for sneaking out."

"Dad . . . I want to be baptized. I made the decision tonight at the Burning of the Cross. I asked Daddy Black but he said no." I stood there looking up at him, the moon now gently spilling across his face. He squinted in the night without his glasses, and he folded his arms tighter, and shifted his weight from one foot to the other again, still trying to adjust to the cold. Finally, he settled into it and stood still. He was listening.

"You asked your grandfather and he said no?" he asked.

"He said I didn't have any sin to be baptized for. Dad, help."

He sighed and looked over his shoulder and then back at me. "Do you have sins you want to be forgiven, Stephanie?" he asked. He waited for a response because I was looking away now, embarrassed . . . because I did.

"Yes." I couldn't bear to look at him.

"Okay. Hold on. Let me get my jacket." And he walked back inside the cabin. He came out wearing his pajamas with a heavy jacket and his glasses, and he brought some socks for me. "Put these on."

We walked through the dark woods together without speaking, his flashlight lighting the path only enough for us to see our very next step and no more. We walked far into the night, through the trees and down rocky paths that had been worn by faithful campers through the years. Finally, we came to the creek. Dad took off his coat, and we both took off our sweaters and socks and made our way down through the creek into the still black lake. My father went in first.

I took a deep breath and braced myself, then took Dad's hand and let him guide me into the chilly water.

With the first touch of my feet to the water, I was filled with peace and love and the light of God. My soul was completely quiet . . . calm and tranquil, and I could feel the spirit of God inside of me and around me. I could feel His warming light inside the cold water, warming it to the temperature of a tepid bath, even though thin white steam rose around us in the chill. It felt perfect.

We waded down in the water together until we came to an opening a little deeper, and continued in even further until we were above my waist. My white nightgown hung like a soaked choir robe as we glided through the water and stepped on the rocky lake bottom below. The water was still like black glass, but for the ripples we made with our bodies. The moonbeams shone onto it in shimmering silence. He put his hand on my shoulder and turned me to my side. I faced the forest and the stars twinkled above the trees because God had asked them to do that; He had hung them there, and they looked like diamonds next to the full moon and I was keenly aware of the hand of my creator. The pine trees formed a wall of safe and private protection around us in the secrecy of the lake that night. Any confusion I held about my dad or hatred I had because of things my mother had told me ceased in this moment; he looked helpful . . . kind . . . human . . . and love prevailed deep into my heart for him and for God.

He tightened his grip on my shoulder, and raised his other hand high as if reaching for heaven. He closed his eyes and breathed deeply. "Stephanie Olive Walters, do you believe that Jesus Christ is the Son of God? That He died on the cross to save you from your sins, went to hell, and was resurrected on the third day? Do you believe that He now reigns in heaven at the right hand of God? And you want Him to be Lord of your life?"

"Yes, I believe that Jesus Christ is the Son of God, who suffered and died to save me from my sins. I want Him to be Lord of my life. I want to be forgiven," I answered quietly.

Dad put his hand over my nose and mouth, held my back, and

dunked me under. Now I felt the shock of the cold as I went down into the water, and I died down there in the water and I arose a new creation. I felt a sense of serenity that I had never felt before and I knew *for sure* that I was forgiven, pure and blameless, washed in the blood of the Lamb. He hugged me and prayed silently over me and we walked out of the water together without speaking, my cotton gown sopping heavily from the water, but my heart weightless with redemption.

THE NEXT MORNING BEFORE BREAKFAST we all lined up in the cafeteria to pray. I felt like a different person than the one I was yesterday. My spirit felt like it was actually floating; I felt pure and as if my life was a clean slate. I felt no sin, no shame. Every sad memory in my life had been washed away and my heart was completely clean like a newborn baby. *This day, this feeling of newness, is the best feeling I have ever known. Dear God, please let this feeling last forever.*

One of the counselors, Carl, led the prayer before the meal. He was a freshman in college and a member of Bayside Church of Christ like us. He was in charge of sixth grade boys and because they had dish duty, they got to go through the line first.

"So, guess what?" I asked Simone and Valerie as we went through the line helping ourselves to powdered eggs and milk.

Simone held up a spoonful of brown fruit to her nose and smelled it. She put it back and shook her head. "I can't wait to go home. Only five days left at this hellhole."

"Guess what?" I asked again. "My dad baptized me last night. So if I'm acting differently, that's why," I said proudly. *My soul face is smooth again. The slashes are gone.*

"Really?" Valerie asked. "Good for you!"

"Cool." Simone skipped everything but toast.

I looked across the room and caught the camp counselor, Carl, looking at me. We exchanged glances for a few short seconds and I turned back to my friends. He was good looking. He had a small frame and short, crinkly black hair. His eyes were peculiar but they added interest like tiny black marbles and they were too small for his face. His shoulders were muscular and he had what looked like a gymnast's body—broad in the chest but otherwise narrow. A few seconds later, I looked up again because my body heat was rising, and I could feel him looking at me from behind. He was still staring at me and smiling. It seemed like he should be hiding it, but he wasn't. I tilted my head to the side and smiled back, pretending to be shy like a kitten, pretending it was the first time I had ever smiled at a boy. *Stephanie, this isn't a boy. This is a man.* Our eyes held the gaze for several seconds and without words he told me a silent secret. He was interested in me. He thought I was pretty. He knew I was accessible. The ugly mark was still on me. He could see it.

I kept smiling on the outside, but I knew that if the saving water didn't take the ugly mark away—if being baptized didn't clean me—nothing ever would.

"Will you guys come with me to smoke? I haven't had a ciggy in four days," Valerie said. It wasn't Valerie's fault that she smoked. Her home life was bad, so we accepted her the way she was. The thirty-five-year age difference between her parents was so weird on top of the fact that they were hermits. Simone and I thought whatever she needed to do to get through it was fine. So we finished eating and walked outside and back around the building. It was mid-morning now, and almost time for devotional.

She pulled out her cigarettes and lit one up. Simone put her two fingers up asking for a puff. Valerie rolled her eyes and gave it to her. "I'm gonna quit sharing with you one of these days." Simone inhaled almost the entire cigarette down.

"Hey, stop!" Valerie laughed. "You'll get sick!" She took the cigarette back, the cherry now long from too deep a drag. She gave it back to Simone. "You can *have* it now," she said, and she lit another one.

"Should I try that? What's it feel like?" I asked. I put my two fingers up like Simone had done and Valerie put the cigarette between them. "I mean, I just got baptized. I probably shouldn't. I'll just feel guilty."

"It doesn't *feel* like anything; it just feels relaxing. But just inhale like a normal person, not like Simone. Take a breath, hold it in your lungs, and then in a few seconds, blow it out," she said.

It's not like it was as bad flirting with Carl. Or as bad as thinking about him in the ways that I was . . . maybe it would even help me clear my mind.

I tried to take a puff, but I instantly started coughing and my eyes started watering. I waved my hand in front of me to get the smoke away and tried to breathe through my coughing. Simone and Valerie laughed. Simone lit up a fresh cigarette. "Stephanie, you gotta just take it slow, don't fight it. Close your eyes and don't think about it so much when you do it. Just take a puff of the cigarette, then right after that, take a breath of regular air. Watch me." She held it up to her mouth and effortlessly took a drag. Before she blew out the smoke, she said, "See? Nothing to it. And I don't care what anybody says. It *is* cool, and all the cool people *are* doing it." She laughed and blew out the smoke into the air.

I did exactly what Simone said. I closed my eyes and pictured the sweet nicotine filling my lungs with searing, effortless comfort. I was determined to make this work. I put the cigarette up to my lips and closed my eyes and didn't fight it when the smoke filled my lungs even though it burned a little bit. I took another breath of the fresh air in and held them both in my lungs together before exhaling. I opened my eyes and searched theirs for approval as I exhaled. "Did I do it?" I asked.

Simone grinned and took the cigarette out of my hand and took a long drag. "Yeah, you did fine, Stephy Baby. There's hope for you, yet."

12

DAD GRIPPED THE STEERING WHEEL tightly as if it would fly away should he let it go even once over the eight-hour bus ride home. He barely spoke unless he had to. My mother tapped her nails relentlessly and mumbled under her breath to herself about how nobody ever listens to her, about how she is always overridden, even when it comes to her own children.

"She's old enough to decide that she needs God," Dad said.

"That's not the point," she answered.

"Then, Lily, what is the point?" he asked.

More silence. I was so thankful that he had listened to me that night and taken me out to the pond, even if the feeling of redemption only lasted for less than one day. That one day was worth it.

We were all openly sick and tired of singing and praying and having devotionals and playing Scripture trivia, so we rode broken up into our own little groups, sunburned and overflowing with indoctrination that would last for another year. Simone and Valerie and I circled around our boom boxes and played our music at a low volume. Katherine, Devin, and Trent played cards, and some others were so tired they fell asleep. I looked around at the bus and could feel the calm and closeness among our youth group as I watched the friends I had known my whole life sleeping and talking. Katherine looked relaxed and happy with the evening sun streaming in the windows; she was laughing at something Devin had said.

But my parents were not closer . . . they seemed further apart, and I was beginning to feel sorry for being baptized, even if it had been the best feeling in the world.

We drove almost straight through and arrived home late that Saturday night. I fell into my bed exhausted and sore from the long bus ride home. My parents' bedroom was directly across from mine and I could hear my mother on the phone, her voice muffled but insistent. I crept out of my bed and into the office and closed the door. I pushed the mute button on the receiver of the telephone and held it down before picking up the phone, knowing my mother could not hear me. She was talking to Mama Black.

"So then he took her and *baptized* her," my mother seethed. "He knew full *well* how Daddy felt about it and he purposely went behind his back. He has nothing but disregard for Scripture. He has no healthy fear of God, and no respect for Daddy or the Church. He was a *Bible* major in college for goodness' sake! Does that mean nothing now? It's all about being 'open minded' now. This is the way he always does things; he's sneaky and snaky and you know what I'm talking about. I'm not just talking about baptizing Stephanie. I'm talking about him molesting Katherine!"

I closed my eyes and sank down the wall.

Mama Black spoke up. "Darling, do you *really* actually believe that? What makes you think such things?"

"What makes me think *such things*? I don't 'think' such things! A mother *knows* what goes on in her own home with her own husband and daughter. Paul is married to Katherine, not me. Katherine has absolutely nothing to do with me, no matter how hard I try, and she never has. And I know it's because he's told her that I would hurt her. When she was a baby, he would sneak up and put ice in her diapers when I was holding her so that she would associate me with pain."

"Darling, these are very serious things to say. If you truly believe Paul is gratifying himself through Katherine, then why don't you ask the elders for help in the matter? Proverbs states that a wise man seeks many counselors."

"Because I'll be demonized in the church and you know it! Nobody will believe me! And Daddy will disown me if I try to leave Paul!"

Mama Black was quiet for a long time. Finally, when Mother let out a long, heavy sigh, Mama Black said, "Lillian, darling, no one said anything about you having to leave Paul. You know full well that you have a covenant to your husband until death. Lillian, I do hate to be crude, but as your mother, I need to ask, are you making yourself available to him? On a regular basis?"

"You know what? Not one single person in this world loves me except Stephanie. Even my own mother doubts me. Paul Walters is a dragon who sniffs and snorts around my daughters, but he wears a navy suit and is a deacon in the church, so he's got the perfect image. I never had any hope with Katherine and it's only a matter of time before Stephanie turns away."

"Lillian, why don't you take an aspirin and go lie down?" Mama Black said. "Or better yet, a little Valium?"

Leave him, Mother! Take us with you!

"And," she went on. "I found another card. A very sexual card. It was from Gail again."

Gail? Who's Gail?

"Listen to this." I heard her pulling a card out of an envelope. "It's a Ziggy card, and Ziggy is eating a bowl of ice cream. That whore drew

legs up around the ice cream so that it looks like Ziggy is eating . . .
oh . . . I can't even say it . . . like he's eating from between her legs. And
she wrote, 'coffee, tea, or me?' Isn't that repulsive? I don't know how
much longer I can live with this liar, this deceitful, evil man. I hate him.
Our marriage is a joke."

I placed the receiver down quietly and walked back into my
bedroom.

I closed my eyes and tried to sleep, but my mind was troubled
and agitated with doubts. I put my hands over my ears to protect me
from sounds that only I could hear, the clanging gongs of confusion
and chaos that were far-off sounds of chime, chime, chiming, in the
distance somewhere deep inside me, the sounds of uncertainty inside
beating with the tribal rhythm of a hazy, ominous drum that ruled my
relationship with my father, bum, bum, bum.

I got out of bed again and walked down the dark hallway to
Katherine's room. There was a light coming out from under her door.
I stood still like a ghost in the darkened hallway with my eyes closed. I
shuddered because I did not want it to be true, and I pictured Katherine
and Dad hiding behind the door having sex, him raping her, but her
loving it because they had been doing this for years. It would be all she
knew by now. It made me sick thinking of my dad being married to
Katherine, but it was true that he seemed to adore her much more than
he seemed to love my mother. Maybe she was right. Maybe they were
married in their hearts.

I took a deep breath and raised my hand to knock on the door but
then put it down again. I shook my head and headed back to my bedroom; I couldn't bear to see this. Then I turned around again. I needed
to know the truth.

My heart raced and my lip quivered and I had no idea what I would
find. I raised my hand to knock on her door, but instead, I pushed it
open without waiting for an answer.

"Get out, twerp. I'm tired," she said. She was changing into her nightgown and her body looked like such a woman; her hips were curvy and her legs were strong. Her suitcases from Camp Blessed Rock lie open on the floor with a pile of dirty and clean clothes she had separated. Willie Nelson was playing his guitar in the background, and her stuffed orange cat, Garfield, was right where he always was on her perfectly made bed.

"I just wanted to tell you good night," I said. I stood staring at her waiting for her to answer, but she crawled under the covers and flipped off her lamp without speaking back. I closed the door and wandered back into my bed again picturing my sister and father doing what my mother had just said and wondered how in the world they were hiding it so well. When and why was my mother able to catch them in the act but I wasn't?

Troubled sleep overtook me and I tossed and turned through the night. *I'm disgusted by them. I'm excluded by them. I want what they have. I'm a sicko for wanting that.*

Mother flipped on my bedroom light the next morning, her hair in curlers. She unwound her bouncy mane out of the pink, can-sized things and her bracelets jingled when she did. I didn't even have to open my eyes; her perfume preceded her. It burned my nostrils, but I refused to sneeze for fear it would wake me up for real. When I didn't sit up she rubbed my head and started singing cheerfully,

> *Good morning to you. Good morning to you.*
> *We're all in our places with sunshiny faces.*
> *This is the way to start a good day.*

"Stephanie, sweetheart, I'm sorry, but we're running late for church. If we don't leave now, we're going to miss Sunday school."

I groaned, "Please, Mother. I'm too sleepy."

"C'mon, Stephanie. This is the day that the Lord hath made! I will rejoice and be glad in it!" she answered.

My head pounded and my eyes were hurting behind their lids. *Noooo.*

"But Mother, we had such a long bus ride home from being away two weeks at Blessed Rock. Can we please sleep in and rest today? Please? Just this one time?" I pulled the warm covers over my head.

"Stephanie, you know the answer to that. Now get up." She walked down the hall and rapped on Katherine's door and I heard the same groan come from Katherine. "Mother, we're tired!" Katherine called. I grumbled about how we never get to have a true Sabbath and we never get to rest as I stumbled out of bed and she called back to me, "Stephanie, get happy! Katherine, get up! Both of you girls get happy! It's time for church."

When my dad passed me in the hallway as I walked out of the bathroom he yawned and patted me on the shoulder. "Hey sport." His eyes were swollen and red and his hair mussed but his navy pin-striped suit was perfectly starched.

We took turns yawning in the car on the way to church, our bodies exhausted from the bus ride and late-night return. None of us wanted to be there. I wondered why we could never just take a damn Sunday off. What would actually happen to us if our family ever just stayed home on a Sunday morning and ate pancakes and read the comics? Dad yawned until his eyes watered. He shook his head because his mouth stayed opened so long. My mother looked in the mirror and continued to line her lips. The light from the mirror made her eye shadow shimmer.

Nobody answered. Instead we rode in silence the rest of the way but for our yawning. When we pulled up to the parking lot, the sign in the church parking lot simply said "30,000." There were white wooden crosses all over the church grass, lined up row after row like tombs at a graveyard.

"What is all this? What's with all the crosses?" I nodded to the sign and asked my mother as we got out of the car. She didn't answer me, but walked ahead of me so fast I had to run to catch up. I caught up to her and put my hand on her arm. "Mother, what's wrong?"

She whipped around and gritted her teeth at me. "I'm not going to tell you what's wrong, and I will never tell you what's wrong! Don't touch me!" she growled. She jerked her arm out of my hand and I stood there cut, hurt, angry, and embarrassed. People passed by and raised their eyebrows like we were a circus side show.

Oh, fuck all these people. What the hell did I just do to deserve that?

"The number 30,000 on the sign represents all the babies that are killed by abortion every month in America. The white crosses are a symbol of all the deaths," my dad answered. "Sport, I'm sorry. She didn't mean to snap at you like that. That kind of thing hurts, doesn't it?" he asked. He went to hug me but I moved away so he couldn't.

Who is Gail? I couldn't get it out of my mind.

"I'm fine, Dad. Forget it," I said, and walked ahead of him. But I wasn't fine. I was seething inside.

When we walked into the lobby there were pamphlets and flyers about our church planning to peacefully demonstrate outside of an abortion clinic in Houston. I picked one up, and there were pictures of little babies floating in the womb, safe inside their mothers. The singing started from inside the sanctuary so I put the flyer down and went in to find Simone and Valerie.

Daddy Black preached that day on choosing life. "Turn in your Bibles with me to Deuteronomy 30:19," he said. The congregation fanned through the thin pages of their Bibles sounding like a room full of moths flapping their wings in take-off. He waited for us to get settled. "The Bible says, 'I set before you life and death, blessings and curses. Therefore, *choose life*, so that you and your descendants may live.'" I turned around and looked at my mother and father, who sat on the pew next to each other, but there were walls between them; his arms were folded and she crossed her legs so that she was turned from him. She looked down at her Bible and tears were in her eyes . . . Mother hadn't chosen life . . . and now, possibly . . . my father's choice in choosing her was over. He was choosing someone else.

As the communion plate was passed around, I took it for the first time because I was baptized now, one of the flock. I pictured Christ dying on the cross, his body broken, as I ate the bread, and I could see his blood dripping from his hands and side as I drank the grape juice. Communion was a powerful worship tool, and I was glad to finally get to participate. I noticed Daddy Black looking at me as I took it and then passed the plate. I felt like I was doing something wrong.

"Let's close in prayer." Daddy Black stepped to the side and my father got up to lead the closing prayer.

"Dear God, thank you for this message today," he started. I bowed my head and closed my eyes. "Help us to remember your lost and hurting world." I could feel someone looking at me. I opened my eyes and looked around the congregation, but everyone had their eyes closed and was praying. "Father we ask your blessings on the Martin family as they grieve the loss of their grandmother." I still felt it, someone watching me, so I looked again down the aisle and caught eyes with Carl. His skin was tan from camp. I kept my head bowed but we stared at each other for the remainder of the prayer. He noiselessly mouthed the word, "Hi."

"Hi," I smiled and mouthed back and looked around the congregation. Nobody noticed because their eyes were closed.

On the way out, Daddy Black motioned to me to come into his office. I sat down across from him at his desk, my eyes surveying the various books that filled his shelves—books about Alexander Campbell, The Crossroads Movement, The Boston Movement being a cult, what constituted a cult, what constituted a sect, what saved us, and multiple books about the role of the Church of Christ, the universal church. "Stephanie, I'm proud of you," he said.

I stared back at him, my eyes wide with surprise. "What? Why?" I asked.

"For being baptized against my wishes," he said.

I squirmed in my seat and looked at him, totally puzzled. "Proud of me? I thought you would be mad at me," I said, looking down at the ground, suddenly embarrassed that I had been baptized. I felt like a toddler who had been caught with my hand in the cookie jar.

"I could hear in your voice that night at camp that you were very much ready, sweetheart darling angel. But I hoped it wasn't because you were overwhelmed by emotion. I figured if you were really ready to accept Jesus, it wouldn't really matter what I said. Your faith is strong, Stephanie. You are washed in the blood of the lamb now. I'm putting a lot of hope in you, dear. You are perfect." I felt invaded that he had tested me in this way with something as personal to me as my baptism. And if his words were meant to help, they didn't, because I knew full well I was not perfect.

On the way home from church, my mother spoke up. "You know, it makes me so sad and angry at the same time that some women would choose abortion when others of us would give anything to have our babies back."

Dad put his hand on hers but she pulled away. We were listening. "The doctors said my baby was probably a little boy," my mother muttered. "I was pregnant with him when I was just a teenager, and I didn't eat enough and I ran four miles one day and had a miscarriage. I was trying to be skinny, trying to make it to where I could count my own ribs in the mirror from across the room. I would give anything if I could take that choice back. I didn't know that running during pregnancy would do that." She looked with lonely eyes out her window and started to cry again, and my heart broke for her. Her tender pain was so clear . . . and it bruised me to watch her hurt. I wanted to reach in deep inside of her and pull it out, pull out whatever it was that was behind those eyes.

"Mother, please don't cry," I said. I sat forward putting my face close to her but was careful not to touch her. She was silent and stared out her window.

My baby died when I fell off a horse.

"Never mind," I said, sitting back. "You cry all you want." I looked at Katherine and she rolled her eyes and shrugged her shoulders.

"Mother, none of this even makes any sense," Katherine said. "This story changes all the time."

Katherine didn't even care. *Bitch*. My father drove staring straight ahead like he had heard the story too many times to care anymore.

"There, there," he said.

"It does not!" Mother yelled.

When we got home from church, our family split down the middle. My mother and I lay down in her bed to take a nap while Dad and Katherine went to run errands. We turned out the lights and crawled under the covers and shut out the rest of the world. She scratched my back and the cool air from the oscillating fan blew my fatigue away. Mother whispered, "Stephanie, I hope you know how much I love you, sweetheart."

I knew that she did. I lay next to her feeling like I was a part of her, literally, like we were a part of each other. She stopped scratching and wrapped her thin arms around me. When I was in her arms, I felt like the entire world was right and safe and good. I forgave her for snapping at me in the parking lot. "Stephanie, can I ask you something?"

I was almost asleep so I just nodded. She kissed my cheek. "I remember when you were a baby, and the sunlight streamed across your room into your crib and I kissed your cheeks like that," she said. The fan blew my bangs in front of my eyes and she gently brushed them away. Her touch was loving and careful. "Stephanie, how would you feel if your father and I divorced?" My eyes were closed but even so, the world got darker. *I could never handle that. I need you both.*

"Please don't do that," I said quietly.

"Well," she sighed.

"What?" I asked.

"We can't divorce even if we want to. If I divorce, I go to hell. I made a commitment before God to stay married for life. God hates divorce and our church doesn't recognize it," she trailed off.

"Good," I answered. But then I realized what she was saying . . . that God would hate us if they divorced. "Mother, He doesn't hate the *people* who divorce," I said. "But please don't divorce. I want our family to be together. That would blow me and Katherine's life up."

"Well I would never want to do that," she said.

I knew I was being selfish; I knew they needed out; I knew there was so much I did not know . . . but I couldn't help it; I wanted both my parents. I didn't want two addresses, to split our family. She scratched my back and I dozed off with her beside me.

When I woke up, she was propped up on her pillow beside me. "Hey, Mother, can I ask you a question now?"

She took off her glasses and put down her magazine. "Sure, sweetheart," she said. "What's up?"

"Well, you said in the car that you were pregnant when you were in high school. Does that mean you had sex before you married Dad?"

She gave a big, heavy sigh. "Well, yes, but, unfortunately, I was gang raped in the back of a supply room at a drug store where I used to work down by the docks. Daddy Black got me the job and wouldn't let me quit even though I begged. We would fight and fight horribly about it and he would beat me black and blue and Mama Black hid under the bed and shook with fear but never stopped him." I pictured Mama Black under the bed shaking and Daddy Black beating my mother. Anger rose up inside me and confusion spun around again. I wanted so badly to believe her but this didn't make sense.

"The men made me wear tight T-shirts and very short shorts and that's where I learned to love high heels. That baby I lost could've belonged to any number of men. I didn't know who the father even was."

I didn't know of a drug store down by the docks. "Oh. I'm sorry. Okay. Well, what drug store? And did anyone call the police? I mean, what did they say at the hospital? Did Mama and Daddy Black press charges on all those men?" I asked.

"Stephanie, what are you getting at?" she demanded.

"Nothing. I'm not getting at anything," I said. "I love you. But Mother, what about the baby that died when you fell off that horse?"

"I never said I had a baby die by me falling off a horse. What are you talking about?"

"Nothing."

"Now it's about time to get ready for church tonight. Do you have something to wear?"

"Yes, Mother," I sighed. "My blue jumpsuit is pressed."

13

THAT EVENING, WE RETURNED TO church for night services, and when my family walked through the foyer, I saw Carl talking with his college group. He watched me as I walked in and made my way to the front of the church where my youth group sat. When I was seated, he came and sat a few spaces down the pew from me. He pretended to read his bulletin, flipping through the pages, and, still looking down, asked, "Can I call you tonight?" My heart raced. Blood rushed to my face and I felt lightheaded.

I stared straight ahead while the congregation mingled and found their seats. "Yeah, call me right at midnight. We just got call waiting. No one will know."

So that night, when everyone had gone to sleep, I set my alarm for 11:45. I got up and crept downstairs and brought the kitchen phone into my dark bedroom and plugged it in. I turned on the light in my closet and went inside and sat in the corner. At 11:55 I called the movie theatre and listened to the selections. As the recording droned on, I sat and waited. When the line beeped, I switched over. It was Carl. My blood started pumping faster. "Hello?" I spoke as quietly as I could. Thank Goodness. The phone hadn't rung where anyone in my house would've heard. It was the first time I had used the call waiting and it had worked. This invention was miraculous!

I sat in my closet talking to him, twirling the curly yellow phone cord around my finger, loving the attention.

"So what were you doing when I called?" he asked.

"Nothing," I giggled. "I was just waiting for you to call and hoping the phone wouldn't ring."

"Well, I just wanted to call you and kinda see what you're like. You weren't in bed, were you?" he asked.

"Well I was but . . ."

Suddenly, the door swung opened and my father was standing there. I jerked up. "Stephanie, what are you doing? Who are you talking to at this hour?" he asked.

"Oh, um, it's Carl Williams, from church," I answered plainly. My father just stood there. I was terrified that I was about to get into some serious trouble. I waited for him to scream at me, to scream at Carl, to threaten him and remind him I was only twelve years old, to say he would kill him if he ever caught him talking to his daughter again.

He looked nonplussed. "Well, young lady. It's a school night and you know that. You need to wrap it up right this instant," he said. And he turned around and walked out the door.

I raised my eyebrows and sighed with relief. He was totally cool. "Hey, I gotta go. My dad is pissed," I whispered.

"Pissed at me or pissed at you?" he asked.

"I think he's pissed at me because it's a school night," I whispered.

"Ahhh. A *school* night," he laughed. "What school do you go to?"

"Weis Middle School." I hoped the fact that I was so much younger didn't make him not call me again. "I'll see you at Wednesday night church. I gotta go." I hung up before he could say anything more.

I went to bed stunned at Dad's response, but giddy with excitement because it was totally what I wanted; and I rubbed myself all over, arching my back and purring, thinking sexy thoughts of Carl on top of me, rocking back and forth until I fell asleep. If my dad didn't care, then I didn't care. I felt ready for this.

The next morning on our way to school, Simone took my hand in hers and then threw it down again. "What's that bubble writing on your hand? Who's Carl?" she asked. I told her it was Carl Williams from church. She twisted up her face. "Yuck. Wash your hands. He's a little *old* for you, don't you think?"

"No, not really. And he's *so* fine," I answered. "Plus, my dad's totally cool with it. He caught us talking on the phone last night and didn't care at all. I just got in trouble because it was late."

"That's fucked up," Simone said. "My dad would kill me if he found me sneaking on the phone late. And he'd probably have a college guy thrown in jail if he even looked at me!"

"Well la-di-da good for y'all," I replied. "Not really your place to judge."

"I'm not judging. It's just kind of fucked up, that's all. Don't be pissed." We walked the rest of the way in silence.

That night, Carl called my parents and asked if he could come over. I listened from my bedroom as my mother cleaned the kitchen and my father talked to him on the phone.

"Oh, hell no!" Mother said in the background. "Paul, hang up on him! He's too old!"

My dad put his hand over the phone and snapped, "Lily, will you relax? Do you always have to ruin everyone's fun? It's bad enough you always feel you need to go and ruin mine."

"Paul, he's too old," she said again. "She's twelve. And goddammit, don't shush me!"

Dad gave him directions to our house and spent the rest of the time asking about how Carl's parents were doing, how his freshman year was, if he had decided on a major. My father and Carl's dad had roomed together in college at Abilene Christian University, and they were both deacons. He hung up the phone and told my mother what a polite young man Carl had grown to become.

My mother loaded the dishwasher and was clanking dishes around everywhere. "Paul, you should chase that boy off with a shotgun. This is not even close to appropriate," she said. She shut the dishwasher and sprayed cleanser on the countertops. "Can you hand me the paper towels?" He tossed her something. "The *paper* towels. Not a damn dish towel. Do you think I need more laundry to deal with from you people?"

"He's a great kid, Lily! He's going to study engineering. And they're just talking and getting to know each other. Why do you have to be so uptight all the time? It's like you think everything and everybody is so sinister, like everyone is just *plotting* to hurt you or Stephanie. It's ridiculous. And I do most of the laundry anyways because you wash everything in flaming hot water and shrink all the clothes. Don't you think that if we make all of her decisions for her, she'll never learn on her own? I love her, too, you know. Plus, age is relative. It's more of a state of mind. Some people are twelve, but they're not twelve." He grabbed a beer from the fridge and popped it open. "Age is relative," he said again.

"Please don't leave your bottle cap on the countertop that I just cleaned. And people are not 'twelve but not twelve.' She's *twelve*. Twelve isn't relative. It's objectively countable. You know what, Paul? Just do what you want, you always do anyways. She'll grow up to hate you for this, you know that, right? And I'm going to sit back and laugh. In fact, I will enjoy watching it. She'll never forgive you. You go on and take just enough rope to hang yourself with, Paul. In fact, go to hell." She flipped off the kitchen light and walked past Katherine, who stared at her blankly and stepped aside so she could pass.

"You're crazy, Lillian! Mad as a hatter!" he called after her, and slammed his beer bottle down on the countertop, now sitting by himself in the dark.

When Carl arrived, I met him at the door and stepped out on the porch to talk. I didn't want to share him with my family, so we walked down the driveway and he leaned up against his tan Corolla. Carl was very sexy in his tight Izod shirt and gold chain around his neck. His white pants were rolled up at the ankles and his deck shoes were new and looked expensive. He pulled me closer to him, his arm around my waist, and kissed me hard . . . flames lapped and the water rose and filled my whole body like a flood . . . two things that should cancel each other out but they didn't . . . heat and wetness combined in a way that drove me into a fit . . . I was drunk . . . totally intoxicated by his mouth . . . by his lips . . . he tasted like mint and tobacco, but not tobacco from cigarettes, I could tell. *This guy dips. I wonder if the neighbors saw if they would report Carl to the police. I dare them. No, I hope they don't. Someone stop me. No, don't. I'm such a whore but I can't help it. I want this.*

We stood at his car and talked and laughed. "The showers at Camp Blessed Rock were freezing cold! I hated that part!" I said.

"Wait, what do you mean? The showers weren't cold," he laughed. "Why were your showers cold?" He leaned down and kissed my neck.

"Carl, all the showers were cold. They were ice cold!" I said, leaning in so he could kiss me more.

He looked right at me and smiled. "I think only the girls' side had cold showers. Our showers on the guys' side were fine."

My dad opened the door and called out to us from the porch.

"Stephanie, it's time to come in. Carl, tell your ol' pop I said 'hello.'"

"Will do, sir," Carl laughed and saluted my father. We touched hands one last time and I giggled the whole way up the driveway, blushing and turning around to look at him once more, thrilled that he was interested in me.

For the rest of the week, we talked every night on the phone at midnight. I sat in my closet and loved the sexy thoughts we shared. "So where would you want me to touch you?" he asked.

I giggled. "What do you mean? You tell me where you want me to touch you!" I said, spreading out onto the closet floor, wearing nothing but my bra and panties. I wasn't very good yet at talking dirty, but I loved every minute of it.

"How 'bout my dick?" he said. "Do you want to touch my dick?" I could hear him breathing heavily.

"Sure . . ." I purred. My closet door opened again. It was Dad. I shot up like a rocket and hung up the phone.

"Stephanie, you need to go to bed," he whispered, but forcefully so I knew he meant it. "I'm going to have to pour cold water on you to get you up tomorrow morning, you knucklehead! It is a school night. That's it. If it happens again, I might have to ground you. Now, go to bed!" I knew deep down that he was whispering so that my mother would not hear.

The next Saturday morning my parents left to run separate errands. Katherine and I had the house to ourselves and we spread out at opposite ends of it so we didn't have to speak. We passed by each other in the hallways but looked down at the ground. She didn't speak much to me or my mother these days. She was absorbed with her friends and my dad, and her face had changed and was bumpy and weeping with pus because it was broken out in acne so she sat in her room picking at it in front of the mirror and I lay on my bed listening to the lawn mower next door.

The telephone rang loudly throughout our quiet house. I stepped into the kitchen and answered it. It was him.

"Can I come over?" he asked.

I peeked around the corner with the phone up to my ear looking for my sister. She was nowhere around so I guessed I didn't need to whisper anymore. I stood with my back against the wall. "Well . . . um . . . my parents are gone. How would you get here?" I peeked around again, still no one there.

"Well," he laughed, "How 'bout I drive over? Would that be okay with you?"

I laughed. "Carl, I totally forgot you had a car," I said.

I waited on the front porch for him to come. It was such a beautiful Saturday. Our neighbors were out washing their cars and planting flowers. The smell of fresh cut grass drifted over to me, and the sounds of children laughing as they rode their bikes were comforting and reassuring. I looked up in the sky for clouds, but there weren't any. Our own lawn was nicely trimmed and our bushes perfectly flowering; my dad always had a keen eye for detail.

When Carl walked up to the porch, we didn't speak. He smiled and took me by the hand and led me through my own house like he owned it. He must've intuitively known where my bedroom was, because we went straight to it; it had recently been painted and decorated in lavender lace by my mother. He walked past the closet where our secret conversations had taken place, shoved my stuffed animals off the bed, and sprawled himself out across the bedspread. He unzipped his jeans and left them pulled up, and pulled himself out. He looked different from Trent and Devin. He was a man.

He guided me down to my knees, pulled my head down, and introduced me to a whole different world. *So this is what men really want from girls.* I didn't necessarily hate it because I felt like I was wanted, sexy, needed, sought after. I was the center of his attention. He laughed when I looked up into his eyes, and I felt powerful because the faint sounds of the lawnmowers outside weren't enough to drown out his deep, sexy moaning. This time, I didn't leave my body or go to the other side of the room or to the moon; I was fully present in my bedroom with Carl as he directed my head up and down with his stubby hands on the back of my head and looked into my eyes. And without warning, tears spilled up and over and out of my eyes, but I wiped them away quickly . . . and I couldn't tell whose thoughts came next, whether they were mine or the thoughts of The Rent House, but they soothed me and injured me both at the same time. *Stephanie, shhhhh . . . it's okay, it's okay, it's okay, it's okay, it's okay, it's okay, it's okay, it's okay, it's okay, it's okay. This is what you wanted . . .*

. . .

The next morning was my family's day to be greeters in the lobby at church. We stood up straight in our stiff clothes, our hair short and tightly curled, mine getting redder as the years went by, Katherine's as blonde as wheat, my mother an embarrassing brunette now. Katherine and I had fought on the way over about who had not complimented whose dress and my mother grabbed us both by the fat of our arms and snarled in our ears, "Both of you, get happy! Katherine, compliment your sister!"

"You look very pretty, Stephanie," Katherine cooed.

"Oh fuck you," I whispered.

"Fuck you," she hissed back.

"Fault-finder!"

"Bitch!"

"Both of you, stop it!" Dad whispered.

"Welcome to Bayside Church of Christ." My parents smiled and shook hands with a few visitors from out of town. My father placed a rose on the lapels of the guests' clothes and my mother took down their contact information. "So are y'all from around here?" they asked. "We have coffee and donuts down the hall." Katherine and I smiled and nodded sweetly as they passed by us and into the sanctuary. The singing from inside floated out into the foyer as the doors opened.

Carl breezed in through the front door with a few of his friends and winked at me as he passed by, but he never spoke to me again. My mother and father exchanged glances and my mother slit her eyes at my father. Dad slit his eyes back at her. My relationship with Carl was a contest between them.

I knew that the Bible said that Jesus loved me.

But I was also deeply afraid of swimming in a lake of fire forever and ever.

I didn't think my baptism took.

I wanted to be innocent. I wanted to be pure. But no matter how hard I tried, I could not carry it out.

I've gone too far. There is no turning back now.

The singing continued and my family filed in line into the back of the sanctuary together. I scooted in the aisle and sat firmly beside my mother instead of with the youth group. The smell of the Tea Rose perfume from the old lady in front of me sickened me. With a stack of our four Bibles forming the same old wall between us, Katherine and my father sat together. None of us picked up a hymnal. Mother smiled and crooned with confidence, loudly, operatically, and we all joined in at the tops of our lungs because we knew all these songs by heart.

KATHERINE AND I GATHERED UP the last remaining towels and sun hats into our overnight bags and loaded them into the trunks of our cars. I loaded mine in my mother's red Thunderbird, and Katherine tossed hers into the back of my dad's silver Crown Victoria. We were staying overnight at a Holiday Inn in Galveston because the inside of our house was being painted.

The last few months had been tense in our house because Katherine had grown into a woman and puberty had come into full swing for both of us. Also, my mother had become convinced that Katherine was becoming a man.

Katherine's body wasn't like my mother's side of the family. Her shoulders were a little bit broader and her waist was thicker, and she didn't have the bird-like features that were typical of the women on the Black side. "Katherine, your face is growing hair," "Katherine, are you growing a penis?" "Katherine, let me pop your pimples, oh how can you stand that?" "Katherine, come here and let me look at you. You stink. Stop crying. You smell like a man. Hold still."

My father and mother argued almost constantly about the numerous doctors my mother was insisting Katherine see and how unnecessary it was. Mother had taken Katherine to see several endocrinologists, but no one was willing to give my sister the diagnosis that my mother wanted of her becoming a man. So they continued to see doctor after doctor to try to get a diagnosis. My father comforted Katherine under his wing when she cried about her weight, and he reassured her there was no way for a young woman to change genders.

"Stephanie, I am so worried about your sister," Mother confided in me one day. "Have you noticed her shoulders are becoming broad like a man? And her voice is deepening? She even has hair on her chest."

"Well, yeah, now that you mention it, kind of. Yeah." I didn't know it was possible for that to happen, but she seemed so sure of it and made it sound so true.

"Your father doesn't want her to get help because that would make him gay," she said. "If your sister becomes a man, then that would mean he was attracted to men since he's been sleeping with her for years, his little wifey. And even though he has slept with many male prostitutes, he would not want to be known as openly gay because that would hurt his banking business."

Dad has slept with many male prostitutes? I motioned for her to come closer and backed further into my bedroom so no one could hear us. "Mother, when did Dad sleep with male prostitutes?" I asked.

"Oh, many, many, times, Stephanie." She flipped her hand as if what she was telling me was nothing more important than the time of day. "In fact, I saw photographs of him with male prostitutes at a swanky bar in Houston. I hired a detective and he showed them to me. His arm was around one and they were about to kiss and he was smiling big. Everyone at church knows but nobody talks about it. Your father was involved in a hit-man industry at the time, and all of them had relationships with men on the side, it was just part of the culture." I felt like I had been hit behind the knees with a baseball bat. Katherine walked up to us and saw us talking privately. She stood carefully facing us in the hallway. We both stopped talking and Mother looked at her and smiled innocently. *Katherine, please help me.* Oh, what was I asking? I'd never helped Katherine. Why should she help me?

"Mother," Katherine looked back and forth from me to my mother and spoke slowly. I was embarrassed because it was obvious we were colluding. "Dad says it's time to leave."

"Well did you pack your tetracycline? Your face looks so awful, sweetheart. It looks like pizza." When Mother came home with the prescription for tetracycline that she had managed to get prescribed for Katherine, that was one of the few actual screaming matches my parents had ever had; they rarely actually fought out loud like that. But that day, my father screamed at my mother; he was getting braver, more willing to fight with her out loud.

"Do you understand the side effects of that drug?" he cried. "She could go into renal failure! She could go blind! She's just a kid! Do you really want to risk that because your child has a few pimples in middle school? Why don't you just leave her alone and love her the way she is? She's beautiful." I listened to his words. I wondered if he thought I was beautiful, too.

"Paul, stay out of it!" my mother screamed. "This is none of your goddamned business! She looks like a monster! Why don't you care enough about her to help her? You sabotage every attempt I make to help our children! You are like every other horrible Christian man I've ever known!" She threw dishes at him and he ducked out of the way. Glasses shattered, pictures flew off the walls, and doors slammed as they moved from room to room.

"Help our children? Help them? By telling my daughter she is becoming a man? How fucking mental can you be? Nobody *becomes* a man! Do you really believe that?" He started crying and banging on the table. He was scaring me now. "Lily, you're crazy. You are fucking crazy." He was sobbing. "You need help if you really believe that!"

"She's my daughter, too!" my mother bawled. "She's my daughter, too, Paul! And you never gave me a chance with her! Never gave me a shot! I can't even get to her!"

"Never gave you a shot with Katherine? Lily, that's a joke! You never wanted her to begin with! And I have no idea what you tell Stephanie in your little *talks* but she won't even look me in the eyes! Who never had a shot?" He cried harder.

"I did the best I could with that baby!" she yelled. "It's not my fault! I could've done better if you hadn't always had to take her on *your* little private walks. And I don't tell Stephanie anything that isn't the truth!"

"You need to take your medicine, Lillian," he said calmly. "And lower your voice. The neighbors will hear."

"And you need to stop trying to make me think I'm crazy! Especially when the girls can hear *you*!" she yelled back.

Katherine and I sat on her bed and listened to the fighting. She turned to me and said coldly, "You know they are fighting because you're such a brat and you cry all the time, don't you?" My insides felt like they were ripping apart.

I turned and looked blankly at her and said, "No they aren't. They're fighting because you're fat." And I hated myself because now I started crying too and couldn't stop.

But still off we went to Galveston to relax together. And since the fighting was still fresh, we decided to take separate cars for the ride to the beach, like a caravan to a funeral procession, me with our mother, Katherine with Dad.

When we got to our hotel, Katherine and I changed into our swimsuits and were about to hurry down to the water when my mother called me into the bathroom and shut the door. "Here, sweetie, put this on," and she slathered white sunscreen all over my back and face.

"Mother, rub it in! Don't leave my nose like that!" I laughed when

I looked at myself in the mirror with the thick white goo on my nose. She laughed and rubbed it in gently and completely. "Now we need to reapply every few hours, okay?" She tapped her own nose like she was making a note to herself and I called down the hallway to Katherine to wait up. "Did Katherine get her sunscreen, Mother?" I called back.

"She sure did!" My mother was smiling and magnificent in her black-and-white polka-dotted one piece. It hugged her tan, slender body. Her short, platinum-blonde hair framed her face like Tinkerbell. Katherine and I rode the elevator downstairs and went out to the pool.

We swam until we got bored of it, then we ate sandwiches we had packed and brought with us, then Mother was tired and returned to the room. Dad, Katherine, and I walked down to the shoreline together to look for shells. We sat with our toes in the sand and let the cold brown Gulf water wash over our legs. I ached for Katherine, all the while being sickened by her deep down somewhere else, deep down where the darkness dwelled . . . where she and my father were together, and she introduced me to a world with no innocence. But I loved being with her today as the hot Texas sun glistened off the ocean. I laughed at a joke she told and we waded into the murky water until we were up to our necks. "Hey, Stephanie, when it's just the two of us, it feels nice, doesn't it?" she asked.

"It does." I smiled at her and she smiled back. It didn't feel right to tell her I loved her, but I wanted to. Instead I looked ahead into the water. It gently bobbed us up and down and we rode the lull of the evening tide. We splashed around and talked in the gentle waves, and then I heard our father's voice calling from the shore.

"Hey, Ace!" he called through cupped hands. "Ace!" he called again until we both heard. Katherine turned around. Her face lit up and she answered, "What, Daddy?"

"Come on out and let's go rent some bikes!" he yelled.

"Bye, Steph. Have fun. Try not to get caught in an undertow!" she laughed and ran out of the water to meet my dad.

"Hey, can I come?" I called out to them. But they didn't hear me. He wrapped a towel around her shoulders and kissed her on the forehead. They walked down the sand together, and as I looked at their bodies side by side on the beach, the sun in front of them caused them to become dark, shadowy figures, and now that I thought about it, Katherine actually *did* look broad and strong like she was becoming a man. I noticed her back was getting pink and I called to her, "Katherine! Katherine!" but she was too far away to hear me over the sound of the tide.

I stayed on the sand for the rest of the day watching the waves crash and listening to the sounds of the seagulls. As I lay back on my towel, I sucked in and counted my ribs. I bet I could count them from across the room. They stuck out high and my stomach was thin and flat and I felt sexy lying there, my thirteen-year-old body now looked like a woman's, too. Katherine wasn't the only one with boobs.

The more I tried to relax, the more my thoughts refused to quiet. I tried to listen to the waves, but the voices in my head wouldn't allow it.

Your father is gay. He sleeps with male prostitutes. He belongs to a hit man group. It was part of his culture. Everyone in the church knows, but nobody talks about it. He has sex with your sister. Like every other horrible Christian man, he's a rapist, like every man I've ever known; the baby could have belonged to anyone; they fight because you cry too much; I never had a shot with my daughter; you're crazy, Lily, mad as a hatter; age is relative; nobody can have any fun; I found a card, a very sexual card; Carl is a good boy, studying engineering; the wages of sin are death . . . I hated my family and I loved them all with my whole heart at the same time. My parents were good people. They were good people who loved their church and helped their community and had good jobs and provided a pretty home for us. We had warm beds with plenty of food and friends who were leaders in the community. We had nice clothes and fun vacations and good schools. My parents were educated, middle-class professionals, and Katherine and I had all the opportunities we could ever want.

And yet, the evaporation of love was happening to us. *Dear God, my family is starting to throb.*

That night we all met poolside for dinner. My parents sat next to each other and I saw their hands accidentally touch for a split second; it almost looked like they were holding hands. "Do that again!" Katherine said. "I want to take a picture." My parents looked at each other and then looked at Katherine and me. They scooted in closer and put their hands together one last time. "Got it!" Katherine snapped a picture with her Polaroid and smiled. The picture came out and she shook it and the faces of my parents became clear. I could see by the forced looks and desperation on their faces. I could see that it was over.

We sat and ate in silence and watched the pink sun sink beneath the ocean's distant horizon. Dusk turned to night and the lights from the nearby cabana lit up our table and zapped the bugs that were attracted. The lights distorted our coloring, making us appear pale and green. But when Katherine stood up to go to the bathroom, I noticed her back looked maroon. "Katherine, I think you got sunburned," I said. She turned her neck around and tried to look at her own back.

"I did?" she asked. She stretched out her arms and we noticed that they were turning the color of burgundy and deep red striations were emerging under the skin's surface seemingly as we were watching. My father furrowed his brow and shoved his chair back. He stood up and walked behind Katherine. He pulled her swimsuit strap down to the side, revealing a thick, stark, paper-white strap mark on her shoulder. He walked over to me and pulled my swimsuit strap down. My skin was even and unharmed.

"Lily," he began carefully, restraining himself. "Did you put sunscreen on the girls like you said you would?" My mother looked back at him vacantly.

His voice rose, "Did you?"

"Yes. Of course, I did," she shrugged. He looked again at both of our shoulders.

"Lily, did you put sunscreen on *both* girls?" he demanded. My mother turned her head indifferently and motioned the waiter over.

"May I have another iced tea, please?" she asked him. The waiter nodded and took her empty glass.

"Lily, you know Katherine cannot go into the sun on tetracycline without sunscreen. Did you put sunscreen on Katherine as well as Stephanie?"

"Oh, good grief Paul. The child is fifteen years old. She should've thought of it herself! You could pretend to be a partner to me, you know. I'm not the only one with access to the sunscreen," she answered. "I put it on Stephanie. You could've helped me remember to put it on Katherine."

"But I was about to put it on Katherine, and you *asked* to put it on both of them! You insisted! Why did you do that?" he asked, pulling my sister's strap back up. "Katherine, let's get you back to the room and I'll go to the store and get you some lidocaine and aspirin." They gathered up their things and left. When Katherine walked away, I noticed white, jelly-like blisters had formed down her back. Her back was beginning to look like bubble wrap.

"Fine! Go!" my mother shouted. "I can't do anything right!" she said under her breath. We sat there in silence, the two of us, until finally she spoke, "So I guess *we're* the bad guys, eh? It's all our fault?"

"Why am I a bad guy?" I asked.

"Stephanie, don't play dumb. You were with her all day. Surely you saw she was burning without sunscreen. Why didn't you alert her?"

I did notice her turning pink, but I had not known she was burning that badly. I thought we both had sunscreen on.

"It's just one more way of Katherine inserting herself between you and your father. Tell me, did they invite you on their little bike ride today?" she asked.

"No, Mother, they did not," I answered. "And I don't want to talk anymore." I didn't want to listen, either. My face felt like it was on fire and the flames were rising inside. It hurt that they hadn't invited me. I wanted to be with them, not her. And I felt horrible for feeling that way because I was all she had.

"Well, don't you find that a little *odd* that they would need to be alone like that? You know, this is how it was back when your father was dealing drugs. They are probably dealing drugs together. You better watch out for them, Stephanie. Especially that sister of yours, with her big blue eyes. 'Oh, Daddy, thank you, oh Daddy, please, oh Daddy, Daddy, Daddy.' It's disgusting. I think she may even be split personality. Of course, that's what incest eventually does. It fragments the psyche if you let it. I should know. Daddy Black raped me repeatedly."

"Daddy Black beat you *and* raped you, too?" I closed my eyes and tried to picture it but couldn't. Daddy Black was a lot of things, but a rapist? No.

"Beat me?" She looked confused. "What on earth are you talking about?"

"I thought he beat you while Mama Black hid under the bed and shook?" I said.

"What? What are you talking about? I never said any such thing. Stephanie, you've been watching too much primetime TV."

I couldn't listen anymore. I felt dirty again but for different reasons now. I was part of the bad guy club, party of two, only I didn't want to be in it but I couldn't help it because I was born into it. *Oh, I don't know what to believe. I have no idea what truth is!* Sharp pains stabbed under my ribs and in my stomach and I had tunnel vision. I looked out at the water and tried to focus on the black vastness of the ocean and how it met the sky, but I could no longer tell the difference between the two. This was like the sickness between my mother and me, and like the sea and sky, I couldn't tell where one started and the other one ended. *I need a different kind of baptism. A stronger one.*

"Mother, I'm tired. May I be excused?" My lips felt fat and tingly.

"Oh of course, sweetheart. It's getting late. Don't forget your towel." She blew kisses at me as I left.

When I walked into the hotel room I shared with my sister, I found her sitting alone on the made bed wrapped up in a white towel, her hair wet from a cool shower. She was poised by the wall unit air conditioner, letting the cool air soothe her. She was beet red. When she turned around to look at me, I noticed that her nose now looked like a bulbous clown nose and her eyes looked like little bitty black jelly beans sunken into her swollen, red face. She looked up at me helplessly. "Hey, Steph. Dad went to buy me something for pain. Can you hand me my drink? I'm a little bit nauseous." I stood there in the doorway and then closed the door behind me. "Did you and Dad have fun on your little bike ride today? Did y'all ever think to invite me?" I asked. "Does it ever occur to you that I may want to be with the two of you?"

"Not now, Stephanie." She had her back turned to me. "I think I'm running a fever."

I felt like lunging at her. I sat down on the bed beside her and started bouncing up and down. I bounced harder and higher until she almost lost her towel. "Stop it, Stephanie," she said feebly.

"Get up, Katherine. I want this bed," I whispered. We were alone in the room, but I knew my words were too cruel to say loudly.

"Don't be stupid." She winced in pain as she spoke. She looked redder now than she had outside. She re-tightened her towel and moved closer to the cold air of the wall unit, gently touching her blisters with the tips of her fingers. Her eyes were tightly closed.

"Katherine, get up. I want to lay here." She opened one eye and looked over at me. "No, Stephanie. Stop it."

"You can't tell me 'no!'" I hissed. "You cannot tell me 'no!'" I pictured her and my father together, walking down the beach without me. My rage took over. I was getting harder. Stronger. Meaner. Weaker. Powerless.

"Get up, you stupid fat bitch." I gritted my teeth. "Get up. You think I don't know what goes on between you? You and Dad are a couple!"

"Stephanie, *what?* Why are you attacking me? Can't you see how sunburned my fucking back is?"

"Oh that does it, Katherine." I calmly walked out of the hotel room and knocked on my mother's door. "Mother, Katherine is in the bed that I have chosen and she will not move," I tattled.

She shook her head and laughed. "Oh, is she now? That little brat thinks she can just take whatever she wants?" She stormed across the hall and opened the door. I shut it behind us. Katherine's protector was gone, and my protector was here now. *Doesn't feel too good, does it, Katherine? Sic her, Mother. Sic her.*

Katherine was sitting as still as a stone, trying to doze off in the coolness of the wall unit. My mother walked up behind her and tapped her on her deeply burned shoulder with her long red nails. "Katherine, did your sister ask you sweetly to please get up out of her bed?" Mother asked.

"No. She demanded I move even though I was here when she walked in," my sister answered, looking straight ahead. My mother turned to me and cooed.

"Stephanie, did you ask sweetly?"

"Yes, Mother. I did. I asked sweetly."

My mother raised her voice now. "Katherine, you can be so selfish! Who do you think you are, dear? Your sister asked you nicely! What exactly does it take to get a little kindness out of you? You can be such a spoiled brat sometimes! It's as if . . . well . . . it's as if you treat Stephanie like she is a stranger on the street! In fact, I bet you would treat a stranger on the street better than you treat your own sister." She leaned in closer and got right up close to Katherine's face and gritted her teeth, lowering her voice into an almost inaudible, guttural growl. "Now you get up out of this goddammed motherfucking bed right this minute, you little brat. *If* you aren't too fat to move."

Katherine stood up, trying without success to retain her dignity by keeping the tiny hotel towel secure around her large body and her drooping, stretch mark–covered breasts. She knew it was no use to argue with us when we teamed up on her. Just as I knew it would've been useless to chase them down the beach today and ask if I could ride bikes. She moved to the other bed, and I heard her hold in a whimper as she situated herself on the stiff hotel sheets and covers; her blisters were angry and dangerous. My mother stood over her. She wasn't finished yet. "Katherine, say you're sorry." Katherine just lay there, pitiful with her short, freshly permed hair. She faced the wall away from us and I heard her say, "I'm sorry, Stephanie."

My mother folded her arms and stood right where she was, not moving a muscle. The air was still with conflict and anger. I was afraid for Katherine. My mother knew she had free rein right now with my father being gone at the drugstore. Her voice changed into a syrupy sweet melodic tone. "Katherine, you know that is not how Jesus wants us to apologize. If you don't sound sincere," she sang, "then you might as well not have said anything at all. That truly does not sound very sorry to me. Does it sound sorry to you, Stephanie?"

I felt like we had gone far enough. I wanted to end this, now. But I saw the flicker in my mother's eyes and felt that this was as good as love got, that right here in this space was the safest place to be, aligned with her, so I went with it. "Nope. She didn't sound very sorry to me. She never apologizes sweetly to me, Mother. She always acts like she's doing me some *favor*."

Katherine finally propped herself up on her elbow as best she could without touching her blisters to the sheets and turned to face me. Her face was void of any expression. She looked deeply into my eyes and paused for what seemed like a long time. "Stephanie, I am truly, truly, very sorry, okay? I'm so sorry. Please forgive me?" She looked up at my mother and prayed to her with her eyes. My mother smiled, baring all her teeth, and looked straight at me. She shook her head very slightly so that only I could notice. I took my cue from her and went in for the kill. *I'm cruel and I cannot stop myself. This is the only thing I know to do.*

"Apology not accepted," I snapped back.

My mother smirked and shook her head disapprovingly. "Katherine, I am so saddened and shocked by your lack of love for your sister. Sometimes it is like pulling teeth just to get a little teeny-weeny bit of manners out of you." She rubbed her fingers up together muttering, "Shame, shame, shame on you," and walked out the door and closed it behind her. I hopped into the cooler bed next to the air conditioner and slid my pale thin body in between the crisp sheets and crisscrossed my legs over and over again until they were looser. I had broken into my new domain. As I listened in the dark to Katherine cry herself to sleep, I thought about both of our relationships with our parents and the lines that were drawn. I lay in my bed and pretended to sleep peacefully but wondered, between Katherine and I, which one of us was really luckier? The one of us she hated? Or the one of us she loved? And once again, just like when we were young, I knew what I had done, and I wondered about my own cruelty, but it wasn't enough to stop me.

"KATHERINE, I SNUCK IN MOTHER'S purse and found these. What are they for?" I asked.

"They're for her psychosis," she answered plainly. "Now go put 'em back before she notices they're gone and get your clothes out for church tomorrow."

Tomorrow was Mother's Day.

"Nobody ever told me Mother is taking these pills or was psychotic," I said.

"That's because you're her baby and you never ask, Stephanie. Just hide your eyes and stay in your own little world with her. It's where you both belong anyways," she said.

"Katherine, I don't *belong* anywhere." I followed her down the hallway to the bathroom. She went in and shut the door.

We went to church as usual, dressed and pressed, and our congregation honored the mothers by giving them all corsages. The elder handed ours to me so I dutifully pinned it on my mother's white suit lapel. She looked distant today and had chopped all her hair off into almost a buzz cut and had shaved the back with her disposable razor so it left little red bumps and scrapes.

"Here you go. Happy Mother's Day," I said as I pinned it on.

She didn't smile.

After church, we all came home and sat down for lunch in our pink wallpapered dining room. We sat at the table in our Sunday finest, the four of us, and the clinking of our silverware was the only noise. Our parents sat at the heads of the table and ate without looking up.

"Happy Mother's Day, Mother," I said again. "The sermon was good, wasn't it? I thought Daddy Black did a good job."

"Yes, Happy Mother's Day," Katherine echoed hopefully. Amazing that after our time in Galveston Katherine was still trying to get Mother's approval. "I thought you had the prettiest suit in the crowd today, Mother. In the whole crowd. The prettiest." Katherine looked at me pleadingly and I looked back at her like I didn't know what to do to help get Mother to talk, because I didn't.

Silence.

The time had come for someone to make a change. We could not go on this way.

My mother finished chewing her bite of food, took a delicate sip of her iced tea, and laid down her crystal goblet. She folded her napkin and placed it across her plate. Dad sniffed and put his elbows on the table and looked at her and waited for her to speak. He had shimmering tears in his eyes and his face was peaceful. She looked across the long table and matter-of-factly said to him, "Paul, I have hated you for seventeen years. The girls don't need me anymore. They're thirteen and fifteen. They are grown. I'm leaving you today."

He pushed his peas around on his plate, took another bite, and chewed slowly. He wiped the corners of his mouth with his white lace napkin and didn't look up, but instead looked as though he were talking to his food. "Okay, but, Lily, we just bought a new iron last week. I mean. What are we going to do with it? Are you going to take it? Or do you want to buy a new one when you get to wherever you are going?" Tears spilled down his cheeks but he didn't acknowledge them.

My mother cocked her head and thought this one over for a minute. "Now, this is certainly something to consider," she said. "You know, I think I'll buy a new iron when I get to where I'm going," she replied.

He nodded his head like he understood. "Alright, yes, Lily, I think you should have things just exactly like you want them. And this? This is just exactly the way you want things?" he asked.

"Absolutely," she answered. "I'm more sure about this than I've been about anything in years."

He began to clear the dishes. Katherine and I just stared at them, our mouths wide open in disbelief, looking back and forth at them and then at each other. I stood up and went to my room and jerked a few of my own things out of my closet. I grabbed my worn-out brown teddy bear and stomped out to the driveway to my mother's car. The trunk of her Thunderbird was wide open and full of her clothes, hot rollers, suits, heels, dictionaries, hat boxes, hot plates, trash bags, and other essentials. I tossed my things on top of hers and turned around to go in and get the rest, only to find my father standing behind me.

"Stephanie, what do you think you're doing?"

"Dad, you heard her. It's Mother's Day. And we have hated you for *years*. We are leaving today!"

Just then my mother walked out onto the driveway carrying more of her clothes. Her face fell and she stopped dead in her tracks when she saw my father and me standing by her car. She put her long red fingernails on my shoulders so she could peek around me and into the trunk. She saw my teddy bear and clothes. She looked into my father's eyes for help but he turned his head away. "Um, sweetheart, see," she stammered. "I hadn't really planned on all this." She started fumbling around, looking up at the sky. She thought for a second.

"How about this? How about I get to where I'm going, and I'll send you a card really, really soon, okay? I'll call you lots and lots and we can visit. But I don't think there's room for you in my new place. I can't take you, Stephanie."

She took my things out of the trunk and draped them over my arms. She kissed me hard on the cheek and got in her car, which was packed with only her clothes, and slowly drove away waving and blowing me kisses. I stood on the driveway alone as my father hung his head and walked back into the house where Katherine waited inside at the window. She looked out and I saw her laughing and crying at the same time and shaking her head at me holding my clothes like a damn fool.

I knew right then that the tables had turned from my victorious night in the hotel at the beach . . . I was in enemy camp now; no one here wanted me; I did not have a home where I belonged. By loving my mother and aligning myself with her so that I could escape what my sister could not, I had dug myself a deep, dark grave. And now I had no choice but to calmly climb down into it and pretend like it had been what I wanted all along . . . rocks, gravel, dirt, and all.

"AND SO THEN WHAT?" SIMONE asked, as she lit up a cigarette and passed it to me.

I took a big drag and gave it back to her. "She just . . . drove off. And Katherine was all, 'I told you so. Where's your best friend now?'" I exhaled.

"You know what, Stephanie? Your mom is a fucking bitch. She's always seemed kinda cuckoo for Cocoa Puffs. I mean, what is up with her *hair* right now?" She dangled the cigarette in her mouth as she looked in the dresser mirror and picked at her crusty cold sore in the corner of her mouth. She winced because she picked the scab off too soon and it started to bleed and weep pus. She dabbed it with her shirt. Valerie wrinkled her nose and handed her a tissue.

"Ahhhh *fuuu-ccckkin A*, that hurts!" Simone held the tissue up to her mouth and cringed in pain.

Valerie peered at it and poked out her bottom lip in sympathy. "Well don't pick at it," she said. "You'll spread germs."

"Well no shit. But Stephanie, your dad does too, for that matter," Simone said.

"Does what?" I asked.

"He's cuckoo for Cocoa Puffs. His knee socks crack me up." She stood up and put a pillow under her shirt. She poked out her belly. "Good morning, Brothers and Sisters. I'm Paul Walters, your local deacon and trusty banker. I lead singing by day on Sundays and jack off to porn every night." She took the pillow out from her shirt and scowled at me. "I've been in his bathroom, too, you know. Your dad's a fucking perv."

I pretended to laugh. "Simone, stop. They're not that bad."

"The hell they're not. Both of them suck if you ask me," she said. "Someone needs to bitch slap both of 'em."

We were at Valerie's house spending the night, and it was cool with her parents if we smoked inside. Valerie's room was small and dingy with one twin-sized bed and Led Zeppelin and Kiss posters all over the walls. Valerie's black hair had grown down long past her waist, and she had gold highlights all throughout the ends of her dark curls, framing her face like a halo. Her nails were long and painted black and her makeup was dark and I had to look hard to see through it and find her kind eyes, but they were there. She could not hide her beauty no matter what she did. Led Zeppelin was playing "Stairway to Heaven," and Valerie rolled a joint. She sealed the paper with her pretty, long nails and licked it slowly closed. She lit it and held it casually like she held her cigarettes and took a drag, then passed it to Simone who was lying down across the pillows on her back. She took it between her index finger and thumb.

"You know who you look like?" I asked.

"Who?" Valerie said.

"You look like Cher," I said.

Valerie shrugged and took another hit off the joint. "Who's Cher?" She closed her eyes and held her breath for a good long time, then exhaled and smiled at me.

"I mean, where the hell did old Lillian go, anyways?" Simone took the joint and puffed on it like she wasn't getting anything out of it. She re-lit it and it immediately went out again and she looked annoyed like it was the joint's fault. "Piece of shit," she said. The cherry spontaneously re-lit and fell off onto Valerie's bedspread. Simone waved and flailed her arms at it fast so it didn't start a fire.

Valerie sighed and rolled her eyes. "My God, give that to me. You are so impatient, Simone." And she lit it again and took a long hit and closed her eyes and handed it back to her. Simone took a hit and handed it to me.

"Should I?" I asked. It smelled like rotten eggs.

"Um, yes, dork," Simone said. "You should. It's not addictive. And it's not like it's mind blowing or something. Smoke it just like a cigarette, only hold it in a minute longer. Don't blow out right away."

I took the joint and inhaled deeply and kept the smoke in my lungs until I couldn't hold it anymore and exhaled slowly. I waited for some feeling of euphoria to hit me, but I felt nothing. "Lemme try it again." I reached for the joint again and Valerie handed it back to me.

"Y'all need to start buying your own cigarettes and weed," she said coolly while holding the smoke in. How she could talk so perfectly while holding in weed I did not know, but I was determined to get there no matter what. "I can't keep funding everything for y'all. Plus, I can only get so much free shit. Then I have to pay for the rest." She exhaled slowly and Simone changed the tape to Ozzy.

"Turn it up," Valerie said. She stretched out across her bean bag chair. "I love 'Goodbye to Romance.'"

"I love this song," I said. "But it makes me sad."

"I'm sure Ozzy would be happy to know his music moved someone."

Her eyes were as brown and gentle as they ever were behind all that dark makeup. Valerie hadn't been to church in a long, long time.

Simone dabbed the last of her toes with hot pink polish and blew on them to be sure they were dry. We turned the music up a little louder and started to giggle.

"You know what?" I asked. I lit another cigarette and held my shoulders back. "I don't really care that my mother left and that I have no idea where she is and that my dad and sister hate me. Who needs Katherine, anyways? I'm *with* my sisters. Simone and Valerie . . . you guys are *better* than sisters." I opened my arms to hug Simone but she dodged me and fell back on the floor coughing.

"Oh, my God! Who POOTED?" she shouted. Valerie burst out laughing and lunged on top of her, putting her brown hand over Simone's mouth. They melted into a rolling puddle of snickering blonde and black curly hair. "Your fart smells like burning tires!" Simone held her nose and gagged.

"Will you shut the fuck up?" Valerie snorted she laughed so hard. "You're going to wake up my dad!"

"Well it's seven o'clock. It's not our fault your dad is a hundred years old and can't stay up past the early bird special." Simone cackled and we all doubled over onto the dirty carpet, laughing and hooting hysterically into the pillows we had piled up.

"Be quiet!" Valerie whispered, but that only made us laugh harder.

"Maintain!" Simone said, but we couldn't maintain. I snorted and tears rolled down my cheeks from laughing so hard. "Stephanie . . . you're stoned."

That night we lay in Valerie's dark room talking. The moonlight came in through the window and put a white light across Valerie's face. She looked different now that she had stopped laughing and with her makeup off. She looked colder and further away, but still her face glowed with kindness and tenderness. "I think your mom is really going to miss you. How can she not?" she whispered as she scratched my back. "You and Katherine don't deserve that. People just give up too easily these days, Steph." Her long nails were soothing on my skin as she gently scratched up and down on the small of my back. "I know," I said. "But I think she'll come back when she clears her head."

"You think so, huh?" she asked.

I didn't answer.

Finally, she sighed, "Well, maybe she will. I bet she will."

We talked for hours while Simone snored. When Valerie finally fell asleep, I lay awake until the morning sun streamed across the room, then climbed out of bed and tiptoed across my pile of friends. I slipped my jean jacket on and headed home, smelling the smoke in my own hair and knowing that Valerie was slipping away.

I was sure everyone would still be sleeping when I stepped into the house, but I stopped in the front doorway when I heard his voice. Dad was on the phone in the kitchen talking frantically, waving his arms in the air. "What the hell do you mean you donated it *all*?" he yelled.

I looked around the house. Every single piece of furniture had been taken out of the house and nails hung haphazardly where the paintings and mirrors used to hang, the walls underneath them whiter and cleaner than the rest of the wall space. The carpet was darker in the shape where the couch used to be, and cheerios and pennies remained under what used to be our chairs. The kitchen was bare, the table and chairs gone, except for the dishtowels that hung on the oven handle, and even the antique wheelchair was gone from the den. The fish were all gone but the aquariums were still there, water emptied from them, the plants inside tipped over and dry. The curtain rods hung bare like embarrassed, naked old ladies. There was not one piece of furniture left in the house.

I passed by the kitchen. Every drawer was left open and empty, and the same was true of the bathrooms. I passed by Katherine's stark, empty room, and when she saw me she got up and slammed her door. Her face was streaked with mascara from crying. She didn't look like a man today; she looked like a scared, angry little girl. I banged on the door. "Katherine open this door! I want to talk to you!" I yelled and pounded on the door with my fists. "What's going on?" I yelled again.

"Stephanie, just go away! Nobody wants you here!" Katherine shouted. I kicked the bottom of her door as hard as I could and it rattled.

My room was just a purple cave now, but my mattress had been left on the floor. I threw myself down on it and stared up at the ceiling. My dad came in and sat down beside me. "Stephanie, kiddo. We're going to get through this, okay? We'll get you some new furniture."

"What the hell did she do with all of our stuff?" I asked.

"Well, she came and got our pictures and family photo albums. She donated our furniture, on the other hand, to the local high school Home Economics and Theatre departments. And all of her jewelry, including her wedding ring and mine and her great-grandmother's diamond ring, and all of her strings of pearls, and all of our china, and light fixtures and paintings, well . . ." he trailed off.

"Well, what?" I demanded. "Where *is* that stuff?"

"She wrapped it all up in plastic wrap and drove into downtown Houston last night and tossed it all at homeless people," he answered quietly. My eyes grew wide with disbelief and my head was spinning.

"Dad, I didn't sleep very well last night. Can I go back to bed?" I asked.

"Sure, sweetheart. Sure." And he patted me on the back and left me.

I thought about Valerie and how dark her eyes looked last night and how old she looked lighting that joint. I thought about my mother and where she might be now, huddled under a bridge wrapped up in a blanket or sipping tea in a mansion, I didn't know. Finally sleep overtook me in my early morning sunlit room with all my stuffed animals gone, and I slept dead to the world until the walls became dark again with shadows because of the nighttime glow of the moon and then bright again with sunshine the next day, and just as the sun and moon took turns and switched places, so did the little girl and woman in me.

I WANDERED INTO THE KITCHEN and saw that Dad had left some plastic bowls and spoons out on the countertop for me. I got out some cereal and poured the milk and sat down on the gold linoleum floor to eat. I slouched with my back to the wall and my dad came in dressed in new linen pants and a flowing white shirt. He wasn't wearing his glasses and his face was all lit up and he sat down beside me.

"Stephanie, I have someone I want you to meet tonight. She's a special friend of mine and she is throwing a little get together at her house tonight and she really wants to meet you. Her name is Gail."

"Is she your girlfriend?" I asked, slurping my milk out of my bowl, something my mother never would have allowed.

"No, no, no, sweetheart. She's just a friend. She works with me at the bank. Katherine knows her well and really seems keen on her; she's met her a couple times, couple times. Anyway, will you come? You can bring Simone and Valerie."

I thought about my mother's conversation with Mama Black about the Ziggy card. But I looked at my father's face and his new outfit, and I hadn't seen him smile in so long, so I said yes. I got up to throw my bowl away but accidentally threw it on the floor before I realized we didn't have a trash can, milk spluttering onto the pantry floor.

"Sweetheart, just lay it down on the counter, I'll get it later. Now, listen, I want to warn you. Gail is not very pretty or anything. What I mean is, well, she's kind of plain. She's not beautiful like your mom. Oh, what am I saying . . . she's a little plump, that's all, but her face is kind and pleasant. And she's really, really nice. And she's been dying to meet you."

"Dad I couldn't care less about what this stupid lady looks like," I said, with my back turned to him. I started rinsing my bowl but then decided that was ridiculous. I put it in the sink and turned to look at him. He was still sitting on the floor. I softened my tone towards him. "I'm not judging her or anything. But why would I care if she's not pretty like Mother? She's just your friend, right?"

He smiled and scurried up to his feet. "Yup! Just a friend. And she'll be so excited to meet you! Call your friends!" And he kissed me on the cheek for the first time in my entire life and literally almost skipped out of the empty kitchen.

Valerie was out at a party and couldn't come, but Simone tagged along reluctantly when I promised her there would be food there.

When we got to Gail's place and stood on her porch, I couldn't help but notice all the flowering plants and wind chimes. My dad rocked back and forth on his ankles and smiled waiting for the door to open. "Whatcha got there?" I asked, nodding to the box in his hands.

"Patchouli incense," he answered, and a little gray-haired old lady opened the door and smiled a big goofy grin. "Paul! Come in!" she said, and they kissed each other on the cheeks. My father and Katherine walked in and disappeared into the party. I noticed the guests kissing Katherine on both cheeks and her smile with them seemed casual and relaxed; in fact, she looked totally at home here. I stepped inside and took a glance around at the warm, crowded, candle-lit condo. There were wooden figurines of giraffes on the fireplace mantle and soaring green plants that reached easily over the couch. Big, plush purple throw pillows were tossed about casually on the love seat, and some people were sitting on the couch and visiting under a big blanket while their bare feet poked out and played footsie.

"What the hell is up with the porn condo?" Simone whispered in my ear the minute we walked in. "Why are there *beads* dangling from the doorways? It looks like a swinger's pad." Dad had evaporated into a sea of friends in the kitchen who were laughing and munching appetizers served out of wooden bowls.

"Shhhh!" I whispered back. I looked around; took it all in.

We ducked under a big leafy plant as we walked over into the lushly carpeted living room. The gold lamps arched and swayed over the record player that nobody noticed was skipping softly and made the place look mellow and dim. There were candles lit everywhere, and it smelled like old pot and roses. "Do you smell that?" Simone asked with a frown.

"Shhh. Yes," I whispered.

"Well, what's up with that? We're the only ones allowed to smoke weed! And at least we have the decency to try to hide it." We both laughed. There were artsy looking people mingling around quietly, with sparkling glasses of wine and flowing linen clothes. Two guys were arm and arm and kissed each other on the cheek and laughed loudly.

My father joined a group surrounding a slender man in round dark glasses with a smooth bald head. He was motioning to a sculpture on a small table that was lit up in an elegant glass case.

"Can you see in the curves my conceptual concerns about the human-scale relatedness to object familiarities without regionalist narrative extrapolations being necessary?"

"Yeeeeesss," the group collectively answered.

"And can you see, in the concaveness, the reflexive reaction anima-tion possibilities of current international politics substantiating how *little* time changes events except for characters?"

"Yeeeeesss," they all sang.

A round brunette walked up to me with a huge smile plastered across her face. She had on a comfortable looking mint green blouse with a long gold chain that hung down between her large freckled bosoms. Her skin was bronzed from the natural sun and her makeup was subtle, with a clear gloss across her lips. Not only was she not wearing high heels, she was barefoot. Her face *was* pleasant, like my father had described. This was Gail.

Simone had left my side and wandered like a sheep into the kitchen and was shoving a large mass of sour cream and onion dip into her face missing her mouth and dropping half of it onto her shirt. She looked around to see if anyone had noticed and licked it off when she thought no one had. "Simone!" I whispered. "Simone!" But she was moving on to the bacon-wrapped jalapenos and cocktail wieners.

Gail wasn't ugly. I don't know why my father had said that. He had pretty much prepared me that his new friend was going to look like the Hunchback of Notre Dame or something compared to my mother. I was expecting someone hideous. She was pleasantly plump, that's true, but her face was pretty, and she seemed so comfortable in her own skin; she didn't seem like she would care if you told her she was overweight. This woman appeared to love herself and her condo looked loved, too. In fact, she seemed to embrace and celebrate herself and had a light and comfortable air about her and in her home.

She took my hands in hers and beamed as she spoke to me. "Hi, Stephanie. I cannot tell you how nice it is to finally meet you. I'm Gail, your dad's really good friend. I have a suuuurrrrppriiise for you. I made your dad a wonderful cake and it has a secret ingredient." She looked deep into my eyes like this was a fabulous game and I was just going to hop right on board with her little fun, fun, fun, frolicking secret ingredient mystery. I didn't know this woman. I looked back into her eyes and took my hand out of hers and put it in my pocket, making a mental note to wash it. "What kind of secret ingredient?" I asked. She didn't know me very well, but she was sure acting like she did.

Everyone was watching now, including Simone and my dad, this first exchange with this mysterious woman. She laughed nervously. "A secret ingredient that you'll never guess! Never in a million years! Now, here, take a little bite of your dad's cake," and she put a little bite onto a fork and guided it up to my mouth.

I glanced up at my father who was smiling and urging me to taste it, nodding his head and grinning like an idiot. All the hippies in the room were smiling little "Oh isn't this sweet, they're bonding beautifully" smiles. I took a step back and looked around the room and suddenly felt very uncomfortable.

"Okay, but seriously, what is the secret ingredient?"

"Stephanie, just taste it. Don't be silly. It's good," Gail said, this time a little less sweetly. She looked around the room, now appearing embarrassed and blushing. By this time, my imagination was running completely wild. *I don't know this woman. I've never met her in my life.* She looked into Dad's eyes and pleaded with him for help like she had known him for a million years, and he reached out and touched her shoulder *like a wife. What the hell is this?* The way they looked at each other, the way they touched each other, the friends in the room that spoke in such casual body language . . . they'd known one another a long time. And all of a sudden, I knew that I was not a stranger here . . . that the people in this room have not only *heard* of me, but maybe even watched me grow up from afar. There was something very well acquainted within this group, but it had nothing to do with anything I knew about. Gail knew me. She looked like she already loved me.

Maybe there were chocolate-covered ants in the cake. What else could it be? What other ingredient could be concealed in chocolate that no one would ever be able to taste? I didn't know, but I sure as hell wasn't going to let this stranger who was so obviously connected to my father and sister feed me cake to secretly test me in front of everyone to see how fast I would trust her. Here was the answer, lady: not this fast.

I backed away farther this time, pushing the cake away. I didn't care what these people thought of me and I didn't care what Gail thought. I was angry with my father for allowing me to be put on the spot this way, and I looked over at Katherine who was flipping through a coffee table book with her feet propped up contentedly. If she had met Gail, why had I never been invited here before now? Simone walked up and stood behind me. She popped the collar of her shirt and her eyes were defiant with mine. *Thank you, Simone.*

"No, thank you. What did you say your last name was?"

"Taylor. But you can call me Gail."

"No, thank you, Ms. Taylor. But I am not eating that. I don't know what your secret ingredient is, or what this game is, but I don't like surprises like this." There was a difficult silence while every guest in the room stood frozen. Then someone noticed the record player skipping and fixed it, and the crowd relaxed again and went back to their chatting and clanking of forks.

Gail and I stood looking into each other's eyes and I sent her a message, from my mind to hers, and her eyes widened because she received it. *Nice to meet you, Gail. I'm your new stepdaughter, aren't I? I'm Stephanie, not Katherine, so I won't be that easy to reach, because unlike Katherine, I am not happy my mother is gone. I am and always will be evidence of my mother. And right off the bat, I don't like you. You are not my mother. My mother is not here, but I deeply wish she were. You are not my family. You are not my friend. My mother left. I mean she just left on Mother's Day, and I don't really know where she is or if she will ever come back for me. My family is blown to hell. Do not touch me. Do not look into my eyes after tonight. Do not ask me to trust you even with something small. This is not a game.*

"Stephanie, I'm sorry. I went about this wrong," Gail said.

I could see fire behind my father's eyes, and Gail shook her head at him as if to tell him not to be angry with me. She was embarrassed and now I was embarrassed, too. "Honey, it's just sauerkraut. I found this recipe that said sauerkraut made chocolate cake really, really moist. You can use it instead of eggs, which are full of cholesterol. Your dad said you were kind of trying to be a health nut, so I thought I'd try it for you." I stared at her indifferently.

"Don't call me honey," I said blankly.

"Got it," she replied.

Simone and I spent the rest of the evening whispering and sprawled out laughing in Gail's bedroom about the absurdity of it all while everyone else partied the night away. The room had a big, flowing canopy above the bed, and there were large wooden bamboo sticks in vases on the sides. Every few minutes the group down the hall collectively erupted in laughter and I could hear my dad's laughter over everyone else's. He was happy. Really, really happy. I was confused. I had just met someone who my father obviously already cared about and could not wait to introduce to me. And I hated her with everything that was in me. She was nothing like my mother and her life was nothing like the life I knew and these people were nothing like our church family and I had never seen my father this way. Something about him, though, seemed totally authentic tonight, and I knew in my heart he felt at home in her condo, that he had stayed here many, many nights. He had been on those couches. He knew from which cabinet to reach for a glass of water, where to hang his jacket, where the bathroom was. He maneuvered in the space of the condominium like it was familiar, like it was home. He looked different tonight . . . something was there in him I hadn't noticed before. His face was relaxed; his body was relaxed; he didn't wear his glasses; he smiled and waved his hands easily. He was genuinely in his element.

Tomorrow would be exactly one week since Mother's Day, and we were pretending tonight that Lillian Walters never existed.

THE NEXT SUNDAY MORNING, KATHERINE and I sat next to each other with our youth group and Dad and Gail sat on the last pew in the back of the church. While we waited for the singing to start, Katherine said, "You look pretty today, Stephanie."

"I do? No, I don't," I said.

"I'm serious. You do. I was thinking that this morning. Your hair looks good," she said.

"Well . . . thank you. And I like your nail polish. That pink goes really well with your eyes." I had no idea what that meant, but she smiled and handed me a hymnal.

Gail wore a flowing lilac-colored sundress with sandals that strapped up the calf of her bronzed, voluptuous legs. Dad showed her the hymnal and ran his fingers across the words so she could follow along. She sang the hymns loudly like Mother but off key, which was so unlike Mother, stumbling on the words and beginning the verses too soon and coming into the harmony too late and all wrong. I looked over at Katherine and we couldn't help laughing. We tried to be serious and kept singing.

> *Up from the grave He arose! With a mighty triumph o'er his foes.*
> *He arose the victor from the dark domain,*
> *and He lives forever with His saints to reign!*
> *He arose! He arose! Hallelujah! Christ arose!*

I looked back and my father put his arm around Gail and she nuzzled her head into his shoulder and pretended to bite his ear. I looked to see what Katherine thought but she was laughing at something Trent said as if she hadn't noticed. I could feel the stares of the congregation. I shot daggers from my eyes at Dad and Gail, but now they were pretending to bite each other's lips. We all placed our hymnals back into their sleeves and Daddy Black struggled through a sermon on Revelations. Every few seconds, he glanced in the direction of my father and Gail and lost his train of thought.

The congregation noticed. We all noticed. The men and women alike wiped sweat from the backs of their necks and smacked their kids when they turned around to stare. Nobody knew what to do. They were in utter panic as to how to respond to this outward display of adultery. Daddy Black ended the sermon early for the first time in my life, and after the service, Dad stood proudly in the vestibule with Gail at his side introducing her to everyone. Nobody knew what to do or how to respond. The women tried to ignore her while the men fretfully shook her hand and then wiped her heathen, godless germs onto their freshly creased slacks. They nervously hurried to get their children from the nursery and darted past my father and his "friend," anxiously shooing their children ahead and averting their eyes on the way out the door.

They rebelliously stood in the church lobby arm in arm while Katherine and I milled around talking with the youth group. This did not last long before twelve elders split up into groups of three and whispered into Dad's ear for us to join them in my grandfather's office. My father told Gail to go wait in her car, and their hands lingered as they parted. "I'll go on home, baby," she purred. Her voice was distinctly un-southern. He winked at her and motioned to Katherine and I to go into Daddy Black's office.

Carl's father, Carl Sr., stood beside my grandfather's desk. Daddy Black sat erect behind his desk with his hands folded like the Godfather.

Carl Sr. began. "Paul, you know we here at the church love you. Your separation is breaking our hearts. We weep for what you and Lily are doing to your girls. But you know that First Corinthians says, 'But I am now writing to you that you must not associate with anyone who claims to be a brother or sister but is sexually immoral or greedy, an idolater or slanderer, a drunkard or swindler. Do not even eat with such people.'"

He continued as Daddy Black nodded him on in approval, "Paul, you are also in flagrant disobedience of Scripture by taking up with this individual whom you brought to services with you. What kind of message are you trying to send?" He shifted his attention to my father, who stared out the window. I thought back to Carl lying across my bed, his pants unzipped, erect and smiling down at me with the smell of Skoal wafting down from his breath and his hands on the back of my head. I thought back to him mouthing the word "Hi" to me when I was twelve years old during the church prayer and the late-night conversations that took place in my closet.

"We, the body of elders of Bayside Church of Christ, in accordance with the original church of Corinth, have decided that you are not living a spiritually clean life. This is defiling to the body of Christ, His Church. Brother Paul, would you like to repent of your sins in a public confession and re-baptism?"

Katherine and I both sat helplessly waiting. Daddy Black sat silently, nodding his head in agreement to what was happening.

My father's lips were pursed together into two little lines. He looked angry and after a few quiet moments, he turned his head from the window and looked straight into the eyes of Carl Sr.

"No, I would not. I am not sorry for anything that is happening right now. I have been a part of this religious system, trapped under your thumbs, fearful of disfellowshipment, fearful of hell, since I was a little boy. The teachings you spout from the pulpit, Victor, have not served me well. Not only do I not want to be re-baptized, I want to live in freedom, no matter what I lose. Because I've already lost everything a man could lose . . . I've lost my marriage, my family, the hopes I had when I was young, my furniture, my household, my dreams. Do you really think I set out to do this wrong?"

"You are stiff-necked, Paul. Like the Israelites," Daddy Black said.

Dad interrupted him. "I am not stiff-necked, Victor. Lily walked out on us. She said she hated me and wanted to leave. Why, then, do I need to be sorry for bringing Gail to church?" he asked. "How am I an adulterer? I've been abandoned."

"You need to be re-baptized because you're still married and are fornicating. In fact, you've been fornicating with Gail for twenty years, haven't you?" Daddy Black asked.

"Lily hasn't let me near her in almost twenty years! She won't even let me hug her, let alone sleep with her! She doesn't even let her own children touch her! I've struggled with her mental illness every single day, and guess what? Nothing worked! If something would have worked, I would have done it over and over and over again. I had no choice but to turn to Gail. You all should be happy I have her. I'd have wanted to kill myself if not for her!" my father screamed. His voice trailed off and reverberated off the dark hallway walls. Suddenly I was keenly aware that the church was now empty and that everyone had gone home to leave us to this.

Daddy Black closed his eyes and tapped his fingers against his desk, reminding me of my mother. He nodded his head at the men in suits.

They looked like police officers. The group of elders formed a line and the one closest to the door opened it up to show us out. Carl Sr. began arrogantly, "Paul, if Lily has forsaken her marriage vows to submit to her husband and you are not willing to repent for adultery, then we cannot decide which one of you is going to hell the most. Until either or both of you turn from your sins, Lily for forsaking her vows and you for adultery, and make a public repentance regarding this divorce, we have no choice but to disfellowship your entire family, including your children. Mental illness is not grounds for divorce . . . you vowed to love Lily through sickness and in health. Lily is technically scripturally free since you are an adulterer, but she has abandoned her children and that is a sin, according to Matthew 18:6, 'Anyone who causes one of these little ones to stumble, it would be better to have a millstone hung around their neck and be drowned into the depths of the sea.' Because surely . . . Katherine and Stephanie have stumbled. In fact, they have stumbled more than once." Carl Sr. looked straight at me.

"We love you all, Walters family, with the love of the Lord, and we will be here when and if you decide, but until then, please do not come back. In a spirit of Godly discipline, our congregation will no longer accept you as part of our flock. We kick the dust off our shoes, today, knowing that we have carried out the work of The Lord."

Katherine spoke up. "What about us? Why are Stephanie and I being disfellowshipped? We haven't done anything wrong. We're just kids. We need our church now more than ever." She looked hopeful and vulnerable. She folded her hands and pleaded with them. "Daddy Black, please? We're your granddaughters."

Daddy Black looked at my father and then back at Carl Sr. The elders folded their arms and finally Carl Sr. spoke. "Girls, the sins of the father will be visited on the third and fourth generation. If you are hurting, there is no one to blame but your father."

The men stared at us in disgust like we had leprosy.

Finally, Dad shook his head and started laughing. The elders looked at each other in bewilderment like they were confused. He started cracking up laughing and was cackling so hard tears streamed down his face. His whole body shook and he leaned over and put his head in his hands and laughed so hard that his face turned bright red and then he started to sob. Katherine and I didn't know what to do. He sobbed and sobbed and sobbed, shaking and laughing at the same time while hunched over in his seat. Katherine and I shifted uncomfortably in our chairs, Katherine patting him on the back lightly. Finally, he stood up and wiped the tears from his eyes with his crisp monogrammed handkerchief, then quietly walked out the door, still shaking his head and snickering, and Katherine and I filed out behind him. I looked at Katherine and she shrugged. I shrugged too because I had no idea what to say as we followed him out to the car. On the ride home, his laughter stopped and his eyes became distant and apathetic and he seemed so far away and I knew that this was the last day we would ever attend a Church of Christ. God was gone.

WHEN WE GOT HOME THAT afternoon my father called us both into the living room. We had lawn chairs now, and they were swallowed up by the sheer size of the room. My father sat in the least rickety one—the one with metal legs, while Katherine and I tried to make ourselves presentable on the plastic green-and-white reclining patio chairs that were now functioning as our couches. "Girls, Gail and I have decided we are getting married. I know it's soon, but we are ready to begin our new lives together now," he said.

"You know it's *soon?*" I laughed and tried to sit up but the back of the chair kept falling back making me feel foolish. Finally, I gave up struggling with it and let it fall back flat. "Dad it hasn't even been a month. You and Mother aren't even divorced yet."

"Well, we're working on that, we're working on that," he answered. "We're going to leave the day the divorce is final and drive up to Kansas. We'll be married at Gail's mother's house the next evening beside her pool. I want you both there."

I snorted. "Oh, my God, Dad, forget it. I'm not going. That woman is a pig." I dug myself out of the chair and shook my head and started to walk out of the room. My father acted like he hadn't heard me, looked right past me and focused on Katherine instead whose eyes were lit up with joy.

"Oh, Daddy! Can I be a bridesmaid?" Katherine squealed.

"Of course you can," he said. He walked out of the room, leaving the two of us together.

"Katherine, do you even care that Mother is gone? Do you even love her?" I asked.

"Yes, Stephanie. I do care. But she doesn't care. So I'm not going to waste my time on that bitch. I like Gail and I want her to be my mother." She looked deeply into my eyes and said, "Plus, I think it would help things a lot between me and Dad." She looked down at the ground.

"Oh, I see. I get it," I answered. "You're afraid of losing him. Haven't had his attention in a while. You think Gail's going to take him from you, so you're keeping her close, eh? If you can't beat 'em, join 'em. He's not interested in you anymore, huh? You feel replaced." She focused her eyes on the floor and wouldn't look back up at me. "Katherine, you do understand that's sick, what he does to you, right?" She didn't answer. "Katherine!" I had to get out of there.

I walked over to Simone's house and Lynne opened the door and threw her arms around me, pulling me so tight she almost took my breath away. "Stephanie, sweet girl, I'm so sorry." Word had traveled fast.

"Hi, Sister Lynne," I said as I wiggled out of her grip. "Thank you, I think?"

"Lynne, leave her alone." Simone walked into the room. "You'll make her feel weird. Plus, it's none of our business."

"Simone, Stephanie, I am sorry, but, Stephanie, yes, it is my business. Your family is being disfellowshipped, but I've watched you grow up since you were a baby. I can't turn my back on someone I've known since they were little. You are always welcome here, okay, kiddo?" She leaned in closer to me, "You know you have choices, right? You don't have to end up like them. Just because these chapters have been written, doesn't mean you can't write the rest of your story to look different. Think about it." And she ran her hands across my cheeks like a mother would.

Simone rolled her eyes. "I'm almost touched," she sneered.

Lynne stood beside her with her hands in her pockets. Her flipped-up bob looked like a head full of dyed brown cotton candy, the back teased out to create height. Her freshly pressed khaki shorts hugged her trim waist and she popped the collar of her starched white polo, a move I had seen Simone make a million times herself. "Do you girls want some cookies?"

Simone cleared her throat. "No. We're going to Valerie's. I don't know when we'll be back."

Simone shooed her hand at Lynne, "Go, go, go, tend to your housewife duties," she said. "Go on, now, Lynne. Go on, go." Lynne straightened a wrinkle that was forming in the dining room tablecloth and obediently walked out of the room.

"You should treat your mom better," I said. "She's really kind of a gift, Simone."

Simone breathed a heavy sigh and turned to me and put her hands on my shoulders, squaring off. She looked deeply into my eyes. "Look at me. Stephanie, I love you so much. I am not going anywhere. I am fifteen years old. I do not practice shunning and I don't like people who do. Okay, so I'm proud of Lynne. She has her moments. She's doing the right thing. But if you tell her I said that, I'll kick your ass."

· · ·

When we got to Valerie's, she was already sitting on her front step waiting for us, slowly dragging on her cigarette. When she saw us walking across the lawn, she slipped something into the pocket of

her jean jacket and coolly ran her fingers through her hair. She nodded at us.

"Hey, guys, how's it going?" she asked. Her eyes were glazed and
she squinted like she was having a hard time focusing. She pulled her
pack of cigarettes out of her pocket and Simone and I both took one.
She flicked her lighter and brought the flame up to our mouths, and
then slid it back in her pocket, her long nails painted black.

"Valerie, the Walterses were disfellowshipped from Bayside today,"
Simone said.

Valerie tilted her head to the side and held her cigarette in her
mouth between pursed lips while she adjusted her jeans over her black
boots. There was a breeze just then, rather than the thick, motionless
Pasadena air that usually stunk like the refineries, and the sunlight
shone down onto Valerie's face. She stooped down and when she came
up, she brushed her long, shiny hair back out of her eyes. "What's disfellowshipped? What does that mean?" she asked.

"It's church discipline. Shunning," I answered. "It's because my parents are divorcing."

"So they did decide to actually divorce?" She thought about it for a
second. The spirit behind Valerie's eyes looked hard, not soft and mal-
leable like it used to.

"Well, I haven't been to church there in quite some time, and
nobody has even noticed I was gone, and I've managed to somehow
live through it. So what do you care, Steph? Fuck 'em."

But I did care. I cared more than anything. Bayside Church of
Christ was my family. These people had taken care of me when I was
a baby, had clapped when Trent taught me to ride a bike; they had
given me stickers when I had learned my Scriptures, had been with us
when we were sick; they had cared for us when we needed them, and
we had cared for them, too. We ate together every week. We prayed
together and for one another. We cried together when people we loved
died, and we rejoiced together when good things happened to any

one of us. They were my Sunday school teachers and I had watched all their children grow up right alongside me. My parents had loved them and their children and tried to fit into what they thought they wanted them to be. I thought of Brother Hazel and how he accepted me unconditionally, how he hugged me each Sunday and smiled at me when I ran to him, and I wondered if his heart would be breaking now, or if he would stand cold in agreement.

Valerie stood up nonchalantly to walk into her house. "Can we come in?" Simone asked.

"Not today," Valerie said. "I just want to be alone and I've got stuff to do." She stepped inside and shut the door, leaving Simone and me outside on the front porch. Later that night, we got word that Valerie's father had died.

CHAPTER

20

THE NEXT WEEKEND GAIL MOVED in. She brought with her the plush couches with beaded throw pillows and lavender armchairs and slushy lava lamps. Her cozy furniture was welcomed in our bare house but it clashed with the memories of the lace curtains and crystal vases that used to be there.

I walked through the living room watching the movers as she directed them where to put her faux polar bear rug and noticed three large drawings being hung with great care as Gail directed, "To the left, up higher, no, down lower." I stopped dead in my tracks when I saw them. She stepped back with her hands on her hips smiling at their perfect symmetry.

The drawings were of my father and Gail having sex. All three were drawn in swirling black charcoal pencil. The first was of my father kneeling behind Gail on rumpled sheets doing her from behind. Her long dark hair in the picture fell across her grimacing face and on to the bed, while her large, floppy breasts hung down creating a tunnel in her cleavage so that the onlooker could see my father's hanging testicles. His eyes were closed in the drawing as a smile beamed across his middle-aged face.

The second one was Gail on her back in the same lovers' bed with her legs wrapped around my father's neck. His thick head of hair was buried in her mess of curly pubic hair, every detail carefully drawn. Her eyes were closed and a look of sheer ecstasy floated in the swirling lines of chalk, each carefully drawn to show every crevice, every line, every fold of the skin.

The third was of both in the missionary position screaming out right before an orgasm. My father's head facing the sky and Gail rearing, arching her back in elated pleasure. Swirly, black dust danced across the page, giving them both a shaded appearance. I almost spit out my drink when I saw them. "What on earth are those?" I asked, half laughing.

"What, honey?" she asked innocently with her back turned to me. She held up a book called *The Deeper Dimensions of Reality* and smiled, brushing off the dust. "Here it is!" she squealed and placed it on our new coffee table made from the trunk of a tree.

"Those! Those pictures! Is that you and Dad?" I studied the face of the man in the throes of orgasm. I wondered if that was the way he looked when he was with my sister.

"Oh, Stephanie, honey, aren't they the most beautiful display of sensuality expressed through sex? Yes, they're of me and your father." She smiled like we were going through slides of her trip to Disney World and we were talking about the good old days. "My friend, who is a wonderful artist, drew them out of charcoal for us as a wedding present. What do you think?"

Just then, my father walked in with a large box in his arms. He slowly put the box down and walked over to Gail and stood beside her with his arm draped around her shoulder, waiting for me to answer.

"What do I think? I think they're fucking *disgusting*, that's what I think. I think nobody wants to see that. I'm thinking you both look awful and I'm definitely thinking I'll be embarrassed to have my friends come over if you're going to hang these monstrosities in the living room." I laughed but only out of nervousness. I was angry.

Gail smiled like she pitied me. "Oh, Stephanie, this is your response to art? Do you think only thin, beautiful people make love?"

"What? No, I don't think only thin people make love. What are you talking about?" I turned my mouth up in sarcasm.

"Well, you said, 'you both look awful.' I found your word choice interesting. You know, sensuality and sexuality come in all beautiful shapes and sizes and ages. I saw pictures of Jesus on a cross with a stab wound hanging proudly at your church. So violence is okay in art, but not love making?"

"Look, Lady. I don't really give a shit about your fat sense of sensuality or age or Jesus or whatever. The paintings are fucking gross."

"Stephanie, look here, young lady," my father began. But I was not listening. I walked up to the drawings to study them more carefully. The detail in the things really was exquisite. The fat rolls on Gail's stomach were drawn darker towards the middle and her nipples were outlined in black and shaded perfectly to look like they had bumps. No detail was spared on her breasts. They weren't perfect, like a *Playboy* model; they were floppy and droopy, hanging like sacks of flour.

I paced in front of the drawings while my father said something in the background about their wedding and past life soul mates and how this was happening whether I liked it or not; the three large charcoal drawings, framed in the thick black trim. I walked past them and the living room light from behind me stayed right where it was in the reflection of the glass. It didn't move as I moved. I passed by all three slowly and looked carefully at the still reflection of the light from our living room ceiling fan. It stayed motionless.

"You paid extra for the glare-proof glass on these fucking things, didn't you? How much extra did that cost you as we sat here with no mother and no furniture? These things are humiliating to me! Can't you see that? They aren't going to be heirlooms, Dad, they're sickening!" I yelled.

This was not the father I knew.

This was not the man who wore suits on Sundays and preached at the nursing homes and led singing and prayers and took us to camp. My father got up in my face and grabbed me by the arm. He realized what he was doing and he lightened his grip. "Now, you look here, young lady. Your mother is gone and I'm glad. Gail is moving in and we are getting married, and I really don't care if you like it or not. Now you have two choices. You can either get with the program or things are going to get pretty hard for you around here."

I wanted my mother. I jerked my arm out of his grip and leaned back and took a deep breath and with everything in me, I leaned back and spat in his face. He slapped me hard across the face, but the burn on my face was nothing compared to what I was already feeling inside. I went reeling and started screaming hysterically and crying. "My mother is gone and I hate you!" I shouted.

"Paul, stop it!" Gail shouted and took his arms in hers. "Leave her alone, Paul. She's scared!"

"Fuck you, Dad! I'm running away! I want to go live with Mother!" I hit him over and over and over again, crying and shaking.

"She won't have you, Stephanie! You have no choice but to stay with me. Let her go!" he shouted. The enormity of the fact that what he was saying was true was saturating my heart. She was gone. Our family was gone. Our church had turned its back when we needed them the most.

I sobbed into his stomach and chest. I wanted to hug him but I didn't. I just kept hitting him. I wanted him to hold me, but Gail was holding him, and I doubted he would have anyway. I wanted to throw my arms around him, to jump up in his arms and bury my face against his neck like a little child. I wanted my father to protect me.

"I miss her so much," I cried. I could almost feel my heart breaking inside my chest, burning and aching as the loss of my family set in, as the words from Carl Sr. played again in my mind, *"you know we at the church love you, but . . . sexually immoral . . . idolaters . . .*

greedy . . . swindlers . . . do not even eat with them . . . what you are doing to your girls . . . repent of your sins . . . your separation is breaking our hearts . . . we are no longer in fellowship." I didn't understand why my father was so happy . . . how he could be so glad . . . he seemed so unaffected.

I looked up at my father through my tears, hoping he would feel the same way, hoping that we could breathe and talk, but he glared at me and wiped the spit off his face. "You are so much like your mother," he said.

"Paul, no," Gail whispered. He pulled back out of her arms and stood staring at me.

I backed away from him calmly, looking deep into his eyes. There was nothing behind them now, not anger, not hatred, only indifference. "I'm going to spend the night with Valerie," I said, and then I turned around and walked out the door, leaving my father and Gail standing arm and arm in our living room. The drawings of my father and Gail making love held fast to their new spot against the pink satin wallpaper my mother had chosen and remained there as a symbol of the two worlds colliding.

That night I stayed with Valerie, her house even quieter and darker than before now that it was just her and her mother. The dishes were piled in the sink and the refrigerator was empty and the light inside was burned out. Her young mother stayed in her cave watching television, but the stale smell of smoke made the air thick with aloneness and the feeling that everything and everyone was old. Valerie and I talked and talked all night; it had been awhile since it had just been the two of us. Her clean face revealed her big eyes and smile now that she took off her dark makeup, and the streetlights from outside blinked, really showing her youth. At fifteen years old, Valerie was the most beautiful girl I had ever known. We sat by the open window and let the cool breeze blow into her room while the smoke from our cigarettes and joints wafted into her front yard.

"Valerie, have you been okay lately?" I asked, holding the joint up to her mouth while she took a hit. We sat quietly while she held it in, thinking and looking ahead.

"Do you think I'm going to find a husband one day?" she asked. "Like, do you see someone ever wanting to like, marry me? You think I'll have a family?" She motioned for me to take another hit and I did.

"Oh, God yes. I think you'll have a huge family one day. Lots of beautiful babies to call you Mommy and probably a big, strong rich guy for a husband."

She crushed out the joint and lit up a cigarette and took a long drag, blowing it out into the night air. "I've been doing a little cocaine lately, it's no big deal." She shrugged her shoulders, shut the window, and climbed into bed. My heart sank at the thought of my beautiful friend spiraling.

Her eyes were far away and thoughtful. And as I looked at her closer, I could see that whatever it was that used to make her seem so hopeful and encouraging appeared to be gone. "Stephanie, I want you to have this." She took off her tiny gold necklace and put it around my neck. "You're a good friend," she said.

I fingered the gold chain. "Well, you are, too, Valerie. And you know what else? I'm always gonna love ya." And I hugged her close and vowed to pay more attention to her from now on. "And I never want you to feel invisible or like I don't know you're here, because I do. I promise I do."

She crinkled her eyes in the moonlight and smiled back at me and just for a moment, just for a split second, I could see hope in her eyes, but just like that, it was gone again.

We slept in the same bed, holding each other and scratching each other's backs and taking turns singing to each other Camp Blessed Rock songs in the dark while we tried to doze off. I knew she was hurting after just burying her father, and she knew I was hurting, too. We didn't have to talk about it.

"Jesus, Jesus, Jesus, there's just something about that name," she sang. *"Master, Savior, Jesus . . . like the fragrance after the rain."*

When did it all become a lie? Was it Christmas morning when I was three? When I was seven? Was it the church picnic when I was five? Was it a lie all the times we went to dinner after church? Did our life become a lie at church or out of church? Did it happen the day I was born? Is that when it all became a lie?

I cried quietly. "Shhhh . . ." she whispered. Her long nails felt cool on my bare back and she reached around and gently wiped the tears from my cheeks as I lay facing the wall in the moonlight with her. "Don't cry, Stephanie, God loves us. He loves us both. I just know He does. He is with us now." She blew on my neck as she continued to sing and the tender touch of her friendship warmed my aching soul like a salve.

I did not know for sure if God was with me. I could not feel His presence, and I had stopped praying a long time ago. I didn't know where my mother was or what was happening to my family. I knew Valerie had to have ached for her father, too, but she seemed so much stronger than I was in so many ways, and even though her father was not yet cold in the ground, she comforted me and prayed for me the most, and I let her. It didn't occur to me that Valerie may have needed comforting herself. I was so focused on my own pain, and I needed her calmness and peace so badly and she was there like an angel. Just like she had always been.

I STUCK OUT MY THUMB as cars whizzed by shaking me with their speed and steely heaviness. Very quickly, a blue sedan pulled up in front of me and stopped. I ran up to the car and the driver rolled down his window. He was a young man who looked about twenty years old. "Are you a runaway?" he asked.

"No, my dad couldn't pick me up from the mall because he's packing to go out of town, so I just need a ride home," I answered, squinting my eyes in the sun, leaning into his car. My instincts about him were that he was good. I had no fear when I looked at him.

"Get in," he smiled.

"Can I get in the front?" I asked.

He reached over and opened the passenger side door so I jumped in and we sped off.

"G'head. Look for a tape." He motioned to the glove box, so I fished around.

"Queen?" I asked. He nodded so I put it in.

We rolled the windows down and let the music play loudly as we swerved in and out of traffic. He took me right to the front of our neighborhood and let me out. I thanked him and started to walk home ahead of his car, but he pulled up beside me and looked at me as he drove alongside. "Hey, what's your name, beautiful?" he asked.

I thought about giving him a fake name. "Stephanie," I said. He stopped the car and rolled down his window again and I leaned in and shielded his eyes from the sun.

"Can I call you?" he asked. He had a smoky baritone voice that was cagey. His shadowy eyes and crooked smile drew me in. His front two teeth had a small gap between them and his blonde hair was wind-blown. He brushed it out of his face with a lanky hand, and I noticed his nostrils were red and inflamed.

"Sure," I said, and I wrote down my number and gave it to him. "Thanks for the ride. What's *your* name?" I asked.

"Luciene. But my friends call me Luke. I'll call you later, Stephanie." He winked at me and slowly drove away. My heart was racing. I knew right then and there I had just met someone I would love for the rest of my life.

I walked down the street and passed The Rent House; it was a friend from a long time ago now, just someone I used to know. A family with kids was living there now; their colorful Big Wheels and trikes were scattered in the yard. The paint on the garage door looked chipped around the edges.

"Stephanie, make sure to put your dress on a hanger, not wadded up in a bag," Gail instructed right as I walked through the door. "We're all packed to leave for Kansas. You are the only one who's not ready. You're dragging your feet."

. . .

That night, Dad and Katherine were putting batteries in our radio for the ride up to the wedding when the phone rang.

"Stephanie!" Gail hollered through the house. "Luke is on the phone for you!"

"I'll pick it up in my room!" I yelled back. "Hello? I've got it, Gail."

"Hey, beautiful," he said; his deep voice melted me like a chocolate kiss in the sun. Gail hung up saying something to my father about how the plants on the back porch would bloom next year if he would trim them now. *Next year? Gail, you're still going to be here next year? You dumb bitch. You'll be long gone because my mother will be back by then.*

My heart zipped around like a firefly at the sound of his voice. We talked about songs that we loved and art we had seen and God. "Hey. Did I tell you I have to leave town? My dad is getting married this weekend. He's making me be a damn bridesmaid." I applied a third coat to my mascara in front of the mirror.

He laughed. "I have a better idea. Why don't you stay with me?" I stopped what I was doing.

"Well, I wish. But they're going to be gone for a week. I have school." But then I thought about it more. There was no point to me going to the wedding. My father didn't really want me there, and neither did Katherine or Gail for that matter. "I'll go ask," I said.

He laughed again. "Sweetheart . . . sounds like your dad's got his balls in Gail's hands. He's not thinking of you. You don't ask . . . you tell."

. . .

I walked out onto the driveway to find my dad. He was loading up the car and checking the tires for pressure. I took a deep breath. "Dad, can I talk to you for a minute?"

"Can't it wait, Stephanie? You know we're trying to pack." He answered without looking at me, then walked past me with grease on his hands and into the house where I followed him. As he washed his hands, I said, "I'm not going to your wedding."

He continued to scrub up his arms and in between his fingers. The white sudsy bubbles turned gray as the grease rinsed down into the sink. "Oh, really? And why's that?"

"I don't want to celebrate your marriage. I don't like Gail. You cheated on Mother with her. I think she's slutty and I don't agree with your choice. If it weren't for her, you and Mother would still be together. I want to stay with my new boyfriend, Luke. He said I could stay with him."

My father turned his back to the sink and dried his hands off, one finger at a time. He neatly folded the towel and replaced it on the countertop. "Well, if that's how you feel, go pack a bag. Don't forget your toothbrush. Whether we know it or not, people judge us by our teeth. I'll run you to his house now."

I laughed at him. "You don't care if I spend the week with Luke? He's twenty years old," I said.

"Nope, not at all," he said. "Some people are ready for sex and love at twenty and some are ready at fourteen. Age is really just relative. Now, go on. Go get ready. If I'm going to take you, we need to leave now."

I went to my room and packed a week's worth of clothes, slamming one thing in the bag after another. I called Luke back and told him I was coming and got directions to his apartment. My father loaded my suitcase into the back of the Crown Victoria and we drove the half hour to Luke's apartment in silence. When we arrived, he carried my suitcase for me up to Luke's door. We stood without speaking, together, waiting for Luke to answer the door and I looked around the hot parking lot. The apartment complex was old with dilapidated run-down cars in the parking lot. The door of his apartment was beat up and the paint was chipping off. "If you think this is a bad idea, Dad, we can go home. I mean, if you think it's not safe for me or something," I said.

"Nah, Sport. I think it's fine. Looks like a nice place," he said.

My father knocked again, shifting the weight of my suitcase to his other hand. Finally, Luke opened the door. His pupils were large and he looked high, but my dad didn't notice or didn't care. He shook Luke's hand and handed him my bag. "We'll be back in a week. I'll call the school in the morning and tell them you'll be out for a while. School can wait. Luke, can you bring her home next Friday or Saturday?"

"Sure thing," Luke replied.

And he left. He walked back to his car and left.

I stood there, not knowing what to do, but Luke quickly ushered me in and shut the door behind us. "Can I get you something? Want a Coke?" He opened the fridge and handed me a soda. I sat down on the couch looking around nervously.

"I like your posters," I said, nodding to the poster of a mystical dolphin on the wall. He laughed, tossing his hair out of his eyes.

"That's just there until I can afford something new. I have some paintings on layaway and when I pay them off, I'll hang them there. They're really dark displays of the sadness and healing of mankind. I love them because they are a woman who dries all the tears of the world with her hair." He sat down beside me. "You should let your hair grow, Stephanie. I love the color. It reminds me of garnets." He started kissing me, but I was stiff, still thinking about my dad and Katherine and Gail having a wedding without me.

"Hey, listen Stephanie, do you want something to help you relax?" he asked. He stood up and got his wallet off the kitchen counter. He took out a small sheet of paper with tiny clown faces on it. He handed me the sheet. I looked at the clowns and some were laughing facing forward, some to the right, some to the left, and some were shown from behind. As soon as he gave it to me, he took it back. "Do you want one?" he asked.

"What is it?" I asked. He put it back in his wallet and into his pocket. "It's acid," he said. "We'll do some tonight. Why don't you go put your stuff in my room?"

I walked back into his room and put down my bag. I wondered what my family and Gail were doing now. They were probably glad I was gone. Luke's bedroom was dirty. In fact, the whole apartment was filthy. There were piles of dirty laundry in all four corners of his room, and his sheets, which were pulled off the corners of the mattress, were gray and balled-up. He had papers of music he was writing thrown all over his room, and it looked like he was in the middle of several books, because they were stacked up on his night-stand with bookmarks fixed like flies in a web into the gummy rings left a long time ago from his coffee cup.

He walked in after me, embarrassed for the mess and picking up his clothes off the floor as he went. "Sorry, Steph. It's not usually this bad." He piled them all up and threw them into the empty hamper. His carpet was worn and flat, like the floor of The Rent House. "Hey, want to go grab some ice cream?"

I smiled. He was trying to make me feel comfortable. "Why don't you go and bring me some back? I'll stay here and clean. In fact, why don't you leave for a few hours?" I said. He protested that he didn't want me to feel like I had to do that, but I shooed him out the door and started to pick up. I cleaned the kitchen first, whistling and danc-ing with his stereo turned up loud.

When I got to his bathroom, I scrubbed the dark ring around his toilet feeling like a wife. In my fourteen-year-old mind, I pictured myself as his wife. I pretended this was my home, and that we were a family. I scrubbed the dark black ring on the bathtub until it came sparkling clean. I twirled around the living room, hugging the vacuum cleaner like my dance partner. It was amazing how clean everything looked just by being picked up and fluffed. This felt like a new home, safe and secure.

When I got to his room, I picked up his writings and art and couldn't help but look through them. His drawings were all of men, very dramatic poses of faces and bodies with beautiful muscles. The eyes in every drawing were unique because no matter how strong the man was in the drawing, each of the eyes was drawn in full makeup. He wrote about fire and burning and hearts breaking and love and sex and God and poetry and nature and his mother. He wrote about how he hated her for hiding who his father was from him. As I sat on the floor deep into the mind of Luke, buried in his most intimate writings, he came up behind me and grabbed me, startling me, sending papers flying. "Boo!" he shouted in my ear.

"Oh, my gosh, Luke, I'm so sorry. I was just cleaning. I'm so sorry. I wasn't trying to snoop." I stacked the papers unsuccessfully, my hands shaking.

"Sweetheart, it's okay. Here's your ice cream. It's a little bit melted." I took the ice cream from him and we sat on the bed together.

"Luke, where is your family?" I asked.

"Ah, I never met my dad," he said. "My mother said he came to meet me once when I was two and taking a nap. She let him peek in on me, but I've never met him. Mom is a really strong woman. She's a nurse, but we don't talk much. She lives on Westheimer, and I don't really think she's very proud of me. She thinks I'm gay, and she hates faggots. Not my word, hers."

I looked at him carefully for a moment in silence while we ate our ice cream together. He was beautiful with very pretty features. His eyes were deep-set and his mouth was smooth. He looked like a tall blonde Italian who had been on the beach all summer long, his skin tan but smooth. I licked the ice cream off the spoon and wiped my mouth in the corners. "Are you gay?" I asked.

"Oh, I don't know. No. I don't think so. I mean, sometimes I think maybe I am. I'm attracted to some men, sure. Who isn't?" He lay flat across his bed and looked up at the ceiling. He thought about it and then sat up with such purpose it startled me. "But I don't think so. I don't really like to assign labels like that to people. I think love can come in all kinds of different forms, so I can't really say, 'Oh, I will love only women,' or 'Oh, I am someone who only loves men.' I like to think I look more at the spirit than the body. What about you?"

I almost choked on my ice cream, surprised at the question. I sputtered, "I'm not gay." Just like that, I didn't really need to think about it. He nodded his head and got up and turned on some music. His strong back had a tattoo of a colorful peacock feather on the right shoulder. We lay down beside each other and listened to The Cure until we couldn't stay awake any longer. He wrapped me up in his arms and just as I drifted off, he roused me and asked, "Stephanie, how old are you?"

I turned over and studied his face. His angular features reminded me of my mother's. I missed her so much. I missed my father, too. I missed the sister I never knew, and mourned the gap between us. I didn't want a stepmother. I needed Luke tonight. I felt so safe there in his apartment, even though it might have been wrong to need him. I knew I should have been turning to God, but I could not help but feel like God gave me Luke. I looked up at him and smiled sweetly. "Seventeen," I lied. I had just turned fourteen.

The truth of my age would've turned him away and I couldn't risk it, couldn't risk him taking me home to an empty house, to a broken family; I wanted to stay right here with him forever where I was welcome and wanted. He wrapped the sheet around his slender waist and smiled; we fell into the motionless calm of sleep, he and I. He held me like a friend through the night without touching me like a woman at all, although I wanted him to touch me so much. I woke up several times in the night and rolled over and looked at his striking face, so peaceful as he slept, and I knew he had come into my life to write on my soul, even if he was only a part of my life for a little while.

His arms were not the arms of permanence, but when they held me, my soul was calm and peaceful. I woke up the next day in his arms as the midday sun warmed the still and quiet room. My back and legs were covered in sweat from the stagnant apartment air. I rubbed my eyes and turned over to glance at the clock on his nightstand. We had slept the morning away. He was already sitting up in the bed propped up on a pillow when I woke. He put his cigarette up to my lips and I breathed the smoke in easily. "Good morning, cutie," he said smiling. His face was fresh and rested. He rolled over to reach for his wallet, his cigarette hanging loosely from his lips. "Are you hungry?"

I sat up and stretched, remembering my family was driving to my father's wedding, remembering it was the beginning of a new school year, a new school day, that eighth grade was still happening somewhere for some people. I looked at the ceiling, remembering where I was, remembering I was going to have a new stepmother, remembering that my mother was pretending to be someone else's mother, remembering I was alone. I pushed the images out of my mind. "No, not at all. Let's sleep all day." I smiled and yawned.

"We can arrange that," he said, getting up to turn on a fan. His body moved through the room gracefully; his strong chest was chiseled, smooth, and svelte. I got up and walked into the bathroom and looked in the mirror. I looked like a whore; my makeup was smeared down my cheeks because I hadn't bothered to take it off the night before and my teeth were dirty because I had fallen asleep without brushing them. My God, my eyes looked *swollen*. I splashed cold water on my face hoping it would be different when I opened my eyes, but no. What did he see in me? I heard from inside the bathroom the music of The Beatles, "The Two of Us," and when I walked back into the room, he was propped up in his bed on a few dirty pillows again, reading the back of the album. His black cat, Ophelia, purred at his side as he stroked the top of her head. Lennon and McCartney filled the room with contemplation and the fan circulated cool air, which made the room feel fresher.

I opened up the small bedroom window and climbed back in between the sheets. I put my head and hand on his warm chest and took in the smell of his earthy skin. He looked at the album cover and held me without talking. His arms weren't too tight and they weren't too loose, either. I closed my eyes and realized how much I needed to be touched, to be held. "You're beautiful, Stephanie," he said as he caressed the side of my stomach. "You really are. You are like a sculpture," he said. "Do you mind if I take your picture?"

I sat up and pulled the sheets around me. "Sure," I said.

"Do you want to try some acid first?" he asked.

"What does it do?" I had never heard of acid before.

"It's a psychedelic drug. It makes you feel totally uninhibited. It awakens your mind to another dimension and feels like you can create anything, like you can be anything, think anything. It makes me a better artist." He pulled out the sheet of paper clowns and tore one of the faces off for me and put it in my mouth. "Just hold it on your tongue." He tore off another one and put in on his tongue and then tore off another one and let Ophelia lick it until it disappeared.

"Do you really think the cat should eat acid?" I asked. I was shocked at this, and worried about what it would do to her. But Luke was so smooth when he talked, so mentally engaging, so physically beautiful, that everything he said sounded true.

"Sure. It's funny. Why should we have all the fun?" He climbed back in bed and propped himself up against the pillow again, reaching over in his nightstand to pull out a camera. He loaded a new roll of film and looked up and stuck his tongue out, tapping it lightly, motioning for what he wanted me to do.

I put the paper on my tongue and waited for it to disappear. We lay there talking and listening to the music. I stood up and took off my clothes that I had slept in and arched my back and pulled one leg up higher than the other on the bed, revealing just enough of myself. I reached down to touch myself between my legs, to show him my most private places. I didn't need to be taught; I knew exactly what to do. "No, no, no, sweetheart. That's beautiful, but that's not what I want. Come here, sit down and put your back to me."

"But that's not very sexy," I said.

"Oh, *yes, it is*. I'm trying to do something beautiful here, and you're making it dirty. You need to open your mind to yourself being beautiful, not so sexual. Here, put your back towards me and turn to face the wall."

"This is dumb. I can't even see what you're doing. I'm just going to look fat," I said awkwardly, suddenly feeling embarrassed, but I let him direct me. He sat me down on the corner of the bed with his gentle hand, and positioned the gray sheet that was originally white so that it wrapped around my waist and he turned my face to the side. "Look down," he said, guiding my chin with his hand. "These will be black and white," and he started to snap pictures of the curve of my back and the curve of my waist and my hands as they held the sheets. "God, you're gorgeous," he said as he snapped pictures of my mouth up close and of my eyes. "You need to let your hair grow, Steph, you really do. Hold this," he said, as he put a cigarette in my hand. "Hold it up to your mouth," he said. So I did.

He said, "Act like you're crying. Can you cry? Maybe think about someone that you love that has died. Let the acid do its job. Come sit with your face in the sun," and I moved to where the sun streamed in across his bed. "Cover up your body, Stephanie; I just want the smoke as it covers your eyes, I want to see your soul, your face, or your body." I took a drag and exhaled slowly and let the smoke float into a mellow cover over my face. He put his camera down away from his face, furrowing his brow and thinking.

"I still can't see it. Stephanie . . . show me what's inside of you. Show me your spirit. Sweetheart, think of something sorrowful and mind stretching." And so I did . . . I thought of how I would feel if Luke died; I had begun to love him so hard and so quickly. I thought of how I would feel if we both died right now, if we were trapped in noiseless coffins that were closed too tightly in a cold morgue where the mortician had left for the night, or how I would feel if I were a child again with a second chance to be close to my father, with a second chance to let him love me, and I pictured him dying, but I did not care. I tried to cry when I thought of him gone, but I couldn't. Then I thought of Katherine crying because of something I had said or done, some way I had purposely hurt her without caring, my mother and I ganging up on her, my father having sex with her, too much sorrow for Katherine . . . and tears filled my eyes for my sister, spilling over onto my cheeks. I could smell the fleshy salt from my tears and hear my heart beating. The music was entering me, music of The Cure now.

And let's move to the beat
Like we know that it's over
If you slip going under,
Slip over my shoulder

"Fascination Street" brought me down a dark alley with Luke into a world where I was and I wasn't. I could see the notes of the song in my head; feel every beat of the drum, every keystroke of the piano I heard retroactively as the music was being written. My brain smelled the earth; my nose created images; my senses were interchangeable now. I could speak to my deepest fears, the darkest parts of my innocence gone for such a long time now. I called out to the little girl inside me to tell her to try to cry because that's what Luke wanted us to do. She heard me, and she ran to me, dropping her toys as she ran, pleading with me to protect her, she told me to turn back, to run away from The Rent House, to bury her into the wall, to hold her, but I told her to be quiet. She looked at me from the darkness and blinked her eyes and I heard them blink, her eyelashes smashing down in the darkness like a house burning, but only touching my face lightly. "Oh, my God, that's perfect, Stephanie. I love it. Cry. Do not change anything, your spirit has strong knowledge and purpose," and he clicked the camera over and over, taking pictures of my soul.

I had given my body over before, but this was the first time I had given over my mind and my soul.

When the film was all used up, we lay back down in the bed. I wanted him to have sex with me. I wanted him inside me. I even wanted him to get me pregnant, to end my teenage years, to take me in and make us a family. "Luke, please." I pulled him close, but he pulled away. I put his hands on my face and he traced my lips and eyes with the tips of his fingers. "You are an artist, Stephanie. But I don't know what kind," he said softly as he traced my cheeks. I felt hot from the inside out, like I was boiling with life-saving fire. I looked down at Ophelia, but I felt like I could only open my eyes halfway. The cat was chasing her own tail. I was scared. "Luke, what is she doing? What's happening to her?" I sputtered, sitting up quickly.

He looked at her and laughed. "She thinks her tail is after her! Ophelia, stop it!" and he threw a pillow at her. The cat hissed and ran into the corner of his closet, her eyes flickering madly, and she started meowing loudly. He laughed so I laughed, too, because Luke was truth. I thought of Ophelia falling down a bottomless black hole, swirling and swirling, singing "Let It Be." I looked at the wall and the texture of the sheet rock looked like my mother's face. I stared at her while I felt her emotions after the death of her little boy. I knew her whole past, present, and future, and I watched her face swirl like a melted candle. I saw her baby's underdeveloped head with the beginnings of veins running through and his body perfectly formed only tiny. It felt like only five minutes had passed when the moon shone in through the window. My muscles were tired and my teeth were sore like I had been clamping down. I looked over but Luke wasn't beside me. I walked through the dark hallway and found him standing in the dim light of the refrigerator. He looked up at me and grinned. "Hey, girl. We had some fun, didn't we? Are you still tripping?"

I thought about it, feeling like everything in the world and my mind were working simultaneously. His apartment seemed like a place that didn't exist, a dark place, but everything around me felt good and looked new. It was all very interesting and I felt like a baby who was just discovering my fingers and toes. "I don't know. I, I think so," I answered. "What are you eating?"

"First of all, you're coming down." He handed me another hit. I put it on my tongue and let it dissolve. "Smell this. It will feel *so* good," and he opened up a small brown vial of clear liquid. He put it under my nose, but I instinctively shoved it away. "Stephanie, you don't want it?" he asked. He looked like a sad puppy dog.

I wanted whatever he wanted. "No, I do, I do," I said. He put the bottle up under my nose and I smelled it gently.

"No, you have to huff it hard. Sniff it hard, like this." And he closed one nostril with his hand and took a big whiff. He closed his eyes and handed the bottle to me. I closed my nostril and did the same, and immediately I felt a sense of my brain opening up and allowing all the blood in my body to enter in through my cheeks. It was a quick and fleeting sense of euphoria, and then my entire body relaxed.

We went back to his bedroom, the moon pouring in and mixing with the blinking light at the tennis court outside. His bed was cool and rumpled and we climbed back in together and hid under the covers.

"So tell me your views about God," he said. "What keeps you balanced?" I could feel everything he said to me; I could hear his thoughts and he could hear mine. He rubbed his hands on my body and I could smell the blood coursing through his veins, putting his heat onto my body.

"I don't even feel like I know God anymore," I said. "But I think there's a God. I can't say for sure either way. My church has confused me. I don't know anything now." My soul sobbed inside at the silence of our church, the coldness of the elders. The hypocrisy of it all disturbed me. The thought of Carl Sr. looking down at my father made me want to murder him. But I didn't say it. Luke nodded and lit a cigarette and the cherry burned orange in the darkness as he inhaled.

"That makes sense. But Stephanie, those fools aren't God. I think it would take more than them to drive God out of you. I feel God in music and in the love of those around me," he said. "I don't know much about Him, like, not about the Bible or anything, but I can feel God inside me, you know, here," and he pointed to his heart. I saw vibrating waves of his body heat lifting from his soul into mine and he put his mouth on mine and breathed warm air into my mouth. He slowly let his saliva drip into my mouth and I swallowed it, knowing he wanted to *know* me. He kept breathing, in and out, into my mouth. His breath was hot and stale but I loved him and loved his raw, organic smell. He stared into my eyes and pressed his nose right up against mine, making his eyes as close to mine as he could . . . he was so close he was blurry. I heard his thoughts, "I love you, Stephanie. Stay with me this way forever."

I heard his heart beating and I wanted him near me, as near as possible. He filled the hole in my heart that was in the shape of my father's arms; he filled it because he was Luke, and I wanted him to have me entirely, mind, body, and spirit. I pulled myself on top of him and faintly heard his voice in the distance, the only thing around me that wasn't amplified, "no, Stephanie, no, please don't do this," and I rocked back and forth, back and forth gently, holding his long blonde hair in my hands, feeling the darkness from the room around me like a heavy private shelter on my body.

His hands slid over me and as he touched me, he entered my body and soul and knew all of my secrets. He held my thoughts and unanswered prayers in his safe hands and he memorized my body in the night and I needed him to know me. I needed him that way, that night, I needed his hands on me. He made me stop wanting my father and a family. He was with me; he was willing, and he needed me, too, I just knew it, and even though I heard him say, "Stephanie, stop, please stop, this isn't what I pictured," I moved on top of him seductively and kissed him all over his beautiful face. As I moved and moaned on top of him, I heard his heart secretly tell me he was gay, but our connection transcended that, our bodies were not the extent of us. He let me stay; he said he loved me; he held me tight; he listened to me; I listened to him and we did not let each other go; we did not let go, and the night itself grew stronger with us; his truth about what he saw in my soul became more convincing. The night and the moon itself was breathing hard, accepting us for what we could give.

CHAPTER

22

"OKAY, OPEN YOUR EYES," HE said as he took the blindfold off of my face. I saw the end of an open airport runway, surrounded by thousands of twinkling blue lights lighting the way for the pilots. The jet plane sped towards us with massive force as we waited at a safe distance in the open field where he had driven us. The plane swooshed over us and into the sky, and we followed it with our eyes and heads as the wheels retracted. The noise of the jet engine blustered and the wind from the force blew our hair as we laughed.

"Aren't they beautiful?" Luke yelled, his eyes dancing. This was the first night we had been out of his apartment in a week. We sat on the hood of his car watching each plane take off. "Where would you go, Steph? If you could go anywhere in the world?" he asked.

"I would live in New York," I said.

"I would stay right here. I know it's not glamorous, but it's home," he said. "It's where everyone who loves me lives." There was a side to him that was very solid and made a lot of sense.

We sat watching the planes, remarking how they seemed too heavy to be up that high. After a long stretch of silence, I asked, "Do you think you could ever become a Christian?"

"I am a Christian, Stephanie," he answered, looking down at me like he was injured. "I love God, too, you know," he said.

"But you don't go to church," I said. "I want to baptize you, Luke."

He laughed. "You want to baptize me? Why? I've been baptized. I was baptized as a baby."

"You haven't been immersed and if you die tonight you will go to hell. I just love you and I worry about your soul."

"Stephanie, I'm not going to hell. Is that what you think? Because I haven't been baptized into the Church of Christ? Do you really believe in a God like that?" He looked intently into my eyes, searching them for answers. But when I didn't answer, he knew what I was thinking.

"Luke, have you ever doubted God?" I asked. "I mean, like, do you ever wonder . . . if God hates us?"

"Sure." He took a drag off his cigarette. "Seems to me even Jesus felt that way. But God doesn't hate us. He doesn't hate you, Stephanie. God loves you."

"Jesus did not feel that way! Luke, don't be blasphemous!" I kind of felt stupid when I said that. I took the cigarette from him and put it to my lips and inhaled deeply.

"Sure he did. What do you think he meant when he was dying? 'Father, why hath thou forsaken me?' Seems to me, the only reason he would say something like that is because he felt pretty much alone. It's normal, Stephanie, to go through times when you don't feel God. It's part of being human."

"But you aren't baptized," I said. I took his hands in mine because he needed to be saved. Even though I had been amputated from my system, it was still the only thing I knew.

"Stephanie, God loves me. He created me. He knows every hair on my head, and yours, too, for that matter. If He is the one who made me and knows me best of all, don't you think He's big enough to draw my heart near Him?" he asked.

I wanted so much to believe it. "No, Luke. Because you have to be baptized into a Church of Christ. Why would you risk that?"

"Why would I *risk it*? Stephanie, that's a God of fear you're talking about. Not a God of love," he said.

"No, Christ said, 'I have a baptism to undergo and how distressed I will be until it is completed,'" I said. "That shows how important it was to Christ for us to be saved. And God *is* a God of fear. That's biblical. Nahum 1 says, 'The Lord is a jealous and vengeful God; the Lord is vengeful and strong in wrath.'"

"Stephanie, 1 love you, but you're flinging scripture around like a weapon, both arms swinging, and you are so lost, sweetheart. God is so much bigger than all that. I wish you could see that. You're living in bondage. It's so sad," and he put his arms around my shoulders and squeezed.

He lit a joint and we shared it in the cool breeze. "I have to go home tomorrow," I said, letting the breeze do what it pleased with my hair. Luke and I had made love several times a day every day for the week, sometimes with our bodies, sometimes with our minds, but always with our hearts. He was a part of me now. I knew he was gay, and since he had trusted me with that part of himself, I loved him like a friend the most.

"I know." He took the joint from me and took a long hit. "I'll call you every night and I can come get you next weekend. Let's not think about it. Do you think you're going to be okay with the fact that your dad's married? Guess you've gotta be." He exhaled and handed it to me.

I shook my head. I was enjoying the sounds of the planes as they took off and defied gravity. I didn't want the night altered. "One more year and you'll be done with school, it won't matter." He pulled his keys out of his pocket and walked around to my side of the car and opened my door. I got in the car and he smiled at me. "You're fabulous,

Stephanie. The most passionate person I know." He winked and shut the door.

We drove through the sleeping neighborhoods on the way to his apartment, and he pulled into a parking lot of an elementary school. He turned off the ignition and turned to face me. "Let's break in," he said calmly.

I laughed and looked at the school building, its windows covered with finger paint art. "For what purpose?" I asked.

"Just to say we did. Let's break in and just sit and visit inside. It's the environment of the young mind. C'mon." We got out of the car and walked up to the school and crouched down behind a bush. I looked around for cars, but nobody was around. The houses on the streets around us had some lights from within their windows, but mostly they were dark.

He took a rock and hit the window. When it didn't break, he picked up a bigger rock and smashed it, causing me to jump at the sound. He reached in and opened the window and climbed inside. I followed him into a room of tiny desks and plants and maps. There was a reading corner in the back full of plush stuffed animals. I could hear the sound of children laughing and pencils sharpening during the school day when sunlight filled the place, but tonight, only the silence of the inanimate things remained . . . one coat and a few forgotten lunch pails, the teacher's coffee cup. He took a seat at a desk and motioned for me to sit down. We sat and visited until we just couldn't keep our eyes open, and just before the custodians arrived, we slipped back out the window the way we came and drove home.

The next morning, he drove me back to my tree-lined neighborhood. It seemed like I had been gone for years. We turned on to my street and passed The Rent House. Simone was outside checking her mail. She waved as he pulled into my driveway, wrinkling her nose up. As we drove past her, I saw her mouth the words "What the hell?"

She made a beeline over to my driveway and tapped on my window before he had even had a chance to put the car in park. I laughed and got out of the car, smoke wafting out onto Simone when I opened the door. "Where the hell have you been? I thought you were in Kansas at the blessed union."

I ignored her and walked around to Luke's side and he rolled down the window. "Don't get out," I said. "I love you."

"I love you, too, Stephanie. I'll call you when I get home, okay?"

"Okay. Thank you for letting me stay with you this week, Luke." He stuck out his hand like we were the best of friends, and I pumped it up and down and laughed. He waved at Simone and drove off and I turned around to walk in but Simone's face was scowling right into mine.

"What the hell is going on, Stephanie?" she asked.

"What? I stayed with my friend, Luke," I said, walking casually past her with my bag. She marched through my yard following me.

We walked into my house and Dad and Katherine were playing a game of Scrabble in the living room. Gail sifted through her new wedding pictures and carefully pulled back the plastic sheets and placed them neatly in an album. They looked up at me, Gail's eyes smiling. "Hi, honey! How was your week with your friend?"

Katherine looked up and said, "Hey, Simone. Want to play Scrabble?"

"Gail, I told you not to call me honey. And um, no, Katherine, that's weird and we are not going to pretend to be one big happy family." We breezed past them without further acknowledgment and walked into my bedroom with Simone following like a puppy.

"Stephanie, that guy is so FINE. But isn't he, like, kinda old?"

"He's twenty," I said.

"So you spent the night with him?" she asked. When I didn't answer, she asked, "Oh, my God. Stephanie, did you spend the *week* with him? Holy shit. Does your dad know?" Her eyes were lit up. There was a note on the bed in the handwriting of my father. *Your mother called. Will call you back tomorrow.*

"So tell me everything!" she said.

"Well, Luke is really special," I began. "We talked all night long one night . . ."

"Shhh, hang on, I totally want to hear this, but first let's turn on MTV." She popped her gum and turned on the television to an A-ha video. "Oh my god, I totally love 'Take on Me.'"

I tossed my bag in my closet and plopped down on my bed and read the message again.

"There's really nothing much to tell. He's just my friend," I answered, but mostly I was talking to myself, not to Simone.

• • •

The next morning, I came downstairs to the kitchen and found my father and Gail drinking coffee and sharing the newspaper before work. My father was pointing out an article. "And they said someone had broken in the night before so it was definitely pre-planned. The whole thing is going to have to be rebuilt from the ground up. Can you believe that? Who would do such a thing?" I tuned them out while I poured my cereal and drank the last of the juice from the carton. "Stephanie, don't drink from the carton," my dad said.

"I'm sorry." I yawned and shuffled my feet towards the clean glasses in the dishwasher. My hair was getting longer and I brushed it out of my face and yawned again. I teared up from such a big yawn and then I yawned even bigger and then drank down the last of the juice.

I rubbed my eyes and closed them again as I considered going back up to bed. "Is there any fruit?" I asked. They ignored me and continued their conversation, so I mindlessly sat down at the table and searched the cereal box for a prize.

"Well, I guess those kids will have to be bussed, huh? Is there even room for them somewhere else? Poor babies. They are the ones who will suffer." Gail shook her head. I opened up the paper and looked for the comics.

"Hey, how come the comics aren't in color?" I asked.

"Because it's not Sunday. That's only on Sundays," Dad answered. "And gallons and gallons of gasoline lying around and whoever did it had scoped it out the night before by finding ways in and out. The bastards who did it were lucky they didn't kill themselves in the process." My father sighed and folded up the paper and got up to get another cup of coffee, placing the front page casually down on top of my comics. He shook his head and muttered something about how these neighborhoods were going down. My heart pounded in my chest when I saw the picture peeking out of a flag pole waving the American flag high beside a flattened pile of ashes. I could see the front of the school building and recognized it from the night before. I waited until they left for work to read the article. The elementary school where Luke and I had talked the night before had been burned completely, utterly, and totally to the ground.

I ran to the bathroom and splashed cold water on my face and stared at myself in the mirror, my hands shaking uncontrollably. *Pull yourself together, Stephanie. Pull yourself together!* I really didn't know anything for sure, did I? I had no way of knowing for sure if Luke had anything to do with burning down the school. He wasn't like that. Luke was full of everything good, everything true. He would never hurt anyone or anything. He was too calm and good for that. Then I remembered him giving his cat acid and my mind started swirling with questions. I came back into the kitchen and picked up the phone and called him.

His phone rang several times as I leaned up against a kitchen wall and waited for him to pick up. When he finally did, my heart started racing with fear. I could see his face in my mind, etched into my soul as being near my face, beside me, between my legs, above me, under me. Luke was my family.

"Luke!" I whispered into the phone frantically. "Where are you? I need to talk to you." The other line beeped . . . someone was calling, and I knew it was my mother. I needed to talk to her and if I didn't answer now, she may not call again. But I needed him too badly; I needed to know the truth now. "Luke, did you burn that school down?" I hissed. The line beeped again and I let it ring, then something told me she was gone. "That school was in the newspapers this morning. Somebody burned it down!" I said.

"I did," he answered calmly.

My heart sank and I closed my eyes. "Why?" I asked. "Luke, why would you do such a thing? If you get caught, you'll go to prison. Luke, you could have caught yourself on fire!"

His voice was still and calm. "I don't really know why," he answered. "It was like an internal phantom itch that needed scratching, you know? Like a pain from inside my soul, on the inside and out, but I couldn't scratch it. I tried to get up the nerve to ask you to help me that night, but couldn't. Maybe I was hurting for you, I don't know. Maybe pissed at my father who I never met? When we left there that night, you and me, I was just so sad that you were going home the next morning. We had had such a good couple of days. So I went back by myself and burned it down. And the itch went away."

"How did you do it?" I asked. "No, don't tell me, I don't want to know." The line beeped again and I ignored it. "Okay, tell me."

"I went around it and doused it with gasoline then lit a match. It wasn't that hard to figure out," he answered.

"Oh my goodness, Luke!" I slid down the wall and closed my eyes. "Weren't you afraid you'd get caught? Have you ever done anything like this before?" I asked.

"Just burned a few fences. And a dumpster behind a supermarket once," he replied.

"Were you high?" I didn't want to pry but I couldn't stop myself.

"Well, yeah . . . I was a little high. Stephanie you won't tell anyone, will you?" He spoke fast and panicky now, keenly aware that I held the power to keep his secret or not.

"Oh, God, Luke, no. Of course not. Everything about you is safe right here with me. I would never tell anyone anything about you," I answered. I breathed hard into the phone because his secret now weighed heavily on my shoulders and the realization that something was extremely wrong with the person I loved invaded my memories of him but did not change my feelings.

"Luke, can I be honest with you about something, now?" I asked.

"Of course you can. You know you can," he said.

"Luke, this is all kind of a lot for me. The truth is . . . well . . . I'm only fourteen," I said.

"Jesus Christ on a cross, Stephanie! Are you serious? But you look so old! Are you trying to pin me for *rape*?" he squealed.

"No! Luke, you didn't rape me, please, please, please, don't feel that way. I *am* old! In my heart I'm old! Please! I needed you. I still need you. Please, Luke! I love you! I would tell any judge that. You're not a rapist! Please don't be angry. My dad does not care about stuff like that. He thinks age is relative. He says some kids are ready for sex sooner and I was! Even Katherine was. We're just born that way in my family. You know that empty house two doors down from my house?" I told Luke about The Rent House and the boys when I was ten. I told him about Katherine and the boys behind the church. I told him about Carl.

"Does anyone else know about what happened in that rent house? Or what happened to your sister?" he asked.

"No."

"Stephanie, oh sweet girl. What would make you go in that house with those boys?" he asked. "Were you trying to be like Katherine?"

My face felt flush. "I don't want to talk any more about that!" I snapped. "Forget it. I'm sorry I said anything."

We sat on the phone without speaking for several seconds. I

wrapped the cord around my finger until the tip of my knuckle turned blue. *Dear God, please don't let Luke hate me. Please don't let him leave.*

Finally, he laughed again but this time his tone was sinister and he gritted his teeth. "Ahhh *fuck*. Age is relative, huh, Dad? *Ready* for sex at ten or twelve? Well then, I guess now we all get to keep a few secrets, don't we? Your dad, you, and me."

·   ·   ·

I kept the phone close to me and waited for it to ring again, praying she would call back. Not very many moments passed before it did. It was her. "Hi, sweetheart!" she said. "How's it going?"

I was taken aback by her happy tone. "Good, good, Mother. Everything's good. I mean, Dad got married this week, did you know that?" I asked.

She got quiet and didn't answer for a long time.

"Mother are you there?" I asked.

Finally, she spoke, "No, I didn't know, but I bet it was a beautiful wedding, wasn't it? Your dad always had such good taste in things like that. That's what I told myself when I married him, 'this guy has such good taste in food and decorating.' In fact, it was his idea to wear a navy tux at our wedding because he was always so fashion forward. He married Gail, I assume? Oh, what am I asking, of course he married Gail. Who on earth else would it be? Were you and Katherine brides-maids? I bet you both looked beautiful."

"Yes, Katherine was. She wore a peach dress. I stayed in Houston with a friend," I replied.

She was quiet again. "Well I'm sure that worked just as well. And peach looks so pretty on a blonde, doesn't it? I've been thinking I should go back to blonde so I can wear a summer palette. Please thank Sister Lynne and Simone for having you. I hope you girls behaved yourselves."

I didn't correct her. "So what else is new? I can come visit you . . . if you want."

"Well, I'm considering becoming a missionary. The whole world is a mission field, Stephanie, and we could build an unmitigated mansion for ourselves in heaven. Unmitigated."

"Uh huh," I sighed. "I bet that's true. Well, could I come check on you?" I asked.

"Darling, I would say yes, but I'm not sure it's a good idea. I've been so busy lately," she said. "Stephanie, your voice sounds strange. Are you crying?"

"I'm just tired."

"No, it's something more. A mother knows these things. Is there something wrong?" she cooed.

"Well, Mother, I have this friend . . . he's in trouble . . . oh never mind."

She was quiet a while, and then finally spoke. "Oh, don't cry, sweetheart. Oh, Stephanie, okay, I think a visit sounds like a great idea. In fact, I just had a marvelous idea! Why don't you just come and stay?"

I wiped my eyes. "Stay? Well, I don't know about *stay* . . ."

"Oh forget I said that. You've simply had too much loss and too many decisions to make lately, haven't you, darling? I shouldn't ask any more of you. Your dad always said he would get you in the end, and if you feel like you need to take his side, that's fine." But a part of me wanted her to ask me to come stay with her. I didn't want to stay where I was. I didn't want to go with her, either.

"No, no, I'm glad you asked," I sniffed. "I want to come. I'm just crying because I'm tired. But I just don't know if I can stay that long, Mother. But, Mother, I'm not trying to take Dad's side." I was crying from a place so deeply within that when I spoke bubbles came out of my mouth. "I've missed you so much I've wanted to die. I want to come."

We decided she would pick me up the next day.

I PACKED A BAG OF clothes and waited on the porch for my mother, all the while thinking over and over about Luke and I sitting in that classroom together in the dark. Luke had only left me alone once to go use the bathroom. Was that when he found his way in and out, like the papers had said? I thought about the sweet classroom with the pictures of the happy families that the kids had finger painted and hung up to dry.

Mother whirled into the driveway in a beat-up gray Ford Fairlane that sputtered and coughed as she slammed on the brakes. She stepped out of it and books and a blender fell out, and as she struggled to shove them back in, I saw that she was wearing an expensive white suit with five-inch zebra stilettos. "Hi, sweetie!" she sang loudly as she fought to close the driver's side door, finally kicking it hard. She smiled and smoothed down her hair and her suit and walked up to the porch. "Can I take your bag?" she asked.

"No, I've got it. Did you tell Dad?" I asked, walking with her towards the car. "Where's your Thunderbird?"

"You know what? I decided the Thunderbird was bought for me by your father and I'm no longer accepting gifts from white Christian men because the men and the gifts are always the same. So I sold it and paid cash for this car and gave the rest of the money to a Mega Church named Lakewood and some homeless people. You know, the homeless community of Houston really is full of amazing people. They have no expectations, no fear. You know, Stephanie, there's no condemnation for those who love the Lord," she said as she slammed my door shut. She walked around and got in the car and faced me, still smiling. Her powder was on too thick and made her face look much darker than her neck.

I looked for a place in the back to put my bag, but it was filled to the rim with dishes and quilts and books and wrappers and pink rollers and photo albums and a large lamp. I carefully placed it on top of a hot plate and wondered if it would block her view out of the back window. She yelled, "Not there, Stephanie! That was a gift!" She pulled out from under it a small, hand-painted wooden bird. "One of my students gave that to me my first year of teaching. It's very special," she said. I tried to put my seat belt on but it was stuck.

"Mother, are you living here? In the car?" I asked.

"Oh, good grief, no." We drove in silence for a little while. I tried to turn on the air, but it blew heat, so I rolled down the window. We drove into Houston over the soaring overpasses and freeways. The skyline twinkled with energy in the warm night sky. "Don't you just love Houston when it's all lit up like that?" she asked. "It's like watching a heartbeat."

We drove past the city proper and into the Fifth Ward, a place so separate from my safe world on Orchard Lane, where I used to ride my bike freely and without care. My parents used to point to it when we drove past and say we didn't belong *there*. This place was for the *other people*, they had told me. Surely my mom remembered that.

She parked our car. I asked, "Mother, what are we doing *here*? Where's your house?"

"We ARE home," she said gleefully. I looked out and there before me was a bustling homeless shelter called The Jesus Center with lots of people meandering about outside the entrance with grocery carts full of belongings and paper bags overflowing with what little they owned.

"Mother, you've got to be kidding me." I stared out the window and saw that one of the women had a little boy who peeked out from behind her legs. "What is this?"

"Stephanie, this is home to me now. I decided to toss away everything that was holding me down, everything earthly, and live among the poor. This shelter is my mission field."

"This doesn't look like a mission field," I said as I got out of the car. The darkness was heavy and the people milling around looked like ghosts. They looked dirty and like they smelled and they were loud, asking for blankets and a place to stay for the night. We stepped out of the car and suddenly I was keenly aware of how nice the clothes were that my mother and I were wearing. "Mother, we don't belong here. We're from the suburbs. This is a shelter for people who are homeless." But she was already walking ahead of me, smiling and waving as though she were walking into a place she had known intimately and forever.

We breezed right past the people waiting in line out front and the man at the front desk inside said, "Hi, Miss Kasow. Looking good tonight."

She smiled and waved back, "Doing well. God is good, He's good all the time."

"Yes ma'am, He's good all the time," he echoed.

"Who the hell is Kasow?" I demanded as we walked through the large lobby and towards the long, stark hallway. We passed by a toy area shoved off to one corner of the room where a thin, pleasant-looking woman who was playing on the floor with her children looked up at us and smiled. Some of her teeth were missing. The kids were smiling but they had dried snot all over their faces and they were slobbering on the already dirty toys. "Miss Toujours, is that you Stephy? She pretty like you be sayin'."

"It is. Say hello, Stephanie," she said sweetly as we kept walking. I nodded my head at the woman and muttered, "Hi." The place smelled like old macaroni and cheese and bleach. There was a clanking and banging of pots and pans coming from the kitchen, which was lit up bright with several people working and wiping down the tables from the dining hall. Steam rose from the industrial-sized sink as they rinsed the many plastic dishes with hot, soapy water. "Mother, stop walking ahead of me like this is fucking normal," I cried.

She stopped walking and faced me. Her eyeshadow was white and caked up in the creases of her lids. "Mother, you have on way too much eye makeup. You don't need to put it all the way up to your brow like that, geez." The one dangling light bulb responsible for lighting the entire hallway flickered.

"Stephanie, this shelter is my home now. I'm living here because I want to," she sighed. "It's something I've always dreamt of doing since I was a little girl."

"Bullshit! They don't let you do that. You can't just 'live here' because it's a dream. You're living here because you *have* to. Mother, what is this? And why are they calling you by that name?" I asked.

"I legally changed my name to Kasow Toujours. I never really felt like a Lillian, to tell you the truth. And I hated the nickname Lily even more because I am not a flower. K-A for Katherine Ameilia, S-O for Stephanie Olive, and W for Walters. Toujours is the French word for always and forever. Kasow Toujors. I don't want to be a 'Walters.' That's your father's name. My name is now my children. Always," she said. "And I named you Stephanie 'Olive,' which was a name I insisted upon, by the way, because during the flood of Noah, no matter what succumbed to the waters, the olive branch survived.

It was the most important tree to the Israelites. I want that interest and strength as part of my name, too."

"Dad said you just asked if you could name me Stephanie Olive and he said sure. He didn't say you insisted," I said. "So your name is just . . . gone?" I asked. "Mother, I want to call Dad."

"No, not now, Stephanie. I want to show you my room and where the showers are."

"Where the *showers* are? You don't have your own place to bathe? But you have a room?" I had always thought of shelters like on TV, with cots lined up and stuff in a big room.

"No, I don't have my own shower, and yes, women have their own rooms so we don't get raped, so I'm glad you're here and you need to be sure to wear shower shoes, Stephanie, because they really are subpar when it comes to being clean. Sometimes there's hair in the drains and whatnot, so I have a caboodle for you with some flip flops and a robe."

"Oh well, thank you, Mother. You seem to have thought of just about fucking everything. I don't want to stay here! Does Katherine know about this?" I asked.

"Stephanie, please don't talk so trashy. You know that's very common and shows you can't think of anything more creative to say when you use words like that. It shows a lack of intelligence. And will you just give this a chance? Let's just go to sleep and talk more in the morning, okay? Now can we go to our room? Please?"

I rolled my eyes and nodded. We walked down to the end of the tiled hallway to the last door on the right, and there was a cardboard cutout in the shape of a star on her door covered in aluminum foil. I laughed and motioned to it. "Did you put that there?"

"Yes. It makes me feel more authentic that way," she answered.

She opened the door to a humble white room with a wire clothesline that hung across the back of the bed that held her beautiful suits. There was an ordinary twin bed in the center with a blanket my father's mother had made and a plain wooden nightstand to the side of it. Her worn-out Bible sat on top of it. There was one dim light in the center of the ceiling that had tiny black bugs gathered at the bottom of its shadowy dome. I let my bag fall to the floor in wonderment and mumbled, "Mother, you have a master's degree for goodness' sake." A small black rat emerged out of a pair of her heels that were lined up on the floor, hopped up onto the clothesline, and scurried into a hole in the wall. I jumped back and hollered, "Oh my God. I mean goodness. I'm sorry for saying 'God.'"

"Stephanie, don't worry about things like that," she said. "You have to look at the bigger picture, the spiritual realm. This is what I've always dreamt of. I grew up in beautiful homes with sparkling crystal and fine china. We wore the prettiest dresses, went to nice schools and churches, but it wasn't *real.* I didn't know God. I thought I did, but I didn't. I married the man I thought I could turn my life into a dream with. He met all my criteria, and I thought I was doing right and I tried to be a good mommy but I can't. I always dreamt of living poor because all that lying and struggling for *the dream* disgusted me. The hypocrisy of it disgusted me then and it disgusts me now. We had the look; we just didn't have the love. All those years, I was told by the church I was perfect, better than others. I'm nowhere near perfect . . . it was just a lie. Is that how Jesus acted? No. And now all that fraudulence is totally stripped away." Her face looked honest and lucid. "I don't have to fake things here. I don't have to pretend not to have made mistakes—big mistakes with consequences that will always be a part of me—and nobody asks me to."

I dug through her shower caboodle. "Mother, is this dog shampoo?"

"Uh-huh. It really takes great care of my dandruff. No more flakes," she said, and she shook her head.

"Mother, you do know this is not a long-term solution, right?" I asked.

"Well, Stephanie, you do understand that houses are really just a Western concept. There are many cultures that sleep under trees when it rains. They don't need to *hide* behind houses to feel safe," she said.

"Well, they may be a 'Western concept,' but in America, it's kind of considered deviant to sleep outside, isn't it? And I don't feel like wanting a house means anyone is *hiding* behind them," I said.

She leaned back against the wall and folded her arms. She leaned forward again and took me by the hands. Her childlike eyes pleaded with me. "Oh, Stephanie, I hope you can understand and support me on this. I know you've had far too much to adjust to already, but do you think you can find it in your heart to try? The people here really need me."

Just then, a quick rap at the door and a firm voice from the hallway said, "Okay, Kasow, it's ten p.m. Lights out."

"Listen, Stephanie. Let's get some rest. Tomorrow is a new day, okay?" She pulled back the covers of the worn-out bed and patted it for me to lie down. I slid in between the linens and the plastic mattress pad crackled as I did.

I nestled beside her, both of us in our clothes. And the night passed noisily with jerky bouts of sleep interrupted by the many voices of the shelter workers murmuring outside our thin door in the hallways as they made arrangements for today and tomorrow and forever. The traffic on the streets and the buses stopping and starting and the yelling from those who didn't make it in tonight, and the spirit of the homeless rose and fell from outside as the people roamed the city with their shopping carts full of broken lives. They were all eerie reminders that the wandering souls of the city's homeless were not resting . . . and whether inside here or outside there, by choice or force, my mother was now one of them and I prayed to God to make that not be so. I opened my eyes and our room was lit up by the lights outside, blinking from the bar across the street, and I looked over at her resting tranquilly despite the sounds of the scratching rats in the walls and the profound nighttime bustling that was happening all around us, and I understood that it *was* so . . . and I prayed to God again from the bottom of my heart to at least keep the weather warm until I could come up with a plan to help her and I tried to sleep again but failed. I began to grasp that my mother Lillian Walters, as I had known her, was now Kasow Toujours. She was gone again along with her name. And it felt like an innocent death.

Fear and Worry came traipsing into our room that night and even with all the noises outside they worked their way into my dreams like a couple a' thugs, all tattooed up and wanton. I told them to get out, fought and thrashed about with them and screamed that they had to go, said I was a child of God, a daughter of The King, and they couldn't have me. But Fear put his big, macho hairy arms around me and laughed, decayed teeth and all. Worry grabbed me and jostled me around a little and said he *belonged* right there with me; he thrusted himself hard up against my back, said he had a right. They stunk; smelled like stale smoke and humiliation, like their familiar brother, my first love, the brother who knew me best of all, Shame.

And they snuggled in close, stuck their sweaty bodies right up next to mine from the front and back, next to my mother and me in our small shelter bed, but she didn't wake and protect me from them. I prayed *Dear God, wake her up, make her get 'em away from me . . .* but she was sound asleep. They wrapped their strong, muscular arms around me even tighter and mocked me and whispered dirty things into my ears, breathing hot and bothered. They said that above any other guys in the whole wide world that they belonged there, that they loved me the *most*. And so because they said they loved me and made it sound like truth, that night I rolled over, opened my legs and heart, and breathed heavy with them, and gave myself away to them too.

• • •

"Stephanie! Hurry up! It's time for church!"

"I *am* hurrying, Mother. Church is right out in the lobby. I don't think it's going anywhere if I take five minutes to dry off," I said as I wrung the last bit of water from my hair, which had grown almost to my neck. I pulled back the moldy shower curtain and stepped out.

"You're going to miss the praise and worship and that's the best part. The music is really different here. Hurry up! I'm going on in. Come find me. Everyone who stays at The Jesus Center has to go to worship so if you don't come they'll kick me out," she said.

"I know that, Mother. I'm coming."

All the chairs had been taken from the dining hall and put into the lobby and the place was packed with men, women, and children of all ages. They were dressed in rags and oversized coats and shoes that were too big and floppy, but they were smiling and swaying back and forth with one another as they sang. People were standing with their arms raised high in the air and I found my mother on the second row in between an old hunched-over woman and a fat, bulbous-nosed man who looked like he had tartar sauce in his gray beard. Mother's eyes were closed and her hands were raised high and she was singing at the top of her lungs with the rest of the crowd, *"I am not afraid! I am not afraid! Cuz I'm walkin' in faith and victory, that's right, I'm walkin' in faith and victory!"*

The instrumental music terrified me. The beat of the drums felt Satanic and the guitar felt like a sin. "Mother, why aren't you afraid? This is the scariest place in the world! Why is everyone raising their arms?" I whispered.

"Because they're full of the holy ghost. Just hush," she answered. I looked back at the rest of the crowd. Their faces were smiling and peaceful and joyful and they continued to face the sky with their eyes closed as they swayed and rocked to the music.

The preacher came to the front and picked up a microphone. He wore a plaid button-up shirt and baggy shorts. He raised his hand in the air, "Pray with me, will y'all? Father God, we honor you, Father. We love ya, God, we lavish you with perfume Loooord, and with holy present fire. You are worthy, Father. Oh, you are worthy, worthy, worthy." He swayed his arms from side to side as he spoke.

And Mother started to mumble and mutter under her breath, "Tski wah miy sha," she said. "Ohmalama shabakiseeka." Her eyes were tightly closed.

"Mother, stop it!" I hissed. "What are you saying?"

She opened her eyes and smiled and whispered back, "I'm speaking in tongues. It's a gift of the holy ghost."

And others around us started muttering, too. "Hallelujah," someone said. "Praise you, Jehovah Nissi," someone else shouted. "Oh, Jehovah, you are our banner." A man with long black hair, a leather jacket, and knee-high black leather boots shouted from the back, "And Devil, Man! You better get thee behind us, dude!" And the crowd erupted in loud applause. A woman twirled up the aisle with a hula hoop decorated with streamers and began to dance and the loud, thumping music began again.

This is a sin. We're going to die and burn in hell.

"Hallelujah!" the preacher yelled, and the crowd began to jump up and down as if they were at a rock concert.

My eyes filled with tears and I began to feel hot and light in my face. "Mother, I feel dizzy." I tugged on her shirt, but she was overcome with emotion and was somewhere else. It was as if everyone around me was in a trance. "Father God, give us a miracle, Father God!" the preacher shouted.

I ran out of the lobby and into the bathroom and as I pushed the door open, the strong smell of urine wafted into my nose and I barely made it to the stall before I started vomiting into the already filthy toilet. I heaved and gagged and sputtered and cried alone in the stall until I thought I might actually die from the confusion and fear and in between each wave of vomit I cried, "I want my dad."

When I came back to our room, my mother was sitting on the bed. "I went to the bathroom to check on you, sweetheart, and I heard you crying for your father. I called him for you but he was leaving for the day. He said to keep your chin up and that it's not a good time for him to talk, but he'll call soon."

"Asshole," I said.

"I'm so sorry, Stephanie. I tried to pick out a good father for you. I failed you. You know if he can't be worshipped, he doesn't want anything to do with you. That's why he loves Katherine so much more than you or me. She worships him and you never did. You were always too strong for that," she said. And she handed me a cool rag. "Come lie down and let me blow some cold air on you. Are you sick?"

"No, Mother. I'm not sick. I'm scared to death. That church service was . . . terrible." I put the rag across my forehead and lay down beside her. "How can you like that kind of thing?"

"But different isn't always bad. Sometimes getting a good look at something from a different angle can be the best thing that ever happens to us. Learning that there are different ways to worship God and to live and to love can be very freeing. Stephanie, I love *you*. You know I will always be here for you. I have always just been so proud of you." She caressed my head. My nausea began to subside, and I snuggled in closer to her.

"Is there something else wrong, dear? You seem so sad. Your heart is so heavy. You know, if there's something else wrong, God will let me sense it in the spirit, because that's the power of God," she said.

I closed my eyes and buried my face into her. I wanted so badly to be close to her and to be locked up inside her love. It would be the most beautiful prison I could ever hope to find. I breathed in the smell of her skin and almost spoke but then thought better of it. "No, Mother, everything is fine. I'm just . . . confused."

"Stephanie, if you don't tell me, I won't know how to pray for you," she said. I leaned back and looked up into her eyes. They were full of hope and love and she smiled at me as the dim light overhead seemed to smooth any lines on her face. The roots of her hair were growing out to their natural color with strands of silver shining through the brown. She began to hum and scratched my back. She looked so . . . centered. I ran my hands through her hair. "I like this," I said.

She began to pray over me sweetly and softly, "Heavenly Father, soothe Stephanie's heart, Lord. Let her feel your love . . ."

"Well, Mother, stop just for a second. If I tell you, will you promise not to tell anyone?" I asked. "Mother you have to promise."

"Of course, sweetheart. You can trust me with absolutely anything. I'm your mother. If you can't trust me, who can you trust?"

"Well . . ." I propped myself up on my elbow and the washrag fell to the bed. I looked in her eyes and my words came spewing forth. I couldn't stop them. "Mother, please keep this in confidence, because I would never, ever want anything bad to happen. But did you hear about that fire at that elementary school? That someone had burned it down? And do you know my friend Luke?"

Trusted her. Told.

. . . . .

PART 3

My Name Is Now
My Children.
Always.

THE NEXT MORNING, BACK IN my own bed, I woke up to an empty house and someone knocking hard on the door. I answered it, and the man held out a badge. "Stephanie, hi, I'm Detective Deloney from the Houston Fire Marshal. I'd like to ask you a few questions about Lakeview Elementary School. Would you mind coming downtown with me, darlin'?" I looked outside at his car.

"Well, I don't really think I can help you," I said, staring straight into his eyes. "I don't know anything about that. And I'm not dressed to go downtown."

"You didn't hear that it burned down a while ago?" he asked.

"No sir, I hadn't. Did it?" I asked.

"Stephanie, why don't you come get in the car with me and let's go downtown and have a little chit chat. Your boyfriend, Luke, is going to get a little visit today, and if you want to help him, you won't lie." He stood waiting for me on our front porch in his cowboy hat and boots. He looked like Boss Hog, with his big pot belly.

"I need to get my purse," I said. I was shaking inside.

"You won't need a purse darlin'." He spit off the porch and into our flower bed. "Throw on some shoes and come with me, please." I slipped on my shoes and followed him out to his car and he opened the back door and put me inside.

When we got down to the station, my mother was waiting in the lobby reading a Hebrew encyclopedia and a guide to understanding the Bible. She was dressed in a suit and heels and her makeup was garish. She waved and smiled a big smile when she saw me. "Stephanie, I'm so sorry, but I had to do what I had to do! When you moved back in with your father without saying goodbye, you left me no choice but to do the right thing. And this is best for Luke! Just tell the truth. He'll thank you, baby. Just do the right thing," she said. I glared at her as I passed by. Detective Deloney led me down the hallway into a small room and I did nothing but focus on telling my bottom lip not to quiver.

"Stephanie, your boyfriend is an arsonist. Did you know that?" he asked. I stared down at the table and thought of Luke's face, his beautiful face, his wide eyes, his soothing voice, and his loving arms. I sat and remembered his bed, how warm his touch was, how much I needed his friendship. I didn't look up. I didn't speak.

"Stephanie, are you listening, little lady? You've got way too much going for you to go to jail with a guy like that. Now what do you know about him burning down this school?" He was talking to me, but I wasn't listening. I seethed inside at my mother. "Stephanie?" he said. He sighed and shook his head and waited for me to speak. But I couldn't speak. I sat still and looked down at my feet.

"I don't know what you're talking about. I want my dad," I said. "I'm fourteen."

"Young lady, we'll get to that later. Do you know what it means to hide an arsonist? Do you understand that you will go to jail?" He leaned in closer to where I could smell his rotten breath. "Do you understand that Luke has raped you? There's a mighty big age difference between the two of you according to the law, and if you can just help us solve this mystery of this here fire, I'm sure the District Attorney would be appreciative and just look the other way on all the rest. All we really want to know about is the fire, darlin'," he said. I looked up at him and met his eyes hearing his threat loud and clear.

"Nobody raped me," I tripped over my words and my hands started to shake and I couldn't keep my lips from quivering. "Can I call my dad? Or should I like have a lawyer?"

He handed me a large yellow notebook and pen. "Well now," he laughed and coughed thick phlegm into a handkerchief and looked at it before folding it and putting it in his pocket. "The state of Texas says it was rape even if a girl like you loved every minute of it, which I have no doubt you did." I closed my eyes and put my head in my hands.

"You don't want to talk? Writing's just as good a way to tell folks what happened. Write it all down, darlin'. Tell what you know. It's the right thing to do so we can get that boy Luke some help. He needs your help, darlin'. He'll probably thank you for the rest of his life. And I'm sure you're mighty eager to get back in school. I bet we can work something out with the state truancy officer to get you back on track where you belong so you don't end up losing the whole year. Maybe that way . . ." he pushed the paper across the desk closer to me and smiled, "you won't end up in jail yourself, and you'll still get to go to high school and maybe even graduate with your friends. Don't be scared, little lady. First let's sign this nice affidavit swearing to tell the truth." His yellow nails had ridges in them as he held the pen for me to take. For the first time in my life, I swore. I picked up the pen and slowly started to write.

I, Stephanie Walters . . . he's a good person . . . my friend Luke . . . swear this is true . . . yes he burned it down . . . no, I'm not sure why . . . he's not raping me . . . we are just friends . . . no one was with him . . . he never touched me . . .

I filled the pages with my testimony against Luke because I didn't know what else to do.

• • •

My mother was gone from the lobby when I finished, and the fire marshal drove me home. My father was waiting for me at the door. "Stephanie, I spoke to your mother. I know everything," he began. "Luke has been taken to a psychiatric hospital where he can get help. Somebody told him the police were coming for him and he drank Lysol and tried to light himself on fire. He's not in jail. You did the right thing. I know that was hard." He reached out to hug me but I walked past him and pushed his arms away.

"Dad, I didn't do the right thing! Mother turned him in because she was mad at me for not moving in with her at the shelter! I never would have told anyone. And now I don't even get the chance to say goodbye!" My voice shook and I was furious at myself for crying in front of him. He reached out and held me tightly and this time I let him. I shook in the arms of my father and cried until the tears were all out of me. He hugged me and the power of his comfort was a beginning of solace for the loss of Luke. "This is twisted," I sobbed.

"I know," my dad replied. "I know."

Three Years Later

WHEN SIMONE PULLED UP IN her little blue sports car for school that Monday morning, I tossed my backpack in the back seat and slid in next to Valerie.

Simone pulled out of the driveway. "We're not going to school today," she said, rounding the corner out of the neighborhood.

"No, guys. I can't keep skipping. I need to start getting my shit together. I'm not going to summer school again because of truancy this year. I've gotta get ready for the SAT. I can't skip anymore," I said.

"Yeah, but we had fun all those times skipping. There's nothing going on at school anyways," Simone said.

"I have to be there. If I get less than three absences, I won't have to take my finals. Drop me off at school," I said.

"Nope. We're going to Galveston."

Simone fixed her lip gloss in the mirror as she drove. Her blonde curls blew as she opened her sunroof. "It's senior skip day."

"Yeah, well, I'm not a senior. Juniors aren't even welcomed there by ya'll. That would be totally lame of me. Plus, I don't even have my swimsuit. Drop me off at school," I said.

"We'll steal you one," she said. "Murdock's has horrible security."

Valerie struggled to re-light her cigarette while the wind from her open window blew her cherry out over and over again. She cupped her hand and buried her head down and finally got it lit. "Simone, lay off. If she wants to go to school, let's drop her off." She turned back and looked at me. "Go to school, Steph. It's okay. We've had plenty of days at the beach." Valerie, forever the glue.

Simone sighed and did a U-turn in the middle of the road and headed us towards high school. "Fine, goody-goody. But you only live once."

They pulled up to the end of the school parking lot and let me get out and walk from there. As they pulled away, I kicked the dirt. I wished I had gone with them. It was a beautiful day for the beach. There was a cool breeze and the sun wasn't too hot. It was the kind of day that would fool you into thinking you didn't need sunscreen.

The school day droned on and on, and tons of people were absent. I should've gone. I really was becoming a goody-goody. But damn, I needed to graduate. The teachers were apathetic that day and probably wished they were at the beach too. I walked into my sixth period English class, and my teacher made strong eye contact with me. What did I do? I've been here one day.

Standing beside my desk was our student body president. "Hey Stephanie, can I talk to you outside a second?" I looked over at my teacher. She nodded her permission. We walked out into the hallway as the students shuffled into their classrooms just as the bell rang. He motioned me over between the lockers. "Stephanie. I need to tell you something, and you are not going to like it." He stared deep into my eyes. I looked around nervously wondering what was going on. The time it took him to get out his next sentence seemed like years, but I know it was only seconds.

"Stephanie, an hour ago, at a hotel in Galveston, Valerie Rodriguez leaned over the balcony of her hotel room and fell thirty feet and died. I'm so sorry," he said.

I stood there and shifted my weight around and furrowed my brow, going through what felt like files in my mind. "Who is Valerie Rodriguez?" I finally asked. "I don't know anyone by that name."

He cocked his eyebrow. "Valerie Rodriguez. Your best friend, Valerie."

"Who is Valerie?" I asked. I was very confused. I knew he was trying to tell me something, but I had no idea what. "Who is that? What am I supposed to be reacting to?"

He stammered nervously. "Stephanie, Valerie Rodriguez is your best friend. She went to the beach today and leaned over her hotel balcony. I don't know for sure, but I think maybe drugs were involved. It was an accident, but she slipped and fell over the balcony and died. Simone was with her and saw her fall. Valerie."

I stared blankly at him. My mind was vacant of her face. I couldn't place her.

He began to shift around and looked alarmed. "Valerie. Valerie Rodriguez. Your friend."

Blank. "I can't picture anyone named Valerie. Do I have a friend by that name?" I asked. "I don't know her." I stood staring at him and searched and searched and searched my mind but, for the life of me, I could not picture who he was talking about. We stood awkwardly in the hallway and then I realized what was happening. There was a mistake, a mix up. I smiled because now words were making sense and I understood what was going on. "Oh! Okay, okay, I know who you are talking about. You are talking about a girl named Valerie who is not my friend. That mean girl? A junior? Well, I don't know her." I pictured in my mind a girl with long blonde hair who I barely knew and had only seen a few times.

"No, Stephanie. I don't think there is a girl who is a junior named Valerie. This was Valerie Rodriguez, the senior. Your friend. Stephanie, are you alright?"

"Yes, I'm fine. But I guess we need to get this cleared up right now." I still couldn't picture anyone named Valerie Rodriguez or any friend's face for that matter. I did not know anyone by that name. I marched down the hallway and flew down the stairs headed towards the counselor's office. I burst in the door and went straight past the secretary, who didn't try to stop me. I went into my guidance counselor's office and she sat behind her desk. "Who is Valerie Rodriguez?" I demanded.

"Stephanie why don't you sit down . . ." she began.

"I don't want to sit down. I want to know who the hell Valerie is. I only know one person by that name and she is a blonde mean girl who is a junior. Or was."

The woman motioned for someone to go get the school nurse. I turned around and saw the nurse coming towards me with a gentle smile on her face. "Stephanie, let's sit down," she said, but her words were jumbled up.

"Who is she? There are two Valeries at this school, yes? One who is my friend, and one who is a junior and is mean. I don't know this girl who died. The one who died was not my friend. Was it?" I asked. They stared at me. "WAS IT?" I could not piece all this together. I tried again to picture her. I couldn't think of Valerie's face, only another girl, a girl I had only seen a few times. "I don't understand what y'all are telling me. What's happening?" I let the nurse guide me down to a chair.

"Stephanie," she looked kindly and calmly into my eyes. I squinted to make out the nurse's face but she was blurry. "The young girl who died was your friend, Valerie Rodriguez. There are not two girls by that name at this school. The girl who died was *your* Valerie." And she opened up a binder with all the kids' names at our school, and went to Valerie's name and it was highlighted. She brought the binder over to me so I could see her name written. "See? We only had one student by that name."

I leaned across her desk and read it, trying to process. I sat back and pulled my hand over my mouth. "My friend? With the long black hair? My friend?" I whispered.

I closed my eyes and saw Valerie's face, her brown eyes twinkling. My Valerie was careful. Deliberate. Practical. Sensible. She wouldn't ever lean over a balcony.

She wasn't always careful.

I flashed back to her climbing over the wall at the concert when we were kids but just as soon as the memory came to me, it left.

"Yes. Your friend," she answered. Then I realized what she told me was true. I pictured the unspeakable and how it must have happened and Simone watching her fall to her death.

"I need to go home," I said. I turned around and walked out the door, walked through the hallway and swung the door open outside and they didn't stop me. I walked down the road, faster, faster, towards home. The house was stale and empty with everyone at work. I dialed Simone's number, frantic to talk to her, but got a busy signal. I climbed in my bed and pulled the covers up over my head, hiding from the world in the darkness my bedspread provided. I went somewhere far away in my mind, to a stage where I was an actor in front of the spotlights, but the audience was darkened and I could not see them, but they could see me. I blinked and the spotlights turned off and I swept the stage of my mind and closed the curtains quickly, wiping out all thoughts of Valerie. I fell into a sleep undisturbed by the rain that hit my bedroom window.

As I slept hard and deep a thunderstorm began to rage outside and lightning flashed in my bedroom behind my closed eyes. In my sleep I could hear the voices of my dad and Gail downstairs, and I was conscious that the electricity had gone out because the air was unmoving, and that hours and hours were passing, taking me from evening to nighttime. The house was quiet but for the sound of the heavy wind and rain outside and I awoke and remembered that Valerie was dead, and I made my way downstairs. Gail was sitting on the couch with candles lit all around, the room glowing and still.

Once more I couldn't remember what Valerie looked like. "Gail, where are my things that Dad packed when I moved in with Mother?"

"There's a box in the garage," she said.

I walked into the garage and saw the stacks of boxes with my name on them, trying to picture her face, her beautiful face, but I couldn't. I had just seen her yesterday, but I couldn't picture what she looked like now. I reached on top of the stack and took down the first box and ripped it open. The rain beat down outside and the wind blew into the hot garage cooling me down.

As I sifted through old tapes and clothes and shoes I found a picture of the three of us together, Simone and Valerie and me, and something inside me cracked open and I suddenly became terrified of my dear, sweet, funny, beautiful friend lying alone in a cold morgue. I could picture her now, everything about her, and I saw her alone in the back room of the quiet funeral home and thought to myself that it would be a scary night to be alone in a funeral home with a thunderstorm like this.

I feverishly looked for more pictures but I couldn't find any. I pictured her dead in her coffin, or dead in a bag. *Oh, Valerie. What did you do?* I looked up and Gail was in the doorway. She walked over to me and guided me with my hands full of pictures away from the ripped-open box.

I choked out the words, "I can't find our pictures."

She guided me out of the damp garage and into the living room and we sat on the couch as the light from the candles flickered on the ceiling and walls, a reminder of movement, of life—a reminder of the light in Valerie that was now gone from me forever. Gail gently wrapped me up in a blanket. She spoke carefully, "Stephanie I am so sorry that

Valerie died." And she hugged me and I let her. I let her wrap me up in her arms and I let myself cry in front of her and we sat alone in the living room, we two, and she held me. She brought me warm tea and a tissue, and she stroked my face like a mother. She whispered, "Shhh, you are safe. I know you are afraid. Valerie. Don't be afraid. Valerie is safe. Everyone is safe."

"But we don't know that. She may be afraid," I said. "What if she feels scared? Or alone? Or what if they didn't take care of her?"

"Valerie is in a satin-lined coffin," she said. "She's not looking around or frightened. Her eyes are closed in peaceful rest. They probably even rolled her hair. She is dry and she cannot hear the rain. She is not afraid and neither should you be."

I pulled away from her and looked into my stepmother's thoughtful eyes, my lip trembling. The tears poured now in thick, heavy streams down my cheeks. The salt poured in through my mouth and down onto my chest, wetting my shirt with tears. Gail wiped them again and again and continued. "The people at the funeral home have already put makeup on her. Her eyes are lined, her mascara is on, and her lips are colored with her pretty gloss. Stephanie, they've put hot rollers in her hair and put her in her pretty white dress, you know the one she wore with her jean jacket and boots? The one with the lace? Her body is safe and secure."

I sobbed, "How do you know?" The thunder clapped outside. The clouds were angry.

"Because I know. She is not hurting; she is not feeling empty or alone anymore." Her words were like a smooth, healing salve to my heart. It hurt to let her touch me, but I did. I couldn't help it; I needed her love, the love of a mother even though she was a stranger to me, even though I had shown her nothing but hatred. We sat in the flickering candlelight and the rain poured powerfully down outside, pelting the windows with music like yesterday having been and gone. My beautiful friend was dead.

She told me that even though Valerie had died with her last moments being fearful, that she died knowing I loved her. My tears poured slowly down, one after another. They covered me in water. They covered the world. Gail told me that night about her views on reincarnation. She said I had known Valerie before in another life, maybe as a daughter or a mother or sister or friend. I knew it was different than what I had been taught in church, but her words soothed me. She said maybe she was even a husband or son. She said that she was in my life to teach me, and that I was in her life to teach her, too. She talked and talked, honestly, hopefully, and gently to me in the darkness, the golden candlelight shining in her eyes, showing her love and goodness from within. She said I would meet her again one day. She said our time together was never wasted. She said Valerie had learned everything that she was sent here to learn and that she had taught everything she came to teach.

She said if there was anything unfinished at all between us that we would be even better at communicating the next time. She closed her eyes and took my hands in hers and began to pray, but she prayed to Mother, Father, God, Creator of Love and Light. I was so scared not to pray to the only God I knew, the God of Fear, but I was too sad to fight it . . . I let her pray for me in her own way. "God of Love, please wrap my daughter up in white light for healing, God The Good . . . she is grieving. Please wrap her up in your pale pink light of love so that her heart will go on loving and keeping the memory of her friend Valerie safe in her hands."

As she continued to talk and pray and smooth my blanket, I sat still and willingly with my grief and let it come. I let it wrap its dark arms around me; I let it look into my eyes and stare, and the sorrow overtook me, and it felt sincere and real and it *ached*.

"Gail, I don't want to go to her funeral. I don't want to see her dead," I said.

"She understands. You don't have to," she said.

The rain tapped the window and the glow of the room made me drowsy. Gail sat in silence beside me on the couch and wiped my tears and told me she loved me until I drifted off to sleep again but I couldn't answer her. But for the first time since my mother had left, I felt safe within the walls of what used to be our home.

CHAPTER

26

Then the devil took Jesus to the holy city and had him stand on the highest point of the temple. "If you are the Son of God," he said, "throw yourself down." For it is written: "He will command his angels concerning you, and they will lift you up in their hands, so that you will not even strike your foot against a stone."

DAD AND GAIL WERE AWAY at the beach for the day, and even though I didn't have a license, I had taken his car to go visit my mother at her friend's house. As I drove, I pictured Valerie's angels being commanded "concerning" her after she fell off that balcony, lifting her up just before she hit the hard parking lot causing the stone gravel to scatter, giving her wings or causing swirling air underneath her so that she could fly, but they hadn't. I let my eyes glaze over as I watched the road and I reminded myself of what Gail had told me to say when my mind started trying to make sense of something that I couldn't.

I cannot control the day that someone dies.

I cannot control the day that someone dies.

I had forgotten that I wasn't going to the shelter this time, when an aging apartment complex sprawled its tired façade to my right and I passed it by. As I drove down the city streets, it felt like I had gone too far, so I checked the map. That had been the right place. I made a U-turn and pulled into the parking lot.

The complex was run down. The dirty windows were covered in wrinkled aluminum foil and the balconies were the dumping ground for everything from tricycles to dead plants to drying laundry. I stepped out of the car and raised my sunglasses.

"Hi, sweetie!" Mother smiled and waved as she crossed the parking lot. She wore a bright purple suit and Kelly-green high heels. "Where is your dad? Didn't he drive you?"

"Mother, why are you so dressed up? No, he let me borrow his car."

She glanced around like she didn't believe me and that he was going to jump out and surprise her from behind the car. "Did you get your license?"

"No, I haven't been able to get a lift to get down to the DPS. But almost. I still just have a permit. That's good enough. Mother, this place has seen better days," I said, shutting the car door behind me. "Did they make you leave the shelter?"

"Oh, Stephanie, don't be such a killjoy. No, I didn't have to leave. I'm just staying here every now and then because sometimes my new friend Anwar and I study the Bible literally all night long and they have a curfew there, even for longtime residents. I can't wait for you to meet Anwar." She took my overnight bag and led the way through the complex. The cracked concrete veins of a dried-up fountain spoke of a time long past when folks actually might've wanted to sign a lease at this place.

"Who's Anwar?" I asked. We climbed the cement steps and I held on to the stair rail for support and accidentally touched something yellow and gooey. "I thought you were visiting a friend, like, a woman."

"Stephanie, Anwar is brilliant. He's twenty-four years old, from Jordan, and living here with his two nephews on a student visa." We walked up the three flights of stairs that overlooked the parking lot and waited outside the scuffed door of the apartment as she struggled to find the right key. A cat peered from around the corner and stared at us. I wasn't about to pick it up, although it was obvious that was what it wanted. A young man with a beard opened the door and his eyes lit up when he saw us. He threw his arms around my mother, twice his age. "Kasow! Beautiful Leedy! And this must be Steph-ah-nie!" And he threw his hairy arms around me and hugged me too hard.

We stepped inside the apartment and the air became thick as we added to the amount of bodies in the small place. The whole apartment was dark. I hissed in my mother's ear, "There's no electricity here, Mother. Or *furniture*."

"Not now!" she hissed. "Be polite!"

We stood in the living room and he introduced me to his two nephews, but the three of them were the same age and they looked nothing alike. Anwar presented me with a present wrapped in paper covered in multi-colored balloons. "Welcome, Stephanie!" he said, grinning ear to ear. I stood nervously and my mother nodded her head for me to open it. I opened the box, and inside was a real working, color-changing LED mood lamp with flowers that lit up and changed colors.

"It ees magical and stunning, yes?" he asked. I noticed his back tooth was gone.

"Mother, I am not spending the night here. Forget it," I whispered in her ear.

She whispered back in mine, "Stephanie, don't screw this up for me. Take the damn gift and say thank you."

I looked at my mother as she stood taller than him in her heels, which dug into the cheap carpet. I started to sweat under my arms. "Yes, it's great." I looked around for some place to put it, but there was no place. "Mother, will you hold it while I go to the bathroom?"

She smiled like an idiot and took the package from me and I went into the bathroom. I forgot there was no electricity and tried to turn on the light. I opened the window and sat down on the toilet lid, thinking about how far my mother had fallen from our suburban life and about Luke and how pissed I was that Mother had lied to me. I must've been in there awhile, because she banged on the door, "Stephanie! Are you okay in there?"

I banged back. "Yes, Mother, I'm fine! I'll be out in a second, geez!" And I put my hand against the door and locked it as she tried to open it. *This is going to be okay. This is not that weird.* I stood up and opened the lid to go to the bathroom, but the entire commode was filled up to the rim with feces. It was packed in tight and dry to where nothing else could fit, and the smell like death hit me in the face like a wall. I slammed it shut and turned towards the mirror. I turned the handle to splash cold water on my face but no water came out. *Oh my God. What the fuck is happening?*

When I rejoined them in the living room, my mother had her arms around Anwar. "Sweetheart, do you think you can take Ferras and Amit to the store and buy a few snacks? Anwar and I can stay here. Stay gone about an hour, okay?"

I rolled my eyes, sickened, and followed the two nephews out the front door. *This is so confusing!* We drove around Houston looking for a place to buy snacks. We rode with the windows down and the gaseous vapors of the nearby refineries were a fresh fragrance compared to what I had just smelled in the bathroom. They spoke to one another in a foreign language that I didn't understand, but when they offered me a cigarette, I took it. The balmy air blew over the sound of the radio while I smoked. Finally, we found a little Mexican market that was open, and we bought candy and took it home to my mother and Anwar.

As she walked me to the car that evening, I gathered the nerve. "Mother, I wish you wouldn't have turned in Luke back then. You don't know what he meant to me. I could've helped him. Now I don't even know where he is or what happened to him. I didn't even get a chance to say goodbye." We reached the car and I threw my bag in the back seat and turned to face her.

"Well that was a very difficult decision for me to make, Stephanie, but any mother would have done that. I'm not sorry he's out of your life or that he went to jail, and I think as enough time goes by, you won't be either. He was dangerous, Stephanie. That was hard on me too, you know," she said.

"But Mother, this isn't about you. This is about the way you lied to me to gain my trust. And you did it because you felt like I chose Dad."

She stared at me blankly. "Well, now is probably just as good a time as any to tell you that I need to throw a wrinkle in some things. I'm leaving the country to go to Brazil to be a full-time missionary. I want you to come with me. And if you don't want to come, but you'd like to donate to the cause, you can give the money to Anwar."

"Mother, what are you talking about? Who do you know in Brazil?" I asked.

"There are some folks from the shelter who know someone who's building a church there. Anwar is young, and he wants a baby, and Brazil is a perfect, peaceful place to raise a family."

I didn't know Kasow. This wasn't Lily. Kasow was different, bolder, wilder—Kasow was reckless. I took a swig of my warm soda.

"Stephanie, let me ask you something. Do you think Katherine would carry a baby for me and Anwar? I've been trying to think of ways to get closer to Katherine."

I couldn't help but laugh and spewed my soda out. Her eyes got wide like I had been rude, and I wiped my mouth with the back of my hand. "Mother, don't." Katherine hadn't spoken to my mother since she left. She wouldn't visit her, wouldn't take her calls, and she marked each letter my mother sent "Return to Sender." Katherine had embraced Gail as her mother now.

Since their divorce, Katherine was happier than she'd ever been.

"No, I'm serious, Stephanie. Hear me out. I was thinking. Katherine by nature is a nurturer, don't you think?"

"I don't know, Mother." I looked over in the distance at the Ship Channel Bridge.

"Well," she continued on, "I think she is a nurturer. And Anwar and I have decided to have a baby. But I can't have children anymore because I've had my tubes tied. Sweetheart, do you know what that means?"

I whirled around and looked at her. "Of course I know what that means. I'm not an idiot. What the hell are you talking about?" I asked.

She just kept talking like she hadn't heard me. "Katherine has those wide birthing hips, you know. Do you think she would be open to carrying Anwar's baby for me? She loves kiddos, and I think it could really help things between her and me a lot. You know, to have that bonding experience together. Don't you?" I stared at the blinking sign in front of the apartment complex instead of looking at her.

"Are you out of your fucking mind?! Because I *really* need to know! Mother, Katherine is not going to carry a baby for you and Anwar. What would that mean? That he would have sex with her? Mother, that's sick." I opened the car and got in.

"Stephanie, I resent that. I really do. Of course he wouldn't have sex with her. We would use a turkey baster. I'm going to ask her when I see her next."

"Oh no, you're not."

"Oh yes I am."

"Oh no, you're not! Mother, I'm cutting it off here. You need to get professional help and until you do, don't call me."

"Stephanie, don't go!" And she reached inside the car and for the first time in my life, she threw her arms around me. She sounded panicky and she spoke directly into my ear—it was the voice of Lillian, the voice I had known as a little girl, the voice I thought I could trust. "Please don't go, my darling Stephanie. I need you so much." Her voice became a whisper. "I cannot live without you. Please don't go."

It was the first time that I had stopped hugging first. Her face was childlike, and the sharp pain in my chest was deep. It took everything I had, but I closed the car door and drove away. I looked in my rearview mirror at her standing there in the parking lot; she looked thin and frail. I understood that she had set herself on a trajectory of nomadic chaos that would never, never, never change. I had to disengage or spiral down with her, and so I made a decision that someday soon, someday very soon, I would save myself, but I wasn't sure when or how.

WINTER CAME AND WENT AND what should have been the happy stir of spring instead got all over me in a sad and silent way because nothing was changing with her. Mother was back at the shelter full time and Luke was out of the jail and hospitals. Last I heard, he was in an apartment across town doing well. He had tried to call me several times, but each time, Gail answered the phone before I did and she told him she was "insulating" me from him. Not isolating. Insulating. And for whatever reason, I let her get away with that.

On our first visit back together, Mother and I lay in the bed at the shelter after church. "So where is Anwar?" I asked.

"Well, I had a dream where God revealed to me that he had cash bundles of ten thousand-dollar increments in a suitcase and a secret wife. I think he may be a thief and an imposter. I think he may be planning to rob some banks. I don't think those are his nephews at all. I think they are his accomplices. I also have a feeling Anwar may not be his real name and that he may be fleeing from someone. I called the police, but they don't believe me because I'm homeless."

I rolled my eyes, but she didn't see.

"Stephanie, you've just been through too much, sweetheart. Thank you for telling me to get help. You were really right. My weekly sessions with Dr. Leatherman are helping so much." She rubbed my back and her hands were warm. "In fact, there's something I've been working on in counseling that I want to share with you too."

"What?" I asked.

She looked away like she had changed her mind. "Mother, you know I won't tell anyone," I said. "I won't judge you."

"Oh, I know. That's what I love about you most, that we have always been able to share this way. Dr. Leatherman says I should write some things down in a journal. So I've begun writing a memoir because I'd like to tell my truth as it really happened and not have any more confusion, any more secrets."

"Oh, and you want me to read it? Because honestly, Mother, I can't tell what's the truth and what's a lie anymore and in fact I'm going to even give up trying. Or are you about to give me some outlandish recipe for me to pass along to Katherine, to cure her pimples from afar in an effort to make y'all closer, like a mixture of Prell shampoo and Malt-O-Meal?"

I regretted it the moment I said it, because she really was trying to change. Her face was beautiful and innocent, like the Lillian I knew well.

She forgave the insult. "Yes, actually, I'm going to have you read it, and I'd like to talk to you about it if you don't mind. Do you mind? After everything you've put me through, I would think you could at least give me that much."

"Mother, fine. Do I have to read the whole thing? I'm tired."

The lights flickered overhead. "Lights out," someone from down the hall said. Mother got up and turned off the lights. We both slid under the covers and she snuggled in tight behind me. She turned on a small bedside lamp that caused the room to glow and she handed me her memoir.

"No, just start here," she said. "Good night, Stephanie. I love you."

I started to read. Her words were scribbled through at times, sometimes clear at others, but I was able to hear her voice through all of them, and I knew in my heart that what I was reading was the truth.

> I used to skip school a lot and spend all my free time with my boyfriend, Craig. Craig was the love of my life, the flat-out love of my life. He was so sweet. He had this wavy blond hair that he kept slicked back, like he was James Dean. His face was just so sweet. He was just so sweet. And cute! Ah. He was so, so cute. His frame was really thin. Thin, thin, like thinner than mine, and he walked with knowledge of the world around him that made me want to follow him. I trusted him right away. I fell in love with him almost at first glance, and he understood the secrets of my soul.
>
> He respected me when I was quiet; he never pried, never dug into my business. And he exposed me to the music of John Lennon and The Beatles which was just something totally forbidden where I came from. We would lie arm in arm in the woods after school, talking about the world and our hopes for the future. I just loved talks like that.
>
> I miss love like that. Craig wanted to be an astronaut, and when he talked about space and the stars and planets, I closed my eyes and pictured us exploring the universe together. I wanted to marry him. He was . . . such a dear friend.

Luke had been a dear friend, too. I pictured his face next to mine; we had talked about stars and planets, too, and I closed my eyes and wished him peace and hope and love and safety wherever he was. My mother slept soundly, and this time, the city noises outside didn't scare me as much. I kept reading.

Even though I loved my parents, in many ways my heart was gone, far out of their reach. It had been that way for so long. It's sad how hearts get, when they just get out of reach. I was biding my time until high school graduation. I just made a decision to bide my time. Of course, I was hoping to marry Craig, but he was Methodist, so I wasn't really sure how we could. How does Victor Black's daughter expect to get away with marrying a Methodist? They don't even believe anything, you know? I mean, they don't even believe anything scriptural. Craig knew a little bit about God and the Bible, and I just told myself he could be taught and converted. Anyone could be taught. It's not a fault not to know, you just have to be taught.

But of course, I was expected to attend Abilene Christian University and become a teacher, and he was more than eager to serve his country after high school in the Vietnam War. Craig said he wanted to go to the war and fight, that he would die there if he had to, that he loved America that much. That's of course different from Paul, who huffed cleaning supplies and dust and self-induced an asthma attack an hour before his draft meeting so that he would be deemed unable to go. You couldn't go if you had asthma. And it was a cowardly choice Paul made, but I can't say it was wrong, because if he had gone, I might not have Stephanie and Katherine, and of course my girls mean everything to me.

Paul couldn't have handled that war anyways. But then again, what boy could? One Sunday afternoon our whole house was napping before Sunday night services, and my mom knocked on my bedroom door. She had never shown me that respect before, so I was totally taken aback. She opened the door slowly and tiptoed into my room, closing it carefully behind her. She was in her gown, with her black satin robe tied neatly around her thick waist. I can still picture her great big bosom drooped down to her sash, and it reminded me that she was just a mom and a woman herself, just a person, just a woman, a strong woman, a powerful woman, but just a woman. That day, I could see the beginning of gray where her roots met her scalp, and the lines of years of submission to Daddy were drawn deep across her forehead. That was back in the day where women didn't question their husbands. Especially preacher's wives. You just didn't do it. It just was not done. She asked if we could talk, but we had to talk in whispers, so we didn't wake anyone up.

She said, "Lily, I've noticed something about you. You are gaining weight. You have to wear your skirts unbuttoned. Are you eating much more than before?"

I said, "No, not really, Mom. Why do you care, anyways? Are you embarrassed by me?" I lay back down and stared at the ceiling, wondering why I ever thought she was here to try to relate to me. I said, "I'm sorry if I'm a fat pig."

She whispered, "No, no, Darling. It's nothing like that. You are a lovely girl. I'm just wondering . . . are you exercising?"

I said I hadn't felt like it, and that I'd been having headaches. But I knew it was more than headaches, because I had also been tired, like a tired I had never felt before, you know, there was no tired like it and I threw up every time I got outside in the heat.

She asked me how long I'd been having headaches, and when I told her it had been about five months she sat for what seemed like a long time looking at me from the edge of my bed. I suddenly felt self-conscious and pulled the blanket up to my neck.

"Lily," she stammered, as she gently pulled the blanket down, revealing the bump that used to be my flat stomach. "Lily, when was your last menstrual cycle?"

"Mom, that's none of your business!" I hissed, sitting up and slitting my eyes at her. I wanted to scream at her! But I was too afraid to wake anyone up. I knew when my last period was; I'm not trying to be crude but I hadn't had a period since I met Craig. We had spent many moments in each other's arms on a blanket in the woods, loving each other, laughing together, making plans for our future, but we only made love once. It had only happened once.

I could see her face trying to piece things together as she rubbed my leg, you know how faces change? When people feel sorry or sad or when the Holy Spirit tells them something, and you just know deep down, you know how your face changes at a time like that? Well hers did that. She sat calmly and I watched her eyes, and even though I did not feel like I knew her well, her blood was my blood. She was my mom, and I could tell by looking at her, although she said not one word, not one word, I could tell that she was thinking hard and counting. I pulled my leg away from her and turned to face the wall. "It's none of your business," I said again because what else could I say? She stood up and left, closing my door behind her.

As the days and weeks went on, she watched me carefully, without comment, from the corner of her eye as I came and went. My stomach just got bigger and it got harder to hide. I hid it under baggy sweaters and Craig's letter jacket; he was a senior, did I mention that he was a senior with his whole life ahead? He had given me his class ring to wear around my neck, too, and it now rested on the top of my stomach instead of hanging like it used to. Dad never even noticed, he was so busy preparing sermons and writing letters to the editor, writing columns and studying, studying, studying Scripture. He was forever serving our church, taking people here and there, visiting the prisons, visiting the hospitals, taking meals to the sick that Mom had cooked; even prostitutes had been known to turn from their wicked ways when he preached the Gospel to them. He was a minister of the true kind; he loved his church, he lived for his church. He preached from the pulpit about the law of love, that love was the highest value the church held, and about how God loved his people. But we were scared of him. I was scared of him, too. I think everyone in the family was scared of him. I know Mom was scared of him. We feared his anger, his physical and mental blows, and his wrath. His wrath was horrible. He was trapped in his legalism. He was in a prison of sorts.

One weekend, when both Mom and Dad were out, I was looking at my protruding stomach and I felt something like butterflies inside of it. I thought of Craig and his hands running all over my body. I hope this doesn't sound awful or crude, but he was smiling down at me with the blue sky behind his smiling face. I pictured him just a few short months from then in army fatigues kissing me goodbye to go fight a war in the jungle. I can't imagine how scared he must've been. How scared all those young boys must have been. I told him to hide, to just hide in the bushes, to put his head down behind the leaves, you know, that if trouble came looking for him, to fight, of course, but otherwise, just hide and don't go looking for trouble.

When my mom pulled back in the driveway, she screeched her brakes in the garage and knocked over the trash can with the hood of the car. When she came in the house, I was sitting at the kitchen table. Her cheeks were red and her mascara was smeared. She looked like she had been crying, and I was shocked because that was the first time I had ever seen my mom cry. Ever.

She looked flustered. "Lily, pack a bag. We're going on a trip," she said, as she buzzed around the living room straightening throw pillows and folding loose newspapers.

I asked her where we were going and she started stammering her words, like "We are going . . . We are going visiting. Yes, we are going visiting."

I said, "Visiting who?" Now I was getting annoyed. "Is Dad coming with us?"

She said, "It's 'whom,' dear. And no. He's not coming. We'll leave him a note. Now please go pack your bag, Lily. I really don't have time to engage you in every miniscule detail of life." She stood with her hands on her hips and I obeyed. When I came back into the living room with my bags in hand, she had a scarf over her head and thick black sunglasses on.

We drove in silence for what seemed like hours. Every few minutes she inhaled deeply and held her breath, then let it out in a heavy sigh. Her eyes were tearful at times and resolute at others, and I could tell she was struggling inside with something. She gripped the steering wheel hard and sped off into the night like we were running from someone. When we got into the thick of the Texas forests, she turned on her bright headlights. We wound through the roads slowly now, lighting up one tree at a time as we approached them. I asked her again where on earth we were going. This silence was not normal, even for us.

She said, "Lily, dear, we are going to visit some friends and we will stop by and see Uncle R.L. He has a mobile home, it's a sort of movable clinic. He sees patients from there, and is a regionally famous podiatrist, so I think it would be nice if we saw his clinic on our way to visit some other friends."

I said that was wonderful and asked her why she hadn't just said so, then gathered up my bag from the back seat and reaching for a new piece of gum. I offered a stick to my mom, but she ignored me. I shrugged and popped an extra piece in my mouth and blew a huge pink bubble.

When we finally reached his mobile home, my mom narrowed her eyes to make sure we were in the right place. There was no one around for miles and miles, no address visible, but she looked satisfied. She cut the engine, revealing the sounds of the woods, the frogs, the crickets, the tiny mice prowling from behind dried leaves. She left on the headlights and adjusted her scarf in the mirror. I followed suit and reapplied my pink lip gloss, smacking my lips in the mirror when I heard banging on my window, startling both of us.

My heart leapt into my throat and my mom shrieked in fear, scaring me even more. "Dear God!" I shouted. My mom quickly snapped, "Don't take God's name in vain, Lillian!"

But it was only Uncle R.L. He opened up my car door and swung it wide open. "Well, hi there, Little Darling, Lily!" He laughed and held his hand out for me to take.

I laughed nervously and my mom unclutched her chest as though her heart attack had passed. I lowered my eyes out of respect and shyness. "Hi, Uncle R.L.," I said, taking his hand and stepping out of the car into the dirt. "What is this?" I asked, motioning to the mobile home.

He said, "It's a small clinic away from my clinic in town. It's like my weekend getaway! There's a creek right down the road that has good fishing, Lily. And it's a wonderful, quiet place for me to get away from the city and study."

"Well it's lovely," I said. We walked arm and arm towards the warm light shining through the windows. I turned back and Mom had turned off the headlights and was gathering our things. We walked up the steps and he showed me inside. His white lab coat was hanging like an old trusted friend on the hook right by the thin couch. The place was clean, with yellow carpet and minimal furniture. The air smelled of stale cigarette smoke and Pine-Sol. When my mom stepped inside, he said, "Judy, may I offer you a cup of coffee or a nice relaxing smoke?"

She removed her scarf and looked around anxiously, and said "Oh, coffee would be lovely, R.L. Thank you, dear." He put on a pot of coffee and we looked for a place to put down our purses, settling on the floor beside the couch. The place really was very quiet, and his desk, which was where an end table would normally be, was littered with papers and pens and books and medical journals. It reminded me of my father's desk and how it was covered in religious books, Bibles, and Scriptural commentaries. I lifted the papers, looking through them and their titles, sifting through the facts, the proven truths of modern thought and medicine. Two brothers, each equally devoted to their studies—one man of science, one man of faith.

His television was on, and the NBC peacock fanned its colorful wings across the black screen. "Lily, dear, how about you? Would you like a nice Coca-Cola?" He smiled and opened the small refrigerator. I shifted as my mom sat down first at the kitchen table.

I nodded and he handed me the bottle. He motioned for me to sit, and we all sat together at the small round wooden table. He lit a cigarette and my mom handled her large mug of coffee, much different than the delicate china cups from which she was used to drinking. Her wrists looked frail as she shook each time she lifted the mug to her red, Chanel-painted lips. We all sat in silence, staring and smiling at one another. Finally, Uncle R.L. broke the tension. "So, Lily, how is high school?" he asked.

I sipped my Coke and said, "Oh, it's not been bad. My classes are pretty hard, though." I loved R.L. He was one of my favorite uncles.

"Lily, please don't slurp," my mom said, and tapped me on the arm. I straightened up and stopped slurping. "And please spit out that chewing gum. You look like a cow chewing its cud."

"Sorry," I said, rising to spit out my gum in the trash can. I turned from them and dropped it into the can away from them so as not to offend.

"Have you had a chance to meet many friends?" he asked, taking a slow drag.

"Some," I answered, sitting back down. My curiosity as to the purpose of our visit was mounting.

"She has taken up with a nice young man named Craig," my mom said. "They've spent quite a few after-noons together."

He leaned across the table and gently put his hand over mine. "I can see that, Lillian." I looked in his eyes and he glanced down at my belly and said, "Lily, Darling, you are with child, are you not?"

28

I LOOKED DIRECTLY INTO MY mom's uneasy blue eyes, but she couldn't look into mine. The clock on his wall was a large black cat with eyes that shifted with each passing minute. I listened carefully and caught on to the sound of the ticking. I looked down in my lap and took a deep breath and let the seconds go by peacefully. "Yes," I whispered. The sound of the clock was calming, rhythmic.

They looked at each other carefully, and he put his second hand on top of mine. "Well, you've come to the right place, Darling. We love you very much, and I can be trusted. I am a medical doctor, after all. Lily, Dear, have you thought about how your father would feel if he knew you were pregnant?" he asked carefully.

I had thought about it. I had thought about it quite a bit, actually. I had pictured him having to stand up in front of our church and admit his daughter was a whore. I had pictured him crying in shame, screaming at me, maybe hitting me. I had even pictured him killing me. I looked up intensely and searched for my mom's eyes again. This time, she met my gaze. She was frightened. She waited to hear what I would say next. I said,

"I love Craig. We are going to get married." I surprised myself when I sounded certain.

He said, "Darling, do you really believe that sounds reasonable? First of all, not that I agree with this, but your father won't permit you to marry a Methodist, and your mom tells me he is not college bound. Dear, you will want your college diploma, yes?"

I said that was her dream, not mine. I told him I wanted to sell fur coats at Sackowitz at the Houston Galleria. Or to be a waitress. One of those two things. I looked at them both but neither one seemed to be listening. They were staring at each other and communicating behind the eyes.

After a few moments, he knocked on the table and smiled. "Well, Dear, do you mind if I take a look at you? You want to make sure everything is going well with your baby, don't you?"

I started stammering, then. "Well, yes, but where on earth would you take a look at me? I'm not pregnant in my foot," I said, only half joking.

He stood up and began to clear the table. "Well, here, if that's alright with you, Dear." He motioned to the kitchen table. "It's clean and private. I'm quite embarrassed not to have a nurse. Judy? Do you mind assisting me?" She stood up and straightened her skirt and said, "No, Doctor, not at all."

They seemed very certain that this was the thing to do, so I stood tensely as they wiped the table down and washed their hands, murmuring to each other by the sink. "Lily, dear, undress from the waist down, please. Use the sheet on the couch to cover up and lie down on the table," he instructed with his back turned to me. He reached into his black medical bag and put on gloves and retrieved a few instruments. My mom helped me to lie down across the kitchen table and she draped the sheet across my legs.

"Remove her socks, please," he said. She took off my socks one at a time and folded them neatly, placing them in the chair. I clenched my cold knees together and looked up at the fluorescent light overhead. I could hear it buzzing and noticed a few dead flies inside. Uncle R.L. started to hum as if to put me at ease while he positioned himself with a light strapped to his forehead. Mom stood beside my head and held my hand. I tried to pry it loose but she tightened her grip.

"Lillian, stop tensing. You are going to deprive your baby of medical care. Now open up," he said, then he shoved his fingers inside of me.

"Ouch! What are you doing?" I shouted. It felt like razor blades were rubbing across the soft pink tissue of my young body. I had been touched many times before where he was touching me now, but it had never been painful like this. "Uncle R.L., stop it!" I shouted and started to cry. I looked up at my mom who was standing over me but her eyes were fixed over the sheet onto him. She looked like a panicked animal. "Mom! What are we doing?" I pleaded.

She looked down at me and snapped. "Hold still, Lily! He's just examining you. You were a big enough girl to get yourself into this mess, now be still!" And she placed her other hand on my shoulder and held me down. She pretended she was hugging me, but she was restraining me. I wiggled only a little but then relaxed. She was my mom. She didn't have to restrain me. Deep down in my heart, where I truly lived, I trusted her.

I tried to relax my legs, but they clamped together like a vise. He pried my legs apart with his elbows so as not to contaminate his gloves. "Darling, we have a problem." He peered to the right of the sheet so that I could see him.

"What is it?" I asked.

He didn't answer, but instead shoved something cold and sharp inside of me. "Ouch!" I screamed again. "Ouch! STOP IT! Please!" I shrieked this time. I felt warm liquid gush out from between my legs, drenching the table.

"Judy, get the towel, please," he ordered. My mom grabbed the towel from beside us and held it up. He shoved his arm inside me again and I felt tugging and scraping. It was all happening so fast, and Uncle R.L. was using all his brute strength. He used his entire body. I shouted, "Stop! What's happening? What are we doing?"

Mom peered around the sheet and Uncle R.L. whispered to her, "She's further along than we thought. Lillian, close your eyes!" I did what he told, I squinted my eyes shut as tightly as I could, but I couldn't help writhing in pain. I screamed in terror as more water squirted out of me. I sat up and saw his entire shirt sleeve was covered in blood. My abdomen tightened and it felt like boiling water was pouring through my entire body. He used his elbow to put pressure on the top of my abdomen while his other hand skillfully worked under the sheet.

"Am I dying?" I shouted. The pain was shooting through me like fire. I could feel water pouring out and blood was beginning to cover the table. And that's when he delivered my son.

He pulled my baby out by the legs; I could feel him being born. I saw my mom fumble with the towel as he placed him, slippery, in her arms. From the brief second that I saw him, his body was tiny but perfectly formed. He was bloody and blue and his little head was cut. One of his arms was dangling like it was broken. My mom quickly ran out of the

mobile home with him in her arms wrapped up in a towel.
I shrieked and started to scream and cry. He reached in me
again and manually removed the small placenta and threw it
in the garbage can. I put my arms over my eyes and lay sobbing. "Uncle R.L., what happened? What happened to my
baby?" I moaned. "What happened?" I wept and wept with
my arms covering my eyes. I lay on my back on his kitchen
table, trying to understand what just happened.

He jabbed a needle into my thigh. "This medication will
stop your bleeding," he said, and placed gauze inside of me
until the trickling of blood stopped. He stood up and spoke
slowly and distinctly to me over the sheet. His face looked
exactly like my father, but his eyes were cold and hard,
whereas my father's eyes had passion behind them, a desire
to seek God, no matter how weak he actually was as a man,
no matter how much he fell short. "Lily, there was a problem
with your baby boy." He began. "He was mangled, dear."

I tried to sit up. "Mangled? What's mangled? He didn't
look mangled." I howled. "You mean his arm? What was
that, Uncle R.L.? What was wrong with his arm? Is that
what you mean?"

He was totally cool, totally in control, icy. "Why, yes,
dear. That's it. Your baby was mangled. And deprived of
oxygen. He was anoxic. He would not have grown normally. You would not have been able to have him normally.
It's best for him that he died now instead of living a life as
a cripple in a wheelchair."

I mustered all my strength and sat up sharply as best I
could. Another squirt of blood garbled out onto the table.
"He's DEAD?" I cried and cried and lay back down on
the cold, hard table, sobbing. "He's dead? You couldn't save
him? You're a doctor!" I screamed.

He stood over me. He shook his head calmly and

kindly. "No, Dear. I'm sorry. He didn't make it. Sweetheart, I'm sorry. But sometimes these things happen for the best." He took off his bloody gloves and threw them in the trash. He helped me to sit up and he held me as I cried. I shook violently and moaned until there was nothing left in me. My baby, my baby, my baby was dead.

That night, I couldn't sleep. Of course I couldn't sleep. I bled all night, just small amounts, and my arms ached. They ached like they had been wrestled, robbed, and emptied, because they had been. I was afraid of the shadows in that room. They came and went as the clouds cloaked the moon then drifted by it, its light shining again. I pulled the curtains back and looked up at the moon, so white and bright and full. And from my bed, I watched it and I made a promise to myself not to ever let anyone close to me ever, ever, again. But of course, that was before I had my girls.

The next morning, my mom and I woke up early. She spoke with Uncle R.L. as we loaded up our car in the misty haze of the morning. She offered him money, but he shook his head and declined it. I waited in the car as they said their goodbyes. He waved at me as we pulled out onto the road. I waved back solemnly and turned on the air conditioner, letting the coolness blow across my face.

The woods looked different in the morning than they did at night, more alive, more aware. There was a cool fog hovering through the quiet pine trees and the sun was beginning to burn it off. We drove through the winding roads in total silence. The day was noiseless but for the sound of the engine roaring down the hushed, wooded road. My mom did not look at me, and I did not look at her. She looked ahead at the road when she finally spoke, "We'll tell no one of this, do you understand?"

I understood.

"It's important that we move forward quickly and forget this ever happened. Do you understand? We need to focus on getting you ready for college and beginning your life."

I stared out the car window, still sore, still lightly trickling blood from the night before. My legs were sore and it's as if my arms knew they were empty, that I was leaving without a baby, because they ached from somewhere deep within. I pulled my pillow close to me and tried to make that phantom, empty feeling go away, but it didn't. "Yes, Mom. I do." And we buried it, then, she and I, we buried that secret in the pit of hell where that horrible night belonged. We buried it down forever.

· · ·

The next page was blank. And the next. And the next. I closed the journal and looked over at her sleeping, and I wondered where she was. She looked just like a peaceful baby, fast asleep in a world of madness, a kaleidoscope world that swirled all around, only coming into focus in glimpses, and even then, only for a moment. As the bedside bulb flickered, the shadows on the wall behind her shifted and danced like the story of her lost son had shifted and danced through the many years. They were dark and dense, like the truth of what she had just told me, like the truth I had just read. I kissed her on the forehead and whispered, "Mommy, thank you for telling me this," because I knew that it was true. "I'm so sorry for what happened to you that night. I'm sorry your son died." But she was breathing steadily, lost in a dream, maybe of when she was young again, before any mistakes had been made. I reached over and turned out the lamp and we slept all night long, intertwined, the two of us, like when I was little, "two bodies but one heart, two bodies but one heart, two bodies but one heart," and when I left her at that shelter the next morning, the guilt was as giant as Goliath.

I TURNED DOWN MY STREET. Most of the cars that had been there that morning were still there, but a few were gone. The houses I passed by had families milling around through the curtains. I passed by The Rent House, and it was growing darker. It looked to be leaning over to the side a little, and one of the windows was shattered. My heart hurt because my family wasn't together and it seemed that it never really had been, and images of an older brother entered my mind. I wondered if he would have been handsome, if he would have been smart, if I would have ever even been born had he lived, because maybe her life would have been different if she had had that son. I wondered if Craig came back from Vietnam, or if maybe that part wasn't true. Maybe Craig had his own family now, maybe he thought about my mother from time to time, and maybe in the mornings, when he looked at himself in his own mirror and straightened his tie, something gnawed at him as he tried to understand why he felt so empty . . . never imagining in a million years that it was because he had a baby that he hadn't known existed die.

The moment I got home, I took Katherine aside and told her everything. "She said Mama Black forced her into an abortion. An *abortion*."

Katherine rolled her eyes. "I've heard all that before, Steph. Luke called again while you were gone, by the way. He said he *has* to talk to you. He says he wants you to know he's doing a lot better and he forgives you and he wants you to forgive him, too. Wait a minute. Are you talking about a car accident where her baby died or whatever?"

"No! I'm talking about Mama Black! Forcing Mother into a back-alley abortion. Like, an illegal, forced, against-her-will abortion. And *he* forgives *me*? Did you get his number?"

Her eyes grew more serious. "No, he said he'll call back. Stephanie, why are we even talking about Mom's abortion? What difference does it make now?"

"It makes a lot of difference, Katherine. It makes a big difference. Do you understand what that means about our family? About Mama Black? And, Daddy Black's brother performed it! And he was like, an orthopedist or some shit. I mean, how would Daddy Black feel if he knew that? It would kill him!"

Katherine knew I wasn't stopping. "Um-hum, she's told me that before. I think that story is actually true."

"What makes you think it's true?" I whispered.

"Because I asked Mama Black one time. I just like, *asked her* one day in her kitchen because Mother had told me the same story and, I don't know why, it just sounded kind of true. So I just asked, and she just was all, 'Well, I'm not in a position to either confirm or deny that.' Just, 'I won't confirm or deny that,' like no more than that. So I never wondered again if that story was actually true, because I think it is. For me, if you don't deny it, you admit it, you know?"

"You think what story is actually true?" My father turned the corner of the hallway. His speech was slurred and he was holding a beer.

"That Mama Black forced Mother into an illegal back-alley abortion against her will!" I shouted. "Is that true?"

My dad's eyes filled with tears. He said, "You know, I used to be a really nice person."

"Dad, is it true?" I asked.

He wiped his tears. "I mean, when I was young, I sold Bibles door to door for Christ's sake," he laughed. "On a *bike*. God, I was so innocent then. I truly just thought if you did all the right things everything would just work out." He took a swig of beer.

"Dad, if you knew it was true, why didn't you try to help her?" Katherine asked.

"Do you girls think that when I held the two of you in my arms for the first time and looked in your eyes, that I actually set out to do you wrong?" He looked like a little boy. "She was my *wife*! I made a *promise*! I didn't know what the hell to do to help her! It got worse every year! Stephanie, I didn't know how to protect you. I lost everything, too. Every hope I ever had was based in fantasy. Everything I ever believed was a lie." He started to cry. "I lost everything, too. I didn't know how to help her."

I looked at him and Katherine and back at him again. "You could have tried harder," I said. "You whored me out to Carl and Luke because you were too concerned with your own self."

"Now, Stephanie, that's not fair," he said.

"Yes it is fair. You left your post. You left your post and you served me up on a silver platter like a piece of trash. You didn't care about me. You didn't protect me from anyone."

"I didn't know how," he pleaded with me. "I didn't know *how*! You have never belonged to me! You have *always* belonged to her." He put his head in his hands and cried. "I feel like the father who was supposed to take his daughter to day care, and on the way I forgot, and I left her in her car seat and she died. I'm sorry, Stephanie."

I felt something for him, but it wasn't empathy or understanding.

"I'm going to ask to stay with Simone," I said. Knowing I could stay there if I wanted to, I started towards the door because the reasons for me needing to leave were stronger than the love I had for both of them.

"Stephanie, wait!" Katherine said. "Dad, tell her to stay. Stephanie, don't go!" But my father stood flaccid and impotent against my fury and I was already pulling the door closed behind me.

• • •

The street was lined with yard decorations, and cars were parked up and down the street in front of houses—relatives and friends had come to Simone's house for her graduation party. I wished her well from where I was sitting on the couch and wondered if she missed me like I missed her.

We hadn't been as close since Valerie died. I had seen her a few times in the hallway at school, and we had passed each other by and waved. I had called her a few times but hung up when she answered, and I had written letters, all starting with, "Dear Simone, can we talk about Valerie?" and all ending with, "Oh, never mind." I had wanted to bring it up to her time after time, but I didn't know what to say, and after a while, too much time had passed to say anything about Valerie at all.

Simone brought me another cup of punch. "Having fun yet?" she asked, elbowing me in the ribs. "How fuckin' lame, huh?"

I laughed. "I think the party is nice," I said. "I failed chemistry by two points. I have to go to summer school."

"Eh, summer school's not that bad," Simone said. "At least it's over at noon. Then next year? You'll graduate, too," she said. "I'm supposed to like, go to college. And like, pick a major. I have no clue what I want to do. I haven't even officially walked the stage yet. Guess pretty soon high school will all just be one big stupid fucking blur," she laughed.

Simone was looking more like Lynne every day. She looked at me and smiled. "Steph? Are you doing okay?" she asked.

"I'm okay. It's just been a long year," I said. "I miss Valerie."

Simone pulled her hair back in a ponytail and her golden curls spilled out. "Me too. She was the best, wasn't she? I keep thinking about the way she used to smile. They said at her funeral she was an organ donor. That's cool that she signed her driver's license that way. I didn't even know you could do that. Where were you at her funeral, anyways? Seems to me there's only one place you would have been when Valerie was being buried."

"I couldn't go. I'm sorry," I said. "I didn't want to see her dead. It was really selfish, but I was afraid I wouldn't be able to remember her alive if I saw her dead. Hey, Simone? What happened there that day at that hotel?"

Simone stared ahead as she spoke. "Well, I mean, we were all just sitting on the balcony just having fun and V was kind of propped up against it leaning over smoking a joint. She was happy, you know? Relaxed. We were all just laughing and talking and she just leaned over too far. I think maybe the railing was just too low, like it came more to her waist than up to her shoulders." She motioned to her waist.

"We all thought she was joking when she acted like she was falling and waving her arms around and stuff you know, like, we didn't react quickly enough because we were just standing there and actually, I was sitting down in a chair, kind of far across the other side of the balcony, so I probably couldn't have reached her anyways, and it just happened so fast and FUCK, I was so STUPID! We were all just having fun! It just happened so fast! And when she hit the ground, we all just looked at each other for a second and then we ran over to the railing and looked over and you could tell she was . . . we could tell she was . . . Jesus, fuck, Stephanie! She was just gone! She was just lying there face down and I could tell she was dead."

I didn't realize I had been holding my breath. "Simone, I am so sorry. But how? How did you know she was dead and not just hurt?"

I wished I hadn't said it the minute it came out. She turned and looked at me like I was an idiot. "I am not going to answer that, Stephanie."

"I'm sorry. You know what, don't tell me. Simone, I love you so much. I'm so sorry. I'm so, so, so, so, sorry I wasn't there."

She patted my leg. "No. It's better that you weren't. Duh. But it would've been nice if you'd have tried to make it to the funeral. You know, just in case *I* maybe would've needed *you* there."

We sat next to each other and watched Lynne serving punch. Simone came back from peering over the balcony and from seeing whatever she saw that made her know right away that Valerie was gone. "This party sucks," she said. "I need a damn smoke."

Lynne stopped by with a cheese tray. "Cheese puff?" she asked. The music on the stereo turned to "Celebration" by Kool & the Gang and people started pushing furniture aside and dancing.

And because Simone was always brave, she said, "Hey Mom, can Stephanie come stay with us for a while?"

And Lynne smiled and nodded her head and said, "I think that would be wonderful. Stephanie, would you like that?"

And whether I liked it or not, I knew that I should.

Lynne said, "We can go shopping in the morning for some things you'll need, Steph, okay?" Her eyes lit up. "We can all buy matching sweaters!"

I nodded but Simone stepped in. "Lynne, don't get all sentimental and gussy this all up like a Christmas tree. Don't get your hopes up. It's only temporary." Simone helped Lynne move the rest of the furniture and someone told them to pose for a picture. Lynne threw her arms around Simone and Simone smiled and allowed it, and right then and there, as the camera flashed, I could see the grown woman in her.

And I knew that I was safe for now . . . but my thoughts turned to Mother.

LYNNE AND SIMONE WERE IN the kitchen making breakfast and I lay comfortably in the clean, crisp sheets. I could hear their rhythm as they worked together, setting the table and getting out the juice, taking turns and handing each other this or that. Memories of Mother came flooding in, and I thought about the many, many times she reached into the oven with no oven mitt, and the many times we had kitchen fires, and the time she ironed her dress while wearing it, causing burns up and down her chest for me to rub ointment on. These memories seemed like fairy tales to me now, stories told with a twist of irony in the end with whimsical characters popping out of trees along the way and wearing colorful costumes.

It felt good to lie there in Simone's clean room with the smells of maple syrup and bacon in the distance. I rolled over and yawned and the air conditioner kicked on, blowing cool air onto my face. I pulled the covers over my head just to be alone and a part of the private darkness underneath. If I couldn't see the world, it could not see me. A profound sense of peace and tranquility came over me, and I drifted back into a light sleep, but the memories still played like an old broken record somewhere far away in my mind.

"Stephanie, I need you to do me a favor. I've got a phone now at the shelter, and well, you remember what it was like there. Now that you're gone off gallivanting with your dad, no one would know if I lived or died. Does that make sense? Can you start calling me in the mornings before you head off to school to make sure I'm not dead?"

Ring. Ring. I waited alone in the kitchen in the early morning hours with the phone pressed firmly against my ear that last week of school. Ring. The morning sun had not yet risen. I leaned against the wall in the dark before the school day began; calling my mother to make sure she was safe like she asked. I could picture her little curtain-contained corridor at the shelter and her tan phone beside her twin-sized bed that we had slept in together. Ring. Ring. I twisted the phone cord tensely around my finger. I thought about what she had said, about the shelter being a mission field and that she might die and nobody would know.

That Anwar guy, I didn't trust him. I didn't trust him or those "nephews." Ring. I started to feel panicky.

Please pick up, Mother. I'm so sorry I left you there. Ring.

Mom, please don't be dead. Oh God, please don't let my mother die before I get to talk to her again. Mother, please, please, pick up!

I pictured my mother dead in the back of someone's trunk, shoved in stiff like a crash dummy, with her eyes glazed wide open, and a sick smile across her face like the Joker on *Batman*, not having given her killer the satisfaction of knowing he had hurt her when he slit her throat. She would be in a suit with high heels, maybe leopard print or gold lamé, but her suit would be stained with blood, which would have been such a disappointment to her. Ring. Ring. I pictured her dead under a bridge or dragged across the freeway with her head half chopped off from the impact of a Mack truck, or zipped up in a black body bag with a wrist band on that said "Jane Doe." Morgues were cold. Once you were in that body bag, that was it. They tagged your toe and you turned to ice. The people at the morgue would be saying to each other over their tuna fish sandwiches, "If we don't get her claimed, let's donate the cadaver to science. Hey, you dropped a piece of celery in her."

Maybe someone raped her. She would have taken the rape fearlessly, motionlessly, I bet. She would have just lain there and taken it. Maybe they tortured her. In that case, she would have tried to outsmart them, like a rat in a maze, tried to get away, tried to bite through her rope. She did have an animal instinct at times, very fight or flight, my mother. Ring. Ring.

I felt sick to my stomach with regret and wanted to scream and beg for her apology for abandoning her. I thought of our happy times, when she seemed like a child, so vulnerable, so helpless, her smile so sweet, and I thought of how her hurt was so deep I could never help her. I thought of how she used to call me to her side, used to whisper in my ear. Ring. Ring. Oh, there are so many things I would have done differently! Ring. Ring. I waited there like a fool. Ring. Ring. Ring. Ring. I slammed down the phone. *Bitch. How dare you?*

I turned around to walk out of the kitchen, but Simone was waiting behind me. She had been watching me the whole time.

She put her arms on my shoulder for a second, but I walked past her, shaking my head. We drove to the last few days of the school year in a comfortable silence. We didn't need to fill each moment with words. I listened to the music of The Cure and blew my smoke out the window. "Are you okay, Steph?" she asked finally.

"I'm fine. I don't want to talk about it," I answered. My mother was probably sick. Maybe she was hiding her illness because she didn't want to worry me, and had a seizure in the night and had to be taken to the hospital. I was such an idiot to have just left her like that; like I didn't even care.

"That's cool. Will you light me a stogie please?" She fumbled in her purse looking for her cigarettes but we started swerving into the next lane.

"Give me the damn purse, geez," I laughed. I lit her Marlboro and put it in her mouth.

My stomach churned all day at school. I couldn't swallow the right way and I bumped my head on the corner of my locker and bit my tongue. I walked through the halls with my head down; I was in agony with worry. She might have been teaching me a lesson, which just totally pissed me off. I had the right to go live with Dad, or Simone. I had the right to live anywhere I goddamned please! Then I felt horrible for cursing her when she could be dead. Horrible daughter, I was! She might have gotten robbed. My head pounded in the temples and my palms were sweaty. I had left the damn house so fast that I forgot all my homework and my math teacher said I'd never amount to anything. She was probably right. I couldn't even be a good daughter or sister. How would I be any good to anyone else?

I felt an arm around my shoulder. "Hey, what's with you?" Simone walked the halls with me with no textbooks, only a yearbook. She carried no backpack. She was a woman now, a senior whose high school work was done. "Why are you being a bitch?"

"I can't help it. My mother may be dead. I called her at that crazy guy Anwar's house, and then the shelter and she didn't pick up. You know, it's really rough down there, Simone. I'm scared."

Simone laughed. "Steph, your mom is fine. She's like a cat. I'm sure she'll land on her feet. C'mon. Kasow? People named Kasow Toujours don't die. They live forever. Forget about it." And she walked into her class and joined some other friends and they swapped yearbooks. But my mother wasn't like a cat. She was no missionary . . . she was homeless. And she needed me. She needed help. She needed a family.

• • •

"Stephanie! Breakfast is ready!" Simone called from the kitchen.

"I'll be right there!" I answered. I rolled over and picked up Simone's phone and called home. Katherine answered. "Has Luke called back?" I asked.

"No." She sounded annoyed. "Stephanie, why don't you just forget that guy? Why are you so wrapped up in him?" she asked. "Look, I can't talk right now. Dad and I are playing Scrabble."

I hung up and dialed the shelter. I could picture the phone in the common area ringing and ringing until someone finally walked by and picked it up. I asked for Kasow Toujours, God, it felt weird to say it, and I listened to the noisy sound of dishes clanking and muffled voices scooting by. They called in the distance, "Hey! Let Kasow know she's got a call! Where she is? Oh, okay, well letta know someone be waitin' on da phone." The phone got banged around a little and finally she picked it up.

"This is Kasow," she said, sounding professional, as though she were picking up a phone in a busy executive Manhattan office space.

"Hi, Mom. It's me, Stephanie."

"Well, hello darling! How are things going?"

"They're good. I was just calling to check in." I rolled over and pulled Simone's pretty curtain back. The sun streamed in and some kids outside were setting up a lemonade stand. They looked over and saw me peeking out the window and waved me over. I smiled and waved and let the curtain fall back.

"Well, darling, I'm happier than I've ever been. Things are going great. I'm building my Mary Kay business. They say if you ask every single person you know if they'd like a Cadillac or if they need more money, then eventually, one out of ten will say yes. How's your lip-gloss supply, anyways?"

"Um, it's good. But I was wondering, do you think you might be getting an apartment soon? Because like, I would come visit if you did."

"Well, actually, darling, that's why I'm working so hard to build this unmitigated empire. For you and Katherine, of course. Tell you what, let me build my client base and then I can maybe work towards buying a new house? That way, we won't have to be renters? One where you can come, and Katherine, too? By this time next year, I'd like to build my business to where it's at a point that I have a hundred million dollars to invest. MINIMUM of a hundred million dollars. I thought I'd start with the factory workers at the ship channel, start asking them if their wives need any eye shadow. What do you think?"

"I think that sounds good, Mom. I think it sounds really good." And I prayed to God to set me free from the guilt of leaving her there even though my love for her was aching. And He did. God gave me a sling shot and one smooth stone, and I aimed it straight for that giant, and I hurled it at his forehead, sending him tumbling towards the earth, and God set me free. He set me free from Goliath that morning. And the sweet smell of syrup drifted back into the room. The pancakes were ready!

LYNNE HANDED ME THE LAST of the dried dinner dishes and I put them away. "I'd say this kitchen looks clean as a whistle!" she said. The phone rang in the background and I heard Simone answer it. Lynne patted me on the shoulder. "Now, I promised you I'd teach you to crochet, and a promise is a promise. Now let's go get started on those doilies."

Simone stepped back into the kitchen holding the phone with her hand over the receiver. "Lynne, no. Stephanie can't do that right now," Simone said. Simone's eyes were big as she handed me the phone. "It's your dad," she said. She motioned to Lynne and they walked out of the kitchen and Simone closed the door behind her.

"Stephanie, it's Dad," he started.

"Dad, speak up. I can barely hear you," I said. "What's up?"

He was quiet for a long time. "Stephanie, your mother ran a stop-light last night and was killed in an automobile accident. Nobody else was hurt. She was driving over 100 miles per hour."

"I see," I said. This time, unlike when Valerie died, I could picture her face. All of them.

"Stephanie, come home for a few days. I'm not trying to push you to come live here if you're not ready, but just come visit," he said.

"Dad, I don't think we have anything to talk about," I answered.

"I think we have a lot to talk about. Just please come for a visit," he said. "Just come for a few days."

When I walked back through the living room, Simone and Lynne looked up. "Stephanie? Is everything okay?" Lynne asked.

I took a handful of hard candies out of the crystal bowl on the coffee table and put them in my pocket. "Oh. It's my mother," I shrugged my shoulders and sighed. I walked straight through the living room and just before I entered the hallway, I turned back around to face them. "She's dead."

DAD, GAIL, AND KATHERINE MET me at the door. Gail put her arms around me and guided me inside, trying to smile. She closed the door quickly. "Hi, Stephanie. I saved you a piece of pumpkin pie. Are you doing okay?" She looked me up and down. Despite myself, it felt good to be here.

I wanted to have a piece of pie with her. I wanted to let my guard down; I wanted to ask her how they were doing, but I couldn't bring myself to. It still felt like I was doing something wrong to my mother. Katherine had always said she'd rather come from a broken home than to live in one, but not me. I missed our family, no matter how broken.

Katherine patted me on the shoulder. "I'm glad you're home."

"It's only temporary," I said. "Lynne said I could stay with them as long as I need to."

My bedroom looked the same. I glanced around at the pretty flowers on the wallpaper and my stuffed animals on the bed. I propped up my teddy bear who was slumped over. I put my overnight bag down and ran my fingers over the lace on my bedspread, closed my eyes and heard myself laughing and playing as a little girl. It smelled like warm innocence.

"Hey, Sport? Can we come in?" Dad and Gail tapped on the door and waited for me to nod.

He sat down on the edge of my bed and looked up at me. "Do you need help unpacking?" He looked around the room and I wondered if he could hear the same sounds of laughing or if he could smell the innocence, too. Maybe he felt regret. Maybe he didn't.

"No. I'm not staying," I said.

Gail went to my closet and opened it up and sifted through the few tangled coat hangers that I had left behind. "You'll need a dress for the funeral, Stephanie. You don't have anything in here. We can go buy one in the morning."

"I don't want a dress. I just want to wear pants."

"Okay, then we can go buy a nice, pretty pant suit," she said.

"No, not a *suit*. Just pants and a shirt."

"Okay, then just slacks and a nice shirt and maybe a pretty pump."

"No, not a 'nice shirt.' I just want a simple shirt, Gail. And I just want, like, normal pants or something comfortable. Not fucking church clothes and pumps!"

"Okay, then a simple shirt and some comfortable pants," she said. "Linen would be beautiful. Have you ever worn linen before?" she asked.

I shook my head.

"Well, it's very cooling and comforting in hot temperatures. And we can put it with a nice white sandal. Stephanie, whatever you want to wear will be pretty, because it will be on you." She reached over and brushed the side of my cheek. "Stephanie, I'm so sorry about your mom."

We all sat there staring at each other and then finally I spoke.

"But I don't want to go together. Can't I just go by myself?" I asked. "Or just me and Simone will go to the mall."

"No, sweetheart. You aren't insured on my car yet," Gail said. "And plus, I'd like to be there with you. Okay?"

"Stephanie," Dad began.

"Dad, you don't need to say anything about Mother. I don't want to talk to you about her."

"Stephanie, just hear your dad out," Gail said.

She looked at him and nodded encouragingly. "Stephanie, it's just that I wanted you to know . . . I, I mean we, well, more I, but both of us just wanted to make sure you knew one hundred percent that I . . . what I'm trying to say here is . . . I don't want you to feel responsible . . ."

"Dad, can we just not? Crap," I said, searching my bag. "Dammit!" I started to cry and throw out mismatched socks and clothes and my curling iron onto the floor. "Goddammit! I forgot my Walkman!"

He sighed and clasped his hands and waited for a moment. Motioning him towards the door, Gail said, "Paul, she's not ready. Let's leave her alone." She was the first out, but in the doorway, Dad turned and asked, "But someday can we? Maybe we could sit down with a counselor? Stephanie, you'll need therapy."

I nodded and shrugged. "Sure, Dad. Whatever." But deep down, secretly, I promised myself one day we would and that I would listen to the rest of that sentence and what he one hundred percent wanted me to know.

"Your Walkman is in your purse, not your bag, Sport." He motioned to it, and closed the door behind him. I put the headphones on and turned the music up.

That night I awoke to the sound of the phone ringing. I reached over on the night stand and blearily picked it up and it was Luke on the other end. "Stephanie, I just wanted you to know that I love you," he said. "I saw in the newspaper that your mother died. Are you okay?"

I tried to focus my eyes on the clock to see what time it was, but my room was lit up as by a strobe light by a hazy, flickering orange glow. I thought I was dreaming and the strange light in the room was blinking so I couldn't see the numbers on the clock. "Well I love you, too. Of course I love you. I've missed you. Katherine said you called a lot. I'm sorry, I've been busy. Luke what on earth time is it?" I sat up and rubbed my eyes.

"Stephanie, you couldn't have been that busy, but I get it. Look, I'm not angry with your mother, and don't you be, either. You're a good kid, you shouldn't have to look at it anymore," he said. "I want all this to be over for you, and there's only one way for that to happen. I'm sorry in advance for my part." He hung up the phone and the line went dead. Luke was gone.

I heard neighbors milling outside and I could see the lights of our own household glowing through the crack under my bedroom door. The glow from outside rested unsteadily in the dark room. I threw on a robe and walked outside. When I stepped outside, there were fire trucks on our street and we all kept a protective distance in the safety of our own yards and across the street. Just a few lawns away, I rubbed my eyes to make sure I was seeing things clearly. The Rent House was on fire.

The flames blazed in the night sky as the neighbors watched and speculated what had gone wrong. "Faulty wiring," someone said. "Cigarette left burning," someone else offered. "Nah, couldn't be that. It's a good thing this eyesore is gone," they said. "It never fit in. Never looked right."

"Oh yes, it *could* be that," I said. All the neighbors turned and faced me. "It could've been that." Lying, because it had only been once, I said, "I've been in this house a lot and seen live wires hanging everywhere and tons of random people break in and smoke here all the time. That's what happens to abandoned houses. They become hiding places for vagrants. Vandals. People just squat, you know? Because it's empty. Make it their own, you know? Rent houses are vulnerable to stuff like that. It was bound to happen sometime. If you think about it, it's almost like it was meant to be."

They all nodded and echoed with their whispering voices, with their cold-creamed faces and hair curlers bouncing. "My lands, y'all that's so true, that's true, y'all, it was like it was meant to be, it was almost just meant to be. Sometimes things are just *meant to be.*" When a firefighter came around and asked if anyone saw anything, I slipped through them all and disappeared across the lawn. Luke's secret was safe with me forever and going up in flames for good.

The grass had been allowed to grow up and wrap around the front porch columns. The side window had been busted out by some kids playing ball. The sound of the wood popping and snapping as The Rent House burned board by board soothed me somewhere deep inside and immediately when I saw it on fire, I was not afraid to watch it burn. I inhaled the smoky night air and somewhere far away in my memory, the voices of the ghosts from our congregation began singing an old hymn . . . *It is well, it is well, it is well with my soul.*

I worked my way through the small crowd and found Katherine who was in her white pajamas. Her long curly hair was pulled loosely back in a ponytail and tumbled down past her shoulders. Tears glistened in her eyes as the smoldering flames illuminated her pretty face from the side. She looked into my eyes sorrowfully and we watched the house burn together, taking with it my innocence lost there, the voice of my ten-year-old self, maybe the sound of Katherine's voice, too, calling from the upstairs to come, come, come lie down and find love.

"Katherine, can I ask you a question? Did Dad have sex with you?"

She took my hand and said in a voice so low that only I could hear, "Stephanie, Dad never touched me, not like she said. You really have to believe me. He never touched me. All he ever wanted was to be close to you, Stephanie, he loves you so much, but when you wouldn't let him, after several years, he couldn't help but pull away. You should've heard the way he has cried for you."

Her strong hand felt like a stranger, but I didn't pull away. I nodded without speaking, because I didn't know how to understand what she was telling me or what to say, and I let her words hang in the air right where she had placed them. I thought of all my private conversations with my mother, secrets we told, things that never made sense, oh the memories were coming so fast, *Stay away from your dad, Stephanie, you don't want his kisses, Katherine and your dad are having sex, I saw it with my own eyes, she was sitting on him, playing hobby horse, my dad had sex with me, too, be glad he doesn't come tickle you at night, you don't want his kind of love, stay with me, I will protect you, I'm the only one who really knows you, we have to stick together.*

"But it *did* happen. Katherine, don't try to say it didn't. Didn't it?" Even as I spoke them, I didn't believe my own words. They sounded silly. I felt like such a fool. I started to cry because the security of the things I thought I knew, the lies that I believed in, was crumbling with each of her words. A lump formed in my throat. "Mother told me over and over again that it did. And I *believed* that it did, Katherine. And I hated you . . . I hated him. And that's why I hurt you. And that's why I never could get close to him. And now I never will because the distance between us is too wide." The size of the loss and the depth of the fracture began to hit me.

I couldn't let her hold my hand anymore. A few seconds was long enough; it was all I could give and take. I pulled my hand away. I couldn't fathom what I was hearing, but as much as it hurt that I wanted it to be true, I prayed to God that what Katherine was saying was true and as I prayed for it to be true, I knew it was.

"Stephanie, I know she told you that. Stephanie, she was sick. *Really* sick. She wasn't trying to hurt us. In fact, can you imagine what her life must have been like really going through it believing that her husband and daughter were lovers? But it never happened. Please don't do this to yourself. Don't do it." She pulled me close to her whether I wanted it or not and hugged me tighter than I had ever been held before, so tight it knocked the wind out of me. Her love took my breath away, not just because of her physical hold, but because embracing Katherine was new to me and was filling a chasm in my heart that I hadn't even known existed until right then. "But Stephanie, if there was anyone she loved the most, if there was anyone she could love, or that she was able to love, it was you."

I helplessly fell into her arms because it was Katherine, and no matter what I tried, or how hard I had fought it, I badly, hopelessly, urgently, desperately, wanted to give and receive the love of my sister and believe her. The lights from the fire truck sirens, their sound long since turned off, swiveled around us, lighting us up intermittently and each time I caught her eyes and they were tranquil and gleaming, full of hope, full of love, full of understanding. She took my head in her hands and put her mouth right up close to me and whispered in my ear, "I had my own ways of hurting you, Stephanie. Believe me, I did. And I'm so sorry, too."

"No you didn't," I said. I thought of her, a chubby blonde big-eyed little girl, laughing and playing, just like me with all the hope that I had. I remembered all the times she ran to our mother for comfort only to be turned away. I remembered the times we ganged up on her, bullied her. Oh, I could scarcely stand to think on it. "You never hurt me, Katherine. You just took it and took it and took it until you learned to avoid me altogether."

"Yes I did. I . . . we did. We purposely shut you out because it was easier. There was no way for us to get in there, anyways. Steph, I wanted her to love me just as badly as you wanted love from him and I had my ways of getting his attention steered away from you so that I could get what I needed. I know that you are sorry. I'm so sorry, too."

The Rent House's power seemed much weaker now, not the giant force I had once thought. The lapping flames that consumed it sent out just enough heat to reach us and let me know I was alive. The fire that ate The Rent House was more powerful than the water flowing into it. I remembered my baptism and the water that I thought was more powerful than the fire within me, that I thought would save me, that I thought would wash away not only my sins, but the memories of what happened here that day. Even holy water wasn't mighty enough to take away the creepy muscle of The Rent House. But this fire was. These flames were.

Katherine and I stood together and watched The Rent House smolder and I wondered if part of my ten-year-old spirit was flying away in the air with the ashes. Would she? If I really wished hard enough? I wondered if my little spirit girl had been lingering inside in that upper room since that day with Devin and Trent. But as I watched the ashes drift aimlessly like feathers into the bright night air lit by the fire, I knew that, no, she hadn't been lingering upstairs. My ten-year-old spirit was still a part of me, right here with me, and so was my twelve-year-old spirit, and the fourteen-year-old spirit, and all the moments before and after and in between when she reached out for love in any way she possibly could, and she remembered. She remembered but could begin to hear the truth and the soiled part of her wasn't leaving or floating away just because I asked her to. No, my spirit belonged with me for good. All of her.

Katherine stroked my hair like a sister . . . like a *big* sister. "Shhh. Stephanie, it's okay. I understand. I forgive you. We were all just trying to survive."

"You can't forgive me *just like that*." I snapped my fingers and cried indignantly.

She looked at me like I had seen her look at her friends and my dad; like I was someone she loved and had laughed with a million times before. She smiled, "That's what forgiveness is, Stephanie. It's *one* moment when we just . . . decide. And yes, I can do it '*just like that*.' Because love never fails. Because forgiveness is a decision to free myself as well as you. It's not a feeling; it's my action and response. And because you are my one and only sister. I cannot replace you."

We stood holding on to each other and watched the firefighters lose their battle with the blaze. The Rent House burned to the ground, along with its secrets, and as I watched Katherine watching it burn, I sensed that she had known that house as well as I did, known its crevices, its hiding places, known its ugly carpet like I did, known its wobbly fans. I almost asked her, but out of respect, I didn't. Not everything needed to be said out loud. *Luke.*

As the last ember lay crackling in the night air, Katherine turned and looked at me kindly. It was late now, almost two in the morning. "Sweet or salty?" she asked.

"Hum?" I had never had a casual conversation with Katherine before, never heard this comfortable tone in her. "What are you talking about?" I wiped the tears from my eyes and smiled back at her dumbly.

"Sweet or salty?"

I still stared blankly.

"Want something like french fries or ice cream? And you really need to cinch your robe better," she said, and laughed and began walking away toward our house.

I cinched my robe tighter and skipped to catch up to her. "Salty! But what can we do? It's so late!" My heart was racing with gladness because she was including me like a friend, like a *best* friend, and I would've gone absolutely anywhere with her. I laughed and caught up to her . . . my new sister . . . my only Katherine.

"I've got the car keys. Dad won't mind. We're young and free once, Stephanie. Only once. Let's go find somewhere that's open all night and get some fries and talk some stuff out before we have to face Mama and Daddy Black at the funeral. I hear instead of talking about Mom, he's preaching on obedience. Let's face 'em together. I'll stand in front of you and I'll go first. Want to?"

She tossed the keys to me. "But first let's go get some fries. I'll even let you drive."

ACKNOWLEDGMENTS

IT IS WITH HUMILITY AND joy that I acknowledge:

Eleanor Fishbourne, who simply said, "Sure," when I asked if I could send my manuscript, and whose young and talented hands eventually carried my story to its final production spot—there is no one else I would rather scream next to on a terrifying and poorly maintained carnival ride.

My editor, Stuart Horwitz, whose steady hand polished every smudgy crystal of an impossibly heavy chandelier. Your brilliant architectural skills enabled this story to emerge as its full version of itself. My editor, Aaron Teel, whose keen attention to detail provided necessary and crucial corrections at the last minute that if missed, could have sunk the whole project. To Amanda Hughes, for her conscientious and caring eye, Neil Gonzalez for the stunning cover art, and the entire rest of Greenleaf Book Group.

My supposed-to-have-been ghostwriter, Steve Erwin, who could write the story of the Rwandan Holocaust but could not write this story. Thank you for providing me with the opportunity to reach within and write it myself. It was my job to write it all along. To his friend and wife, Natasha Stoynoff, I still think of you as brightly as that disco ball in Times Square, and every New Year's Eve, I think of you and smile. Thank you both for the idea to open this book at the debate scene. It was a stroke of genius, and I cannot think of anything more wonderful.

Angela LaMonte, for the photographs.

My parents, without whom this book would not have been possible, and my sister: The best and worst parts of all of you are in me, and I am proud to be connected to it all. To my grandparents and aunts, special honor and thanks.

My wonderful friends Arlana Taylor Mann and Celeste Proctor Gray, who have provided encouragement through this journey, be it emotional, creative, literary, or otherwise. My friends Leslie Forbau and Emelia Wolfe, for always seeing the best in me. Colleen Winterbauer, for teaching me everything I know. Michelle Stallman, for keeping my deepest truths in trust. Tricia Laubach, there is no one like you. My friends Lauren Enloe and Chayla Horan, who always pick up when I call, and who always have something brilliant to say, and Susan and Jennifer Pruett, who will always be my historical touchstones.

For the souls who crossed over, but were nonetheless a part of it: Lance Rizzo, RIP; Carrie Loughner, RIP; and Gloria Cervantes, RIP.

Rachel Arco, a trusted and enthusiastic beta reader, whose depth and sense of humor is unmatched. I am not sure if you meant all the kind things you said, but they encouraged me to take the next step after the book had been collecting dust. Thank you for seeing Stephanie for who she was and for never judging her. You are a beautiful soul. May the number of people like you increase.

My destructively loved and cherished children and grandchildren: Savannah, Cameron, Josephine and Shepherd Taylor, and Maxwell and Leopold Medley, a.k.a., "The boys."

My priceless and irreplaceable husband, and one and only love, Jason Medley, to whom this book is dedicated. I love you, I love you, I love you.

READER'S GUIDE TO

FROM THE MOON I WATCHED HER

1. How does the setting of a Texas suburb color the story? In what ways is the setting crucial to the story? In what ways could this story have taken place anywhere?

2. In the beginning of the book, we meet Stephanie at a very young age. How does being introduced to the main character as a child affect the way you relate to her? Why do you think it was important to the author for us to hear her voice at such a young age?

3. How does the personification of The Rent House make you feel? Did those feelings change over the course of the novel? Why or why not?

4. After Stephanie's experience in The Rent House, you begin to see a new version of her—a Stephanie who has lost her innocence. How does the author represent this change in the writing?

5. Stephanie develops some troubled romantic relationships over the course of the story. How did you interpret her motivations for those relationships? By the end of the book, do you think Stephanie would continue to pursue similar relationships or do you think her motivations may have changed?

6. Though we rarely see Daddy Black take action in the story, his presence looms large over the other characters. In what ways does Daddy Black influence Stephanie's family and the rest of the town? Do you think Daddy Black actually possesses the kind of influence Stephanie believes he does? How does Daddy Black's presence change over the course of the novel?

7. The expectations of religion weigh heavily on Stephanie's family. In what ways did you notice the effect of that weight on Stephanie and her family? Do you think their lives would have been more peaceful without religious pressure, or would they likely have still faced the same issues?

8. Shunning plays a significant role in the novel and takes many forms. Where do you notice shunning at work in the story? What effect does being shunned by the church have on Stephanie? What effect does Stephanie shunning her family have for them both?

9. How do Lily's words and actions affect your perception of her trustworthiness? Do Stephanie's feelings towards her mother inform your view?

10. Stephanie refers to Lily and herself as "two bodies but one heart." Do you agree? Why do you think Stephanie feels this way? Does this aspect of Stephanie and Lily's relationship seem healthy or dysfunctional and why?

11. In the story, you often see Lily commenting on weight, mostly her daughter Katherine's. How does this practice affect Lily's daughters? How does the arrival of Gail change this dynamic?

12. Lily's story about her past miscarriage changes many times over the course of the novel. Why do you think that Lily keeps changing her story? Do you feel that you ever learned the truth of what happened?

13. Near the middle of the book, Stephanie's mother leaves the family and Stephanie tries to go with her. How would the story have been different if Stephanie had left with her mother? Do you think they would have found peace and stability, or help for Lily's mental illness? How might Katherine's and her father's lives have gone differently as a result?

14. Stephanie's mother takes a big step in confessing the truth of her past to Stephanie. If Lily had not died, do you think Stephanie would have been able to help her mother after learning the truth? Why or why not?

15. In the final pages of the book, you see Stephanie begin to reconcile with her sister, Katherine. What events do you think led Stephanie to feel open to reconciliation? Do you think the same events would allow Stephanie to reconcile with her father and accept Gail, or would it take something more?

16. Elements from nature serve many symbolic purposes throughout the novel. Can you think of a few examples and what they may represent? (Suggestions to explore: fire, water, mud, rocks, the moon, cows, and ticks)

17. Several times throughout the book, Stephanie refers to temperature   things either feeling cool or hot to the touch. What do you notice about these instances of heat and cold, and do you see a connection between those instances and Stephanie's internal emotional landscape? (Suggestions to explore: Texas heat, hot stoves, icy cans of Coke, and air conditioning)

18. What role does music play in the story? What themes do you notice emerging as you examine the lyrics included throughout the novel?

19. At many points throughout the story, you see different characters use coping mechanisms to navigate their experience of

trauma. What kind of coping mechanisms did you notice, and did any of them resonate with you as ways that you cope with stress or traumatic experiences?

20. Throughout the novel, there are depictions of rape, abuse, and consensual sexual activity, as well as an abortion. Considering the conservative religious setting of the novel, what do you think the author's intent was in including these scenes? How do they make you feel when you read them?

ABOUT THE AUTHOR

EMILY ENGLISH MEDLEY IS A writer from Houston. She lives with her husband, Jason.